The Camera Store and Other Stories As Times Pass

by

Richard Selinka

DORRANCE PUBLISHING CO., INC.
PITTSBURGH, PENNSYLVANIA 15222

The contents of this work, including, but not limited to, the accuracy of events, people, and places depicted; opinions expressed; permission to use previously published materials included; and any advice given or actions advocated are solely the responsibility of the author, who assumes all liability for said work and indemnifies the publisher against any claims stemming from publication of the work.

All Rights Reserved
Copyright © 2011 by Richard Selinka
No part of this book may be reproduced or transmitted in any form or by any means, electronic or mechanical, including photocopying, recording, or by any information storage and retrieval system without permission in writing from the publisher.

ISBN: 978-1-4349-0889-6
eISBN: 978-1-4349-5716-0

Printed in the United States of America

First Printing

For more information or to order additional books, please contact:
Dorrance Publishing Co., Inc.
701 Smithfield Street
Pittsburgh, Pennsylvania 15222
U.S.A.
1-800-788-7654
www.dorrancebookstore.com

WHY I NEVER MADE IT IN SHOWBIZ

Eddie Cantor was a big star in the mid-thirties. He had been performing on vaudeville stages for years, singing in his catchy high-pitched voice while gliding smoothly or hopping all over the stage. Often he was in blackface and wore white gloves while his hands clapped furiously together, his large eyes rolling as he entertained. People loved this slight, active fellow. In those years, he was a hit on radio, where his own show aired once a week.

When we were kids at home, our "entertainment" centered around two modes, one of which was radio, whose early form was a boxy affair that the family would cluster around after dinner to capture the news, comedy, music, or drama that was common to the day. The kids loved shows that usually aired earlier, like *The Shadow*, *The Lone Ranger*, or *The Blue Beetle*, for example, but we also joined the family after dinner for the later programs. Eddie Cantor's show was my favorite, even though Red Skelton, Jack Benny, and Fred Allen would compete.

Our other indoor entertainment was our much-traded, dog-eared comic books, which honed our reading skills on the whetstone of those brightly colored squares with balloons of commentary floating over the characters.

I was six. My family lived in New York on Amsterdam Avenue in the eighties in a brownstone walk-up that had four rooms housing eight of us, more or less. My mother was a dressmaker who generally worked in my grandmother's tiny dress store on Eighty-Third Street and Amsterdam, and my father was a salesman. In addition, my sister, two aunts, an uncle, and a cleaning lady (whom I loved) lived there, also sleeping two in a bed, except for Hannah, the maid, who had her own tiny cot in the hallway. The Depression was in full swing and jobs were at a premium, but everybody in our household worked except my sister and me. Though nobody made much of a living, each of the employed contributed to the total upkeep.

I was short and skinny and had blond hair that flew in various directions when disturbed. Other than that, the rest of me was run of the mill. My parents told me I talked too much, my sister beat me up with startling regularity, and the cleaning lady who slept in the hallway hugged me whenever she could catch me. I had a lot of friends. Our playground was the street, where games like stoop ball, stickball, Chinese handball, running bases, wrestling, and fighting took up our time after school. In 1936, there were only a few autos on our play streets, making them ideal fields for our sporting adventures. The public school had a concrete play area where we gathered sometimes. It was surrounded by apartment buildings, which walled it in but never disturbed our concept or the use of it. There were sundry markings on the ground where the girls played hopscotch, tossing a skate key into the boxes they had to avoid. The boys tormented their female counterparts on a steady basis, making a noisy, sometimes hilarious existence of our afternoons.

My teacher, Miss Robinson, after having me read an eye chart that was posted inside a closet door, found that I was near-sighted and sent a note home advising my parents of that fact. My father wanted to know how much glasses cost, and learned that they were seventy-five cents, which he allowed my grandmother to pay. Now I wore large, round-framed, steel-rimmed glasses to complete my description.

We had a telephone. It rang, and my Uncle Harry was on the line. He wasn't really my uncle. My father and he were in the army during the First World War and their friendship continued heartily thereafter. To tell the truth, I wondered a bit later in my life how we ever won the war with those two on our side. I called him "Unk." He responded to me with different unsavory sobriquets, some of which had "head" as the last syllable.

"Meathead," he shouted.

"Yes, Unk, it's me," I admitted simply. He was the richest man in the family, lived on the East Side, dressed like a natty summons server, and usually insulted people at will. My mother told me to be nice to him at all times, referring to his wealth, while at the same time disregarding his reputation. When he mustered out of the service in 1918, he wooed and married my Aunt Sissy, who was not my real aunt, even after marrying Harry (not my real uncle), whose father owned a dress manufacturing business that was very successful. When her father died, she ran the business and soon married Uncle Harry, who looked good in a uniform. Hannah, the maid, told me all that and added that if Harry hadn't married Sissy, he couldn't have gotten a job in the men's room at the Astor Hotel.

"Let me talk to your father. Are you still wearing those idiotic glasses?"

I could handle two questions at once. "He's not home, and yes, I see better."

"Did you ever hear of Eddie Cantor, Meathead?" he roared.

"Sure, he's on the radio. He's one of my favorites."

"He's in a play on Broadway called *Banjo Eyes*. Want to see it?"

He didn't even call me a name after that question, which would have been a pleasing variation in our usual conversation, but I was too excited to think of anything else, so I just said with scholarly excitement, "Wow!"

"Okay," he said. "Tell your father to call me. I have two extra seats for the both of you for Saturday's matinee. Got that, Beanhead?"

"Wow," I said automatically, accepting my newest nickname.

It was only Thursday, but by Friday night I'd told almost every kid on Amsterdam and Columbus Avenues about my good fortune. Everyone had heard of Cantor, but none of them knew that there were Broadway theatres downtown that didn't show two movies and four shorts and the news on a screen for a buffalo nickel. I was never downtown; my father told me it cost a fortune to go there.

Unk was going to meet us at the Saint James Theatre at 12:45 with the tickets. My father and I took the Broadway trolley. He paid a nickel for his fare, and when the conductor pointed at me, he said, "He's only four," and stuck his knuckle in my back, urging me on before I could tell the conductor the truth. We were in front of the theatre a little before twelve along with a sparse early crowd. There was a blind man propped up against the side of the entrance where a large poster was plastered on the wall of Cantor with wide-open orbs and "Banjo Eyes" in bright colors advertising the show.

My education was gaining momentum, for this was the first show-theatre I had ever seen, my first trip downtown, and the first blind man I had ever seen up close. The fellow was middle-aged and of medium height, had dark sunglasses on, and held a cup with four or five yellow pencils sticking out of it. People would put a penny in the cup but never took a pencil. I took one of three pennies I had in my pocket, put it in the cup, and lifted one of the pencils out of it. The blind guy immediately snatched it away from me and put it back in the cup. "They're for show," he explained to my sorrow, destroying my puerile view of consumerism.

A few minutes went by and a fellow approached the blind man and said to him, "How's it going, Ned?"

The blind guy said, "Pretty good, but I'm getting hungry," and with that, he took off the dark glasses, giving them to his friend, who put them on. Ned handed his friend the cup with the pencils and a cane and said, "Take over for about half an hour; I'm gonna get a hot dog," and strode off.

To tell the truth, there was a split second there that I thought the blind guy had regained his sight, but as he left, that thought escaped me as my father appeared with a hot dog for me along with half a bottle of Coke, while at the same time Harry came from another direction and shook my father's hand and said to me, "What have you got to say, Muttonhead?"

We were about to enter the theatre when Uncle Harry pulled out a shiny penny and dropped it into the new blind guy's cup. I tugged at his sleeve and said, "Take a pencil, Unk!" He slapped the back of my head, setting my floppy hair in motion. "Charity is charity," he said. I said to myself, "That's how much he knows."

We had seats in the fourth row center. The theatre was crowded but not quite full, and there was nervous laughter and chatter going on all around me. The hot dog and Coke now joined whatever else was jumping around in my stomach as the lights dimmed, except for the stage, where the curtains parted on the brightly lit boards with about a hundred spotlights circling around Cantor. He immediately began to dance, white gloved hands patting each other, and as the orchestra played, he sang "Ida, Sweet as Apple Cider." Ida, as everybody in the U.S. knew, was his wife, and together they had five daughters, which was always a part of his comedy routine.

The audience went crazy. Cantor's singing and dancing and the skits the actors performed with him hit the spot. I, too, enjoyed the play to the point where I decided that the rest of my existence would be spent on the stage, and if I had felt better just then, this would have been the greatest moment of my life; at any rate, I was thrilled and utterly transported though queasy.

The show ended after one intermission and two acts in about two hours. Before Cantor sent the audience home at the end of the last act, and after all bows were taken and the applause was about to thin out... Bingo—the curtains parted about five feet and out again came the star. The applause started again and Cantor sang one more chorus of "Ida," said a few funny things, and lightning struck me. Cantor pointed to me in the fourth row; the spotlight targeted me and Cantor said, "Stand up, little boy." As I got right up, he said to an usher in the aisle right near me, "Bring him up." The audience now was clapping and laughing as I turned around and waved and bowed to them. The applause got real loud and increased as I was led up to the stage, the spots always following me until I was in front of the curtain, standing alone with Cantor. He said to me, "What's your name and how old are you, young man?" His eyes were rolling.

In my loudest voice I answered, "My name is Dicky and I'm six years old but my father told the conductor on the trolley that I was four."

Well, the audience roared, and Cantor clapped his gloved hands together and laughed out loud, doing a little dance step at the same time. Then when he was able to speak again, he asked in his high-pitched falsetto voice, "Are you married?" The audience now turned to wild laughter as they knew what was coming.

"No, Mr. Cantor," I shouted and laughed simultaneously.

"Well," he said, his eyes wide open and rolling, "you have to come to my house. I can find a girl for you."

The audience thought this hilarious. It was then that I threw up at center stage with all the spotlights on Cantor and me.

Pandemonium. The audience roared.

The curtains closed, Cantor disappeared, and some man grabbed me, telling me as he led me away, "I want to speak to your father and mother."

When I got back to where Harry and my father were, the man handed my father a card and said, "Call me," and left.

My father and Harry took turns smacking me on the back of my head. My hair was flying around and my glasses were at the tip of my nose, but I didn't feel one bit sick anymore. I was a star.

Louella Parsons carried the story in her *Around Town* article the next day without naming me, but the story circulated through showbiz circles and caused much merriment.

The card that my father held while he consulted my mother read: JAMES NAGLE TALENT AGENT—Tel: TR7-3579.

"Should I call him?" he asked my mother, who was busy at the sewing machine.

She said, "Why not?"

So he dialed the number and got Jim Nagle right away.

"I'm the father of the kid at *Banjo Eyes* you met yesterday."

"Oh," Nagle laughed, "the kid that flipped his lunch…did you read Louella Parsons's article in the papers?"

"No."

"Well, anyway," Nagle continued, "I connect kids with radio and Broadway agents and if the kid shows talent, we can get him jobs in the business."

"What do they pay?" my father asked.

Nagle seemed slightly annoyed. "Hey, all I know now is that Dicky is funny-looking and throws up. I want him interviewed at

Jean Justin's studio. She'll see if he goes on from there. Are you interested?"

After agreeing this far, the decision was made to meet at the studio, which was in a hotel on Seventy-Third Street east of Broadway. After school on Monday, my father took me to the Bretton Hotel, third floor, where glass doors read "Jean Justin Studios." I was truly excited, my expectations running wild while questions I had were struggling to emerge, but my father, sensing this, said, "Don't say anything; let me do the talking." I figured I was in trouble with his last statement but obeyed.

After we were introduced to a man who came to the front door and said he was Jim Nagle's brother, Don, and could he speak to me alone first, he said to my father, "If that's okay with you, then we'll talk." So far, so good, I thought.

Nagle's questions were designed to determine my ability to comprehend and converse. He was about six feet tall and had dark hair and a thin moustache between a straight nose and reddish lips. He had blue eyes and wonderful diction. He seemed to like me as he showed me around the studio, which had a small stage, black curtains, and Klieg lights on top of the stage and around it, which gave the actor a true on-stage feeling. There were only a few feet of space in front of the stage for an audience. An upright piano was off to the left and a phonograph sat on the right.

"Pretty soon I'll see what you can do," he said. "I know what you did Saturday at *Banjo Eyes* but suspect you won't be doing that again."

"I didn't feel good," I admitted.

"I know. Let's talk to your father," he said.

It was agreed that I would come down to the studio each Tuesday and Thursday at 3:30 for a few weeks until I could be evaluated. Jean Justin introduced herself before we left. She was short, about five feet two inches, and had dyed blond hair that was cut short with bangs, blue eyes, and a well-proportioned figure. She spoke quickly and indirectly, indicating a detached air. She introduced another young lady as Imogene, her script girl and assistant. Those two and Don were the only obvious employees at the studio.

My one-hour session there consisted of script reading with Don, whose concentrated effort with me would lead to a smooth rendition of the reading. The script girl was the audience and also advised me on how to gesture while I was reading. "That will make the audience laugh," she explained. "It will also make you more aware of the humorous lines."

I had no idea what she was talking about, but I gestured like crazy while reading, and the two of them chuckled often.

"Good, good," Imogene the script girl said. "All the skits you do will be comedic." If she had said "funny" I could have understood her, but I was learning new showbiz words all the time.

After my fourth visit to the studio, at which time Imogene worked with me alone in a small office, I asked, "Where is Don today?"

"Oh," she said, "he's working in the studio theatre and asked not to be disturbed, so don't go in there." To my nature, those words represented a challenge that I could not resist accepting. When Imogene said she was leaving to get a coffee down the block, I said, "I have to go to the bathroom, then I'll go home."

"See you Thursday," she added. "You're doing swell; pretty soon we'll take you downtown to the radio station and see if they like you there. Bye."

She left, and I quietly crossed the short corridor to the studio's stage, opened the door, and went in. Nobody was in sight, but from behind the closed curtain there came muffled sounds that bore no interpretation. Without waiting a second, I parted the curtain at center stage and stepped onto the unlit stage floor. I saw Don Nagle holding Jean Justin closely. There was as much lipstick on him as there was on her. Her blond hair was all messed up and her clothes were crumpled. Don was in shirtsleeves, his tie was off, and he looked quite excited.

"What are you doing in here?" he asked with quiet composure while Jean Justin was desperately trying to straighten her hair and blouse.

"I just wanted to say goodbye. I'm going home now." Then I added innocently a question that has remained with me until this day as the single most ridiculously naive, if not ponderously stupid, words ever to be uttered. "What were you doing back there?"

I thought he smiled when he replied, "We are having a dress rehearsal, so you must leave us alone now."

I left, thinking nothing of it at that time while simultaneously learning a brand-new showbiz word. I was on my way.

On the thirteen-block walk home after my fourth session at Jean Justin's Studio, where I thought I was making great strides in showbiz, I was reliving the scene I had seen behind the curtains. Naiveté must have been circulating through my entire vascular system as well as my intellectual process at that stage, because I totally believed what I had seen was part of a stage play, and I felt part of the production.

I was looking forward to the bread and jam sandwich that maid Hannah always cheerfully made for me, calling it a "foreshpice," a word that baffled me. I walked into the hallway of the brownstone and found myself face to face with Hannah, who put her index finger to her lips and uttered a silent "Sssshhh."

Before I could ask for the foreshpice, Hannah whispered, "Don't say anything. Be very quiet. Your Uncle Harry is in the front room behind the Chinese curtain and I think your Aunt Trudy is in there, too. So don't go in there unless you are very quiet," which meant to my inquisitive substance that was exactly what Hannah really wanted me to do.

Aunt Trudy was the unmarried younger sister of my mother, whose major attribute was a large bosom resembling twin mountain peaks. Her only other mentionable attribute was her behind, which challenged her bosom in size but not in shape. She was short and had a pleasant face and a demeanor that always seemed forgiving.

On all fours, I snuck into the front room and soon enough, from behind the Chinese partition, soft sounds emanated. I couldn't see them yet, but luck was on my silent side because there was a full-length mirror to the right of the partition, which permitted me an opportune view of Uncle Harry standing in back of Aunt Trudy with his hands neatly cupped under her heaving breasts. They were dressed but disheveled as he lowered his hands to her behind. At that point, still in a crawling position, I backed out of the front room quietly, closed its door, and found myself in the hallway with Hannah anxiously standing over me.

"Did they see you?"

"No," I simply said.

"Did you see what they were doing, Dicky?"

"Sure," I said softly. "I saw them."

"Well, what," she asked with slightly more intensity, "were they doing?"

"They were having a dress rehearsal," I whispered. Hannah had a look of complete perplexity. I added, "Can I have a jam sandwich?"

She went into the kitchen to make it. I really believe that those similar scenes urged the beginning of my discarding the coat of childish naiveté that clothed me; however, the covering was not quite off yet.

"What's a dress rehearsal?" Hannah questioned with obvious anxiety.

"It's a showbiz word," I said.

"You get this job," my father was saying, "and I'll buy you an ice cream soda at Schrafft's." We were riding the trolley to Fifty-Seventh Street and Broadway, then we were going to walk the few blocks east to Steinway Hall, where my tryout for the *Less Work for Mothers* radio show was to be held, which was sponsored by Horn & Hardart. It was a Sunday morning program showcasing youngsters under the age of fourteen. It was a variety show for kids with singing, musical instrument, tap dancing, and acting talent. The emcee's name was Ed Hurlahee, but the production people did the testing and controlled the parents, who supported their children vociferously with overstatement and ample applause.

"And," my father said as we neared the studio, "your mother and I will handle all the money you make. We'll open a bank account under your own name."

I was interested in the ice cream soda and couldn't care less about the bank account. We walked into Steinway Hall, explained our mission to the desk clerk, and were directed to the studio, which was in a large theatre with a stage that seemed larger to me than the one on which I had thrown up at *Banjo Eyes*. There were about twenty kids seated on the stage waiting to show their respective talent while all their relatives were in the orchestra seats in front.

A pianist was on stage to accompany the singers and dancers, and a record player was there also if the contestant needed it for his or her act. The producer and his assistant, who held a clipboard and a pen, called each child in turn, depending on the closeness of the chair in which the child was sitting to him. My chair was second to last. Each child would be called to step to the microphone, recite his name and age, and sing or dance while the fellow with the clipboard was busy scribbling.

I enjoyed listening and watching the kids do their song or dance, and I applauded each one that I liked. Some were terrible and some were so nervous they couldn't even get started.

After about forty minutes, it was my turn, and I was ready to earn my ice cream soda, my bank account, and my fame. Desire burned in my young soul.

The producer shouted, "Name."

"Dicky Selinka, sir."

"Age."

"Six and a quarter, sir."

"My assistant tells me you starred in *Banjo Eyes*. Is that true?"

"I threw up on stage." The audience laughed.

"I read about it," he said. I thought, My God, I'm famous already.

"All right," the producer yelled, "sing your song."

"I can't sing, sir," I said.

"Well, do your dance then."

"I can't dance, either."

Exasperated after interviewing twenty kids, he snarled, "Well, what the hell can you do?"

I said straightforwardly, "My mother says if I say 'hell' or 'crap' she'll whack me like a badminton bird."

Slightly embarrassed while the folks in the audience laughed, he said, "I didn't say 'crap,' and 'hell' is what I'm going through right now. What *do* you do?"

"I can read scripts and Jean Justin says that I'm good, and Imogene says my gestures are funny!"

He rummaged through a box, pulled out the script of a skit that had been aired previously, and said, "Read the part that says Jimmy, and I'll be Juniper, and let's see some gestures."

Well, I read and gestured all over the place. Later, each parent was told if their child made the grade. About eight of us made it and were told to be at the studio the next Saturday at 8:00 A.M. and to expect to be there till twelve, at which time there would be a dress rehearsal for the Sunday show.

With some terror in my soul, I said to my father, "I'm not hugging and kissing any grown women."

When we were on Fifty-Seventh Street outside of Steinway Hall, my father said, "Who told you you'd have to hug and kiss grown women?"

I said, "In show business, 'dress rehearsal' means that. I saw it twice in one day: once with Mr. Nagle and Jean Justin, and once with Uncle Harry and Aunt Trudy."

My father said, "Holy God in Heaven."

I was on radio for a year and a half every Sunday for ten or fifteen minutes in skits, gesturing like crazy, which the radio audience never saw. I held my own but never got paid and was never offered a paying job, a fact that soured my father's zeal for that particular career for me. The economy got better in 1937, and during that year, my father was doing well, Grandma's store was enlarged, and my mother went to work full-time for her. We moved to West End Avenue. Aunt Trudy married the handyman in our new apartment house and moved in with him, so now there were only seven of us in the new place. We slept two to a room now, and Hannah had a little room to herself behind the kitchen.

For Christmas, I got a baseball mitt with Lou Gehrig's name burned into the leather, and I decided that starting with the spring baseball season, I would spend all my free time practicing hitting and fielding so that I would be ready for the Yankees when they needed me. I now realized that baseball would be my prime career, replacing firefighting and show business, unless, of course, an opportunity in either of those vocations would present itself.

Oh, yeah! My father told Uncle Harry about what I had seen. He never called me a bad name again, and I noticed a decided hint of respect when he did speak to me.

THE MOHAWK EXPERIENCE

J. D. Salinger wrote a story called "Laughing Man" that, after I read it, brought back lucid memories of my youth in the late 1930s. Those years occurred just after the depths of the Depression, when the black bird of poverty sailed over the unsuspecting ebullience of our young years while struggling parents kindly covered us with whatever cloak of enjoyment they could afford.

Salinger's short story takes place precisely where I grew up on the west side of Manhattan near Amsterdam Avenue in the eighties. His early years preceded mine by about ten years, immediately before the Depression exploded, which had a definite effect on the average family's economic situation but saw little change in the neighborhood.

In the time before Little League baseball or Pop Warner football, kids on the streets of New York formed teams of their own or had choose-up sides where each youngster would be picked alternately by two captains whose reputations were well established as the best athletes in the neighborhood. The guys not chosen would automatically be left standing to start a new team, albeit one of lesser prowess than what was called the first team or the varsity.

As progress would have it and challenges changed the scene, changes happened even to kids' games and their rules, like stage settings of Broadway musicals. What immediately evolved was the appearance of enterprising young male entrepreneurs in their late teens and early twenties who saw the need to add organization to these pick-up groups. In fact, these groups became cells for the organizers that operated on the weekends providing schedules of games, security, and transportation. The group owner/leader charged fifty cents a day per boy for his services, which hard-pressed parents would pay each day their child showed up for the group. The group leader, who had about twelve kids in his charge, would gross six dollars a day, which was good money in the thirties.

Salinger's group was called the Comanches. Indian names were de rigueur, but so were major league team names, birds, insects, and other crawling or fast-moving animals, which all had their genre used as motifs. Our group was the Mohawks, owned and operated by Boots Waldorf.

Boots was eighteen, a floppy blond-haired freshman at City College of New York. He was an inch or so short of six feet, tall and agile—in fact, a darn good athlete who had the propensity to impart the knowledge of sport so necessary to the nine-to-eleven–year–olds who made up what we thought was the fierce and foreboding champion Mohawk team.

To his everlasting credit, Boots was a born instructor bent into the headwind of education with the intent of turning the hurricane into a gentle breeze for his students. This inventive basic element of his personality was a necessity because in foul weather, the Mohawks found themselves in the Museum of Natural History across the street from Central Park or other free-admission institutions in the city. Boots made the trips exciting with explanations of the exhibits delivered with intelligence coupled with a theatrical ability to rivet our young minds to the subject at hand.

Without doubt there was punching, wrestling, and many occasions of similar disinterest in our non-athletic moments, but Boots persisted and we loved him. On the fine weather weekends, Boots would pick us up at two or three designated locations in an old bus with wooden sides and what felt like square wheels, windows that did not roll up or down, and a few spaces in the metal floor where the receding roadway could clearly be seen. There were four rows of wicker seats, hard as rocks, where the twelve of us would sit after the winners of the shoving and grabbing match for the best window seats took place. Others sat disconsolately on middle seats. Boots always announced that his "limo," as he called it, wouldn't start until decorum was evident and continuous, so our youthful energy ebbed as we obeyed our mentor with mysterious respect and a somewhat speedy silent recovery.

All of us brought our lunches along in brown paper bags. In most bags, a peanut butter and jelly sandwich on white bread generally fused with a banana or a random cookie or two, because each of us sat on our lunch bag in the bus while we cradled our baseball mitts in our laps or some football items during that season. When we got to the field, our lunch bags, stained a soft brown and flat as home plate, would be placed in a pile of sweaters and jackets between home and first base.

Boots would let us unwind from the harrowing, bumpy ride to Van Cortlandt Park, and the Mohawks took full advantage of that warm-up time to relax by tackling each other, chasing balls, yelling, fielding grounders, and exchanging nasty remarks with the opposing team warming up in exactly the same way as we about twenty yards away.

When Boots shook a cowbell he used instead of a whistle, the Mohawks would finish unwinding and join their beloved coach where he would be standing out of earshot of non-Mohawks. We would close in on him in a rush, surround him, and squat cross-legged, obediently awaiting the next minutes, during which he would announce the positions each of us would play.

Boots would then pick a subject totally apart from sports, such as a historical topic, and say, "Who knows what happened in 1917?" or "What was the Civil War about?"

Boots, as it became evident in our later years, successfully bombarded us with questions related to patriotism and, of all things foreign to our tender age, the concept of capitalism. At City College, liberalism, unionism, and to a significant degree, anti-capitalism spurred on by Soviet communism that had spread into other European countries and was held in high esteem in the U.S. by a starved and struggling minority, fell on Boots's ears.

His beliefs took an opposite position to liberal positions, and he expounded his feelings to whoever would listen. To the Mohawks, his questions were muted and designed to instruct at a very low level.

When he asked questions, it was in a relaxing tone, and actually inspired us even though we never knew the answers and awaited his own replies to his own questions. "What happened in 1917?" saw all of us shaking our heads negatively. He would reply, "Our country went to war against the Germans and their allies."

"Who won?" nine-year-old Ben asked.

"We won."

"What did we get for winning?"

"Good question, Ben. We stopped bad people from taking the good people's land. But the bad people rose up again, and I think we're going to have to beat them again."

"Will we go to war again?"

"Yes, I think we will. This is 1940, and Europe is in worse trouble now than in 1917 when we went to war. England and France are already at war with Germany."

Yes, that was the early spring of 1940, and war seemed like comic book stuff to us, but we listened, and some of us went home and brought up the topics Boots planted in us like the little seeds in the window boxes our mothers kept.

Capitalism was brought to our eager attention in quite a different way—"eager" because Boots turned concept into realism with a two-edged blade. One of our eleven-year-olds, who happened to be our team captain, pitcher, and best player, said, "Boots and all the other leaders bet on our games. I heard from other groups—from the Iroquois and the Lions."

"With money?"

"Sure."

"How much?"

"Dunno."

"Every game?"

"Yeah."

"Even football?"

"Yeah, yeah." Ben threw his hands up in the air and said, "I don't know any more. Ask Boots."

We didn't have to ask Boots because we were putting two and two together. Before each game and after our history lesson, Boots would repeat something in a whisper, suggesting that we listen even more closely than ever.

"An important thing to know," he began, "is that being rewarded for good work is the American way. Never be ashamed of your reward if you know you've earned it."

By this time, his preamble, which all of us had committed to memory, was followed by the meat of his short pronouncement; if we had known what chops were, we could have licked them.

Boots continued, "Remember, an extra base hit is a penny, a home run is three cents, a strong defensive play is a penny, the winning pitcher is three cents, and if we win the game, everybody gets a soda. Got it? You know your position. The guys not playing, coach until you get in, and you all will get in. The batting order is on this sheet. Get out there and play hard and win that game, Mohawks."

And win we did. We lost a few, but our record was stupendous, and capitalism was branded, sculpted, and tattooed in our every Mohawk soul.

Our fall football record was as good as our spring and summer baseball's was. If Boots was betting enough—Rockefeller, move over. In the dead of winter, from mid-December till the end of March, we all met at the Museum of Natural History, where on the weekends, free movies were shown, and Boots would take us to another exhibit, after which we gathered in the lunchroom and had our sandwiches and nickel sodas and answered the questions Boots would ask about what we had just seen. He repeated a few of his advisory thoughts, and on this day, he gently offered the best of them. "Mohawks, while you're on or off the field, think quickly of what your job is. Use your mind; your opponent may lose theirs. Use your eyes and ears and your brains and your ability will naturally be a part of you." Then he hesitated and noticed that a few strangers in the lunch area were also listening, and said with a bit more emphasis,

"Remember you are part of a team, and never forget you are a part of your country's team, also."

Boots brought along his younger brother Bobby, a sixteen-year-old high-schooler who was a dead ringer for his older sibling. He was a terrific athlete and helped coach us wherever he could on the weekends. We liked him almost as much as Boots because, to begin with, if one of us didn't have the nickel for a soda, Bobby somehow would always come up with it and never asked for any money back.

Our lunch sandwiches of peanut butter and jelly were giving way to salami, ham, cheese, and even egg salad. There was a lot of mirth and ringing laughter on a Saturday around Passover when a religious Mohawk brought an egg salad and matzoh sandwich with him, sat on it in the "limo," and opened his brown bag in front of all of us at lunchtime only to find a flattened mush of running yellow and white covered and thoroughly mixed with matzoh meal. His abject sorrow was quickly assuaged after Boots gave him his salami and cheese sandwich, which he eagerly ate—white bread and all.

In the spring of 1941, a few changes befell the Mohawk reservation. The economic situation was improving in the country, Boots now had over thirty youngsters, Bobby, almost seventeen now, helped every weekend along with two other junior counselors, and the fee for each Mohawk was a dollar twenty-five, but included a soda pop or milk provided by the Mohawk leader.

The word was spreading that Boots was planning a summer day camp or even a sleep-away in 1942, once again employing the Mohawk logo. We were all excited and asked our parents if Boots opened the camp whether we could go even for a week or two.

The pre-scholarly lectures continued, augmented by lucky number drawings, the winner receiving candy bars, chewing gum, and a grand prize of a silver quarter. Interest in these non-athletic moments was always greeted with glee, especially amongst the younger Mohawk braves. The varsity team (now there were three teams of Mohawks), well coached and raring to compete, continued in their winning ways with compensation for extra base hits, homers, good fielding, and pitching much advanced from the penny days, but only for the varsity team, the jayvees striving to make the big team where capitalism flourished.

After the last game of the 1941 football season was played on Sunday, December 7, the Mohawks and their chief and junior chiefs came home to find a far more serious game at hand that knew no season had begun. Japan, on that early Sunday morning, had decided it was a great time to strike our sleeping nation. President Roosevelt called it a "day of infamy" and declared war, and our lives did somersaults.

Though the Mohawks felt the rumblings and even the terror surrounding them, the band played on and our midwinter activities began. Boots grew more serious and the talks he gave targeted the war, which included the horrible European theater now.

We listened, ate our sandwiches more slowly, asked a lot more intelligent questions, and laughed a lot less. In February of 1942, after a movie at the museum, the Mohawks opened their sandwich bags and lunch boxes, which the younger braves all sported, and a solemn-faced Boots with Bobby standing next to him stood straight and tall and waited for attention.

"Mohawks," he began. Some of us who had known him for three years noticed that his lips quivered, which had never occurred before, and his blue eyes were misty as he stared straight ahead, not really, it seemed, speaking directly to us. He forced a smile. "Mohawks," he repeated, "you all know our country, which we all love so much, is in a war that we will surely win. But to win it, all of us old enough to serve must do so. I won't be with you when you take the field in the spring. Bobby will be there with new counselors and you Mohawks will keep on winning with them while I am away with the Army."

The guys bit their lips, some gasped, a few cried, and not one of us said a word as we wiped at our eyes with our sleeves. We all had questions, but nobody asked, "How long? Are you coming back?" and to a Mohawk, we all sought his knowing soul as we thought how we really loved this man, this weekend coach and father.

"Mohawks, when I do come back, I'll get in touch with you and we'll have one of our old-fashioned powwows. Most of you will be too old for the group, but I'll find you and we will get together again. Now I leave you with Bobby. Cheer up and keep winning."

There was another movie that snowy afternoon in February. We saw *Dr. Erlich's Magic Bullet* and went home later to tell our parents about Boots.

I stayed with the Mohawks for the spring baseball season and then left in early summer to prepare for prep school in Connecticut. The country's wartime prosperity mixed with our family members going into the service gave the older kids a test of intellectually sorting out their lives. The war, everybody knew, was a long way from being over.

Bobby and his mother saw to it that we all received copies of letters Boots wrote, first from training camp, and then from strange-sounding places in the Pacific. The letters came after increasingly longer periods of time, but one arrived from Bobby telling us he had been drafted and that his mother would send copies to all of us on the list of all of Boots's and Bob's correspondence directed to us. In the same letter, Bobby wrote that the Mohawk group was out of business till the end of the war.

I was almost fifteen when a letter came from Boots's mother stating in a few lines that Boots had been killed in Leyte in the South Pacific and that Bobby had been wounded in France, but he was okay and would be coming home as soon as he was well enough.

I thought about the limo, the peanut butter, the money I won for the extra base hits, and the four homers. I remembered the dreams Boots had had about plans for summer sleep-away and how that dream surely would have been a reality.

I remembered the questions Boots would ask and how when I was nine, I answered "Who was Andrew Carnegie?" with "He probably was a singer because they named Carnegie Hall after him." There were no Mohawk laughs because they thought I had the right answer. Boots didn't even crack a smile when he told us about the real Carnegie, explaining his steel, charity, and patriotic life story.

I thought about Boots but had a hard time picturing him, yet a much easier time hearing him. I thought about the Mohawk reunion that would never be, and then I thought, Hey! Maybe next year I'll enlist.

A FRESHMAN'S VOICE OF INNOCENCE

It was in 1947, less than a year since the war had ended, that Sam Melon graduated from Jefferson High School in New Rochelle. He was seventeen, a very good student whom his teachers and advisor had urged to apply for college, a wish he had also nourished since his junior year at Jefferson. The problem was his family had just enough money to live on, existing in a walkup, three-story apartment building crowded on both its sides by similar structures in a downtown residential area. Life was pleasant enough for Sam; there was always food on the table for him and his two younger sisters and his parents were intelligent and loving, but both were not inclined to reach for success, to stretch past their limits, or to seek triumph in the business world.

Sam's folks now realized that they could not afford a college education for him and suggested a state or a free school or a scholarship to a better school; however, Sam's graduation year coincided with millions of military personnel mustering out of the service, with all of them being offered free college years under the GI bill. There would be real competition for entry into any school, or, for that matter, any of the better-known and desirable universities that appealed to Sam, who applied only to one college against all the advice his advisors offered.

Princeton was his choice, and Princeton turned his scholarship request and his admission down almost by return mail.

On a sunny, dusty July afternoon while Sam was looking for a job in the city, fate, as is often the case, grasped his arm, spun him around, and placed its smiling face smack up against his own. In this case, it came in the person of a pal of Sam's, a year older, a graduate of Jefferson, an amiable though not an esteemed member of the class of 1946. They greeted each other.

"Where are you going to college?"

"I'm not," said Sam.

"You were one of the really smart guys at school. You're crazy not to go," Phil shot back.

"Princeton turned me down, scholarship and all."

"There's other chickens in the coop."

"Can't afford college," Sam sadly offered.

"Hey, that's crazy." Phil enjoyed using that word. "I go to a free school in Iowa."

"Iowa!"

"Yeah, Iowa—it's Drake University. They are supported by the church or something and all I pay is two hundred dollars' tuition and a few bucks more for other things." Phil's ideas tumbled forth. "You can get jobs out there and pay your way. Food is cheap; you can buy a food card for five bucks a week. You can live with me at the fraternity house for ten bucks a month, and the college might be small, but it's terrific."

"Iowa," Sam said again.

"It's great out there, different—the people, I mean. They're sweet as sugar."

"Iowa, wow!" Sam dwelt for a moment on that state's name. Corn came to mind.

Phil again had answers to Sam's thoughts. "Here, I'll give you the address. Ask them for an application. They're looking for eastern students."

"I wouldn't even know how to get to…what city?"

"Des Moines. No problem—a couple of guys and me drive out in late August. We all chip in and sleep in the car. It takes a day and a half."

Sam's doubts and queries were sorted out quickly by Phil. That gave him the comfort of a constant available helping hand.

Sam wrote for the application sent it back along with the high school records required. He was accepted for the fall term in two weeks.

"Iowa," his father breathed when he was told of his son's decision. Sam told his parents the bosom of the deal, which they eagerly applauded, happy that their boy would attend college. Sam's grandmother, a recent émigré from Hungary, asked, "Iowa? That's in New York?"

An uneventful car trip, a bit crowded and filled with the wafting scent of baloney sandwiches, onions, and coffee and mingled with the sleep-induced breath of three sophomores and one freshman, pulled up in front of the fraternity house on University Avenue to the raucous greetings of fellow scholars and fraternity brothers.

Woman did attend the university, but the postwar period provided far more men then women to enter the school. The sophomore, junior, and senior classes were weighted in favor of women.

An interesting note regarding freshmen college students in 1947: Returning veterans outnumbered high school graduates by at least five to one, and seventeen-year-olds by ten to one, which made Sam feel like a maternity ward object. Conversation with the vets was out of the question until the older group found they had forgotten their high school education and needed some help from the recent grads.

"Hey, kid" was the call word. "What's an integer?" or "Hey, kid, what's parsing mean?" After a few weeks, they learned Sam's name.

The first day in an English 101 class, Sam found himself a child among his elders in the third row of chairs with wide arms used for writing, a bush surrounded by towering evergreens, a shack on a street of skyscrapers—insignificant. He was still in awe of his teachers, and now instructors were called "professor" or "associate" or "assistant professor," titles that guaranteed them absolute reverence from Sam but a contrary reaction from guys who had spent the last four or five years facing enemy fire.

The youngish and pretty professor edged into the classroom and took her place at the lectern in front of the assembled predominately male pupils, who began elbowing each other, keeping at least one eye on the lecturer. She was a knockout, about five feet three or four inches, with jet black hair worn in bangs over her forehead, which fell on cream-colored skin preceding thin eyebrows. Her eyes were black as coal, her nose was straight, and her lips red, and when they parted, white teeth sparkled. Her figure was difficult to discern as she wore a tailored suit with a long skirt, de rigueur in the late forties. A few years later, miniskirts arrived…

She said in a moderately strong voice, "This is English 101. My name is Miss Brent and I welcome you all."

The thumping in Sam's chest advised the lump in his throat that he could love Miss Brent for the rest of his life if given the chance, but abject immaturity throttled all his hopes and confidence, reducing him to shower on her his silent adoration, which would become a trumpet call by earning an A-plus in her class.

The older guys had a different posture. The course was secondary, the professor a primary target. When Miss Brent, now gaining voice strength, finished her introductory sentence, she said, "I will, in a few moments, describe what shall be the aim and substance of this study, but first I will entertain any questions you may have."

Sam, in a semi-embarrassed, entranced stare, avoided her black eyes, which might fall on his. He would fumble the question, probably stammer and turn crimson, so he shrank subtly in his chair and let a braver returning warrior pick up the challenge. One came in haste; he shot back, "If you don't mind, what's your telephone number?"

The guys laughed along with Miss Brent, who did blush a lovely pink. Sam shed a jealous tear. Iowa had its wags.

Sam's parents sent a five-dollar bill to him twice a month, which paid for his room and breakfast at the fraternity house. The house also had a library of textbooks that last year's students would donate to the stacks. For the rest of his classroom needs, he did have just about enough money, but he quickly emptied his coffers. He needed a job. The vets were supported by Uncle Sam, so none of them needed income, but one fellow knew a man named Spittler who had a used car business in downtown Des

Moines. Mr. Spittler sent cars each weekend to Mason City, where there was an auction of used cars each week throughout the year. New car production was slow to start after the war because factories had to retool while demand was strong, especially among returning GIs. Spittler explained the deal: "If you're interested, you must have a driver's license." Spittler was sitting in an ancient caned chair in front of the office, which was a shack in front of his lot. He was whittling a formless block of wood.

"Each man drives a car late Friday nights to Mason City. I take all of you back to Des Moines after I buy you all dinner up there after delivery. If you work Friday night and Saturday mornings, both, you get eleven bucks. I buy you guys lunch on Saturday."

"I have a learner's permit," Sam admitted humbly.

"Good enough," said Spittler, who needed drivers. "I'll get you a real license. I know somebody at the vehicle office. Be here Friday at 5:30."

Sam wanted the eleven dollars, which meant two trips with a malt, a cheeseburger, and fries for dinner and lunch on Saturday. Those meals cost thirty-five cents each and never varied. Spittler did the ordering. His lemons sold for $50 to $150, and he always seemed satisfied with his profit. Sam was a regular employee with a valid license for much of his freshman semester. He approached Spittler one day for a favor. By the third month of his employ, Sam was calling the boss by his first name

"Hank?" Sam had come to work fifteen minutes early so he could ask Spittler, who was whittling another amorphous object, for a favor.

"Hank, I need a car."

"You want to buy one?"

"No, three guys and me want to take Easter week off and drive to the Ozarks. None of us have ever seen the place. We want to rent a car for five days."

"No problem." Hank never looked up from his woodwork. "Pick one out; no charge if you guys return it with a full tank." Hank was a good guy. Gas was thirty cents a gallon then, so that was about three dollars plus some oil.

"Great, thanks a lot, Hank. They all have licenses; one drove a tank in the Army."

The four men came by about three weeks later to pick the car they wanted, with a plan mapped out to leave that Monday morning for the woody and hilly Ozarks.

As they examined the cars Spittler had made available for them, their combined similarity of opinion of these wrecks placed them in an auto cemetery, a moribund or at the least a morbid collection of metal skeletons, all of which deserved a burial rather than to be snuffed out and driven in full view, a wretched tangle, above ground.

The price was right, however, and there were hundreds of miles to go, though their combined bet was that the prewar Ford would not make it out of the lot. After priming and cajoling the ancient motorized clunker, a few violent jerks, lots of smoke, and a sound a collapsing building makes, the Ford twitched past Mr. Spittler, busy whittling, and onto streets whose startled pedestrians alternately shrank in terror or laughed hideously at them.

For seventy-five cents apiece, they filled the tank with gas and added a quart of oil. Over a period of time, they spent as much on oil as gas, but the clunker did clunk along, and Midwestern sights were revealed to buoyant expectations.

The entire round trip of six hundred miles would rattle through south central Iowa due south to Kansas City or to the Kansas-Missouri border, then make a southeast turn to the Lake of the Ozarks. They figured the trip could easily be accomplished in four days. Sleeping in the car or wherever else they could avail themselves of free boarding would be their profit, while bulk purchases of bread, ham, and cheese and a few large bottles of soda would be an adequate answer for provisions.

On the southern portion of the journey, a darkening sky and colder weather proved that the heater was useless, and the onset of cold rain indicated a failure of the passenger side windshield wiper to perform its task. Outside of Saint Joseph, the wind picked up so that when a fellow named Stan, alongside of Seymour, who shared the back seat, got out of the car to gas up, a hefty gust neatly removed the rear right door from its body and slid it ten feet windward on the slick pavement. Sam retrieved the errant door and stashed it in the car until rope could be found to reattach it to its larger member.

The jerry-rigged door rejoined the body in less than half an hour, but spaces in the Ford that had not existed before now allowed cold, damp air into the heaterless car. The boys agreed they had had enough adventure for the day and sought sleeping quarters.

A small town called New Market, a few miles further south on the map, came into view. A roadside sign advertised a police station with an arrowed directional, which they followed. The station turned out to be a small, unoccupied jail accompanied by a smaller office, which had three electric heaters warming the place where one officer took charge of the entire operation.

"What can I do for you fellows?"

They explained who they were, where they came from, and that three of the four of them were veterans, one an ex-Marine. It turned out the officer was a Marine, too, and the comrades fell into happy and animated conversation that ended up with the officer-captain-chief of the New Market Police Department (and the only member of the force) putting up coffee and cake and offering to let the guys use the cell for sleeping, and also to let them shelter the car in a garage. As Sy edged the car into its new space, he noticed that the wind had deftly separated the chassis from the rear bumper, which had disappeared somewhere north of New Market.

The morning found the skies clear, the temperature in the forties, and the Ford difficult to start, but fortified by the officer's coffee and day-old doughnuts, an ambitions foursome coaxed the auto into a southern route toward the Lake of the Ozarks. Route 71 took the boys into Kansas City over the Missouri River, though the big city and out again, where 71 turned into 7 at Harrisonville. There Sam Melon exercised his legal right to drive with his eight-week-old Iowa license. As he exited the gas (and oil) station, he managed to nudge a stone divider, which loosened the left front fender so that it hung perilously to the side body and running board of the car. It sort of dangled but hung on enough so that the unanimous opinion of the riders agreed to let it hang as long as it didn't drag on the road.

Unfortunately, the left front headlight, though still attached to the dangling fender, had cracked; the broken bulb could wink no more.

After four hours of driving on an engine that smoked noticeably, which the boys assuaged by adding oil to the engine block, Sam gladly gave the wheel, one of the few objects in the car still in its original place, to Stan. While stretching on the side of the road at Clinton, part of the reason for the excess smoke was discovered: A substantial section of the tail pipe was missing, accounting for the increased noise as well as the smoke. The college men struggled and made do.

The views from the top of hills of the wildlife area and the outstanding scenery of heavily tree-lined lakes stretching for sixty or more miles eastward and southward made the bumpy, shaky, and thudding ride awesome. They stopped the car often to gaze silently at this beautiful land that they had fought to protect, in wonder, astonished at its daunting magnificence. Sam's tender seventeen years were treated to landscapes and panoramas he only dreamt about before.

The conveyance carrying the men though all this lush beauty was a sorry comparison to it, but a disheartening discovery of the inhabitants of the Ozarks left a sad note to the music. The people they met were poor, living in shabby conditions on rocky soil, land forbidding agriculture; the rider-adventurers could only guess how these people subsisted. Sam and the other three fellows would gladly contribute to these poor creatures, but together they had less to give than the donees probably had. That impression of the Ozarks would play a meaningful role in their college educations; even though they had all seen poverty before, the contrast of the poor living in the midst of splendor caused consternation, and a mellow atmosphere greatly engulfed the occupants.

On the return trip, the same roads were traveled, the same jailhouse was revisited, and the same ham and cheese sandwiches were consumed, but the Ford sounded worse, the sound magnified now as the door hanging on ropes and a front right window that could not be closed let the sound in without shame. The banging, a pervading and cadent report, became a hiss and a swoop and a final clang as a piston obviously escaped the engine block. There were less than a hundred miles to go. Spittler's lot would be reached, if at all, in darkness, which might be a blessing but would only put off the inevitable till the light of morning would shine its yellow brightness on a hardly operable metal heap.

Ten miles from home, the front right tire exploded, flattened, and bent a connecting rod. The last spare, a pitiful rubber tube, replaced the detonated original. Now the car slowly lurched and hobbled to the dark lot, the result of progressive deterioration. If the Ford were a horse, it would have been shot. Spittler had gone.

The boys walked the mile to the campus. They laughed insensibly all the way back to their rooms, stopping only to instruct Sam, the tender, the younger, the employee, the boy who had not yet faced an armed enemy, to face Spittler in the morning like a man, and to make a deal that the other three agreed to guaranty along with Sam.

Spittler commented dryly to a nervous and embarrassed Sam, "The car is pitiful." Hank Spittler stopped carving and smiled up at Sam. "I'm not sure I can get it to the junkyard."

"I'll help," Sam said.

"Oh, never mind, Sam, it wasn't worth more than thirty bucks anyway. Tell you what, Sam—work the next week for free and I'll buy steak dinners for you and me. It looks like you guys had a good time."

Sam wanted to hug Spittler, but instead he gave Hank a whittling knife the boys had chipped in and bought from an Ozark native for a dollar fifty.

"It's a deal," said Sam as Spittler harbored the blade and fondly balanced it in his palm.

"Work one week for free…" Hank reconsidered. "…but if you need the dough, forget it."

Sam's freshman year would last but six more weeks, two semesters that witnessed a determined lad, about to turn eighteen, who had beaten the odds by maintaining an A average but had a failing grade in dating; feminine entanglement eluded him. He did not wish to see high school locals; the older guys would make merry of that, and the college girls dated the older guys anyway.

In truth, Sam was hesitant, a ten spot from being broke, and too aware of ridicule.

Some of the vets glanced sideways at Sam while preparing him for some sport. They sat Sam in the front room and surrounded him where he sat rather low on a cushioned armchair, expecting some fun to be poked at him but surprised by the serious and direct question asked of him in a sociable manner.

"Sam, you, for the most part, haven't been dating. Would you like to?"

"Sure, guys, but you know my problems."

"Yeah, we know—we think we can help."

"Look, next year I'll be eighteen and the freshman women will be younger."

"Yeah, but are you going to be ready?"

"Sure."

"No, you don't know what we mean. Here, have a butt."

"No thanks, I don't smoke."

"Maybe you should start."

"I really don't want to smoke."

"We're not talking about smoking."

"What are you talking about?"

"Sex."

"Sex?"

"Yeah—have you ever had any?"

"Sure—dozens."

"Really?"

"Well, a couple."

"Sam, we're your friends."

"Well, once."

"Once."

"Well, almost once."

"You see?" said another serious voice, again speaking softly and unsmilingly. "If you get your feet wet, you'll have more confidence around girls."

"Um…"

"We're not fooling. The big freshman soiree is coming up. Bet you don't even have a date for the big night."

"I don't," Sam acknowledged.

"You show us some confidence, and we'll fix you up."

"Wow."

"We'll take care of all the particulars; just play along."

The particulars were simply a scheme to have Sam meet a women who, for two bucks, would never say no, who would then introduce Sam to sex and provide him with "confidence," at which time his older brothers would not only have tested his coming of age; they would be both benefactors and audience.

"It's only two bucks?"

"Absolutely."

Quivering, Sam said, "Okay, I'll do it." He was back slapped by the scheme-team, who immediately set the design in motion.

In an area of downtown Des Moines, in sight of the old domed capitol building, a string of shoddy structures sidled up against the only hotel there as if standing guard for it. The Gill-Brand was a four-storied brick edifice; large dirty windows faced Emerson Street and seemed to say "beware" to approaching pedestrians. Its mysterious and aging persona did nothing for its profit, as it appeared to be void of patrons or employees. Sam, escorted by two brothers, one holding each arm, was helped along, urged onward and balanced by them at the same time.

"It's closed," Sam harshly spoke.

"No, it's not."

"There's nobody in there."

"You'll see."

The filmy glass door opened to a narrow vinyl hallway, dimly lit, smelling like old carpeting and mold, and led to a raised desk area where sat the madam proprietor turning the pages of a movie magazine. She barely looked up.

"I know what you boys want. Two bucks apiece, forty-five minutes, second floor."

One of the escorts set straight the situation. "Only this fellow; we'll wait outside."

"Okay, kid—two bucks, knock on any door, when you see what you like, go in. Forty-five minutes."

With nervous, shaky steps, after paying the two dollars, Sam, trancelike, walked up the flight of steps and started down the carpeted hallway, stopping at room 201, the first door he came to.

Before knocking, he almost turned to leave, but he was sure he couldn't face his attendants and survive the telling of his retreat back at the fraternity house. He managed one soft knock. The door opened and he slowly marched right by the girl without looking at her, sat on the edge of a bed—the only piece of furniture in the room—closed his eyes, and bit his lower lip.

The young lady, about Sam's age, stood over him as he sat.

"You're kinda nervous."

"Yes, ma'am."

"First time?"

Sam had no reason to lie to this stranger. "Yeah, it is," he whispered. He still hadn't looked at her and merely answered her voice, but he raised his head now and looked at his forty-five–minute companion. She had on a short skirt and sweater like the girls at Jefferson used to wear. She was fusion-Oriental, quite slim, about five feet three inches, with a smiling, pleasant, unpainted face, deep black hair that fell to her shoulders, and the thin, expressive hands of an artist, which moved carefully.

"Three weeks ago it was my first."

"No fooling?" Sam asked.

"I needed the money, which didn't turn out to be that good. I shouldn't tell you this, but I hate this job; I'm quitting in June."

The simple, direct talk eased Sam.

"What's your name? Mine's Sam."

"Mine's Aileen."

"Are you Chinese?"

"No, my father was Vietnamese, and my mother is American. I don't know where either of them are."

"I'm sorry." Sam was beginning to enjoy Aileen. In the few minutes they had together, he found her conversation free and honest and her manner artless and informal. There were only twenty minutes left and Sam wished for a lot more time, but Aileen put her hand on Sam's.

"Do you want to start?" She stood now, facing Sam, and in a flash, she removed her sweater and let down her skirt; those two items were all the clothes she had on. She then attended to Sam, who, in shock, let her undress him and do what she had learned for the past three weeks.

With about five minutes left before the warning knock at the door, they dressed, and Sam held Aileen's hand.

"Did you like me?" Aileen spoke directly to Sam's face.

"More than I can tell you in five minutes. Can I come by tomorrow?"

Sam kissed Aileen on her forehead and opened the door to come face to face with the woman in charge, who was about to knock.

The two escorts were waiting for him at the entrance, waiting and winking at each other as an ebullient Sam strolled down the street, almost skipping, between them.

"How was it?"

"Can't say."

"What d'ya mean, can't say?"

"Don't want to," and that was that. No longer a virgin, he was a veteran.

The next evening at seven o'clock as prearranged, Sam entered the Gill-Brand Hotel and in quick step stood in front of the madam, down to just about his last two dollars, and said, "Same room."

"201—forty-five minutes."

Leaping up the stairs two and three at a time, he immediately rapped at the door where Aileen, in the same outfit she had worn the night before, awaited. Sam gently kissed her on each cheek and once on the lips. "I want to ask you something."

"You want to marry me?"

"I wouldn't mind, but I'm broke and have school to finish."

"I'm devastated."

"But I want to take you to our freshman prom. You'll be the belle. It's the twenty-fourth."

"I've never been to a prom. But my work…"

"Tell the boss you'll be sick on the twenty-fourth, but wait till the twenty-third to tell her."

"I'm going to do it." Aileen hesitated until the thought she harbored became a question. "Sam, are you sure you want me…you know what I mean. God, Sam you're the first—I mean, it's the first time I ever enjoyed myself. Will you be here soon again?"

"I'd be here every night, but I'm dead broke. I work Friday and Saturday, so maybe next week."

"Would you take me for a walk on Sunday? We could meet in front of the capitol."

"I'll be there at nine o'clock, but I'm warning you, all I can afford is walking."

"Then we'll walk."

Sam's clothes were off before Aileen's.

The group at the house cheered their game, poverty-stricken brother. They planned to appoint him next semester's fraternity vice president, and they promised as formally and faithfully pronounced that they could find him a date for prom night.

"I won't need one," Sam announced.

"You're not going?"

"I am going. I got a date."

"Who?"

"Not saying. You'll see her."

The guys were satisfied; they would all attend the big event at the student union. Their time as soldiers had become a year of hilarity and scholarship.

The Sunday walk drew the unlikely couple together, attracted to each other like the opposite north and south ends of a magnet. They exchanged stories, though Aileen and Sam had short lives to discuss, lives that were totally different yet were magically narrated so that each of them understood the other: Sam feeling sorrow for Aileen's pitiful and tragic past, and Aileen joyfully accepting Sam's happy and humble family experience.

They strolled the shady avenues of residential streets to the outskirts of Des Moines, where the many flat acres of cornfields turned the sunny afternoon into a green and yellow landscape pungent with the warm fragrance of early May sunshine.

Aileen bought a bag of sandwiches, which the couple consumed as they sat by the side of a large brook and watched the slow-flowing water inch along. They held hands and kissed—nothing more. It was Sam's happiest day; he wondered if he was falling in love.

There would be only one more afternoon like this before the prom, and it was equally enjoyable. The term would be over a week after the dance, and Sam wondered if he should go back to Westchester then, or stay in Iowa and see Aileen, get a job, and let things evolve. His parents would be disappointed; perhaps he would bring Aileen back to New Rochelle.

Dance night came amid stringy colored lights in an otherwise dark and decorated student union dinner hall. A student band played Benny Goodman music for the dancers, and long tables of punch bowls, not-too-fancy hors d'oeuvres, and cookies, all of which sat on paper tablecloths, fed the hungry and thirsty while many a sneaky bottle of booze was shared by the more adventurous and reveling attendees.

Sam borrowed a car from Spittler to drive Aileen to the campus. He picked her up on the corner of the street where Gill-Brand was. She wore a black knee-length skirt topped with a tight-fitting white sweater. Her black pumps had low heels.

"You're a sensation."

"Thanks, Sam—you look like Joe College."

There was a nervous aura about Aileen; a well-warranted apprehensive feeling struggled with her will to enjoy a special evening the likes of which her abused youth had denied her.

Dancing in the semi-darkness with mirrored rotating balls showering silvery darts of light over the ballroom and then escaping to the large terrace underneath a crescent moon where romance prevailed brought unrestrained joy to the couple.

When they went back inside, Sam left Aileen alone for a short while to wait in the punch line. Aileen, standing alone, was approached by an older student steeped with more than punch, a flask's top showing in his side pocket. He grasped her arm above the elbow and spoke directly to her face, his alcoholic breath accompanying his corrosive message.

"You're one of ladies from Gill-Brand. I've seen you there."

"Leave me alone."

"If you're here looking for business, I'm your man."

"Get away from me." She pulled her arm away from his grasp and moved quickly toward the door to the terrace. Fear, along with the destructive recall of her scam existence, turned her evening into an illusion; she considered herself valueless and abused, a soul-deep feeling of acting out of context and in fantasy blundering into an affair with a decent boy. Aileen, more than sensing the evening to be a mistake, felt that she was a mistake.

When Sam found her, Aileen was standing alone at a terrace door. She was crying and avoided her date's arm, which he tried to put on her shoulder.

"Sam, don't ask me what happened. I'll tell you on the way. Please, let's go now."

Without questioning Aileen, he ushered her out to the terrace and around the corner of the building to the lot where the borrowed car was parked. He started to drive while Aileen dried her tears and attended to her nose. She remained silent for a minute and then related the chance encounter with the drunk.

Sam listened to the story. "I'm going back there. Point him out; I'll break his neck."

"No, Sam, I don't even know him, I don't remember him—leave it alone. I'll feel better tomorrow. Pick me up at the hotel at noon."

Sam did as she wished.

At noon he was at the doorway of Gill-Brand. Aileen was not outside. Sam waited five minutes and walked down the dreary lobby hallway to the desk, where the proprietress did not recognize him as she put her magazine down.

"Two dollars, second floor…"

"No, no," Sam interrupted, "I want to see Aileen."

"Is your name Sam M.?"

"Yes."

"Aileen left an envelope for you. She left it this morning. She won't be coming back. I know these girls; they don't leave any forwarding info."

She handed Sam the envelope; he accepted it and walked a block to a park bench, where he read the note.

Dear Sam,

    I know we cared for each other a lot, but before it goes any further, I don't want either one of us to really get hurt. You have to finish your studies. I know you'll be a huge success someday. I have to change everything. If it makes you happy, I want you to know I'll never do this work again—I swear it. I have to change my life and where I live. I think I'm going west; I'll never come back to Iowa again.

I really loved you, Sam. I'll probably never find another person like you.

Aileen

Sam's first year at college was over; it looked down at a heartbroken lad who had become a seasoned vet, accepted by men six years older than he. He was eighteen but never would forget his seventeenth year or the circle of men who celebrated his success of top grades, struggling with empty pockets, coming of age, and falling in love.

Over twenty percent of the vets would not return the next year for reasons like marriage plans, different schools, economic endeavors, and grade failures. He would miss them and wondered what the next contingent of brothers would be like. A downhearted Sam would no longer be the youngest or the most inexperienced, and he would desperately try not to be the poorest.

MARGIE'S WEDDING

Monte and Margie were brother and sister, though two more diverse siblings would be as difficult to discover as rocks bearing uranium. Monte was a successful lawyer, especially proficient in real estate matters, an owner of property, and well-known in a field that made him prosperous. More important was his charitable side, his good nature, and his ability to reason and readily understand the difficulties of others. He was not profligate, flighty, argumentative, unscholarly, imperious, or unrestrained, as was Margie.

To list Margie's virtues, one would have to begin and end the list with "good-looking."

As a young girl in elementary school, Margie had no interest or intention to open any of the books provided by the school system free of charge. For the fact that she learned how to read one would have to applaud movie magazines and comic books for her success, if it could be called such. The words in the magazines, when compared to the colorful pictures ascribed to them, gave Margie the rudimentary skill needed to apply the meaning of words she could pen in handwriting only she could decipher.

Whatever homework children were asked to explore at that unsophisticated age was not only ignored by Margie; she considered it an imposition, an obstruction, really an interruption of her comic book scrutiny and her survey of Hollywood. A bit later in her life, she gradually advanced to cosmetic and fashion journals, as long as they were saturated with glossy pictures, but for her grade school years, she remained complacently semiliterate compared to her peers.

She did impress her fellow school chums with her good looks and her carefree demeanor. Though she appeared unconcerned with schoolwork, her insouciance appealed to many youngsters who admired her nonchalant attitude toward order, and her fondness for treating severity with good nature and an impish quality of chuckling at difficulties and taking nothing seriously.

As a child, she wore her black hair short; her bangs hung a few inches down her forehead, under which her clear blue eyes sparkled. Her nostrils flared, her nose was straight, and her lips spread constantly in a mischievous smile, which predicted future smile lines around her mouth, which would be joined by pleasant creases on the corners of her eyes. Even as a youngster, she sported a trim figure, dressed in short pleated skirts, cute tops, panty hose, and perennial black patent leather shoes—this charm concealing her errant attitude toward enlightenment.

Both parents worked at well-paying positions and contributed mightily to the family fortune but neglected Monte and Margie, leaving them in the care of a nanny-maid, whose responsibility was to keep the two clean, fed, and off to school. Neither parent was mindful of their offspring's progress, instead content with their exterior appearance and their comfort in a well-funded household.

As it turned out, Monte required little if any assistance, as his schoolwork was excellent and his posture confirmed the probability of a bright future. His sister's future was as uncertain as a summer storm, and Monte knew from early on that Margie would depend on him to stay trouble-free, guided, and capitalized steadily. He accepted that responsibility not as a burden, but as a warm-hearted duty.

The first school from which Margie was evicted was a private institution whose teachers and principal refused to believe a fifth-grader's grade average could be so low. Her mother sat in front of a frowning principal.

"Perhaps she couldn't relate to her instructions?" she posed as a question.

"Madame." The reply was not meant to be taken lightly. "She not only failed in every academic study; she never took an exam."

"Oh, my," Margie's mother sighed. "What should we do?"

"For one thing…" The principal swallowed. "I would save my money if I were you."

"Money is not our problem. It seems Margie is."

"There's no question about that," came the exclamation. "Secondly, I would try private tutelage."

Margie's mother stated that she had to get back to work. "A meeting," she said, and asked if there were any way Margie could stay at the school and be privately tutored.

The principal, as serious as he could look and speak, said, "Madame, it's either she goes or I go. Other kids are trying to emulate your beautiful daughter. You can see the problem."

Margie's mother and her twelve-year-old daughter, who waited outside the dean's office, left. Two years later, the scene was repeated.

The headmaster of the fine private academy at which Margie had spent two years in a dormitory with privileged, non-studious pupils spoke with obvious exasperation.

"We have problem boys and girls here, but Mrs. Weston, your lovely daughter plainly refuses to be educated." He opened a manila folder. "This is from an art class where fourteen- and fifteen-year-old students draw and paint."

The picture, which bore Margie's signature, was a stick figure of Mickey Mouse smoking a cigar. "She is either putting us on, laughing at us, or else she is an abject learning failure who derides education. The trouble is the kids really like her—especially the boys. I think she could do much better, but we can't motivate her. She is a healthy and beautiful girl, but we cannot keep her here."

The next educational facility that Margie attended bore a similar script after she poured a vial of sulfuric acid into the chemistry instructor's teaching notebook; though it was poured in the spine, minutes later, the notebook turned brown and disintegrated. Being dismissed became a habit.

The Westons sent their daughter to Europe with an academic traveling group, where Margie enjoyed the scenery, the kids, the camaraderie—in fact, everything but the studies. Europe was a comic opera for her. The museums were a mirthful collection of odd novelties, and the churches were structures that desperately tried to unnerve her; she felt they destroyed her gaiety. In a Catholic church in the south of France, Margie hid in an empty confessional booth long enough to hold up a bus full of kids for an hour while the hunt for her went on in earnest.

Trifling with the world and its inhabitants would never cease for Margie, or so it seemed until deep into her seventeenth year, after all attempts to educate her had been exhausted. She had modeling jobs in New York, which saw her shifting between high-end department stores and showrooms of clothing manufacturers in the fashion center. She spent her earnings on taxicabs, trinkets, and clothes, and often would supplement her income with her older brother's largesse.

A horrible small plane accident close to the Swiss border in the Austrian Tyrol took the lives of eight people when it smashed into the cloud-enveloped Alps. Among the deceased were the Westons, leaving Margie and Monte seventeen- and twenty-four–year–old orphans who certainly mourned their loss but found solace in one another. Sobriety engaged Margie, but her youthful antics left smudges on her canvas that were not easily colored over.

Though Monte's counsel came often, Margie still had the blemishes of frivolity and stubbornness staining her perception of reality.

Monte, in his mid-twenties, was an instant success and shared his prosperity with his sister whenever she requested it. Though he helped her momentarily, Monte sought self-compensation by extending advice.

"Marge," he pleasantly offered, "don't you think it's time you seriously consider your future? You'll be eighteen pretty soon."

"I'm trying."

"You're a beautiful, whimsical lady."

"Monte, I am what I am."

"Young men will soon want to marry you."

"They already have."

"You never mentioned that."

"There was never anyone I seriously considered. That is, until two weeks ago."

Monte recovered quickly. "What happened two weeks ago?"

"I met the man I'm going to marry."

"You know that in two weeks?"

That impish grin so peculiar to Margie appeared as it constantly had years ago. "I knew that in two minutes."

Monte, who had stood as he talked to Margie, now sat down in front of her and moaned. "We'd better talk about this. Tell me about him. What's his name?"

"His name is Jason Bolen. He's a personal trainer, works for Body in Motion, and wants to open his own oven business."

Monte formed about thirty questions he wanted answered, but knowing Margie's manner, slowed his mouth down while his mind caught up. "How old is he?"

"Thirty-four or -five."

"Ever been married?"

"Yeah, divorced, I think, and he has a son, about ten or eleven. Monte, he is the cutest man. He has red hair, a build like Superman, he's fun to be around, and he's friendly with a lot of show business people—you know, singers, dancers, actors, waitresses."

Monte, now sensing concern, issued a statement—really a warning. "This fellow is twice your age and sounds like he's been around. Can he support you? Where are you going to live?

Margie, now in shallow water, became defensive, protective of her choice. "I'm going to continue modeling. He doesn't make a lot of money, but when he opens his own place, he will. We'll live in my apartment to begin with."

"Where is he getting the money he needs to start the business?" Monte stealthily approached the nucleus of this atom, which began gnawing at the answer he correctly suspected.

"He asked me if I could loan him some money. Since the folks died, I really have more than I need."

"How much?"

"Thirty-five thousand. He tried the banks, but they won't lend him any unless I cosign."

"Don't sign anything."

"Well, I did."

"Great God."

"Monte," she said with emphasis, "we *are* going to get married."

A long minute of silence followed until Monte spoke again. "I want to meet this fellow. Arrange a dinner for us at my place next week."

"Oh, Monte, that's grand. Will you make the wedding? The girl's family usually pays."

A week later at Monte's apartment in the east seventies in Manhattan, he awaited the appearance of Jason the body builder and his preteen, whose father advised Margie he would be bringing him along. Monte did some surreptitious background checks on his proposed brother-in-law, and what he found was disturbing. Jason had never been married; the child was his, but the mother was unknown and never saw the boy after giving birth to him. Jason was never jailed but owed city, state, and federal taxes, unpaid now for over two years. He had also been named in a paternity suit.

Monte did not discuss these findings with Margie, knowing her carefree manner would throw sand in her eyes, causing disbelief, some friction, and possibly hostility. He thought it best to let Margie discover some of these worrisome details herself. Facts uncovered are treasured by the finder, while events to which one listens are often misconstrued, fathomed Monte.

Margie arrived ten minutes before Jason and Jimmy. Father and son were lookalikes. They had red hair, similar features, direct approaches, and athletic shapes. Jimmy had a Coke before dinner and asked for a second one. The others had wine. Jason also had a scotch.

At the dinner table, where food was served by a young lady coming in and out of the kitchen via a swinging door, Jimmy, a letter in hand, asked his father, "Should I give it to him now?"

"Best time is the present," answered Jason.

Jimmy slid the letter to Monte, who read it and puzzled at its contents. "This is just a list of hockey equipment: skates, pads, sticks, goalie stuff…what does it mean?"

"That's what my team needs."

"Your team?"

"Yeah, there are seven of us and we need equipment."

"So why don't you and the other six buy it?" Monte, a bit annoyed, asked.

"We don't have the money."

"Ask your father to buy the things."

"He doesn't have the money. He told me to ask you or Aunt Margie."

"Work for the money. Don't go around asking strangers or people you hardly know to pay."

"My father said you wouldn't mind."

"Well, I do mind," he said as his gaze went from Jimmy to Jason and then to Margie, who agreed.

"Uncle Monte is right. Earn the money."

Jason, an unsettled look on his face, turned to Margie but spoke to Jimmy. "Forget it."

"But you said…"

"I said forget it," he repeated a bit louder.

The rest of the evening was spent discussing the future, likes and dislikes, and a relevant exploration of Jason's finances, which turned up the reality of a serious deficiency. Jason's focus on other people's money was likened by Monte to a young child placed on a beach who immediately begins to dig in the sand.

Besides money, Monte did not trust Jason's truthfulness or his relaxed view of relationships, children, and marriage. God, he thought, Jason and Margie are both cavalier. Which one will carry off the nonchalant trophy? Who will hurt the other first and foremost?

After less than a month, the date for the wedding was set. Monte's apartment would be the hall. He would hire a piano player, buy the flowers, pay for the caterer, and pay the minister picked by Jason. Margie agreed to pay for the honeymoon trip, but Monte secretly bought trip insurance and informed Margie's bank that she was not to cosign for anything without his own signature on the document as well.

The mystery of love at first sight, the solving of which confounded Monte, was left by him to be unraveled by time rather than by confrontation. Margie, if she suspected a mistake in the match, did not admit it. A further request for an additional loan was thwarted by a forewarned bank, Margie assuming she had exhausted her credit line while Jason fumed.

Her happy but short engagement partially filled with wedding plans cut into her buoyant and lighthearted nature, and like a ship edging into the past, she slowly glided into a more purposeful berth. She invited about fifteen friends (there were no relatives), while Jason submitted a list of over eighty people, few of which Margie knew except for a clutch of minor showbiz folks whom Margie always judged to be boisterous and high-spirited—even more carefree than she. One had a band, others would entertain, all would swallow alcohol like thirsty animals at a trough, and one aspiring thespian claimed to be a legitimate minister capable of administering vows.

The hall, Monte's large apartment that he, with serious reservations, had donated to the cause, was fitted with a runway of white fabric, its sides, down the entire twelve-foot length, bedecked with an array of colorful blossoms that had surely emptied a flower shop, which one of Jason's guests managed.

Liquor, ordered by Jason and charged to Monte, filled a large space behind a rented bar arranged in the far end of his spacious living room. Easily ten cartons of booze rested there while four cases of Champagne awaited opening. Caterers in the kitchen and pantry busily prepared hors d'oeuvres and the balance of the menu, which a female artistic friend of Jason had planned, carefully timed, and charged to the host. The combined odors from the kitchen and the fragrance of the floral pageantry were quite enthralling in the empty apartment, soon to be a circus.

Margie was being dressed in one of the three bedrooms. She wore a white knee-length wedding dress, tight-fitting about the waist, which had a red velvet bow around it. The neckline was a low U decorated with lace. Her white high-heeled shoes emphasized her well-shaped legs. Monte, who wore a black suit, marveled at his sister's grand appearance. The brother and sister and the guests they invited were properly attired for an informal wedding. The balance of the invitees, all of whom were the groom's guests, began to arrive. They wore an assortment of clothing ranging from appropriate to ridiculous—"appropriate" being skirts and blouses or sweaters and men in slacks and sport shirts and an occasional sport jacket and tie, but the majority of those guests wore jeans, sandals, and t-shirts. A few ladies wore leotards. Two men, obviously dancers, wore sleeveless tops. All came primed for a bash, a party meant for the self-serving, for food and drink-starved, festivity-minded patrons fresh out of their early twenties yet seemingly reminded of their fore-twenty revelries.

Drinking and general hilarity began in earnest at one P.M., with the nuptials scheduled for four. Dining was spaced in between those afternoon hours.

Just after one, a black-suited gentleman with a string tie dangling over a soiled white shirt entered the scene. He carried a bible. Many of the guests greeted him, winked knowingly, and escorted him to the bar area, where he quickly joined the back-slapping camaraderie of drinkers who, though it was early in the festivities, were already deep into their alcoholic endeavors. The parson joined the noisy throng, mislaid his bible, and never bothered to greet his host.

Monte regarded the scene with deep concern but let it act its way out. His few guests, in astonishment, were the audience, viewing the stage as if it were a Grecian carnival without the togas. Monte, in his discrete, intellectual attitude, needed little to grasp the wild plot being acted out. Jason, already in his cups before the ceremony commenced, had his arm around a beauteous guest, who kissed him repeatedly. The "minister," who enjoyed his semi-besotted state, joined in song with a throaty trio.

Margie emerged from her dressing room and joined her friends and Monte in a less turbulent corner of the shady room. Few of Jason's friends greeted her. She watched those joyous guests from across the room. She saw Jason, in the grasp of his admirer, let go of her and stumble toward his fiancée and kiss her. Jason then turned to Monte and asked, "Would you mind paying the minister before the ceremony?"

Monte, playing his part superbly, answered, "Tell him to meet me in my bedroom. I'll see him in there."

Jason staggered off.

"Monte," Margie asked with an uncharacteristic, thoughtful tone, "aren't I supposed to sign marriage papers?"

"Don't sign anything."

"But the license?"

"You were supposed to have that a while ago."

"Jason said we had that. I went with him to City Hall."

"The license is preliminary. You're not married yet."

"I know that. Monte, I don't like what's happening here. Jason is kissing that girl again."

"We all see that."

The "minister" was shown to Monte's room, where he waited in an unsteady manner for Monte, who joined him a minute later.

"What's your fee for performing?"

The minister, whose words came in unintelligible clusters, managed to say, "Hunnert dollars."

"You've had about a hundred dollars' worth of booze already."

"Nothin' like it," slurred the minister, his string tie now six inches below his open shirt collar. "Not drunk enough."

Monte wanted to get right to the core of this apple. "You're not a minister, are you? If you are, show me some ID." Margie now stood inside the bedroom, the minister's back to her. She was listening carefully.

"Can't show ID, jus' a fren' of Jason. Told him I'd do the job."

Monte grabbed his lapels, pressing the issue. "So this is a hoax. This whole affair is a deception, a little joke." Monte's face was up against the minister's, his grip tightening, his voice rising. The minister, frightened, his words jumbled, shrank as he spoke.

"Supposed t' make hunnert dollars, marry them, and leave, but can't even find my bible."

"Why is Jason doing this? As if I don't know." This was said so Margie could hear the explanation firsthand.

"F'money, I suppose. Don't tell him I said that."

Monte looked at Margie, whose shoulders shook as she cried.

"So there was to be no wedding—just a big party, a big prank, really, a caper. Here's twenty bucks. Get out and go home—if you can find it." To Margie, he said, "Would you mind if I throw Jason out?"

"No," she said tearfully, "go ahead and throw him out."

Monte gave the minister twenty dollars, showed him the door, and closed it behind him. Nobody saw him leave; the caterers were serving and guests were busily eating. Many were drinking Champagne as they dined, while gas-filled balloons, their strings hanging down, bobbed on the ceiling.

Monte let the gaiety continue until the frolicking died down like the last moments of a wind-up clock. Then he told Jason to leave, told him that the "minister" had left an hour ago, that there would be no wedding, and that neither he nor Margie wanted to ever see him again.

"Lemme see Margie. I'll splain."

"First of all, you have lipstick all over your face, and secondly, she wouldn't see you if you were the mayor of New York. Now get out while I announce the end of the party."

Monte returned to the bedroom, where Margie waited, now sitting on the edge of the bed. She stopped crying and looked directly at her brother.

She appeared, for the first time in her life, to understand a lesson, to grasp the significance of a message truly aimed at her. In the few moments following the explosion, she realized that during her lifetime, she'd lit the firecrackers, fired the weapons that made the important battles of childhood and teen years one continuous, merry party, a party with no purpose and a battle with no victor played out as the blare of the trumpets sounded.

Her apology to Monte was accepted with a smile.

"I'm terribly sorry. I know how much trouble you went through. How much money—"

"Margie, the money, yours *and* mine, was well spent. So was the affair and the way it ended. You went to school for the past few months. It turned out better than a graduate degree, even a doctorate. And as far as the money goes, it cost a helluva lot less than college."

The party was over; the caterers were busily cleaning up a catastrophic mess while Margie honestly began to clean up hers. Monte helped rearrange some furniture. He found, behind the bar, a half-filled glass of vodka standing atop the misplaced, wet-ringed, stained bible.

THE NEWEST GRIFTER

Off Federal near Hallandale there is a small bar called Smokey's where after the races, parking lot attendants, waitresses, grooms, and an occasional jockey would stop in for a beer or a shot of whiskey before their evening pleasures commenced.

The beery smell and the purple thickness of cigar clouds hung heavily over the long, slippery brown wooden bar and the few small tables against the wall. Few women inhabited the place; there were no waiters. If you wanted a drink, you gently pushed or elbowed your way to the bar, and when one of the barkeeps looked at you, your order was given and delivered in a splash.

Mike slipped up to the counter between a few drinkers, ordered two beers, wiped off the wetness in his area at the bar with a swipe of his sweater's sleeve, and carried the two beers back to a tiny table in the corner. His best and only friend, Matty, sat there guarding the spot so that none of the crowd could take the table or join it.

The two sat with their bottles in front of them and took cigarettes from separate packs. They lit up from a match that Matty struck, adding a snap-quick flash and a strong but minute wisp of phosphorous to the already pungent atmosphere.

Matty drew in heavily and softly blew blue smoke into the density. He said, "You're my best friend here. I've only been around a few weeks, and you're my only buddy."

"Same here," Mike replied, taking a swig of beer from his bottle.

"This ain't much of a job we've got; I mean, parking cars at the valet's. I'm knockin' down about forty bucks in almost six and a half hours in tips plus the minimum."

"Not too great," breathed Mike, smoke bubbling out of his mouth as he spoke.

"Yeah," Matty agreed. "I wouldn't bring this up, Mike, but being as you're my best friend and my only one here, I want to ask you something."

"What's that?"

"Well, you're here only a couple of weeks, and you know I don't want to look at your underwear…"

Mike interrupted, "Go ahead, ask; I won't hide anything from you."

"Well," Matty began, "we're here about the same time, doing the same job and workin' the same hours for the same minimum, but you're comin' away with five times more cash than me."

Both men finished their beer; Mike pulled away from the table, edged his way back to the bar, paid, and brought back two more bottles.

Mike was about five feet seven inches and thin; his face had a wise smile that seemed never to fade. He had short-cropped blond hair, twinkly blue eyes, and big ears that he could wiggle separately.

Mike lit another cigarette and offered Matty one from his pack, which he plucked out and lit.

"Look," Mike confided in a hushed voice, which was difficult to hear in the noisy room. Matty leaned forward, his head almost touching his friend's, so that he could hear better. He sensed that Mike was going to say things secretly that he didn't want to share with anyone else.

"Look," Mike said again, "the season is almost over here. I don't know where I'll be next, so I'm putting my brain to work same as my feet running for cars."

Matty listened, drank, and smoked as he bent forward with an obvious deep interest in Mike's success story, which was about to unfold. Matty was darker-skinned, the same age as Mike, and taller by three or four inches. His floppy black hair, which glistened, hung over his forehead as he leaned toward Mike. Matty's dark blue eyes neared the tops of their sockets as his interest grew.

Mike whispered, "I can do the same thing wherever I park cars, only there's got to be a crowd. You can always get a job parking where there's crowds."

"Sure thing," said Matty agreeably.

"Well, anyway, rich guys that use the valet always have large bills. It's only two or three bucks to park, but most of the time they give you five or ten or even twenty, and you give them change."

Matty's interest swelled.

"Well, when they give me ten or twenty, here's what I do: I make believe that I have to take care of another car, disappear for ten seconds, then come back to the first car, where the driver is nervous and wants to get into the track ahead of all the others."

Matty said, "And all that time you have his ten or twenty."

"Sure," said Mike, "but I act like he never gave me anything yet, and I haven't given him his car check."

Matty's head was now flat up against Mike's.

"So I ask him for the three bucks to park, and he'll say, 'I gave you ten,' and I'll either say 'No, you didn't,' or I'll show him a five."

"I got it," said Matty, "I'm no dope."

Mike went on. "So while the crowd is building up, he'll say, 'Okay, give me change of the five,' when he really gave me ten or twenty; or he'll forget altogether that he gave me anything and come up with another five or ten. Then I give him change."

"Jeez, Mikey, you're a genius."

"Well, you get pretty good at things when you put your mind to it."

Matty asked, "Does it always work?"

"Hell, no," said Mike. "If I see they're serious or suspicious, I say, 'Sorry…it's so damn busy.'"

Matty finished the sentence. "And then you give him the right change."

"Right," Mike said, "but it works a lot of times." With the smartass smile that was always there, Mike put an index finger to his nose and winked.

Matty then sat back in his chair and asked, "Do you think I could pull it off?"

"Sure," Mike said. "Watch me when you can, then try it out. You'll be surprised how easy it is."

The next day was Saturday. There was a Grade I, million-dollar race, with the winner not only winning the largest part of the purse, but becoming an obvious pick to run in Louisville at the Kentucky Derby. The crowd was overbearing, immense, and frothing to get into the track. Their thoughts at the valet parking were to get rid of the car and nothing else. Get out of the auto after waiting in the lineup, stand at the door of the car, wait there with heat- and nerve-inspired perspiration to pay the attendant, and dash inside.

Matty could only watch Mike work this crowd once or twice as he was busy running and driving off to the lot, as were all the parkers. The bank cash he was given to account for was one hundred dollars in singles and fives, which he had to return later, after keeping his tip money.

The first time he tried the scheme, it worked like a charm. For ten bucks, he gave the driver change of five and pocketed the seven dollars. The second time he went to work, he was given a ten, kept the anxious driver waiting while he disappeared for about fifteen seconds, came back, and asked the same driver for the parking fee.

The guy said, "I gave it to you."

"No, you didn't," Matty said, showing him an empty hand.

"What the hell?" said the guy. "I could swear I gave you something." But in his haste, he had to get rid of the car, which now had many others in line, some honking furiously behind him. He gave Matty another five and got two bucks change.

Matty now had visions of success, leading to a life of extreme leisure. His face had a wide and wise, non-disappearing smile, extremely similar to that of his best friend and mentor Mike's. Matty was now thinking of going into this grifting business in full throttle, working over every car in his charge. In fact, whatever mathematical ability his eighteen years of life and minimal schooling could muster was working methodically on the profit he could amass by screwing, say, fifty cars a day.

Matty's reverie was interrupted by the next car that pulled up to his station. In this eight-year-old Mercedes sat a sixtyish, rather large man whose square face was the color of a rare steak. The top of his head had a stubble of gray hair, which surrounded the totally bald dome. Two beady pig eyes peered out on either side of his wide, flat nose, where the nostrils had hairs protruding long enough to be braided.

Unbeknownst to the world at large, this particular specimen's son was a night watchman in a meatpacking slaughterhouse on Eleventh Avenue in New York City. The son had presented his father with a silver police badge emblazoned with a gold-colored star surrounded with the words "Special Police." Also on the front seat of this Mercedes was a copy of a magazine titled *Police Benevolent Society*. This whole arrangement of badge and magazine was designed to ward off tickets for illegal parking or similar minor offenses, hopefully left in the front seat for a real officer to see. Matty didn't notice this adornment when the car drove up and the driver got out to get his car receipt after paying.

Matty announced, "Three dollars."

The big guy handed Matty a fiver and waited for his change. Matty disappeared for ten seconds, approached the driver again, and said, "That's three dollars."

"I paid you," hissed the driver.

Matty held out an empty hand and said, "You forgot to pay me. That's three dollars."

The big guy stuck his hand in his pocket, and instead of coming out with money, flashed the badge.

Matty's non-disappearing smile disappeared, and he paled with miraculous suddenness as the big guy put his face right up against Matty's, and with alcoholic breath joined by a wafting odor of stale armpits, sneered menacingly and snarled, "I gave you a fifty; now give me my forty-seven in change or I'll run you in right this second, you little thieving rat."

Matty counted out nine fives and two singles and gave the money to the big guy, who took his car receipt and, laughing quietly to himself, pocketed his profit, and as quickly as he could, shuffled into the grandstand area.

Mike saw Matty in the parking lot area, where Matty, still shaking, told him of the transaction and said, "I'm quitting right now. He'll kill me. I'm not even going back to the valet area. I'm getting out of here now. Give the boss my hundred bucks back. If that slob sees me again, I'll be in big trouble."

Mike was standing by his friend, who was shaking perceivably. Matty bent down on the side of "Big Guy's" car, where he had just let the air out of all four tires.

"I might see you at Smokey's later," said Matty with a shudder as he looked up at Mike.

THE CONTEST

A Greek Revival structure with four high-ceiled floors stood east of Broadway on Fifty-Third Street in Manhattan. Its gray fluted columns guarded the newly installed wide glass doors at the entrance while at either side of the conservatory and across the avenue, other buildings paled in comparison and seemed like soldiers waiting to be received by their superior.

Built in the late 1870s as a school for art students, it had etched in its façade "Academy of Creative Arts." Its grandeur was never questioned, but economic vicissitudes had visited in the past and were once again at its doorstep. The year was 1936, and the Depression, though abating, had gloomily descended like bone black oil poured into a glass of clear water and affected the lives of all except those whose wellbeing was assured beforehand.

Dedicated art students and those who could be called artists struggled economically to attend classes at the Academy. The large, high-ceilinged floors had huge rectangular windows facing north, which helped ventilate the odors of paint, linseed oil, turpentine, and polish, which kept the wood floors gleaming. Overhead lights strung on long chains along with the brightness from the windows adequately lit the work area. Easels were set up on the floor in a haphazard manner for the water colorists, oil painters, and sketchers, while sculptors worked on a different floor. Instructors walked among the easels, making a charcoal correction here or a color remedy there, administering aid deftly. A small area for models rose a few feet off the floor, a stage in the center of the room, the students depicting posers from different angles.

The high quality of art produced at the Academy enhanced its reputation. Promising art students had their work juried by professionals at the Academy before they were admitted, and in spite of the dull economy, the halls were fairly well filled. There were exhibitions of artwork each month, and finished work could be sold to the attending public, which, in a small way, helped the artists cope with living expenses. Those artists who didn't sell usually left the school and were released into the workplace arena like sown seeds in a new field, but most held on, and some became successful in the advertising or illustrative fields a bit later in life. A very few succeeded in creative or aesthetic art.

In 1937, two outstanding oil painters easily outdistanced the rest of the class to a point where students and instructors would gather around their easels to watch the technique and nuances applied to the canvases on which they worked. Their sketching and preliminary drawings were magnificent, each line an emotion of its own and each finished sketch a collector's delight. Both artists sold at every show, and their reputations, even at this early stage, developed and promised maturation.

The childhood years of the two could not have been more varied, one growing up on a farm near Kansas City, the other in a slummy neighborhood called Hell's Kitchen in New York. Peter Schoen's parents had emigrated to the U.S. from Germany at the turn of the twentieth century to help farm 150 acres for an uncle who had died soon after the Schoens arrived. Peter's parents were extremely religious and fit into the area on the prairies perfectly. There were many husbands and wives there whose religions believed that very large families were the will of God, that each child was a blessing, and that each blessing would earn a reward in heaven. Numbers counted. Peter was the third-born child of sixteen—eight boys and eight girls—all of whom survived under conditions of servitude, for the girls over six years of age immediately had as their charges the younger offspring. The boys over six would be put to work in the house, in the barn, or in the fields. All of the kids over five walked to the schoolhouse, which was about a mile from the farm. School started at eight A.M. and its day ended at two thirty, at which time they would walk home together to jobs their pregnant mother assigned them.

The terror of their family was their overbearing father, an easily agitated martinet who switched the boys anytime he found them lackadaisical. He did not hit the girls but screamed at them when he considered them to be lazy or noisy. The mother rarely disciplined the children, but would say continually, "God is watching," or "The way of the Lord is such and such," or "Hard work is the Lord's way." Hearing this constantly, some of the kids, Peter included, wished there was no such spirit as God, but all of them were herded off to church on Sundays with their father switching the slow boys and their mother advising them about every two minutes that God was waiting and both parents hollering and directing to and from church.

Sunday afternoons were study time, however. Their mother, large with child, was fatigued, and their father was off to work on something or other so that there was no instruction or homework helping from anyone other than an older child who was solidly incapable of assisting the younger ones. Whenever Peter had free time and neither parent was looking, he would find a secluded spot, and with paper, crayons, charcoal, or pencil, which he mysteriously produced, draw whatever came to sight or mind. After his first year of school, his teacher noticed in his notebook sketches the boy had made of other kids, of the schoolhouse, and of the scenery all about, and especially one of her, which was a true likeness. She had never seen drawing talent like that in a young boy, and after school she gave Peter the paper and drawing utensils he "mysteriously" had, and told him keep drawing and coloring.

"My Pa won't like this," Peter said with some trepidation.

"I'll talk to him," answered Miss Neville, the teacher. "You have a real talent, and I'll tell him."

"He's gonna get real mad."

"Then I'll speak to your mama."

"She'll tell you God don't want me to."

"God wants you to do the best you can, long as you're not hurting anyone."

"My Pa will think I'm hurtin' him if I don't do my chores. "
"I'll talk to them."
"I'll get switched good."
"I declare," said Miss Neville with despair and disappointment in her voice.

Miss Neville drove a Model A Ford over to the Schoen farm one evening as the sun was setting over the wooded area to the west of the fields, leaving a red line under the darkening blue sky. "It's a lovely sky tonight," she said as she got out of her car and approached Mr. and Mrs. Schoen, who were standing with arms akimbo, facing her.

"What is it we can do for you, Miss Teacher?" Mr. Schoen said directly in his decidedly German accent.

"I won't take much of your time," Miss Neville said clearly, "but I want to tell you that Peter has a real talent for artwork and should be encouraged."

Four children were nearby, including Peter, who expected his father's reply.

"You teach in school. I teach here, and I won't let him waste time when work is to be done."

Mrs. Schoen added immediately after her husband's sentence, "And God says his work should be done—"

"But..."

"—because work is the way of the Lord." Mrs. Schoen finished her thought while Mr. Schoen finished the conversation, saying, "If I catch him wasting his time drawing, I'll switch him good."

Miss Neville got back in her car, said a goodnight through the open window, and drove off.

Frustration often leads to defeat, destroyed hope, and disillusionment, but the thwarted action of denying one's talent had an opposite effect on the young artist. Peter blindly kept at his love of depiction and his innate desire to reproduce life's yield on any surface available to him. His teacher taught him more about the spirit of God and the existence of angels than all the preachers and church buildings Peter imagined existed. Peter was a less than average student but a savant in his beloved skill. He marveled over reproductions of master paintings that Miss Neville continually found for him, and she watched him stare at the colors and then reproduce them on a flat board, his palette, from tiny tubes of oil colors mixed with delicacy and applied to a surface with firmness, the assuredness of talent. He was often allowed to sit in the back of the classroom doing his artwork while the rest of the class pursued the general level of work that Miss Neville tried to imbue in them. Peter could read and write but suffered from the lack of an extended layer of knowledge. Schools on the prairies and farmlands in the twenties were changing into more sophisticated workplaces, becoming larger and adding classrooms, which of course eliminated the one room, one teacher concept.

Peter at fifteen had assumed the dawn of his manhood. Taller than any of the Schoen siblings, he had a triangular face, dusty blond hair cropped close over a high forehead, light eyebrows, metallic blue eyes nicely spaced, a straight nose, and a wide, unsmiling mouth. His complexion was ruddy. He was not unfriendly, but he had no friends—lots of relatives, but no friends, unless Miss Neville could be considered thus.

Miss Neville, in her mid-sixties, died suddenly before Peter's sixteenth birthday, which had a grievous and depressing effect on the boy. She left him a large box of oils, paper, and drawing implements, and a number of canvases, some blank and some with rude pictures that could be painted over and reused. Inside the box, she left a note that read, "My dear and talented student, never cease to do what your heart and your ability tell you to do. You will be a great artist one day. I know that now, and the world will know it later on. Your friend, Mary Neville."

For the first time in his life, Peter wept, and he put the short note to his cheek. He would carry the letter with him for the rest of his life, and often removed it from his wallet and reread it, knowing always that his teacher was the mother he wanted, her love and understanding the fuel he missed that the family never provided.

At sixteen, he said his goodbyes to the family, who showed no sorrow for his leaving, packed two satchels, and began his journey to New York. He left all the canvases and drawings piled on his bed, expecting that they would be destroyed but not caring, yet enjoying the notion that his parents would shrug and say, "He was strange. He was different than us." And his mother would add, "Gott ist mit uns."

Peter's destination in 1933 was the big, noisy, crowded city he had only half imagined. The Depression was a few years old, causing the discomfort of poverty all around him, but the ever moving and shifting tableau crushing about him gave him energy. He worked in a free lunch bar, cleaning up mostly, but also allowed to wait on customers. His large chubby Irish boss liked his work ethic.

"Augh. Straight off the farm, are ya?" he'd laugh, and discovered soon enough his employee's penchant for drawing. Peter sketched many of the bar patrons, who would give him a dime or a quarter for their likeness and bring friends to the place to see his work. The boss was ecstatic about the increased business.

A tall dark-haired fellow came into the bar one day, had a beer and some free food, and watched while Peter was sketching a patron.

"That's damn good," he said, adding, "Tell you what—I'll sketch you sketching."

"Go ahead," said Peter. A small crowd gathered around the two teenage artists drawing at the bar, while all the time the boss was enjoying the action. All of the pictures sold, while the drinkers ordered their beers and asked to be drawn in what seemed like an endless succession. Harley's Irish Pub was becoming a neighborhood sensation, its fame stretching its tentacles to Fourteenth Street and down to the Bowery, while the two boys, both not yet seventeen, with no hesitation, sketched madly. They no longer cleaned the place or waited tables; they were resident artists, pocketing six or eight dollars a day and making Harley's a lot more.

Peter and John became fast friends and decided to rent a loft together near Eighth Street on the third floor of an old converted factory that had been a hospital during the Civil War. The large space had three rectangular windows, providing plenty of light, a concrete floor, and in one corner, a sink and a toilet, which could be partially closed with a swinging door and a piece of string. The boys bought an icebox, a stove, and two cots, which concluded the furnishing except for easels and paint materials.

They worked at the bar from noon till midnight, and considering the dark era of the Depression, were doing extremely well. They had a few hours in the morning to work at their easels, and at times after midnight they would struggle with the poor light to paint. This lifestyle continued for two years. Both boys, now nineteen, had a decision to make. They had savings that could hold them for a while, and both wished to pursue full-time studying and creating fine art. They notified Harley of their plan and the boss had no trouble replacing them, though the new artists were clearly inferior. Harley gave them each twenty dollars as a parting gift and made them promise to "come back anytime for free booze."

John was John Still, the son of a large, attractive woman whose sobriety was severely tested on a daily basis. Her husband, John's father, was long gone, forgotten, and never missed or spoken of. John was over six feet tall with jet black hair on top of a square face that generally looked like it needed a shave, though he shaved often. He had steel blue eyes, a large straight nose and a wide mouth, with smile lines all over. Most noticeable were his hands, which had long, sensitive fingers almost too fine for a well-built man who would be called handsome.

His painterly talent and Peter's were on equal footing, both of them realists who disdained abstraction but eagerly accepted all new forms of art. Color and form were their specialties, and to the cognizant, they were exceptional. They were introduced to the executives and managing director of the Academy, who had heard of them and fairly swooned when their work was shown. They were regarded as equally talented.

Peter and John attended the Academy's classes twice a week for four hours each day and were viewed as stars, but a crack in the concrete of their relationship appeared. Peter's austere childhood molded the clay of his early manhood, making him apprehensive and retiring compared to the normal activities of others his age. To females who showed an interest in him, Peter would appear shy and uninterested, and the girls felt a diffidence in him, perhaps feeling it would take hard work on their part to dispel the complexity of his disturbing personality. That was the underlying feeling, perhaps, but in truth, it was not the case, for Peter was on a straight-line course, one rail with no signals to guide him and certainly no signs to stop or derail him. He was the complete artist.

John, on the other hand, whose artistic talent was equal to his roommate's, had another face. Born and bred in New York City, where on every block hordes of kids played, fought, shouted, or conversed in their own way, seemingly free from parental interference, John grew into maturity self-confident while deep in his breast there was the magnificent gift of artistry. He was outwardly friendly, good-looking, and attractive to the young ladies. As John quickly realized, the girls became more important to him than merely painting them, using them as models who generally undressed as they posed in the loft. The nudity didn't bother Peter, who worked at his easel twenty feet away, often depicting models of either sex, clothed or nude, but it was apparent, to say the least, that John was doing a lot more than painting his female mannequins. The distraction was disturbing to Peter's work ethic, and when John persisted in mixing job and amusement to a higher degree, the roommates parted.

John moved three blocks away to the third floor of another old loft building, where he set his easel and his equipment back about ten feet from the large windows common to those edifices. With some difficulty, he replaced his old cot with a large, comfortable bed, on which he generously piled cushions and pillows.

Both artists continued to work, each with their own mentality and ethic, quite apart from one another, except on the days they would travel together on the Broadway trolley to midtown and then walk east the three blocks to the Academy. Once there, the two were truly on stage. Even though the instruction was helpful, the models were exceptionally well chosen, especially for life drawing, and the ambiance was settling and a comfort, John and Peter were regarded as masters. The monthly exhibitions of the students' labor steadily continued, with ribbons offered as prizes for watercolors, sculptures, and oil paintings, and though there were varied winners for watercolors and sculptures, the oil competition was constantly won by Peter or John.

The executives at the conservatory met and agreed that the oils presented a problem, as competition, they argued, would be stifled if nothing changed. The two were always winning, even though the students and judges were content with the outcome. Also, John's and Peter's finished works always sold for an amount three or four times the other pictures would get if the others would sell at all. Other works would be compared with Peter's and John's and would be a poor second in comparison. One member of the governing board's idea was seized on by the others, immediately applauded, and sentenced to completion by a unanimous vote.

There would be a contest between Peter and John using the same model.

The time for completion would be two months.

The medium would be oil.

The Academy would promote this competition wholeheartedly, spending more money and energy on this venture than ever before.

The winner's painting would earn its creator one thousand dollars and an agreement with the Metropolitan Museum of Art that the painting would be on view there for a period of one month, after which time it would be auctioned at New York's leading auction house.

The excitement at the board meeting was interrupted by one board member exclaiming, "Who is the model to be?"

"We will pick the best we have."

"No, no," one advised.

"Then who?"

"Let the two decide. They will be painting the subject; they must agree on the model, but certainly not on the subject."

"Good—vote. Vote."

The whole idea was unanimously approved, depending on the acceptance of the contest by Peter and John. The artists were consulted and questioned on whether the model should be male or female, and who that person should be. John and Peter huddled and quickly decided on a female. There was no question about accepting the contest and its rules, but the model? Both agreed that nobody posing at the Academy would do.

"Let's ask them to see new models," Peter suggested.

"Absolutely," the board president agreed, and he asked the principal instructor to arrange candidates to be reviewed by the two artists, who would choose one of them.

The principal had a list of many female candidates and said he would arrange for some of them to be reviewed in a week's time. One week later, with the two artists closeted in a private room at the Academy, eight models were asked to undress and pose nude. All were rejected. A week after that, seven more potential candidates were brought into the private area and asked to pose nude one at a time. The first three were rejected quickly, and a fourth young lady stood in front of John and Peter. She was asked to undress. "No," she flatly stated. "I won't do that."

The principal answered, "But you must. We are all artists here. There is nothing to be ashamed or frightened of."

"I do not pose nude. I will not undress."

"Then we can't use you."

"Wait," said John. Both he and Peter were staring at the girl, studying her with deep regard, hardly blinking. John again said, "Wait. Would you mind posing just as you are? Lift your head up. Toss your head so your hair flies, kneel, and spread your arms out. That's it. That's it. What do you think, Pete?"

"She's perfect," Peter whispered. "Perfect. What's your name?"

"Sally," she answered. Sally was advised of the contest and the rules and was further informed about her hours and salary and schedule, which would place her for two days at John's studio and two days at Peter's each week. "All that is okay with me," agreed the model. "But I will not pose nude."

After Sally left the Academy, John poked Peter playfully, saying, "She's got some kind of hang-up, but for certain, from what I do see of her figure, she's got nothin' to be ashamed of."

Peter slowly nodded but said nothing.

The artists heard Sally's short life story as she carefully discussed her earlier years with them in episodes. She was of medium height, about five feet five inches barefoot, as she always posed. She had a way of walking, sitting, standing, or just squatting that exuded the quality that had influenced the artists at the interview. When she was not in motion, there was a hush and languid sexuality veiling her, and beneath that filmy curtain, a sensed nudity flourished. When Sally slowly moved to change her pose, a persuasion of carnality seemed to surround her, projecting an invitation to examine her forbidden flesh that she swore would be eternally concealed. Short black bangs extended down from the inky blackness of the soft hair on her round head. Her hair, easily set in motion by a breeze or the simple stirring of her body, was cut short enough to cover half of her ears and straight across the back of her neck. Her forehead beneath the bangs was not high; it was smooth and creamy white, as was the rest of her complexion. Black arched eyebrows knowingly curved over her unflinching blue eyes, which penetrated other eyes that looked into hers. High cheekbones rose slightly on the sides of a straight nose whose nostrils flared when she wanted them to. Sally's lips were always rouged red, and they were rarely smiling, hiding her small white teeth. She appeared to be silent, serious, and sullen, which with her beauty established a mysterious yet striking sensuality about her. The clothing she wore added to the mystery. Tight-fitting black costumes like ballerinas wear Sally covered with a transparent chiffon coat, so lightweight and sheer it floated over the inner formfitting outfit and sailed away from her body when she walked. She seemed to be dancing to an eerie serenade, barefoot and lustful.

Sally was not yet seventeen. Her mother's oddness, authorities determined, had been caused by a combination of pathological intoxication and psychosis stemming from her years as a prostitute. Sally and her mother were separated by law, and Sally was placed in the care of an aunt when she was thirteen years old, but by that age, she had been subjected to her mother's bouts of madness and the furor of her sullied earlier years. Her mother regularly scolded her young daughter, warning her of men and especially of exposing her body to them. The warnings were harsh and recurring and becoming more threatening, more menacing.

"Let no man see your naked body, you hear me? No man. Kill before you show your body."

"Yes, Mama, yes."

With her eyes and her mouth wide open, she heard repeated a hundred times, "Kill before you show your naked body to a man." And after, she would add, "Look what it did to your poor mother. Oh, look what it did to me."

Sally lived with her aunt for three years, went to school, and was quite friendly, getting pleasure from interpretive dancing and rudimentary ballet, all the rage then. Some of her horrible childhood memories were dispelled by whirling or leaping dance steps, but she wasn't ready or qualified to be a professional in that field. Instead, she modeled when a job was offered, always obeying her mother's hysterical advice. When she was called by the Academy to be interviewed for a modeling job, she responded positively.

When Sally worked at Peter's atelier, she found him to be a soft-spoken, determined young man, sincere and serious about his work at hand. The pose he immediately asked Sally to take was a dance position just before the leap, which he sketched in charcoal. The gauze of her outer attire would fly behind, both feet off the ground, and in her arms, a silver tray of some sort. Peter marveled at her beauty, sketched and painted her for hours, brought her early dinner, worked some more, sent her home.

The next day she would work for John, and Peter smiled hesitatingly as he thought of John's reaction to his model and Sally's response to him. John sketched Sally for twenty minutes before he spoke to her, merely gesturing with his hands how he wanted her to posture. Her lovely form reacted to his wishes, and when she faced him without a sound, their eyes would meet, his milky blue and slightly moist, hers large and bright, blue-gray, seeming to challenge.

John spoke softly, inquiringly. "Would you undress?"

Sally, staring right at John, only her lips moving, answered, "Never ask me that. I can't."

John walked toward her, put his hands on her shoulders, and whispered, "Wouldn't you do it, if only for an hour?"

She removed his hands from her shoulders. "Don't ask me to do that," she answered. In a softer, almost accommodating voice, she repeated as she looked away, "Please don't."

The next few sessions at Peter's loft found Sally in the original pose, Peter now studying her form carefully, her mood, ready to paint not the form but the emotion, the passion, the very soul of his poser. He could paint from memory now, but having her facing him, there was a meeting, perhaps even a closeness. The contest now had no meaning.

Sally posed for two weeks, performing each move asked of her and submitting more willingly to the artist's beckoning. Peter noticed the change in Sally's reaction to his requests; he thought she was more fluid, dreamlike, even frothy, in a newfound fanciful softness. He imaged that Sally truly enjoyed these sessions, and in a reverie of his own, Peter danced with Sally, her gown of chiffon sweeping behind her, his arm around her waist as they coasted.

When Sally would be at John's studio, Peter found himself envious of the hours she spent there. He wondered how John saw her on canvas, how he spoke to her, if he touched her, and, knowing John's personality away from the easel, if there was more. Peter searched his thoughts and the apparent answer was jealousy, a feeling he'd never had before, which confused him. When he was alone in the loft with his unfinished portrait and his thoughts, which perplexed him, his dilemma slowed him and, like the haze of the spring mornings in the fields of his childhood, surrounded him with vague self-doubt. He stared at the painting for a long time and didn't add a pigment to it but explored it and his beating heart at the same time.

Sally would be at John's studio the next day, and the day after that, the artists would meet at the Academy, at which time Peter planned to ask his friend about Sally and the progress John felt he had made with his work. When the second day came, Peter called John when it was time to meet for their trip to the Academy. There was no answer, which often was the case, as John could be sleeping late or he could have walked to Broadway, caught the trolley, and finally arrived at his destination by himself.

John wasn't there and never showed up that day. Peter spent uninspiring hours at his easel painting a prosaic and somewhat barren portrait of a nude male model. He left his easel a few times to call John, but no one answered. At five o'clock, he packed and cleaned up and remembered that at six o'clock he had promised to meet with two instructors and the principal for dinner. When they met at the restaurant, John, who was also invited, never showed up, leaving the four men for the next few hours to enjoy their meal and wine together.

The evening was hot, the night air hardly cooling the crowded street where slow-moving humans filled the avenues, and Peter moved with them, feeling compressed and sweaty, while he pondered the missing John and his floating Sally. At some point, he decided to end his walk and ride the rest of the way downtown. When he got to the Village area, he decided to go directly to John's place seeking a solution. His mind turning, unable to invent answers, he became fearful, and a nervous throbbing shook him.

He approached the building and stood in front of it, looking up to the third floor where a dim yellow light shone in the window of John's studio.

Peter slowly walked up the concrete steps, steadying himself by holding onto the iron banisters in the stairwell, which was not well lit. He was sweating profusely, his white shirt now wet and dark with perspiration, his short hair soaked, and his face streaming and dripping. On the third floor, he found the door to John's loft apartment ajar, with the yellow light from inside leaving a yellow stripe on the gray blackness of the hallway. Peter gently pushed the door open a few inches more and hoarsely called, "John." Silence. He opened the door wider and again said, "John." Not a sound in reply. He now stood in the loft, his eyes slowly adjusting to the dim yellow gloom.

Near the rectangular windows but not in front of them stood the easel with the large canvas on its low crossbar. It rose six feet off the floor and partially hid what was behind it, which looked to Peter to be canvas covers or drop cloths crumpled up. Step by careful step, Peter approached the painting, obscured by the shadows of the dark loft and distorted by the glow from the lighted images of the street below, which left only a muted radiance.

Almost by the side of the painting, Peter stepped on what he conceived to be the drop cloths and caught himself before he tripped over them. He looked down to find to his abject heart-stopping horror that he had tripped on the foot of John's naked corpse; he lay on his back, spread eagle, his arms straight out on either side of him. In gasping terror but transfixed on the scene near the easel, Peter saw Sally's nude body, a pistol still in her hand, her dried blood mingling with John's in a dark stain around their heads, which touched.

A terrified Peter steadied himself on the easel and turned to look at the painting resting on it. He was struggling for air, crying now, and through his tears, he saw the naked body of Sally on a crude wooden crucifix, the realist's exact replica of the pitiful, suffering position of Jesus. Sally's face was lovingly smiling down on a perfect image of John kneeling at the foot of the cross but sadly staring up at Sally.

Peter, shaking and crying, found the phone, dialed the operator, asked for the police, and gave their address.

The wail of the police sirens groaned to a halt in front of the loft. The police jogged into the building and climbed the stairs three at a time.

THE AFFAIR

On every man's travels along life's torturous pathway, going astray from time to time is common; erring trivially, fortuitously, and thoughtlessly, he struggles and remedies those moments with a correct heading, a new channel. An error that affects a lifetime is the poison in the porridge of this story.

Wilson Goodwin made a decision in his twenty-first year that turned out to be a bomb among firecrackers. He married for the wrong reason, mainly because of his personal circumstances and the unfortunate directions received from his parents in his teenage and early college years, which were well meant, but like a rowboat with one broken oar lock, the resulting advice steered him off course, and Wilson stayed that course with only one oar dipped in the water.

Wilson was a winner in high school; everybody called him Willy the Winner. He was a track star, running 220s and 440s, beating other sprinters from opposing high school teams and becoming a champion in his time, and in the milieu of his town, he became famous. The girls smiled at him, some aggressively approached him and followed him, and some yearned for him. The guys liked him, hung out with him, envied him, and made him class president.

Wilson was a hair under six feet and had a medium crew cut on top of a square, honest face, blue eyes that were watery and nothing special, a slightly curved nose with flared nostrils, and a smiling mouth. His grades were below average, and he rarely led a conversation, saying little, and in a quiet way, not adding to the grip or grasp of discourse. What Wilson did have was aura, an assumed intimacy, an athletic bearing, and bashful good looks. He never argued or fought, though he appeared to be able to defend himself in either case.

At home he was attentive, mindful of tasks expected of him, and loving to a huge degree of both parents, who worked full time at jobs that were not attractive, coveted, or well paying. His parents struggled to maintain a mediocre lifestyle—no decorations, fringes, or icing, just plain pie—and Wilson reflected his nurturing with reticence and a lack of design.

In his senior year of high school, his class voted him most respected and second most popular behind the football team's quarterback, but when the voting came for "most likely to succeed," Wilson's name did not appear. He attended State University in the same county where he lived and soon found that his high school popularity had disappeared as the foliage of the quest for knowledge surrounded him. He ran track and found that stiff competition from runners from all over the state held him in an ordinary position on the team, a fact that made his normal moderate character even more mellow.

The girls were still attracted to Wilson, but the depressing circumstance of teetering on an impoverished brink narrowed his social qualification. Wilson worked in a cafeteria near campus to stay afloat economically. No monetary help came from his parents, his father's illness having shaved the family income to a subsistence level. When Wilson's mother asked him to come home over a weekend so she could discuss the family's plight, he nervously felt the icy chill of a hopeless situation envelop him, but he accepted the invitation.

She picked him up at the bus station in the family car, and before she had driven a few blocks, she pulled over to the curb and said, "Wilson, things are real bad."

"I know they're bad, Mom. How bad?"

"Dad's not going to live much longer. The insurance mostly covers the costs, but there's no salary coming in. I got a job at the department store, which can just about tide me over, but

Wilson…oh, I hate to ask, but I need you to work full time for support so's we don't lose the house."

Wilson's silence was somehow his strength. When he didn't have to answer immediately, he would hold his breath and think the question through, digest it momentarily, and without anxiety, would good-naturedly answer…

"I can do that," he gently said. "I can leave school for a while and go back to it later on."

His mother wept openly and held Wilson's hand in both of hers. "I hate doing this to you. I don't know if I'll ever forgive myself for it, but I don't know how else—"

"I'll go back to the university on the next bus, take care of things there, pack up, and be back in a few days. We'll be okay, Mom. It'll work out."

That was Wilson, an unquestioningly agreeable person, without a plan or even a hint of the path to take, but already on it. He was never a long-distance runner, rather a sprinter, a dash to the finish line, no time for deep thoughts, get it on, finish it, and worry about it later. It'll work out—don't know how, but it will.

When Wilson returned, the job he needed had to be near home so that he could live there, help his invalid father, and help with expenses—all this at age twenty. The position he got at the department store in which his mother also worked was that of a floor manager, the hiring supervisor remembering his temperament and his fame in the area of a few years before. He wore the same navy suit with a red tie on a cuffed white shirt every day, and customers also remembered him, liked him, and asked questions for which they didn't need answers.

Weibrook Department Store, a chain of over fifty similar units, was wholly owned by Simon Weibrook, the sole scion of Simon Weibrook, Sr., deceased some five years and probably as miserable underground as he was treading on the earth. Senior was a Napoleonic nightmare, about five feet three with red hair that turned orange and finally a russet gray, which he wore flattened on his round head. His sallow complexion, a grayish pink that rarely greeted sunlight, often turned to the color of raw hamburger when its owner was upset. Dark, beady eyes were set back by his puffy cheeks, the eyes glaring constantly, no matter his mood, on whomever was faced by them. His wide mouth gave vent to his throaty exuberance, a loud, clear expression that could roar when he felt the situation called for warning thunder. He had small hands and dainty feet, shod daily in patent leather loafers, which extended neatly from his rotund figure. His suits were expensive, tailor-made outfits that covered cuffed white shirts and solid colored ties. His son, Simon Junior, was a clone, almost a twin likeness, who had the same habits and demeanor as Senior. If anything, he was cleverer, richer and craftier than his father.

Junior, whose family's wealth could not wholly compensate for his chubby appearance, married a young lady who in the spirit of charity would be called plain. Her name was Rose, obviously a misnomer, for her complexion was more the hue of scrambled eggs than the lovely flower for which she was named. She also was short, had brown hair, wore glasses over her large brown eyes, and had a small nose, slightly uplifted at the tip, and heart-shaped lips that covered small teeth. A rather large bosom rose over the balance of her form, which was trim but bore no curves.

Her tone was direct and terse; no quick wit, but a sharp, designing intellect was obvious. She, too, came from wealth. When Rose was twenty-one, she gave birth to a daughter who was named Camelia and whose age was now twenty. Camelia was in her senior year at the university and near the top of her class intellectually, but near the bottom in sociability and appearance and ability to obtain dates.

Camelia's reputation centered on wealth, and her desire not to hide that fact set her popularity back more than a fraction. She was short and sported her mother's full bosom on a thick body. Her face was slightly more oval than either of her parents', and her complexion, though marred by some skin imperfections, was freckled. She had straw-red hair worn long; her light brown near-sighted eyes were magnified by lenses whose large round frame sat perilously close to the tip of her upturned nose. Her lips were rouged red and usually rested unsmiling and thin over good teeth.

There was talk on campus among high school acquaintances from Wilson's town that he had left college to support his mom, and that he had a job at one of Camelia's father's stores. The conversation about Wilson was always favorable, even laudatory, commending his fleeting fame, his good looks, and especially his good nature and accommodating attitude. Camelia was included in some of these conversations and paid close attention to a number of facts that, when combined, added up to a craft in her astute and shrewd behavior that also encompassed the intrigue she had inherited from her father. Wilson became a target for the oft-overlooked Camelia.

Wilson worked hard and saved whatever he could, but almost all of his salary supported the family, where expenses were still outdistancing income. His father passed away less than a year after Wilson started work, which caused an immediate ballooning of expense and then a lessening pattern, but when money was needed, Wilson produced $2,500, which assuaged the shock of adversity that existed.

Wilson met a fellow worker whose job was similar to his on a different floor. He had known her for the six months he worked at Weibrook's and saw her after work many times, a relationship that widened and expanded like the cumulus clouds that rise in a summer sky. Her name was Maria, a girl whose Hispanic family knew poverty intimately and resided in an area of town where few white families lived. Her black hair was soft and cut short and rested in bangs over her dark eyes, which gleamed. Her straight, short nose and smiling mouth on an oval face made Wilson happy as he often stared at her. Her slender body added to the attractiveness of her overall appearance.

Their many hours together passed joyfully in a manner unlike other couples whose more carefree, less strapped lives moved swiftly toward unplanned goals. Maria and Wilson fell in love as reddening sunsets descended on the hills and treetops at which they gazed on their walks in the countryside. They waded together in the summer in the cold shallows of pebbled stream beds and sunned on the grassy hills overlooking the town they laughingly called Povertyville.

Maria had saved $2,000, which she loaned to Wilson when she heard of his family's problem, and together with $500 that he had been able to put away, his tiny family lifted itself out of the insecure ditch in which it found itself and crawled toward a hazy future.

Wilson and Maria's relationship grew emotionally, yet both realized that lurking behind them like a ghostly shroud was the veil of poverty, under which both of them were living, and they yearned to escape.

Wilson fondly explained his feelings: "Someday we'll be able to be with each other when these money problems are over."

Maria agreed. "I'll wait. I don't want to marry with the problems we both have. I've come to love you, Willy, and to lose you would be terrible."

"You'll never lose me." Wilson said these words in no way seeing the future or the fate concealed in the mysterious screen of times to come.

Camelia's artifice was planned with an officer's knowledge of the battlefield. The object of her offensive was Wilson; his weakness was exposed, his location could not be less protected, and his army was his family. She began the attack by softening up the objective with the aid of her intelligence corps. One day the old man Simon Weibrook, with a squinty eye and a faux smile, approached Wilson, who nervously greeted the boss by offering his hand, which was firmly grasped.

"They tell me you're doing a fine job. I want you to keep it up. Stay the course; I'll keep an eye on you." This said in a loud and direct voice, Weibrook, Jr., let go of Wilson's hand and jabbed him playfully above his elbow, turned, and strode off like a tank leaving the field of combat.

A few employees who saw this encounter congratulated Wilson. "Never even saw the boss before. You're the fair-haired guy now for sure" were the comments.

A day later, Wilson noticed a young red-haired lady advancing toward him with an arm extended.

"Hi, I'm Camelia Weibrook. Dad told me about you at dinner last night. He's heard a lot about you and the work you've done in the department."

Wilson was stunned; his handsome, ruddy face reddened as he thanked Camelia. She continued immediately. "Dad would like to meet you in a more personal way. He'd like you to come for supper tomorrow. Here's the address; seven thirty all right for you?" She handed Wilson a card with the address.

"I'd be honored."

"We'll see you then—bye." She turned and left much like her dad's departure, except the flounce of her skirts flew behind her like a battle flag on a windy day.

Wilson was left with a high that comes of a sudden signal, an exalting one that promises good tidings. He stood alone and unmoving for a few seconds in his department, exhilarated yet nervously pondering the invitation.

Dinner went well. A lot of attention was spent on Wilson's past, his father's sickness, his mother's love, and her problems and his own ambitions. Made clear to him was the headway available to him in the organization, which had plans to add to the fifty stores in operation presently, and the hinted need for more executive help in the expanding office. More meaningful from a different direction were Camelia's invitations for lunch at the club and for Wilson to attend her graduation exercise.

Wilson accepted each invitation, followed by more of the same, this groundwork leading to the contrivance to date Camelia regularly. He examined carefully his objective and found that though he saw Camelia regularly, in fact almost daily, there was no growing love for her; the way he felt toward Maria was nothing like his relationship with Camelia. The heartfelt adoration of Maria remained vivid in his memory but faded with the palpable presence of Camelia; the real promise of abundance, which lifted the weight of inadequacy from his chest, filled his mind.

Maria left the scene like the closing of a play, the dark theatre abruptly lit by house lights thinly illuminating emptiness, the audience and the actors gone. Maria with strange suddenness no longer worked at the store, left home, and could not be reached, leaving Wilson in bewilderment, his conscience bothered by impropriety and a moroseness brought about by self-doubt and uncertainty. Reality, he reasoned, was the direction in which Camelia led. The rationale of wealth made jelly of his moral strength.

In six months' time, Wilson and Camelia were engaged. Wilson was placed in the executive offices three doors down the corridor from Junior's; his salary was an enormous amount that Wilson had never expected, nor could he comprehend it at first. He made arrangements for the complete renovation of his mother's house and for a solid income that would come to her from his salary. He made certain she had no debts, and told her in a kindly manner, a wide smile on his face, that she was fired from her job at Weibrook's.

Camelia had gotten what she wanted and set about to secure her victory after the wedding by having Daddy buy them a four-bedroom home on three acres in the best suburban area in town. She furnished each square inch of the house without Wilson's concern or advice, added a swimming pool and a tennis court and trees and shrubbery to rival the grounds of a palace. After completion of her homestead, Camelia decided to become pregnant and notified her husband of her resolute wish.

Wilson found himself an object of Camelia's life, almost a possession; never consulted, instead he was informed, not asked to counsel but to be judged. He was constantly given reminders, found his clothing purchased for him, and received warnings of advisability from his wife regarding social affairs, while his father-in-law constantly recommended the expedients Wilson should follow in the business of retail department stores.

His mother-in-law wholeheartedly agreed with the wishes of Camelia communicated to Wilson, and reminded her son-in-law of wonderful things in the offing, especially the birth of twins Camelia was expecting. She would, when her visit with Wilson ended, offer her sticky mauve cheek to be kissed and move off.

Wilson was kept busy at the office and by his many visits to stores within and outside of the state. He found time slipping past him quickly, one event at a time, either business or social, but he discovered few pleasurable occurrences. What was most disturbing, Wilson opined, was the total lack of love in his life except for his mother's deep affection for him. After his twin sons were born, Wilson thought love of them would foreshadow all else, but Camelia produced nursemaids who blanketed the newborns with the care and protection entrusted to them and shared not their job with relatives or outsiders.

Wilson often realized that there would never be love shared with his wife. He knew the marriage provided each of them with what they had wanted in the first place and perhaps what they deserved: for Camelia, a lifestyle, and for him, relief founded on the fears of paucity. He thought of the barren condition of loveless life promised and he asked himself if a trap was set, if he were caged, if all this largesse was worth the pain. To question Camelia would be fruitless, and to survey the family would be dangerous, if not ruinous.

When the boys were toddlers, Wilson played with them on the bedroom floor, often to the dismay of the maids, but with fatherly austerity, he made his feelings known to the help.

Camelia intervened. "Will, the nurses really don't want you to play on the floor with the boys."

"You know, I really don't care what they want."

"Well, I want the nurses to run the show in the nursery."

"When I'm not here, they can run whatever they want." Wilson reddened. "For God's sake, I'm their father. This is crazy; I want some time with them."

"Calm down, Will. I'll talk to the nurses."

Camelia by now knew her man, his pliancy, his relaxed exterior like a soft cushion on an unyielding sofa, his gentleness and love of family, but she also cleverly realized that Wilson had been a determined young athlete, had known popularity, and could be pushed only so far. She knew her husband had limits, like a stream whose banks would overflow its shallowness after a heavy rainfall, but Camelia also realized that he had a desperate need to succeed, and that would be her trump card. No one, however, knows another person's entire story—the complete mind, the complexities borne of the past.

As time passed, the boys, now five-year-olds, enjoyed the hours Wilson spent with them. The twins were not identical, but as luck would have it, both resembled their father in looks and stature, and even at this early age, an athletic similarity was noticeable. Wilson often brought the twins to see their paternal grandmother, who adored them and showered on them the affection they missed at home from the maternal side of the family.

Wilson became a vice president in an extremely important post and in good standing with Junior, now in his early sixties, still irascible, hard as iron, and gruff, but not as loud as before and dependent on Wilson, now in his late twenties, to travel for him. Wilson gladly made these trips because, as always, when he was by himself, he could reflect and take enjoyment out of thoughts concerning personal things instead of challenging affairs of business. He found that business problems could be solved, but it was more difficult to resolve and tolerate an unloving attitude at home and the emptiness he felt.

Arriving quite hungry in Columbus, he drove his rented car to a restaurant that had been recommended to him, parked, went in, and waited to be seated. He wasn't looking directly at the approaching hostess, but she stared at him and said, "Willy?" and he turned and faced Maria.

Wilson wanted to hold her, kiss her, and, as in a storybook fantasy, lift her in his arms and fly away, but could only stand motionless. Tears filled his eyes. "Maria."

She held back her emotions; there were others waiting to be seated. "Stay there," she said. "I'll be back."

When she came back, Wilson quietly said, "I can't eat now; I don't think I'll ever eat again." He handed her a note that he had quickly scribbled. It read, "I'll be at the Hilton across the highway. Will wait for you in the lobby. Say when you can come."

She read the note, said, "Eleven o'clock," and with tears in her eyes, ushered another couple to a table.

A few minutes before eleven, Wilson was waiting at the hotel's front entrance when Maria walked up and wrapped her arms around her lover of years gone by. Wilson's strong arms were tight around Maria and both silently cried in that position. In the short time that followed, Wilson's mind swiftly returned to their sunsets together, to the wooded roads outside of town where hand in hand they had struggled in snow higher than their boot tops and where mouth to mouth they had hesitated in their walks to linger and feel one another's cold cheeks as their breath condensed to a fine mist.

Maria's tearful and faraway look reflected Wilson's thoughts, and though their memories coincided in what should have been the bliss of yesterday, the hurt they both felt was today's sharp pang of love.

Wilson put his arm around Maria's waist as they entered the Hilton and led her to the barroom. "It's quiet in there; let's talk." At a small round table, in a corner of the darkened bar, the two said nothing, staring at each other with tears in their eyes, and in Maria's case, down her cheeks, which she dried with a table napkin.

Finally Wilson spoke. "You disappeared. You left the store. I spoke to your mother and sisters; nobody knew where you were."

Maria held Wilson's hands in hers. "I don't know where to start, but when you began seeing Camelia, for weeks I didn't see you except at work, and all I heard there was 'Willy and the boss's daughter' kind of talk."

Wilson's interruption came with a hushed admonition. "I know. I'll explain. I...I..."

"Don't, Willy—let me finish. Somehow I've thought and dreamed about this for years. Please don't apologize." Grasping Wilson's hands more tightly than before, she continued. "A few weeks after you started dating Camelia, I was fired. Willy, I don't care why; I had to go on with my life anyway. I went home, told the family I was leaving, packed, and left." She hesitated a second, trying to recall facts that were seven years old. "A friend of mine worked for a restaurant and said she could get me a job. Willy, I don't want to remember the way you said 'Maria.'" She cried again but went on. "So I changed my name, first and last, and went to work in Toledo and other cities, and a year ago, I wound up in Columbus. Everywhere I saw a Weibrook store, I saw you, my love. Three years ago I met a man. Please, Willy, don't ask me about him. I was looking for someone to love. We never married, I got pregnant, he left...I had an abortion. Lord forgive me, but I couldn't bring a child up in my circumstances." Wilson took his handkerchief from his pocket and wiped the tears from Maria's face. "I have a good job now; I make enough to live nicely, with two girlfriends."

Wilson listened intently, then thought deeply for only seconds of how to answer and explain to his lovely heartbroken lady what he must say, but Maria softly added, "Willy, I must go on. I'll always love you and probably only you, and for you my thoughts will always be there. Always," she said again.

"Let me explain. Don't stop me." Wilson started to speak in his typical direct manner. Maria felt his honestly as their eyes met and their hands remained clasped together on the tabletop.

"People react sometimes too quickly without waiting for alternatives to what they perceive, what they think they must do. My situation was the same as yours. I was desperate. The condition of my family then was horrible. I was nineteen or twenty, dead broke, when the sky opened up, and I could act no other way. I selfishly grabbed that hand coming out of the sky. Maria, if I could relive those hours I would ignore that helping hand and throw myself at your feet."

"No, Willy, no."

"Yes, I would. The only happiness I have comes from the twins and my mother's newfound satisfaction in her life. Maria, I never told her about my miserable, loveless home life. She revels in my good fortune and the two boys."

"Willy, you might not know it, but like in your high school days, you are famous again. Everybody knows about your success; they don't care about the boss's daughter or Weibrook Junior. They talk about you. Willy, that's all I'll ever care about: you and your good fortune. You are in my every dream."

"Maria, nobody ever said that to me before; I know my mother feels that way and I hope my boys grow up to love like that."

"They will, Willy."

"I want you back, Maria."

"No, Willy—let's enjoy these hours."

"But I want you to come back."

"It would be one of those mistakes you mentioned before. Be happy, Willy, knowing you'll never lose me."

"I said that to you once."

"I remember, Willy, and I know I never really lost you."

They left the bar late that night, stepping into the elevator together without hesitation.

Wilson spent the next five days in Ohio cities where Weibrook stores were located, finished the business he had there, and managed to return to Columbus to meet Maria each night at eleven. On the second night, he reminded Maria of the $2,000 loan, which he had never repaid.

"Oh, Willy, I never gave it a thought."

"Maybe not, but here is the payment with some interest for six and a half years."

Wilson gave Maria a cashier's check for $50,000 and explained that it was the same as cash, so she couldn't rip it up.

Maria gasped, "Why, Willy?"

"It's been on my mind for all these years."

"But so much."

"Money is the least of my problems. I'm going to help your mom also."

The kiss Wilson got was warm, long, and promising.

After three nights of traveling back and forth from Columbus, Willy was dressing in the morning. Maria was out of the shower, still in the bathroom. "I'll be back in three weeks, Maria. I have to be back in this area and we'll be together again. Where can I phone you?"

"Just call the restaurant."

"What name do you use there? You never told me."

"Just ask for Mary."

Maria emerged from the bathroom half dressed and completed dressing in the bedroom. Wilson was standing near the bed, admiring every move she made.

"I love you, Maria."

"I love you, too."

"I'll dream of these days. I can't wait to see you in a few weeks."

Maria, standing in front of the large mirror over the bureau, spoke to his reflection.

"Willy, don't dwell on this. You have an important life to lead, much to accomplish, and many people who depend on you: your children, your mother, your employees…"

"You didn't mention Camelia," he joked.

"No, I didn't, and never again will I. If she makes you unhappy I'll feel the same way. But Willy, live for what is important to you and remember: no more big mistakes."

"One is enough," mused Wilson.

"Maybe it wasn't one."

"The biggest of my life."

"Forget it, Willy. Know that I'll always love you."

Wilson got up from the bed, turned Maria around, and embraced her. "You'll be in my dreams every night till we're together again." He faced Maria again and said, "This is not an affair, Maria. I'm going to find a way to make it permanent."

"Dear Willy, my love for you is speaking for itself. Do good, and many people besides me will love you. Now get your suitcase. Let's go; you'll be late." Bravery was in her voice. They left.

"Good trip, dear?"

"Yeah, Camelia, the firm looks like it will add another small chain to the fold. Told your Dad we're going to need some public money if we keep expanding; right now, though, I think we'll be all right."

Camelia was facing away from Wilson. It seemed like she was listening to the window. "You never mention money, Will. Are you worried about it again?"

"Again?"

"You remember—like before we married."

"Those were bad days; talking about that would bother me. We have no problem nowadays, and I want the firm to stay solidly solvent."

Camelia countered, "I don't mean the firm."

"I said talking about before we married would bother me."

Camelia responded, "I don't mean to bother you, Will, but sometimes it does not hurt to recall the past and learn from it."

"There's nothing in my past that can teach me anything. I'm best off forgetting what used to be and hoping for good things that might be."

"Hoping."

"Yes, and dreaming."

"Dream when you're asleep, Will; think and act when you're awake." She changed the subject. "We have dinner plans with the Fosters tonight."

Wilson nodded assent as his wife left the room. It occurred to him that Camelia was either reading his mind or knew something. "Don't make any more mistakes." Maria's advice came to mind. His immediate thought was, I don't care if she knows or what her intuition is. Play it safe, Willy the Winner—play it safe.

He stepped out to the back lawn to have a catch with the boys, but before a ball was thrown, the twins tackled him and smothered their dad with affection.

Dinner at the Fosters' went well and the liqueur and cigars in the library were enjoyable for the two men until Wilson almost dozed off. Ben Foster shook Wilson awake. "Too much traveling, Will. You look bushed."

"You're right, Ben, I am bushed; think we'll head home."

In the car going home, Camelia said, "All that traveling seems to be wearing you out, Will."

"It's for the business. Your father isn't up to it anymore."

"Well, all the same, you shouldn't be traveling this much."

"I've got to do it again next week."

"I'll go with you."

"Too hectic, Camelia."

Two days later Wilson had a meeting at a dinner club in town. He used a public phone and dialed the number of the restaurant in Columbus. A lady's voice announced the restaurant's name and hers.

"Could I speak to the hostess, please?"

"One minute, I'll put Charles on the line."

"No, no. I want the hostess."

The lady who had answered the phone obviously put it down while she called for Charles.

"Charles speaking."

"I'm sorry, Charles, but I want Mary, the hostess."

"There is no hostess named Mary here."

"I mean the Hispanic lady."

"Oh," Charles said. "I'm the manager here. You must mean Francesca. She resigned yesterday. Worked here for over a year, gave no notice, no forwarding address—just picked up her salary and left. Did she owe you anything?"

Wilson shut his eyes, covered his mouth with a cupped hand, and almost inaudibly answered, "No, she didn't owe me a thing."

His shoulders drooped as he hung up the phone.

A GOLF STORY

"Stop me if you've heard the one about the priest who went to heaven and somehow was lucky enough to play a round of golf with God. Well, the first hole is a par three and the priest hits a honey of a four iron to within six inches of the cup, and God says, 'It's a gimme,' and the priest is happy with his birdie deuce. Then God hits a four iron; good height, but it sails over the green, hits a tree, rattles around some branches, and falls to the ground, where the ball bounces on a rock, then rolls toward the cup and into it for an ace. The priest, who lost the hole, looks at God skeptically and says, 'Are we gonna play golf or are you gonna play God?'"

The guys in the card room, still sweaty in their golf clothes, are drinking beers and having sandwiches while they laugh and listen to the wag tell jokes or gab about the round he just played.

"I heard it."

"Me, too."

"I thought it was good—not bad."

"So did I."

The card room is crowded; smoking is allowed there, which gives the place a purple haze that subdues the soft white light from the neon tubes overhead. Pictures of famous golfers and of picturesque holes on Westchester County courses are all over the walls, and are also obscured by the smoke. The smell is beery, smoky, and armpit-sweaty. There are about thirty tables, all but a few occupied by foursomes who have already played and some who will tee off later in the afternoon. Almost all the men are under forty. The older fellows have either retired or taken their higher handicaps to Florida or are lunching upstairs with the women, who on Sundays play after one P.M. in mixed foursomes with their husbands. The club is exclusive, meaning it's expensive—the reason why the younger Wall Streeters, lawyers, and other professionals apply and enter while less prosperous families play at clubs further north and or at public courses where a round can take six hours on a weekend.

Exclusive nowadays doesn't mean restricted, where only a particular faith or race or nationality join in a bigoted channel to play golf with equally narrow-minded athletes. Eagle's Perch is thoroughly mixed with rich blacks, whites, Hispanics, and Asians, all playing together, but rich they must be. Initiation fees range up to $100,000; less for singles, juniors, and the occasional older family that does not opt for golf membership. Dues are close to $20,000, and assessments are to be expected also. With all that money hovering around, dice are constantly cast for lunches and drinks, and money bets on golf games are standard. There are a few cliquey foursomes who play $100 to $500 Nassaus, or one-on-one stroke or match play contests, with other foursomes. To lose or win a few thousand dollars on a typical day before lunch is not uncommon, and at one table, the losers are shelling out without any adverse spirit, thinking that the next match will reverse their luck.

In fact, the wag, who was a big loser today, says, smiling, "Did you hear about this thirty-five handicap who's playing alone and comes to a water hole? Well, he opens the ball pocket in his bag and pulls out a cut-up range ball, and puts his new Titleist back in the pocket. He's about to hit when a thunderous voice comes out of the sky and says to him, 'Put the old ball back in the bag and take out the Titleist.' The golfer figures it's God talking, and why argue? He takes out the new Titleist and puts it on the tee. The voice booms again, 'Take a few practice swings.' The golfer does what he's told, and the voice cries out, 'Put the old ball back on the tee.'"

"I heard it."

"Me, too."

"I thought it was sorta funny."

"Me, too."

"There's a zillion God and golf stories around," says the teller.

The wag isn't through yet. He tells a few more stories involving God, with a beer accompanying each new tale. The room is thinning out as the afternoon wears on, while the wind outside the window is blowing leaves against it along with raindrops, which are falling harder, leaving streamlets on the glass. As the gloom on the course deepens, members are either leaving or have already left. The other men at the table excuse themselves and leave Pete quite alone with a final beer in front of him. Even the bartender, after wiping dry his working area, excuses himself.

"I'll leave a few lights on for you, Mr. Stengler. I have to go upstairs and get the bar ready for the dinner crowd."

"Sure," says Pete. "I'll leave soon. Give me another couple beers before you leave."

The beer is delivered, the bartender disappears, and Pete is left alone in the room, where the haze has lifted and the lights above him are few and dim. A very light breeze from an open window brings a fresher smell to the room, chasing almost all of the barroom odors out. Pete is still somewhat sober—not entirely—but he is feeling a lager-fed comfort in his solitary setting while a soundless atmosphere in this yellow chamber bathes him in thoughtless reverie. He tries to tell himself golf stories and lifts his head as if to think when his unclear eyes see a figure sitting in a corner near him.

"Somebody there?"

"Yes. I've been watching you for some time. Mind if I join you?"

Pete responds, "Sure, but can't offer you a beer. Place is closed, unless you want to go upstairs or share my last bottle."

"No, no," says the stranger. "I want to be here alone with you."

Pete looks more closely at the man, who has slowly approached the table and sits opposite Pete, who asks, "You are a member here? I don't recognize you."

"Well, I'll come to that. Just call me Chris." Chris is an old fellow. His thin face is hidden by a white beard, which also makes it difficult to make out his complexion, though his nose is grayish pink, and in the dimly lit room, blue eyes peek out of the bushy gray eyebrows. His lean, wrinkled hands are clasped on the tabletop. He wears gray pants and a gray jacket, which covers a white shirt and a black tie. On his head he wears an old flat checked cap of the kind that golfers wore long ago. "I got dressed for this occasion," Chris quips.

Pete, who is semi-inebriated, leans forward, mystified but amused and interested in the older gentleman, who begins talking immediately with a purpose obviously only known to him.

"I wish to tell you a story—a story to a storyteller, which I noticed as I sat listening to you."

Pete nods and starts drinking the last bottle of beer available to him.

"You know," Chris begins, "this club, Eagle's Perch, has been here a hundred years, and I visited it long ago, because I enjoy stories myself, and there was a fellow here much like you who told jokes all the time. But I think there was a big difference in personality—yours and his, you understand."

Pete listens as intently as he can, considering the calamity of beer that he has poured down his throat, which has also caused the narrowing of his watery eyes.

Chris continues. "His name was Corey—last name not important—and he was nasty. People felt they had to listen to his jokes or be handled roughly by the unsavory character. Also, he happened to be one of the best golfers at the club, and by far the biggest gambler here. He bet on every match, every hole, and every stroke. Other players loved to contest him, even though they were subjected to his rotten banter, mostly using God as the topic in a vain manner."

Pete is annoyed at being compared to this joker Corey, but he can sense the varied comparison through his alcoholic fog.

Chris continues on as if there is a necessary urge to the chronicle. "Corey needed an adjustment, and his day came on a Sunday morning. The betting before the game started was brisk and heavy. The first hole was a par four, only three hundred eighty yards long. Corey laid his second shot on the green and sank a ten-footer." Chris winks and says, "He then made a big mistake. He said to the losers of the first hole, 'You guys should be in church praying.'" Chris frowns, then looks at Pete to make sure he's paying attention, and administers a playful shot in the arm to the singular soul in his gallery. "Well, they got up to the second tee, with Corey still jibing the others. The hole was a par four, a bit longer than the first, but there was a deep wooded area along the left side of the fairway. Corey hit a wicked hook, which, after flying two hundred yards, made a sharp left turn into the woods. The other three guys were nudging each other and sensed a turn of events." Chris sits back in his chair, satisfaction obvious on his bearded visage. "Well, Corey went into the forest by himself, the others content to let him look for his ball by himself before helping him locate it. Corey's caddy, who was carrying two bags, was helping his other customers before coming to Corey's aid. Corey, now quite alone in his hunt, came to a shaded clearing where a fellow who looked just like me was sitting on a fallen tree, which served as a crude bench. There were rays of shimmering light shining through the tops of pines, beeches, and maples, onto this little old man wearing an ancient golf cap, while at his feet was Corey's ball."

Pete's eyelids are widening now, striving to gather the pieces of Chris's tale into a meaningful one. He says nothing.

"Well, Corey was pretty upset with the situation at hand, and roughly said to the stranger, 'Move out of the way so I can hit my ball out of here.' The little bearded man said, 'I will, but hear me—it will only take a second.' Corey, without hesitation, tried to push the man off his perch, but found he was as stout as the trunk of a tree and quite as immovable. 'Listen,' the little man said again. 'Change your ways, do not be blasphemous, mind your tongue, and calm your actions.' Corey answered, 'Mind your manners. I belong to this club, not you, and I'll darn well say and do as I please here.' 'Be not blasphemous,' said the man again, and he left his perch and walked further into the woods. Corey laughed after him."

Chris continues, "Corey's caddy appeared at the place at which ball and golfer stood. Corey took a swing, another, and another before emerging on the fairway. His face was the color of raw hamburger, and he angrily finished the hole three strokes behind the others. The next holes were a nightmare for Corey. His balls found lakes, streams, rocks, and roughs, and by the ninth hole before the halfway clubhouse approach, another obstacle arose. On the right side of the fairway was a line of willow trees where green threads of branches arched softly to the ground. Corey teed off last in the foursome. By this time, a curse between every third word was wildly spat out. Corey's drive started out flying off the tee, a seemingly straight flight, but sliced off to the right, headed to the willows, and landed under the lovely green canopy of one of them. He was now six holes behind in the contest after winning the first hole and losing the next seven, and he had doubled the bet on the ninth, where he found himself in the spaghetti-like cage of the tree. Corey sized up the shot, took his stance, and on his back swing, his five iron caught in a willow branch, where it hung, his swing ending up clubless. The cursing was loud, sustained, and blasphemous. Corey quickly walked in the direction of the clubhouse, paying neither the caddy nor his betting debt, got into his car, and with his golf shoes still on, drove off into a light drizzle now falling."

    Pete hears the whole story, he thinks, but the suds bring on a dismal drowsiness. He does not acknowledge Chris, puts his head over his arms, which are folded on the table, and falls asleep. Hours go by while Pete sleeps in the empty darkened card room, but the arriving Sunday evening dinner group noisily awakens him. His mouth has a horrible taste, his head is spinning, and his golf clothes, which now have been worn eleven hours, are creased and smell of sweat, smoke, and beer. Pete struggles in a hazy awakening to rise and walk up the stairs. On the landing, he comes face to face with a dinner guest in a blue suit who has a white beard and a funny flat cap on his head. The next male guest is wearing a brown suit and has a white beard and a plaid flat cap on his head. Three men, who next pass Pete while on his way to the parking lot, all are suited and have white beards and flat caps of different designs. Pete is given his car by the attendant, who cheerfully accepts a two-dollar tip as he lifts the flat cap off his head, displaying some white hair and a bushy white beard.

THE PARTNERS

Louis, who owned the Toyota Camry, picked up Nick and Ben and drove along the Hutchinson Parkway on the way to the cemetery. It was the rainiest April on record. For days at a time, the drops did not stop, sometimes lightly in a steady drizzle, but now heavier, the raindrops sounding like marbles as they splashed and splattered on top of the car.

The Westchester countryside was turning a light green, a soggy but lovely green partially obscured by the early spring mist and the splattering on the windshield and windows of the car. The newborn leaves on the trees glistened with moisture while the host of pines that never lose their deeper green crowded the roadway and cared not a drop for the weather.

This was the first opportunity in months for the three men to get together. Louis lived in Woodmere out in Long Island, Nick lived on West End Avenue in Manhattan, and Ben lived in New Rochelle, so it fell on Louis to drive to the city and drive up the Hutch to New Rochelle, thence to the cemetery. They planned to have breakfast in a diner/luncheonette in Eastchester before driving north. They hung their raincoats and sat at a comfortable table, where a waitress took their order and gave them extra paper napkins, remarking, "You look clammy."

Louis started the conversation. "Nick, you went to the funeral. First of all, why?"

"To see who would come and to hear the lies the preacher would say."

Louis said, "Well, who came?"

"None of his three sons were there; in fact, since his wife died, no family was there at all that I could see," Nick said.

Ben asked who did come.

"Not many, maybe thirty people. I recognized the three lawyers, some of the church members, the two accountants that we used to see in the office, and a few of the brokers from Nuveen and Smith Barney."

Ben said, "I'm sure those leeches would be there, but who were the others?"

Nick explained, "I didn't recognize any of the others, but listening to the sermon, I think they were from the hospital and from other charities that got his money."

Louis said, "It makes sense. The church got millions for guarding his soul, the hospital got millions for watching his ass, the attorneys got millions for keeping him out of jail and making sure their fists and eyes were on the estate, and the college fundraisers were there to annoy the lawyers, same as the brokers."

"You have that right," answered Nick as he continued out of context. "And not a tear was shed the hour that I was there."

Ben added, "His sons had no use for him. From what I know, and I knew John J. since college, he was a tyrant coming out of the womb, in school, in business, in marriage, and in fatherhood."

Louis sipped his hot coffee. "You knew him the longest, Ben; how did Bernice hang in there?"

Ben said, "She was sweet and sort of pretty; he was strong and smelled of success and the sure approach of money. She was swept away. She was as good to the boys as he was nasty. She was as protective as he was damaging. Right after Bernice died, the three boys left the roost. One lives in Canada, and the other two live in Europe somewhere."

Louis had a manila folder with him, which he opened, taking a newspaper article out and spreading it on the breakfast table. "Did you guys see this in the obituary?"

Both men said, "Sure."

"Couldn't miss it," added Ben.

"Makes John J. sound like Saint Christopher," Louis said. He continued, "Every word sounds like hands clapping and complete adulation. His charity contributions, adding up to over fifty million bucks, with each charitable organization applauding and extolling."

Nick said, "Not a word in there about the hookers, the kid out of wedlock, the lawsuits, the IRS story, and worst of all, how he screwed his partners."

"You'll never see that in the obit. Whoever wrote that was probably in on some of the dough."

"Did Bernice know any of this?"

"She knew of the daughter he fathered. The girl caused plenty of trouble to the family until John paid her off."

"How about the hookers? Everybody around him knew of them. Every week there was another one coming to the office or meeting him somewhere."

"Bernice was told he traveled for business."

"She was a nice person."

"She was."

"Suffered plenty."

"Sure did."

"I remember her funeral," Louis sadly said. "She had lots of friends and some family there. Do you guys remember her gravestone?"

Ben said, "Sure, a big granite one, and a picture of her in some sort of see-through frame embedded in the granite."

Louis said, "She had a big smile on her face, which sort of faced left toward the empty spaces in that huge plot."

"Well, John J. is supposed to be buried to her left. We'll see. I don't think there will ever be anybody else buried in that plot."

Smiles all around.

"I never got over the screwing the three of us got."

"The worst scenario ever."

"The attorneys did the dirty work."

"Yeah, but John thought it up."

"No question."

"To promise us each ten percent of the business while it was so profitable."

"While he drained the capital out of it."

"The secret secondary."

"The lawsuit those lawyers won for him."

"Then the recession, the loss of business while the money disappeared."

"And we sat there and let him do it."

"The promises he made."

"The hookers coming around every week for huge dollars."

"Bernice died and the boys scrambled."

"The business failed."

"We had to face the public."

"The accountants and lawyers knew how to get their money."

"We didn't."

"What asses we were."

Louis said, "Hey, we're alive and managing."

"Thanks to some income."

"And some awfully good children."

"You bet."

Louis paid the check. Nick laid down the tip, and the three agreed to leave.

The rain left large streams in the parking lot, and the puddles the Toyota went through splashed onto other cars from Central Avenue to the highway. The rain distorted headlights, throwing flashes of glaring lights on the roadway. Traffic was light on the Bronx River Parkway, but the poor visibility made all the cars move slowly northbound.

They finally arrived near Briarcliff, where the side road led to the cemetery. There was a small traffic circle in front of the brick building, whose wet sign read: "Office, Heaven's Gate Cemetery." The three men went inside, where the only person in the place sat at a small desk. The walls had a few large photographs of the cemetery layout. One picture had the plots all numbered. Louis asked the girl at the desk where they could find John J. Grimes's plot. She went to the picture map and showed them. "Easy to find," she said.

Ben had a big black umbrella opened under which the three men huddled as they made their way to the car and jumped in.

Finding the plot was rather easy, but the rain had made the grassy area around the large gravesite soft and muddy. There were now two very large tombstones. Beatrice had a wide smile that mysteriously, with dripping streamlets running down the portrait, looked like she was grinning. John J.'s picture, which was also installed in the granite above the usual lettering, had his visage facing forward. As in life, there was no attempt at a pout or a smile, only a straightforward peering past anyone facing him. No recognition attempted. It seemed to say, that face and tightlipped, red-complexioned picture, "I lived and died and what's it to you or anybody? You got what was coming, and I got what was coming to me."

About twenty yards away, two gravediggers leaned on their shovels and watched the three men at John J.'s grave. They obviously wondered why these visitors would stand in the rain under one black umbrella. They watched as Louis, who had brought a long package that had been stored in the trunk of his car, unfolded it and handed one object to Nick and one to Ben, keeping one for himself. What the gravediggers could not see clearly was that each man held a sturdy stick of wood with a dancing figure on each in plastic affixed to the pole.

Each man, one at a time, approached the muddy mound that covered John J. and pushed the stick with the dancing plastic figure firmly into the ground.

Then what the perplexed gravediggers saw was each of the three men take a position at the foot of the mound and, one on each side, unzip their flies, and together with the rain, which was now just a sprinkle, add to the watering.

The gravediggers got the picture. They leaned on their shovels and laughed till tears rolled down their already wet faces.

The three men, now zipped up, faced Bernice, apologized to the picture, and walked briskly back to the Toyota.

The gravediggers were still convulsed with laughter and the dripping of raindrops on Bernice's picture made the grin wider in a downright mirthful smile.

The sky brightened as Louis, Nick, and Ben drove off.

THE HERMIT OF THE LOWER EAST SIDE

Martin Wesselman lived in the same apartment in Peter Cooper Village for almost forty years, and not a stick of furniture or a new carpet had been added to the place since he had married and moved there. It could transform itself into a really nice, livable set of rooms, but the neglect and detachment showed it could be compared to an old sawmill or a sunken ship lying on the bottom of the ocean at one thousand feet.

There were two bedrooms, a living room, a dining area next to a small kitchen, and one and a half bathrooms. The couches and armchair were threadbare. The rugs looked like Civil War flags, and all the sink and kitchen fixtures had looked great forty years ago. The kitchen area mysteriously had no food odors, the stove being used as a cabinet for pots and pans, which lay fallow as an unused acre of farmland gone to seed.

The refrigerator had a few bottles of milk in it keeping company with some forlorn jars and containers of condiments like ketchup and mustard. Oddly enough, the fridge worked and kept its few occupants cool.

The beige walls were completely blank. There were no pictures, religious symbols, or photographs, not even a calendar on them. The curtains on each window were the originals, hanging limp, and in a few cases, torn. This ancient apartment's appointments, however, were clean as a whistle.

Books in a chipped and colorless bookcase were dust-free, as were the well-vacuumed, tattered rugs and ripped curtains. The unused kitchen sparkled even though the sink fixtures, as well as their counterparts in the bathroom, clean as they were, refused to work too well, as they were designed to do, probably because of unseen rust in their anatomies.

This conundrum was simply explained through the labors of a single house man who never stopped caring for Martin and never, ever hesitated in his travails to clean and polish every reachable item with tools either readily available or borrowed from maids he knew in the building.

This house gentleman's name was Pellegrino, obviously an Italian name attached to an ethnic Latvian who could speak only enough English to understand Martin's repetitive requests. Martin, on the other hand, never spoke to Pellegrino except to request something he knew his man would understand—nothing more.

When Pellegrino had started working for Mr. Wesselman fifteen years earlier, an ad Mr. Wesselman had placed in the paper found Pellegrino with an interpreter, ad in hand, explaining to Martin that Pellegrino could read numbers and nothing else. He was extremely quiet; in fact, he seemed to be slightly deficient mentally. The interpreter also suggested showing Pellegrino pictures of what was required. The salary arrangement included cash payment only, payable weekly. He would appear for work at eight A.M. and stay till seven P.M., at which time he would go home to a flat in Chinatown where his invalid wife, who was equally deficient in languages other than her native tongue, awaited him.

The arrangement sounded perfect to Martin, who was not given to wordiness or worldliness, and the two men had lived their silent daily lives for the past fifteen years, as is quite understandable, without an argument.

There was never a meal cooked in the apartment, which adequately answered the odorless nature of the kitchen. Each dinner was circled on a menu of items to be picked up at the same delicatessen and charged to Martin's account, and the leftovers were saved for the next day's lunch. Martin never paid for Pellegrino's food. Pellegrino brought a sad-looking paper bag with him each day that obviously concealed his meager lunch.

In fifteen years, Pellegrino had never gotten a raise or a vacation. Birthdays, Easter, and Christmas went by without a present or a greeting. Pellegrino never learned the English language, which obviously created and answered the equation. Martin, of course, never suggested new topics; in fact, he only used pictures and one-word requests for his limited contact with his loyal man, and the two spent entire days, weeks, and years together in the apartment in silence.

Martin Wesselman was sixty-two years old and had worked for over thirty-five years in a maintenance department's bookkeeping section for the city. He was born in New York on the lower East Side to parents who owned and solely operated a bakery business on Houston Street. He was the only child of two consumptive parents who worked seven days a week for nine or ten hours a day and therefore never had the time to attend to Martin, who was introverted, unfriendly, homely as a log, and good with numbers but with nothing else in an intellectual sense. He was short and nearsighted, with bluish eyes magnified by the lenses he wore, and had sparse gray hair that always needed trimming and covered the top parts of his ears, which were large but lay flat against the sides of his head. His nose, which had visible hairs in each nostril, was wide and a bit flat. His complexion was generally sallow and varied in color with his moods.

Martin had stayed single till a young lady, Maxine, in his actuarial department, who could have been his clone, showed a mild interest in him, enough to gently urge each other into matrimony. The ceremony took place in a justice of the peace's office/home in Las Vegas with a witness provided by the JP. Neither Martin nor Maxine had any family and certainly no friends to fuel the engine of their peculiar romantic origin.

The Wesselmans honeymooned for a week, during which Martin never moved from the gaining tables and Maxine would never find him till he fell exhausted in bed in their hotel room late at night.

Martin was discovered to have one active point of interest, and that was gambling—an adventure that required no contact with other human beings except with the bookie who handled his habit back home. Parimutuel betting, as well as machines and table games, were all impersonal. Martin had to talk to no one, which satisfied the essence of his personality.

Maxine, in her spare time away from the office job, read magazines by the rack-full and soft cover romance and adventure novels, which depleted her income to some degree, but really only dented her net worth slightly.

The couple furnished their Peter Cooper apartment, remained childless for all their years of marriage, and lived in a silent atmosphere like a submarine slipping through deep seas, hardly producing a wake.

A horrible jolt in their life occurred early in the twenty-fifth year of their marriage on a day in April with rain pelting down. Maxine was hit by a city bus on Fifth Avenue as she stepped off the curb and died on the spot.

There was a large insurance settlement; money was also provided by a savings plan Maxine had.

Martin decided to voluntarily retire from his job with money coming in from that plus some other savings accounts, and Social Security would start soon. With all this largesse, he increased his gambling activity and hired Pellegrino.

There were many trips to the Off Track Betting place a few blocks away from the apartment, bus trips to Atlantic City and the Indian reservation in Connecticut, and of course, the sports betting with his bookie, who showed up often in the apartment, taking bets and making money settlements with Martin.

Gambling was always a large part of Martin's life and really his only pastime. Maxine had never complained about her husband's hobby. There were always salaries coming in, and the inheritance Martin received when his parents passed, so that Martin's living expenses were never threatened. The rent was always paid on time, as was Pellegrino and whatever other expenses existed. But trouble seemed to be lurking in the darkened wings of Martin's stage, where his pitiful life story was acting out without an audience.

Wesselman aged badly, probably a reminiscent visit of his parents' health problems and their early departure. He left the apartment less and less and depended on Pellegrino a lot more. Martin would leave the fold once a week now, spending less time at the OTB and stopping off at the corner candy store for his weekly lottery tickets, which he figured brought him back about 15 percent of his weekly forty-dollar investment.

Pussy Panetella, Martin's cigar-chomping bookie, came up every day now, and there was no question that Martin's losses were gradually increasing. Pellegrino furtively watched money moving steadily in Pussy's direction, and Martin was sending Pellegrino to the bank to cash checks more often with larger amounts written on them. Pellegrino would have liked to warn Martin about the checks, but there was no way he could communicate. He would make a face when Martin wrote out a check, and with dutiful service, do exactly what Martin silently conveyed. Nothing complicated would be considered.

Pellegrino understood the lottery and its giant payouts for the winners, so once a week, with one dollar of his cash salary of $150, he would buy one ticket for the New York State numbers game and eagerly await the results in a few days' time in the newspaper, which Martin read, making markings on the spot where the results were recorded. Martin had four numbers correct fairly often and, as mentioned, won back around 15 percent of the money spent, but Pellegrino with his single ticket showing one set of six numbers never had more than two correct.

With the cost of living rising and Pellegrino's salary stagnant as standing water, he found himself and his infirm wife in debt and teetering on the brink of abject poverty. His knowledge of English had improved slightly after fifteen years of living in this country, so with trepidation and servile shivering, he stood in front of his employer one morning. If he'd had a hat, it would have been in his shaking hands when he stammered softly, "Mr. Wesselman."

Martin was seated at a table in the dining area with a newspaper opened to the page where lottery results were posted and about twenty of the little square paper receipts of his numbers spread out in front of him.

Martin had not yet studied his tickets and their relationship to the correct winners in the paper, but Pellegrino, as he brought the tea for Martin, carefully looked over his shoulder and spotted one set of numbers that matched about four in the winning column. There was nothing wrong with Pellegrino's eyesight, but he could not possibly convey his surprise and excitement to Martin without spilling the tea and getting the boss totally upset with an incoherent sentence.

Besides, he wanted desperately to notify Martin of his paucity first, and then to proceed to the numbers situation, where his muddled thoughts said four right would pay over $200.

His teacup had almost reached Martin when he looked up at Pellegrino, startled at being addressed by his silent employ.

"Yes," he would only answer.

"Mr. Wesselman," repeated Pellegrino as he searched for some English words, "have no money. Wife sick. Need more money." He set the tea down in front of Martin.

Martin lowered his eyes, shuffled some receipts around, and looked up again, but past Pellegrino, and spoke slowly. "I don't know if you understand me."

Pellegrino nodded a moderate assent.

"But I can't give you any more money." Martin was slowly shaking his head negatively. "I am having trouble now with money myself."

"Need more dollars right away, sir."

Martin, still moving his head, said, "No. No more money. I'm in trouble myself."

"Just a few dollars I need." Pellegrino meant an increase in salary, but the words came out wrong.

Martin put his hand in his pocket. He was obviously aggravated and completely alienated by this particular conversation, which he had never before encountered. His lips were quivering and a dark frown appeared under narrowed eyes and knitted brow. The color of his face changed from a grayish pink to a beefsteak red as he took out a roll of bills and shoved four singles and a five-dollar bill, which he peeled off, toward Pellegrino.

"I expect you to pay me back," he said loudly.

Pellegrino didn't understand his boss, but the look on Martin's face, his shaking, and the tone of his voice caused

Pellegrino to take the nine dollars out of some mistaken sense of respect and concern for Martin's shaking and rising voice.

There next came a knocking at the door; Pellegrino, still clasping the money and obsequiously bending toward a trembling Mr. Wesselman, backed away and opened the front door for Pussy Panetella.

Panetella, with his ever-present unlit cigar exiting from one side of his mouth to the other, chomped down on it, took off his coat, which he slung over a bridge chair, and sat down at the dining table facing Martin. Martin, who had been expecting the bookie, was still shaking, particularly his hands, which played with the receipts.

Pussy, without smiling and without having greeted Martin, grumbled, "I hope one of those numbers is the winner; you're gonna need it."

"I haven't looked yet."

"Chances are one in a billion. You're wastin' your time."

"Probably right." Martin's eyes focused down on nothing.

"I wanna get to da point." Pussy was staring at Martin, who continued to shake and didn't meet the bookie's eyes. "You ain't paid me nothin' for two weeks, and you owed me for four weeks before that…understand? And," he went on, his voice rising in emphasis, "you keep placin' bets and I keep takin' 'em."

Pellegrino was looking out of the living room window nervously, hearing the bookie's voice becoming more threatening. He turned his head toward the meeting twenty feet away and saw Martin's back, which was shaking along with his shoulders, moving now as if he were crying. Pellegrino couldn't understand what was said, but he knew exactly the context and the dramatics going on.

Pussy now emphasized his words while his fist softly pounded the table. "I gotta have money now—understan'?"

Martin put his hand in his pants pocket, pulled out of the wad of bills he had, and without looking at Pussy, shoved them across the table in front of him. Pussy started counting immediately. He finished flicking the bills and growled.

"Eight hundred and twenty-three bucks. You know what you owe me?" He banged harder on the table. "Nineteen thousand, that's what."

"That's all I've got now."

"Get the rest outta' the bank."

"There's just enough for the rent and things. The bank account's almost empty. I've been losing at everything." Martin was now weeping, and Pellegrino could hear the sobbing and nose blowing across the room.

Pussy's fists came down hard on the table. "Goddammit, stop cryin' and pay what you owe. I ain't waitin' much longer. I'll be back tomorrow, an' I wanna see some action, understan'?"

Pussy got up, and before he grabbed his coat from the bridge chair, he leaned over the table and with an open hand smacked Martin in his face, hard enough to send his glasses flying into the kitchen. Martin put his hands to his face and his head to the table as Pussy, coat in hand, raced out of the apartment.

Pellegrino rushed over to the table, where Martin was slumped over, face down. His face was a rusty red and wet. Pellegrino, now with a towel in hand, wiped the top of Martin's head, pulled the shoulders back so that the torso was more or less erect, and began to wipe his face. Martin's glasses were still lying on the kitchen floor. Pellegrino started to dry the wet face, which kept slumping toward his chest. Martin's left eye was closed, while the right one was wide open, the pupil on the very top of the eyelid only showing half of the shiny brown eyeball. A clear slimy fluid oozed out of Martin's mouth, and his nose seemed to be running.

After wiping off Martin's face, Pellegrino gently laid his head down on the table, where it obediently lay, the rest of the body slumped over. Pellegrino went into the kitchen, picked up the glasses, and placed them on the table next to Martin. He then filled a tumbler with water from the sink, put it on the table, and gently shook his boss. "Mr. Wesselman, wake up. Wake up and drink water." He then moved the water closer to Martin and repeated, "Drink water, you feel better. Mr. Pussy leave, he gone." He then tried to lift Martin's head. It just slumped back to the tabletop, but when he pulled back on the shoulders, he upset the glass of water, which spilled over the open newspaper and on some of the little square lucky numbers receipts. Quickly moving the paper and piling the wet and dry receipts together, he bumped into Martin's side, which sent the slumping man off the chair and onto the floor, face up; one eye remained closed and the other eye, along with Martin's mouth, were wide open.

This finally activated Pellegrino's mind and aroused the correct perception that Martin was indeed dead. For a few minutes, he thought as deeply as he could about the next action he should take.

The decision made, he gathered the moist tickets together and put them carefully in his pocket and then folded the dampened newspaper, prudently opened the door, and ran down the hallway at full throttle, screaming with what seemed like insensibility to neighbors who opened their doors. One of them ushered Pellegrino, who was screaming and seemed insensible, into his apartment and heard the words, "Dead, dead," which immediately instigated a call to 911.

By the time the police came, Pellegrino had calmed down enough to take them to Martin's apartment, where he pointed unnecessarily with the drying newspaper at the deceased. The cops took his name and address down and sent him home. Martin had obviously had a fatal stroke.

"What I do, what I do?" Pellegrino repeated as he left.

"Go home and relax," a cop suggested.

The flag a person carries through life displays the colors awarded to him or her by God, by birth and inheritance, by one's vicinity and surrounding mores and enveloping circumstances, where by sheer luck or mental ability one adjusts, succumbs, or succeeds. Martin Wesselman's flag did not flap in the breeze; it hung limp, and its faded colors never inspired. It just hung where it was planted in a dingy fortress called "Recluse," which was attracted by a gray spectrum whose banner was inscribed "Failure."

Pellegrino started life in the U.S. with an insignificant banner to say the least, but as luck would have it, he had good eyesight, which improved with startling ascension when he and his wife reexamined the ticket with a mistaken supposition propelled by a hasty glance to have four correct numbers to a reexamination that had all six correct digits.

The five and a half million-dollar lump sum payout easily allows them to fly back and forth to Latvia, where they have no problem with the language—or with anything else, for that matter.

OUT OF THE FRYING PAN

Florida is home to my wife and me in the winter. Florida, Alaska, Timbuktu—it doesn't matter where one lives when you have chronic ingrown toenails; there has to be a local podiatrist available, which, as it turned out, is always the case in Lake Worth. A doctor was recommended to me whose office was off Lake Avenue on Federal. My appointment was an early one on a Friday morning.

The office was spacious, the walls lined with magazines of fantastic variety from health subjects to beauty, sports and Hollywood rags shouting headlines like "Britney Scores Again," "Oprah's Book Picks," and "Bobby Hits Them Wherever." I walked past this dog-eared and colorful library to the pass-through, where sat on the other side a lovely office manager who handed me a questionnaire common to all medical offices, which I filled out and handed back. I was told Madelaine would be with me soon.

The magazine racks faced a row of sturdy chairs in the waiting room with just one other patient sitting placidly in one. She was an older lady who unexpectedly said, "Madelaine is some character."

"She's the nurse?" I whispered.

My waiting room companion adjusted her hearing aid deftly with one finger and whispered, "No, she's the attendant. Some character!"

I waited a few more minutes for the "character" to open a door, mention my name, and say, "Follow me."

I expected to see a circus clown or a fat lady or something out of the ordinary, but Madelaine was a painfully thin young girl with sandy hair, about five feet three, with pleasant features that exhibited no emotion whatsoever. I followed her down a short corridor with a polished linoleum floor that gleamed, past a few examination rooms. The smell of disinfectant mixed with a soapy and iodine odor was no different than that of other medical facilities.

We reached a small room the size of three or four broom closets. The two of us went in; I sat on a chair in front of a footbath that looked like the whirlpool we used in our college training rooms in the athletic department area.

The other podiatrists I had used didn't have such a room. The doctor would spray your foot, wipe it off, and get to work. I guessed correctly that my Lake Worth man sanitized all his patients with the hydro system that Madelaine wanted me to use.

"I took a shower this morning."

"The doctor requires all his patients to use this."

"Why?"

"It's supposed to clean and soften the foot."

"My feet are soft enough," I joked. "And clean."

"Take your shoes off and put your feet in the tub," she announced without changing her expression.

The impression she presented interested me. She looked unhappy, even bored, and her motion was a wooden one not fraught with determination; her manner was uninspiring, to say the least.

She closed the door to our little room, obviously to allay the noise emanating from the hydro bath as it filled with soapy water and emulsified with a churning action that sounded like a dishwashing machine gone wild.

"Takes about fifteen minutes," she said. A pout that turned down the corners of her mouth appeared.

"Why do you look so sad?"

"I really hate this job."

"You better not let the doctor hear you say that."

"I don't care."

"How long have you been here?"
"Two weeks."
"Give it a chance."
"I hate it."
"Go to school?"
"Dropped out."
"How old are you?"
"Eighteen."
"You really should go back to school."
"I need the money."
"Did you have other jobs?"
"I cleaned offices. Worked for an office cleaning outfit."
"How was that?"
"I hated it."
"Why don't you like it here?"
"All I do is clean up the exam rooms and wipe off people's feet."
"You mean after the bath?"
"Yeah. You should see some of the feet I wipe."
"If you don't like feet, I think you're in the wrong business."
"The money's better than office cleaning, and I didn't like the night hours and the Sundays. That's when you clean offices."
"I imagine."
"Some of the feet are twisted, the toes are crooked, and I keep thinking what they would smell like if it wasn't for the bath."
"Why don't you ask the doctor if you could do office work?"
"I'd hate office work. It's like school. Besides, I'm not good at writing; my penmanship is horrible, and if there's any math, I'd screw it up."
"Sounds like you're going to train right here until you're ready for the next step."
"I hate wiping off feet."
"Jesus did it."
"I know. I learned that in church, but I doubt if he wiped crooked feet or ones with bent-up toes or smelly ones."

The hydro machine suddenly went off, the timer doing its task effectively. Madelaine took a pair of paper slippers from a shelf, put them on the floor, and then reached for a towel, saying at the same time, "This is the part I hate, but your feet look normal."

I said, "Hand me the towel. I'll wipe them off myself."

"Oh, no," she said, "that's my job. Then I have to clean an exam room. I'll show you to your exam room first."

I slipped my dried feet into the paper slippers and stood up.

"Thanks for taking such good care of me. I hope you get to like the job better," I said.

"I hate it. I hate cleaning up things all the time."

She opened the door for me and ushered me into the examining room and disappeared.

The doctor expertly completed his procedure and told me to make a follow-up appointment in two weeks.

Early in the morning two weeks later, I tapped on the pass-through office window and was cheerfully greeted and told that Miriam would soon be with me. As the window closed, I said to myself, "Miriam?" and thought this was no surprise.

A smiling Miriam greeted me, and I followed her to the footbath room knowingly. She closed the door, sat me down, and with cheerful abandon, started the machine. While the tub was filling up with warm water, I asked Miriam, a chubby, pink-complexioned, red-lipped, active lass who smiled broadly, "Where's Madelaine?"

"Oh, she left."

"When?"

"About a week ago."

"Did you know her?"

"Oh, sure. We went to high school together. She dropped out; so did I, but I go to night classes." Speaking rapidly and with wholesome animation, she continued, "I'll be studying nursing after I finish this semester."

"I'm glad to hear that; I'm sure you are going to be successful."

"Thank you."

"By the way," I carefully asked, "what is Madelaine doing now?"

"She got a job at the animal shelter. You know, it's funny; she doesn't like animals."

Hopefully, I asked Miriam, "What does she do at the shelter?"
"Oh, she cleans up. Stuff like that."

THE CONDO AND THE SEABIRD

F. Scott Fitzgerald and I were alone in the fifth-floor apartment of a fifty-year-old building whose terraced floor faced east with only the vast expanse of the Atlantic in view. F. Scott, of course, was present in book form, and I held him tightly while his imagination soared and caressed me from the leaves of Paradise.

The sea was wind-whipped, arriving on shore in mildly exploding wave rolls whiter than the clouds approaching from the east not far above the Gulf Stream, whose warmth birthed them.

It was not a beach or pool day; the wind and the absence of sun precluded the routine enjoyment of the outdoors.

The wind was strong enough to create a howling that wavered, increased, halted, and screamed again like the sirens of ambulances, fire control, and police vehicles prominent on A1A in Palm Beach. As I peered over the book, a large gray-white gull struggled with the adversarial wind and headed straight toward my sliding doors, obviously seeking companionship with its reflection in the glass. The impact was softened by the bird's braking action but was enough to deliver a stunning blow to the gull, which fell senselessly to the cement floor of the terrace. It quivered there, unable to avoid human help or take flight. Its tiny black bead of one eye (the other was missing) regarded me, probably in terror, as I opened the sliding door and picked up the bird, which attempted a mild erratic flapping.

Never having held a seagull before, its lightweight, dry, soft feathered form amused me. It seemed to accept its unimaginable fate while enjoying the petting I performed, smoothing its feathers. I walked through the apartment out the front door, creating a draught from the still-opened terrace sliders that mildly propelled me to the elevator. I managed to press the door button and entered the elevator, which had an octogenarian female inhabitant facing the gull and me as the door slid open. This was the same lady with whom I had shared the elevator a month before. At that time, I was on my way to the garbage area to deposit an abstract painting I had completed and immediately hated after it dried. The woman regarded the work, which I held upside down, and exclaimed with a seemingly knowledgeable admission, "I know who painted that picture."

I went along with this short conversation as the elevator slowly descended to the basement, saying, "Really? Who?"

"Why, Jackson Pollock, of course," she said with a touch of excitement to her voice.

"Would you like it?" I asked.

"You would give this to me?" she asked, a startled query on her lips.

"It's yours," I said, saving me the foul-smelling job of depositing it in the large garbage bin. She made me famous in the building, describing that transaction as an act of love for a fellow condo dweller.

Presently she faced me while I was holding the subdued bird.

"They won't pluck it for you in Publix."

Having no intention of relating the history of my acquisition, I leaned toward her and said, "The bird is not dead." Indeed, the perfume wafting from my elevator companion revived the gull slightly, and its little beak weakly shot out and snatched at a butterfly appliqué on her jacket.

She thought that to be adorable and asked if I would give her the bird. I thought to myself, A painting and then a bird. What next?

"No," I said. "I want it to be with its family."

"My God," she uttered, "you have more of them in your apartment." Then she hesitated and whispered, "I won't tell the manager you are keeping animals in the apartment." She winked.

The elevator door opened in the lobby as I said, "That's very kind of you not to tell."

"You're a nice man," she admitted.

As the three of us left the elevator, the gull quietly digested the tiny butterfly appliqué.

If one surrounds reality with the soft, fluid body of imagination, results can be mystifying. Florida condos, wherever they were constructed, seem to be monastic; not in a religious sense per se and not even in a comparative concrete or pictured sense, yet there is a cloistered and a severely limited aspect to life in these buildings.

Inhabitants arise, dine, dress, pill, visit their doctors, and entertain themselves with endless similarity. They dine again, tire, and bed down, often forgetting to extinguish lights and TVs, which in fact awakens them in an hour or so. When they wake, they visit the salle de bain, darken the bedroom, and proceed through the night, often with physical interruptions, to wake again at the same early morning hour only to repeat yesterday's refrain.

There are no cells. Apartments are spacious, nicely furnished, and kept as clean as a once-a-week, three-hour-long cleaning lady's appearance can manage. Poverty is rarely visited. Food and drink is adequate and as close as the nearest Costco or Publix.

There are no monks, Mother Superiors, rabbis, or any other spiritual guide at hand; however, there is a manager and staff to ensure that etiquette and rules are mildly followed. Unlike a monastery, there is very little the tenants still have to be taught, having spent many years learning at the knees of their early schooling and then at the muscular and often cruel attitude of daily work and the often wrenching emotions of family affairs.

In other words, for the largest part, Florida condo dwellers are older, and though they never admit anything so illuminating, except to joke about somebody else's age, they think young, dream of youth, and live with painful reality.

My intent, after walking through the lobby, out the side door leading to a wide grassy area, and onto the beach, was to deposit the bird there amongst its numerous peers. The wind on the shore was milder than expected, but still created a miniature lower-level sandstorm where the sand was dry, but nearer the tidal area, it was wet and hard. At the edge of the tide where the bubbly foam of the waves came to rest after riding the rollers, hundreds of seabirds, some of which were mirror images of my wounded package, were busily pecking at the sand or flying low over the waves.

The birds were attacking tiny seashells that were tossed onto the beach. These little mollusks are prime fodder for the sea- and shorebirds. Small sandpipers on delicate spindly legs flit across the edge of the tide, spying tiny food particles, nimbly nabbing them, and then speeding along to their next microscopic quarry.

This minor riot of white and gray against a dark sea and shouting breakers I hoped would be home to the nonchalant bundle of down cradled in my arm. As I gently placed him on some hard brown sand, he wobbled for an instant and immediately thereafter sat where I placed him, his belly hiding his legs and all of him quite immobile, his head tilted to one side, allowing one little black eye to gaze up at me. In that instant I thought he entreated me not to leave, but I backed off, expecting him to join others of his lookalike fellows or have others approach him, but he was totally ignored, as outcast as a wrong note in a lovely melody.

Obviously he looked like the others but was not part of the family. I regarded this disparaging scene for a few minutes, watching my bird sitting in the same position while his feathers were disturbed by the breeze and his fellow flyers flew away in a feathery explosion of abandonment.

In nature, animals die constantly, often consumed and sometimes not, but always accepted by humans as an undesirable fate to be accepted as an ordinary occurrence; but once a living creature is helped and held, it becomes a part of decent human experience to continue to help even a lowly species of the Kingdom of Animals.

I lifted him again and brushed the sand off his belly. No struggle ensued, and I carried him back to the building and into the lobby, where a few penitents sadly gathered in the cool luxury of the condo chapel. They quietly yet eagerly examined the bird, and with hushed sighing, paid their respects with questions.

"What medicine do you give a sick bird?"

"Do veterinarians take care of them?"

"What do you feed it?"

"Where will it sleep?"

One really older wag whom people called "Colonel" stated, "It will probably walk around all night, squawk, and make on the furniture."

As I walked slowly toward the elevator, some of those seemingly inane questions aroused interest in me.

The doorman, with sensible informality, had put a large empty television carton in front of my apartment door. It had "Sony" in large letters printed on it.

Great name for the bird, I thought. I'll add an "N" and call him Sonny. If I find that it's a female, I'll call it "Sunny," but I decided not to examine it that closely.

Inside the box sand from the beach was spread down on the bottom, and two basins of water—one salty seawater and one fresh—sat on the sand. Food. I bought littleneck clams, the smaller cousins of the larger quahogs, and placed them with the shells closed in the seawater. I sprinkled breadcrumbs, an occasional worm, and some chopped-up fish particles in the carton and cleaned the box every day. I was never sure if Sonny dined on my largesse or if visitors helped themselves, but the box required revisiting often.

Around the pool, the sun, looking like a fried egg sunny side up, directly overhead in a light blue Paul Newman-eyes expanse, spread delicious heat on appreciative wrinkled sunbathers. Their heads were covered in a stunning array of straw bonnets, floppy prints, and baseball caps. Bodies were lying on lounge chairs or propped straight up on matching uprights. Some of the infirm tenants sat reading while their maids were nearby in a shaded area waiting to be called to comfort their employers.

The swimming pool floated no swimmers on its intensely blue water colored by the paint on the pool bottom; however, there were some standees in the shallow end bobbing up and down like the heads of yes men at a religious seminar. The standees admitted this activity to be their only exercise and could be seen in their immersed condition for hours at a time. When they emerged, huge towels were wrapped around them and they considered the added wrinkles issued on their tanned skin drying in the sunlight.

A religious Catholic lady approached me and sweetly asked about the condition of Sonny.

"He's about the same," I said.

"You know," she said with as much solemnity as a worshipper in a one-piece bathing suit could utter, "God sent him to you for a reason."

"And what might that reason be?" I asked her as drops of water from her recent immersion left a small pool at her feet.

"To be honest," she continued, "I mentioned this to my priest, and he said we all breathe the same air and share the same God-given planet, and helping even the smallest creature pleases Him, and you will share in His blessing."

She then grasped my hand and kissed it.

Another woman, a Mrs. Kline, came to my chair and said, "I only wish someone could've helped my husband the way you're helping that bird."

Still another lady came over and stated that the animal shelter could offer advice, and then she added, "You know, I'm Mrs. Salter in 711. If you're not busy some evening, we could have dinner and talk some more about the bird."

I smiled and thanked her for her interest as the Colonel approached. He elbowed me as he said in couched phrases, "Good way to meet the girls—that bird, I mean. It's probably shitting all over the place…right?"

"No," I answered, accepting his less than gratifying disclosures. "Sonny is a perfect houseguest and spends his time snug in his carton on the terrace."

The Colonel left my chair showing mixed disbelief spiced with a dash of disdain.

Sonny was a hit topic, and small groups of elderly tenants discussed him amongst themselves, sometimes appointing one of the groups to discuss their feelings with me. Health concerns were a subject, as was noise, and the possible attraction of other birds to my terrace. I thought my listening to all these suggestions was graceful, and my answers were suggesting perhaps that Sonny was becoming more important than them in our sanctuary, raising the puzzled perception of resentment. "He-he! There his lily snaps!" came to mind, as one monk jealously muttered about another's garden, which was more attractive than his own. It was a line in a poem I read long ago.

Relatives of my neighbors came to visit once in a while but stayed only a few days, sometimes paying their respects grudgingly as if the visit was a duty and their stay was a short sentence to be served before being released to the frozen north whence they came. Many times, however, the visit was a grand occasion and accompanied by a grandchild or two, a happy moment for the lucky tenants who found that after the family left, melancholy revisited.

The momentary visits were merely a break in their existence, only to have monotony press upon them again, bringing a need for unlikely events to punctuate an overlong paragraph. The event was usually a treatise on a neighbor's misfortune, a health issue, or, if there was a married couple involved, the parsing of an argument—or worse, a quarrel—that was overheard. The tongues in motion stirred like the sound of eggs being scrambled, and the varied solutions offered were as useful as fallen leaves shifting in a breeze but rarely as colorful.

One day while Sonny seemed to be recuperating in his carton, which I peered into, he twisted his head so that his good eye stared at me, but to my knowledge the rest of him didn't move. I cut a hole in the carton big enough to let him out for a stroll on the terrace if he so wished, yet he made no use of this exit.

I walked the beach each morning, weather permitting, wading on the edge of the tide and beachcombing for shells that were storm-tossed or otherwise deposited on the sand by waves.

The wonder of millions of shells on every beach is the story of the untold quantity of life in the seas. These live creatures exist in ocean depths of thousands of feet to sand in the inter-tidal zone of one inch, and each mollusk, whose lives vary from less than a year to thirty years, can reproduce up to 100,000 exact replicas of itself in less than a year. Reproduction can be hermaphroditic, having both male and female abilities within the same animal, or in the human sense, to be one or the other and procreate as we imagined.

The sizes of mollusks vary from less than one thirty-second of an inch to the giant squid and octopuses of over thirty feet, but they all have commonality. They are common because early in their existence mollusks secrete calcium oxide and an enzyme called conchiolin, which begins to make the shell immediately after birth. They all breathe, excrete, and reproduce, and their soft bodies have a head and foot and visceral mass, including kidneys, hearts, gonads, and teeth. All these components do differ in certain classes, but their history goes back some 400 million years to the Devonian Period—lots longer than seabird history.

All shells or valves, as they are called, that are on shore have no life left in them, having been attacked by other carnivorous mollusks or fish and finally by shorebirds, which enormously add to their diet those little snails, clams, mussels, oysters, or scallops that survive death in the sea. They remain the bottom of the food chain for shorebirds, which include egrets, gulls, pelicans, sandpipers, and the occasional hawk, which all other birds avoid and to whom they give deference as would a lightweight to a super heavyweight.

In addition to bivalves or mollusks with two shells, their compatriot single-shelled phylum called gastropods also are found on the sand quite lifeless, their shells all beautifully sculpted and as varied as 40,000 species of snails can be. There are over 30,000 species of bivalves.

Beach birds as well as other families gather together in groups of species and act together while seeking nourishment.

Besides fish and many other genre of marine life, mollusks are an extremely important food element to humans as well as to their fellow sea dwellers and shorebirds.

In the pool area, where about a dozen denizens gathered, I was approached by an aging gentleman whose name was

Schoenbun. He spoke in a loud voice common to deaf people and aimed a microphone at me. Adjusting a wire attached to his earpiece, he half-shouted, "Don't you have better things to do than play doctor to a bird?"

Not offended by this pronouncement considering whence it came, I explained into his microphone, "It more or less fell into my lap, and I'm really not that busy that I can't take care of the bird." I continued speaking into the machine while noticing Schoenbun was squinting. "I'm retired now, and caring for the bird gives me something to do."

"How's that?" yelled Schoenbun.

"I like doing it," I responded with a louder tone directly into the mike.

Another person, hearing my increased volume of speech and guessing what topic was being discussed, came slowly to my side, as she leaned on a walker and stated, "I'm not complaining; you should take care of the bird. Personally I wish they would allow pets in the building, but a seagull—what do you care about a seagull?"

I knew her name. "To tell the truth, Miss Coniglio, I never kept pets when my wife was alive, but all animals can have problems and they can't ask for help, so I thought it would be a good thing."

She interrupted, "But a seagull?" and slowly edged away.

The Colonel then strolled over and elbowed me, as was his habit, and said, "It's still shitting all over the place, right?"

I winked at him, patted his shoulder, and closed the curtain on this pool scene by going back to the beach for a walk.

After a week of watching Sonny recuperate, I visited him one gray morning, heavy clouds stationary in the sky above the condo, a slight warm breeze urging its way toward the terrace. He was pecking at some remaining items in his sandbox but stopped abruptly as I peered down at him. His head tilted so that his good eye focused on me, as if to beg me for something in the way of conversation. Believing anything as impossible as that to occur, I made a few idiotic bird sounds and whistles while his position and attention to me remained the same. People in the building were beginning to question my mental credentials and resolute desire to see this escapade to an unlikely finale. Their flapping came back to me from a few better friends amongst the rest to a point where actually conversing with Sonny seemed to add credibility to my adversaries' opinions of me. The terrace was insulated enough to hide the craziness there surely was in speaking to my patient.

In a whispered coo I started in. "How are you feeling today?"

No answer.

"Would you like more food and water?"

No answer.

I then sensed the severity of miscalculations in expecting a response, so I reached into the carton and stroked the top of Sonny's head, trying to communicate a feeling of commiseration and friendly love at the same time. I kept talking to the bird, not expecting an answer and not caring if anyone heard. The hushed words reminded me of a churchgoer praying by himself to nobody, but deep in his soul hoping that a holy spirit could hear the entreaty and somehow, with an extended hand, promise aid.

I whispered, still stroking the bird's little head, "I know all of this is strange. You're a true and lovely product of nature, totally unlike others in every way except one. We all need help, especially in a condo full of older people whose longevity is so questionable. You are different also because you can't ask for help, whereas humans can and do constantly, and for that reason, dear friend, you are getting help; and I swear that I want nothing in return from you, or from the spiritual world, except to find that you're gone from here, feeling fine, and that you are among your fellows."

I wanted to say "Amen" after that prayer-like, one-sided conversation, but I stopped petting him, which he had never disapproved, and I cowardly looked over my shoulder to see if anybody had overheard me, then left my apartment after closing the sliding door.

To my surprise, one morning the Sony carton was empty. A line of clouds in the eastern sky hid the sun, which had not risen above the horizon, but lit an orange-yellow lining on the underside of those fair weather cumulus clouds, promising a clear day. I was on the beach marveling at the early morning show, actually witnessing the sun climbing slowly into the light blue horizon. The scene on the beach was boringly similar to all clear days when the surf cruises onto the sand calmly and noiselessly, the warm seawater creeping up to my ankles and then sliding back, only to be met by the next incoming wave.

I waded ankle-deep along the shore for about a mile, the same shorebirds walking, flitting, darting, preening, or merely standing, planning an attack on the next available morsel of food. Suddenly a few gulls flew past me not a foot above my head, followed by more about shoulder height, and then the last one, whose white wing barely touched my elbow as it followed the others low over the ocean. I saw only one eye on the right side of its head. It might have had another eye, but I had no chance to see it. As the flock skimmed over the ocean, I followed the course of the last bird that had touched me until it was directly in between me and the sun, now clearly above the horizon.

Gazing into the sun blinded me, and the flight of this formation was lost in the glare.

LINDEMANN'S SOLUTION

Lucille usually awoke around nine A.M. with the eastern sun blasting through the bedroom window like a firebomb. It was ten o'clock on a warm Tuesday morning in July; a bedsheet covered her whole body, including her head, in expectation of sunshine, but when she pulled up her knees and the sheet uncovered her face, she saw a gray picture outside the window.

There was a soft drizzle misting the light green bushes on the lawn, and as she lifted herself on her elbows, she could hardly see the low tree line across the street because of the foggy wetness. As Lucille sat up in bed, she rubbed the dryness out of her eyes with the backs of both hands and turned her head to the right to see her husband still sleeping on his stomach with the sheet slipping off his shoulders. As she tried to cover his bare shoulders, he stirred with a mumbled, "Wuzzatime?"

"It's after ten, dear."

A little over a year ago, both Lucille and Mr. Lindemann—Morrie or Dear to his wife but Mr. Lindemann to the rest of the world—had decided that their clock had only so many ticks left. They retired from a very successful insurance business, where a side venture in a stock brokerage arm and real estate holdings added to the trophy of good fortune that accompanied the policies they sold. The Lindemanns were thorough, honest, and intelligent, which was noticed by their clients; however, they were not particularly friendly or forthcoming. Their ability was their reputation, and their reputation was the only facet the world at large knew of the Lindemann diamond.

The couple were childless, relativeless, yet not exactly friendless, but not overwhelmed with social fellowship. Lucille and Mr. Lindemann were the same age, mired in the muckish latitude of their mid-seventies. They had been married fifty years. When somebody asked them how many "happy" years they had been married, both Lindemanns hesitated long enough with their answer to embarrass the question. The business was their life.

Lucille was short, about five feet two, and plumpish. Her hair was dyed once a week at Signorelli's Salon, which produced a blondish crest on her head and never had enough time to show the dull brown-gray roots struggling to emerge. She had a low forehead under her golden canopy and brown eyebrows obviously not at odds with her true root color. Her eyes were brown, large, and slightly crossed, as were her husband's. Her small ears were hidden by her perennial 'do, and her nose was a pinched affair above her heart-shaped lips, which were rouged a light pink. All of this had a surrounding cream eggshell complexion, smooth enough to belie her age.

Mr. Lindemann's appearance in no way complimented Lucille's. She was a foot less detectable than his six-foot-two frame. His bald, broad head was fringed with a light gray, which made the dome seem to rise out of a misty shell. There were hardly any eyebrows, though what there were of them moved up and down when he spoke. His eyes were slightly more crossed than Lucille's. They were a pale blue, intelligent set, even though one seemed to gaze longingly at the other. His nose was long and straight, descending to a well-shaped, wide set of lips that covered straight white teeth.

Nobody made fun of the appearance both made when they stood together. Even though a "Trylon and Perisphere" silent thought might be aroused, the respect the Lindemanns commanded in their milieu brought out a subdued reverence bolstered by their obvious wealth—a wealth that was never flaunted, but was perceptible in their outwardly conservative demeanor, spiced by their evident charitable ways and their sober living circumstances.

Mr. Lindemann, now fully awake, looked out the window at the soggy scene.

"Depressing," he wheezed.

"Yes, but let's make the best of it."

Mr. Lindemann continued fault-finding while he was sitting on the edge of the bed, his long legs over the side and his fleet flat on the floor. "Another depressing day made worse by the rain."

"Yes, I suppose," Lucille said.

This early-morning conversation was similar to many they had shared since they retired. When they were busy working, they arose before seven and were out of the house by eight, he clean shaven, thoroughly showered, and dressed in one of the many dark suits he owned over a white cuffed shirt with a solid colored tie. His black shoes were shined by the maid, Lorena, to a point where they reflected all lighted things.

Lorena was as silent as the dead. Except to say "yes" or "no," she could have been mute. She was a short, thin spinster; a bun of gray and black bobbing on top of her head added some desperately needed height to her diminutive frame. She had a narrow head and face, black eyes, a long nose, and tight lips, all of which rose above her thin, flat-chested torso. Her arms and legs were shapeless. This attenuate figure was far from hapless, however; with little weight to hold her back, she moved like the mercury ball in a pinball game. She kept the home spotless, took all the calls perfectly, did the food shopping, and like Lord Jeffrey Amherst, "looked around for more when she was through." She had been the Lindemanns' angel for twenty years, not necessarily out of love for them or the job, but suspiciously for a salary and perks three times what others in her profession were earning. A fixture, Lorena's inexpedient side was her total lack of cooking ability; she could burn boiling water. This imperfection had no effect on the Lindemanns because they ate out three meals a day and never had parties or had guests to their home. Their kitchen had a lonely aura; in fact, when no light was on in there, it was ghostlike. Lorena had her breakfast in her small apartment before work, had tea and cake for lunch, and ate a late dinner after work.

Lucille was always ready in her working days to join Morris on their ten-block walk to the office. On bad weather days,

Lorena would drive them to work in the Cadillac and pick them up when called to do so. Lucille was coiffed and otherwise ready often before Mr. Lindemann for the A.M. march to the office.

The work ethic of the naught-but-business Lindemanns was well known in the large community in which they lived and served, as well as in an extended area around the community, and had stretched statewide for years. The fourth quarter, the ninth inning, or the last period of the game made manifest their decision to sell the agency.

Now that the game was over, they slept late while Lorena started her day the same as always. The old eating habits of the Lindemanns kept step as before. Except for coffee upon rising and dressing, they went out for the balance of their consumption: a light breakfast and lunch and a heartier dinner. Every so often if the weather was poor, or if a health reason threatened, they would send out for sustenance, the kitchen remaining unused except for heating water.

The drizzle continued throughout the day, the delicate greenness surrounding the lonely house; the sun never appeared through the fog. Mr. Lindemann's mood turned slowly into a hollow sense of desolation. He put down the section of the morning paper and addressed Lucille, sitting opposite him reading another section.

"This retirement farce is getting to me."

"Oh, dear, this mood will pass. The weather has a lot to do with it."

"Maybe, but I miss the work," moaned Morris with an obvious concession to weakness.

Lucille answered with steadfast realism. "We've spoken about that many times and we always agree that we should find alternatives, like exercise—"

Morris interrupted. "Too old to start exercising; besides, the both of us are arthritic old birds now."

"True, true," Lucille agreed as she put down the newspaper, the couple's crossed eyes somehow meeting. "We also talked about travel or meeting people—you know, entertainment we could handle."

Morris was ready with his response. "We just never got into travel or friends, and I know you feel the same as I do regarding those things." He went on, "We don't feel well enough for trips, and I hate to admit it, but after our busy days, new friends would have been a bore. I'm not even sure I'd know how to act around them."

The gloomy day wore on. On pleasant days the Lindemanns would take short walks, go to favorite lunch places for a bit, walk some more, and go home to nap, read, or watch TV. The two would also pore over investment and portfolio statements, call their favorite broker and their old office, and then settle back in a relaxed position into a mindset of gnawing emptiness. No matter the condition of their emotions, Lucille and Morris never argued with the other's opinion; theirs was a peaceful convergence of attitudes. It can be argued that an excited or even a violent clash of feelings leading to contention and argument could spice things up, even lead to solutions that precede the splendor of hope. Not the case with the Lindemanns. Without change, they always came to an intelligent agreement.

"Ready for dinner, dear?"

"Yes."

"Should we drive?"

"Weather's still bad."

"We can send Lorena."

"Maybe call for a takeout."

"Good. What would you like?"

"I think Chinese. Haven't had any lately."

"Love it. I'll get the menu from Ma Lum Sung. It was really good the last time."

Lucille, menu in hand, called in the order: wonton soup, two egg rolls, fried rice, egg foo young, and a vegetable lo mein. Lucille sent Lorena home. "We'll clean up the little white boxes."

Lorena put on her raincoat and left. The Lindemanns awaited the delivery, which would lead to a surprising fate. In about a half hour the doorbell rang, and Morris opened the door. He came face to face with a dripping, ancient Chinese fellow standing in the doorway with two shopping bags with vapor steaming out of them, one in each hand.

"My God, come in, dry off."

"Thank you very mush."

"Lucille, please get a towel. This poor man is drenched."

Lucille appeared with two towels. One she placed on the floor where the man was standing in a small puddle, spreading where he stood. He gave the two bags to Morris, who put them on the breakfast room table, while Lucille took off the man's soaked cotton raincoat, handed him a towel, and hung the coat on a clothes rack in the hallway.

The man began to dry his hatless head, his face, and his arms.

Morris queried, "You walked here?"

"Sorry to say, car not working."

"We could have picked it up."

"No, no; not the way to treat good customers."

"Why didn't you send the young man who came the last time?"

"He my grandson. Has bad cold. Ma told him stay in bed. Nobody else to deliver. Jus' Ma and me there."

"You'll catch your death," Lucille pleaded.

"Seventy-six years; never sick."

Morris said, "Who cooks?"

"Ma and me. I'm Lum."

"Who's at the restaurant now?"

"Jus' Ma."

"And you have to run back and deliver?"

"No other orders. Ma takes phone and then cooks. Food good. Business bad."

Morris said, "Let me pay you."

Lum walked to where the shopping bags were and pulled out a soggy bill, although dry enough to read.

"Twenty-six dollars," Lum said quietly.

Morris gave him two twenty-dollar bills and pressed them into Lum's damp hand. "Your shop is in a bad spot. A block off the main street and three blocks from the new strip center."

"I know," said Lum. "Also, new Chinese restaurant in center and new Thai place on Main Street."

Changing the subject for a moment, Morris said, "You shouldn't be out in the rain at your age. You're a year older than me."

Lum had a big smile on his face, exposing yellowed teeth, which were missing a few neighbors. "When have business, must take care of it."

Lucille and Morris looked at each other and sadly nodded assent. Morris took Lum's arm and led him to the kitchen table. "I want to talk to you. Call Ma and tell her you'll be back in about twenty minutes."

Lum did that and said, "Only one more order. Will take twenty minutes to cook. Then I'll go back and deliver it."

Morris, showing impatience, answered, "I'll drive you back and then the two of us will deliver the next order."

Lucille beamed. Lum, with an eye misting over, could only say, "Ooo, that veree good." He was sitting opposite Morris, who had his clasped hands on top of the table, while Lum's arms hung down his sides.

Morris quickly began talking, sensing that Lum would need to be back at the restaurant soon. "We have a good idea for you." Morris automatically included his wife in his instantly conceived plan, knowing that her welcome approval would be forthcoming. "I've got a great location for an oriental fusion restaurant."

"Please, Mr. Lindemann, we have no monee."

"We have. Let me finish. Do you know anybody else in the same business?"

"Have cousin on East Side. Has same problem. Good food. No money."

Morris, now excited and happier than Lucille had seen him since his retirement, patted his hand on the table and said, "Fine. We'll have two restaurants, each called the same name, serving the same great food. We'll advertise the hell out of the new stores and we'll be the biggest hit in town."

Lum now openly wept, dried his eyes with his handkerchief, and said again, "But the monee."

"We have enough to open a hundred stores—don't worry."

Lum and Morris drove back to the pitiful location, picked up two orders, and delivered both by Cadillac. Lum was finally delivered back to a mystified waiting Ma, who fainted when Lum explained the Lindemann plan to her. The next day, the East Side cousin, after fifty questions and explanations by Lum and Morris, fell back into a kitchen chair, and with an expression fraught with disbelief, hope, and exhaustion, put his hands over his eyes and wept.

After four months of planning and building, the two restaurants were opened with a staff of relatives and expatriates groomed in black and white oriental magnificence serving the best fusion-oriental comestibles so far relished in the entire surrounding area.

Lucille and Mr. Lindemann once again arose at seven each morning. By eight, they were toileted and arranged and out the door. Their 50-percent Chinese partners insisted on calling the sparkling and spanking new restaurants "Lindemann's Oriental."

Lucille was often seen in a silk Chinese-style costume, her hair dyed black.

Mr. Lindemann, when asked about retirement, simply answered, "I'm too busy to discuss the matter." There was a wide smile on his face, which remained there as if painted on.

AN EPISODE IN THE OZARKS

A Play in One Act

    The Time: Not long ago.
    The Place: A secluded mountainous area in the Missouri Ozarks.
    The Characters: Ma and Pa, easily in their eighties, neither of them knowing their true age nor of their dementia. They are uneducated and have raised a parcel of children, none of whom are anywhere near the area since disappearing when old enough to decamp or rather flee from what they deemed to be life's dead end.
    The Scene: Ma and Pa's log shack, which looks too large for only the two of them. An outhouse and various broken-down and rusted parts of old autos and farm equipment occupy the back yard. There is a cleared field of perhaps a few acres totally surrounded by dense woods and rocky outcroppings. A stream, its water tumbling downhill, rapidly passes

through the property and disappears into the trees, leaving its constant burbling to compete with bird and animal sounds. There is a large hound sleeping on the porch, unbothered by flies circling, landing, and biting him. Loose chickens are everywhere. Emma, the horse, lazily grazes on the front yard. There is no need to introduce the characters as they speak because there are only two of them and it is obvious who is speaking to whom.

It is about five o'clock in the morning, already hot. Ma and Pa are in bed, awakening. "Hot."

"Shore is."

"Dreamt my bar'l was empty."

"What bar'l you talkin' of, Pa?"

"None in p'ticular, jis a bar'l."

"What'd it look like?"

"Ordinary, wood slats an' iron belts holdin' it together."

"Wut's supposed to be in it?"

"That's the mystree, Ma—was a empty bar'l, thinkin' would hold our life's 'complishments."

"Good God, Pa. Whit 'complishments you speakin' of?"

"Not sure, Ma; bresh me up wit wut we 'complished."

"Well, we alive, for one."

"That's so. What else?"

"Well, we had chillen'."

"How many?"

"Not sure, but they was a parcel of 'em."

"Wher'r they?"

"Gone."

"Why'nt they call?"

"No tellyphone, you fergit, Pa."

"Why'nt they write?"

"Wut good'd that do, Pa? We can't read."

"Still tryin' to figger out wut to do wit the bar'l, but we'll put the kids in."

"Use it to ketch water off 'en the gutter."

"No such thing. Ain't no rain bar'l, Ma. It's our life bar'l. 'Sides, there ain't no gutters. I'm puttin' in the facts we still alive an' we had chillens. Wut was they names, Ma?"

"Can't even remember how many, an' you want names? Jes' put 'em in the bar'l."

"'Member that dress you made yourself from the checkered tablecloth you had? It was right purdy."

"My, yes, and I'm glad you thought of that. It was the purtiest dress I can remember. Put it in."

"I will. 'Member I rode Emma into town to buy 'nother tablecloth?"

"Shore, I remember, Pa."

"Can't figger why I didn't buy you 'nother dress so you wouldn't haf to cut up 'nother tablecloth."

"Oh, I don't mind, Pa."

"You was always easy to git along wit', Ma."

"Put that fact in the bar'l."

"I'll squeeze it in."

"Had a good crop of tomatoes last year."

"I'll put 'em in."

"But the animals ate most of 'em."

"I'll take 'em out."

"Emma's been good to us."

"Don't think it right puttin' a horse in the bar'l while it's alive. After she dies maybe."

"Pa, if she's in the bar'l, what good's she gonna be to us?"

"Yore right, Ma. Only if she's dead, she won't be much use either."

"How 'bout all those chickens? That's shore a 'complishment."

"Can't see puttin' chickens in thar. They'd mess up everything. Anyways, wouldn'ya rather eat 'em?"

"Good point, Pa. Leave 'em out. How 'bout the hound dog?"

"Same's the horse and chickens, Ma."

"Well, Pa, that purdy much sums up what we got, 'ceptin' our home, the farm, and the outhouse. Cain't think of any 'complishments, and ef you puts them things in the bar'l, the bar'l won't be big 'nuf."

"Well, that the case, I'll dream up 'nother bar'l."

"Pa, you can't jes' dream whatever you wants; a dream gotta come to you in itself."

"Well, I'll try."

"Pa, life's not like that. You'd be wastin' good sleepin' time tryin' to make a dream."

"I made the bar'l."

"It jes' came to you by itself."

"Well, yore right, Ma. Corse dreams are more important than real things, 'specially people."

"Why's that, Pa?"

"Well, when we mixed with town folks, we found out lots 'bout people."

"Like what, Pa?"

"If they tell you how much money they has, they don't has it."

"That's true, Pa."

"And when the boys are alone, they talks about all the lovin' they gettin', Ma…that's why they ain't gettin' any at all."

"I believe that, too, Pa."

"And if they tells how good they are at sports and horseshoes, they cain't hit the ball nor get even a leaner."

"Pa, you tryin' to say dreams is better than live people talkin'?"

"Shore, 'ceptin' if they tells you 'bout all the troubles they got."

"What, then, Pa?"

"Then, you'd bitter believe 'em, 'ceptin' nobody wants to put troubles in their 'complishments bar'l."

"So, Pa, they's nothin' 'bout other people we can put in the bar'l, is there?"

"Nope. I s'pose they have to dream up their own bar'l. And if they do, I'm bettin' it stays empty."

"We shore are blest our bar'l is full up, Pa."

"Not full yet, Ma. There's you an' me goin' to fit in that bar'l."

"Now that's a real 'complishment, Pa. I can't wait."

Epilogue: They happily climb out of bed.

DON-BOB'S LEGACY

A hot summer morning in July—in fact, it was July 18, 1989—found Don-Bob Fecker sitting motionless on his veranda in a rocking chair. His hands were clasped on his lap, a sealed white envelope resting under his fingers, while a small white dog slept at his feet.

He was not rocking as he stared at the pasture spread in front of his house. This was not an ordinary pasture because beyond it, the oil wells, looking like the skeletons of giraffes, pointed at the sky and seemed to hold up the low gray clouds.

There were lots of wells and pumps. The pumps looked like small dinosaurs, their heads moving up and down as they sucked oil out of the ground.

Don-Bob's wife of sixty-eight years had died at eighty-seven, two years before, leaving her husband a very rich, old, and lonely Texan. About a year before she passed, her favorite spaniel also perished, and Thelma-Louise, Don-Bob's hyphenated mate, ardently desired a replacement. The Feckers drove to a dog show in Amarillo, where a breeder attracted their attention. He bred Bichon Frises and produced an example of one and handed it to Thelma-Louise, who immediately became enthralled with the tiny white specimen she was holding.

She sighed, "Oh, Don-Bob. Did you ever?"

"What in hell is it?" came the response in what was almost a shout. He scarcely recognized the genus of what was rolled up looking like a fuzzy baseball cradled in the crook of his wife's arm.

Thelma-Louise, a big smile spread all over her face, cooed, "Don-Bob, ask the man what it is and if I can have it."

Don-Bob faced the breeder. "What is it, and how much cash you want for it?"

"Well, it's a purebred Bichon Frise, and for cash, it'd be two hundred and fifty dollars. I'll give you a book on how to take care of her, and the right kind of food for a few days." Don-Bob thought the man had told him the dog's name. It sounded like Bitch to him, and he couldn't give a snake's rear end about the breed of any dog except a hunter. Anything Thelma-Louise wanted was the law. He counted out two hundred and fifty dollars from a wad of large bills, asked for a basket to carry the pup in, got it, and the happy couple strode off as Don-Bob remarked, "Funny name for a hound, Bitch, but it's probably used to it, so that's what we'll call her."

Don-Bob's grandfather was a soldier in the Mexican War, serving with old Fuss and Feathers General Winfield Scott on the border and in Mexico. After the hostilities, he remained in the territory that was northern Texas where the current state of Oklahoma, borderless at that time, nudged the two thousand acres that Granddad decided to farm. Granddad found a wife whose rationality must have been distracted by a good-looking, heroic ex-cavalry man. She married him and undoubtedly suffered the life of a plains settler alongside her husband. His grandparents farmed in some very difficult years, but stayed with the land. Don-Bob's daddy was born on the farm in the 1870s and led the same hard existence as had his folks, but stubbornly stayed and fought the elements, married, and Don-Bob was born in 1900.

Early in the twentieth century, oil, seeping out of the ground, was exploited to the amazement and ultimate satisfaction of landowners in many parts of Texas. As is usually the case, the big money wise guys tried to pry loose the Feckers' land, but the same stubbornness the ancestors showed resembled the attitude of the current family.

The decision to stay where they were for close to a century had nothing to do with education. All Don-Bob's antecedents, himself now included, had had little education. In fact, reading and writing was the last chapter of their book of formal learning. The similarity of three generations of male Feckers was astonishing. They were attached to the land, intent on making a living off it without anybody's succor. The three Fecker men all had one son each, all had few friends and few relatives on their wife's side, and all the men and their wives had hyphenated names. Don-Bob even thought the new dog had two names. In reflection, as he and Thelma-Louise were driving back home from Amarillo, he said, "You know, Thelma-Louise, that there pooch's real name is Bitch-Freeze. It's what the owner called him, but damned if I can figure out how that name came about, so we'll leave it as Bitch."

When Don-Bob was born, his parents and a few hands worked the farm before oil was discovered on it, and as soon as the boy could handle chores he went at them furiously, hating the mornings he was sent to school, which was a mile and a half down the dirt road toward the town of Blue Fly, population 190. He attended the same school until he was twelve and rejoiced when his daddy declared one early spring morning, "That's 'nuf schoolin', Don-Bob, 'less you want some more. I can use you on the tractor now; you can drive it. 'Less you want more schoolin', you can start working full soon's school's over next month." Don-Bob had two good farm boy pals with whom he shared the good news and found that both of them were ending their scholarly instruction at the same time to be full-time ranch hands.

The next five years were spent happily as tiller, plowman, and cultivator and whatnot, with one added ingredient: oil. The Fecker family still resisted all attempts at buyouts and strong-arm methods to get them off the land. They owed nothing and stayed glued to their real estate. Don-Bob's dad had one dear old friend who lived nearby. He had a nice house, wife, and one son, and no land to speak of, and didn't need any in his business. He was a lawyer, tried and true, and a hunting and fishing buddy of Fecker, and they were as close as two men can get without being attached at the hip. The lawyer's name was Ben Williams, and his son's name was the same.

Ben handled all the dealings Fecker had with the oil people, keeping the vultures scattered while he worked out a venture with the drillers and the big oil companies to buy the unrefined product from the Feckers. All this new business was going on without an end to the other farm work; however, the money accumulating was stupendous. But without question, this incredible largesse had no effect on the family except that they rebuilt their home in expectation of Don-Bob getting married one day and raising his family there.

In 1917, the war in Europe exploded on the American scene, in the cities, in the small towns, and on the farms. The patriotic fervor was inescapable, affecting all the young men and women in the land, and saw the men enlisting in the service in droves. Don-Bob, his two old school pals, and Ben Williams, Jr., all decided to join a battalion raised in Texas, and off they went to train and soon to fight for their country in France. The horror of trench warfare, frontal charges at entrenched, well-armed Germans, the gas, and the unceasing screams, whistling, and explosions of shells at the front were never to be forgotten by the combatants. For Don-Bob, there was a greater horror. Both of his boyhood friends were killed on the battlefield, one of them dying in Don-Bob's arms, pieces of him blown away. That scene, never leaving Don-Bob's memory, made a quiet man speechless for quite awhile. Don-Bob and Ben lived through the war with nothing but the horror of it as their wounds. Ben went on to college and law school and joined his father in their law business. Don-Bob went back to the farm and the oil fields and slowly recovered from the depression from which he suffered. A young lady also helped. Thelma-Louise was a wholesome lass whose allegiance for her first nineteen years was to Mom and Dad and to the soil around their small farm in Oak Bluff, thirty dusty miles from Blue Fly. Her worldly enlightenment was shallow, her blue eyes deep, her pleasant features had a dark blond topping, and her figure met with Don-Bob's approval, as did her unspeakably kind temperament. She made him comfortable. They laughed together, married, and were inseparable for sixty-eight years; but for a single tragedy, they stayed healthy, prosperous, and genuinely content.

A son who, with no imaginative impetus, was named Don-Bob was born in 1925 and unfortunately was never joined by siblings. Thelma-Louise had a problem with the birth of her only child and could not bear any other. Their boy showed a stronger desire for learning than any other Fecker to date, but upon graduation from high school in 1943 was drafted into the army, thrust into battle in Europe, and killed at the Bulge. His parents were grievously shaken for many years and visited his grave on the farm daily. There was a simple stone monument on a green hilly ridge overlooking the farmhouse, the pastures, and the constantly working oil wells, all of which the son had had pitifully little time to enjoy.

As years pass, time heals, and life as the Feckers knew it plied on like a heavy ship in a ponderous sea. Time was spent daily in the gardens and fields. Ben Williams worked with Don-Bob continuously. The oil business was a complicated one, and Don-Bob needed more time to understand the lawyer's and the accountants' explanations, figures, and plans.

He did comprehend what was told him, the unexpected intelligence coming from repetition and the kindness and ability to teach that Ben showed his old friend. As Ben realized Don-Bob's gradually increasing grasp of his estate's value, he urged Don-Bob to do more with his money than invest and accumulate it. Don-Bob would answer with his typical aversion to discussing money. "Ben, let's think all that over. Thelma-Louise and me don't want to answer that right now."

With the old folks long gone and Don-Bob and Thelma-Louise in their mid-eighties, there obviously should have been some comprehensive thought given to the huge estate, but the Feckers, with no relatives, had no idea how to dispose of their wealth. Charities were always after them, and with their mailed-fist approach to donations from people they did not know, turned man and wife Fecker away.

Colleges and other such institutions wrote constantly, crying for the necessity of building their endowments or merely begging philanthropy for a ton of needs. Needless to say, the Feckers had never had contact with higher education and didn't trust the bright boys who forever tried to wrest away their land with deals impossible for them to understand.

Religion also played no part in the lives of Don-Bob, his wife, or any of their ancestors. Their beliefs were centered on self-help, self-preservation, self-esteem, and ultimately self-assurance. They distrusted the preachers and the bible-thumpers who railed at them and promised fire and brimstone for sins they had never committed in the first place. The Feckers were different. Don-Bob remembered his daddy hollering at a black-frocked circuit sermonizer after he called Fecker a damned, no-good atheist from hell, "God is no better 'n me. I never sinned neither, and if there's a God, he knows it. Now get."

The poor were unknown to Don-Bob. In truth, he never met any of them, except for the suffering soldiers in the war, and the people who were not warriors but who were caught in the massacre of hell on earth. Don-Bob never for a second wanted to remember that year of 1917 when he held his best friend who bled to death in his arms, and both he and Thelma-Louise never faced again the thought of their son dying in the frozen woods of the Bulge. The proposition of to whom to leave this wealth was a mind-bender and bent the Feckers' minds into a pretzel. They didn't want to think about a problem that anybody else in the world would love to have, and they always answered with a put-off: "We'll think about it real hard."

Ben Williams's son, now in his forties and a third-generation lawyer, did all of his father's work now that retirement smothered the older man like a collapsed canvas tent. Ben III was soft-spoken, kind, and generous of his personality with Don-Bob, now in his mid-eighties, as had been Ben Junior. Ben III did persist in urging a reply on the estate question, and Don-Bob would say, "We's working on it. We'll have it for you in writing soon enough."

Nothing was forthcoming, though.

On a cold, windy day in February 1987, with the trees in the fields swaying and soil flying with the wind and the scudding clouds sailing eastward, Don-Bob woke about a half hour earlier than usual, sensing the unusual. He could see that Thelma-Louise in their large bed was not breathing. He shook her and cried,

"Lou, Lou," and realized that his long-term love had died in her sleep. Thelma-Louise was buried next to her son's grave on the ridge. Don-Bob was silent, but tears rolled down his face for many weeks, and his silence was respected by the few people who saw him by remaining silent themselves.

The change in Don-Bob was evident to Ben, who didn't press him with the estate problem. But Don-Bob, on a number of occasions, muttered, "I know, I know. I've got to do this myself. Thelma-Louise and me always did things ourselves, and I'll do this. Don't worry."

A year passed since the passing of his wife and still no answer to Ben's soft manner of pursuing the missing will. Don-Bob, still reticent, seemed to be more thoughtful. He surprised Ben one day when he handed his lawyer a blank sheet of paper on which he had printed, "Last Will and Testament of Don-Bob Fecker." He said to Ben, "Sign the bottom, notarize it, and have it witnessed by your wife or your father."

Ben, never skeptical with his dad's best friend, looked Don-Bob in the eye and said, "The sheet's blank. Are you gonna fill it in?"

"Me and Thelma-Louise always did our own thinkin'. Sure, I'll fill it in the way I see to."

Time passed slowly in 1989. Ben Senior would sit on the veranda of Don-Bob's home for hours with Don-Bob, neither of them speaking for much of the time. Ben was smoking an old meerschaum pipe around noon one day when a car drove up the driveway. Out of the car stepped a lone occupant, a woman of about sixty-five, a large, white-brimmed, floppy hat shading her face. The face had a determined look. She wore square-shaped sunglasses, which rested on a straight nose that flared slightly at the nostrils. Her lips were bright red and shiny. She wore a yellow sundress, showing some cleavage. Don-Bob turned to Ben and said, "You know her?"

"Never seen her in my life."

"Me neither," said Don-Bob.

The lady walked up the wide stairs leading up to the porch and stood in front of the two men, who remained seated, basically because it was difficult for them to do anything else.

"Can I sit down with you?" she asked as she dragged the chair over to where the men sat. They didn't question her as to who she was and why she was there, because it was obvious she would do the explaining shortly. Speaking to Ben, who was puffing his pipe, she said, "Mr. Fecker, I'll tell you why I come by."

Ben pointed his pipe and said, "He's Mr. Fecker."

"Oh," she said, turning her head to Don-Bob, and without apologizing, went right on. "My name is Lillian. I live over at Oak Bluff, and everybody talks about you and how nice and quiet you are, and that your wife passed 'bout a year ago."

Don-Bob listened without changing his expression and stared straight at her while a sly, knowing smile crossed Ben's face. "Well, anyways," Lillian continued, hardly drawing a breath. "My husband died six months ago. Drinkin' and smokin', but he was a decent man." She picked up a white handbag resting on her lap and put it on the floor between her legs.

"What's the dog's name, Mr. Fecker?"

"Bitch."

"I hope that's really his name," she said, taken aback.

"Her. Bitch's a female."

"Well, she's cute. You've got any ginger ale or soda? I'm parched," Lillian announced.

Don-Bob called out loud, "Sarah." The housemaid appeared, and Don-Bob told her to bring out some soda.

Lillian went right on. "I was a good wife, made Samuel very happy. You see, he loved his food, and I'm the best cook in Oak Bluff. 'Course, he ate too much, was real chubby, and with his drinkin' and smokin'…" She didn't finish her last sentence, because Sarah put down sodas for the three of them. Lillian took one and drank half of it before she went on.

"You know, Samuel was only sixty-four and still active, you know what I mean? But all that drinkin', eatin', smokin', and such…"

Ben covered his smile with his pipe and concealed a laugh with a false cough. Don-Bob shifted in his chair.

"Anyways," Lillian continued, after taking another gulp of soda, "everybody in Oak Bluff knows how good a wife I was.

Why, all the single, mature men don't stop bothering me, and some of the married ones, too. But I pay them no never mind."

The point was clearly made, and the two men now sat back in their chairs and decided to enjoy the show. Lillian was now unstoppable, but even she knew that the time had come for the climactic conclusion before the curtain was lowered and the audience would respond.

"Anyways, I want to offer myself to you, Mr. Fecker. I mean, my taking care of you since the passing of your dear wife. What was her name?"

"Thelma-Louise."

"What a lovely name. Anyways, I'm a terrific cook, a very loving person, you know what I mean, and I'm ready to settle down here and be a good wife to you."

The pause was significant. Lillian actually expected an affirmative answer. The two men sat, Don-Bob not quite expressionless as he glanced over at Ben, who looked ready to burst like a pricked balloon, his face reddening.

Don-Bob spoke to Lillian in his patented straightforward manner and said reverently, "Thank you for coming by, but there is no need for you to press this here idea of yours. You see, Bitch and I are gonna stay single for the rest of our lives. Now I'm going inside to sleep for a while. Good day, madam."

Lillian stood up, straightened the crease in her sundress, picked her handbag up off the floor, and said, "Well, I've never been put off so abrupt. Without even a goodbye." She turned her back on the men, walked down the steps, got into her car, and slammed the door, which caught the flouncing end of her sundress. She reopened the door, slammed it again, and drove down the long driveway and disappeared in a dusty cloud.

Ben, who doubled over with the wildest laughter ever heard in Texas, was joined by Don-Bob, whose laughter was more an uproar than a guffaw. They laughed like that for quite awhile, then stopped, and Ben said, imitating the departed Lillian, "Anyways, I'm still active; you know what I mean." The laughing started again and continued for about five minutes, until both men were out of breath.

Don-Bob gasped and said, "I never thought I'd ever laugh like that again." As it turned out, the two men did laugh every time one or the other would mention Lillian.

The effect of that absurd spectacle loosened the tight knot of Don-Bob's brain. He sat alone one night with the blank will in front of him. On the desk was the executed blank will, a few pens, and an eight-by-ten framed photo of Thelma-Louise propped up right on the will. Bitch was asleep on the carpet. Don-Bob spoke to the photo.

"Thelma-Louise, you and me never took care of this. There was supposed to be a survivor, Ben said, who, after one of us died, would own everything. You felt the same as me. We talked about it, cried, remember? We never could think of the other as gone." Tears from his eyes spilled onto his cheeks and into the corners of his lips. He wiped away the wetness, played with the pen, and continued the conversation with the photo. "Well, you went first and left me to make a decision. I hoped we'd make it together." Don-Bob cried again and fumbled with a handkerchief, which dropped from his hand and seemed difficult to hold. He wiped away the tears with his shirtsleeve and managed to grasp the handkerchief. He used it again, and once again it dropped on the floor near the sleeping dog. "You and I never talked money. It was something we had so much of, we never thought about it, and now I know my thinkin' was runnin' in that direction, but I'll write something and show it to you. I wish you was here, though." He wrote on the already legal will, spoke the written words of it to his wife, and as best he could, folded it in thirds and put it in a long envelope, sealed it, and went to bed.

Early in the morning of July 18, 1989, Don-Bob drank a cup of coffee that Sarah had prepared for him, and after finishing it, he shuffled out to the veranda and eased into his rocker. Bitch followed happily and rolled up at Don-Bob's feet and promptly fell asleep.

Ben Williams III was about to leave home for his office when the telephone rang and Sarah's excited voice pleaded for him to come right over. He drove to Don-Bob's home and quickly ran up the broad steps leading to the porch. Sarah stood crying beside Don-Bob's unmoving, sitting figure. Sarah and Ben stood shaking in front of Don-Bob for a few moments, as if in prayer, when Ben noticed the envelope under Don-Bob's hands. The envelope clearly had "Ben Williams" written on the front, and Ben gently removed it from under the clasped hands. Ben called the police in town, told them what had occurred, and said he would take care of things with the funeral parlor people. He put his hand on Don-Bob's bare arm and said something so quietly that Sarah couldn't even hear. Then he went inside the house, called his father and said he'd be right over, and then sat at Don-Bob's desk, where Thelma-Louise's framed photo now was facing him. Bitch came bouncing in the room to play at Ben's feet while Ben opened the envelope and read it out loud.

"Last Will and Testament of Don-Bob Fecker. To my best friend, Ben Williams, and his son, Ben, who is my trustee and executor, I leave everything I have—land, companies, banking, and investments—to do with all of it as they wish, and as they know Thelma-Louise and me would approve of. Leave money for Sarah and the hands, and take care of Bitch for us."

Don-Bob Fecker
July 17, 1989

GHOST STORY

Isadore sat in his favorite rocking chair, which was supported by soft pillows on the seat and back. He was barely rocking in front of an actively burning log fire. A plaid wool blanket covered him.

The only light in the study flickered from the fireplace onto walls where stacks of favored books lined up in tiers reflected the reddish-yellow flecks and sparks from the pungent and glowing wood.

Shadows danced about the room while outside the home, a January storm promising heavy snow blew its wailing wind against the house and shook windowpanes as curtains shivered inside.

Isadore sat motionless, sucking his meerschaum pipe, which long since had gone out, his bespectacled eyes exploring the firelight until he became transfixed by staring at it.

Thoughts of his life slowly marched from their mind's origin across his blurred vision and in the semi-light appeared real enough to touch. Thoughts and memories appeared in cloudy yet vivid sketches. Ninety-six years of life had been spent happily in childhood, struggling in early manhood, and cheerfully laboring for many years by writing constantly of renowned, far-famed persons whose lives either thrilled or chilled him to the point that his stories, written or spoken, had brought a modicum of fame to him. His literary work made him financially stable, allowing him the comfort a nominal barrier against poverty affords.

His son appeared first.

"Sorry we had to leave, Dad. Tiny Midwestern town left us no chance to expand. You and Mom were really to blame, you know; all the reading, all the stories, all the knowledge you pressed into our heads left us nowhere to turn but to what we hoped existed out there."

"I know, I know," Isadore mumbled. His white pipe fell into his lap, scattering the burnt-out ashes on the blanket wrapped around him. "Still, I would do it all over again. I mean, all those books, all that information—it's just not fair to keep it to oneself. All that science and history is meant to be shared."

The visions and voices answered, "We know; we did the same for our kids and they're gone, too." The fluttering specters were moving away but managed to speak. "Sorry to leave you alone like this; we thought there would always be Mom there, but you fooled us all. Outlived all of us, you did."

"And keep on living, Iz." His wife now floated in the light, touching his hand. "Keep on reading. You never could squeeze enough facts into your head. You could never tell enough stories or discover enough famous ancients, and Iz, some of them want to talk to you about what you said about them in your stories. Sorry I had to leave you. Sixty-eight years were fun together, though there were troubles along the way. Sorry I had to leave, but I just had to." The voice faded.

The old man reached out to grasp his wife's hand, not wanting her to disappear, but she was gone in the darkness. His blanket fell off as he slowly stood, straining as he bent to pick up a log to place on top of the others, which now spat sparks and showered fiery embers. A few more logs made more tiny particles take flight as they now began to flame furiously, the fire spreading its warmth to its master nestled back in his chair, his plaid blanket once more comfortably wrapped around him.

From out of the smoldering blaze, a figure in a toga stood towering, glaring down at Isadore.

"You know who I am."

"Of course. You are Aristotle, student of Plato."

"You called me a pagan; what nerve you have," Aristotle said angrily.

"And pagan you were. You believed in demons," boldly answered Isadore.

"And the church after me, they believed in demons. Here is St. Augustine next to me. Is he also a pagan?" The two glared at Isadore, awaiting his answer, which came quickly.

> "You, St. Augustine, said man occupies the lowest regions; demons are above men."

"And so I believed."

"You had no faith in man."

Aristotle interrupted, "I had faith in man. Democracy was mine. I had faith in democracy and an intellectual approach to the world as we know it. We Ionians began the search for answers to the unknown in nature rather than the superstitious howling of earlier civilizations. Every element had a God, an invention of early man, who instead of uncovering the hidden answers of nature merely stated that each God controlled his particular area. What folly."

Isadore responded, "You had slaves, Aristotle; is that democracy? And both of you believed in demons. If you were alive today, would you still believe in this craziness that led to the burning and torture of young girls and women in witch hunts? Millions were killed."

"We could not divine the future. Man corrects himself constantly, like your scientists today: they discover things, then refine them." St. Augustine, with frustration and anxiety, continued, "We cannot refine religion; for the most part, we accept dogma. Aristotle probably would have been a great latter-day scientist, while I would not change my concepts. Bah! You blame us for what we did not know." Their voices were already dimming. "'Tis a simple task to blame. We have little time."

Isadore answered, "'Tis a simpler task to speak idly," but they were gone, replaced quickly by a cantankerous bearded figure, rather heavy, who held a beaker that exuded a clear while cloud.

Isadore gasped. "My lord, if it isn't Isaac Newton."

"'Tis," Newton snorted.

"I hope you are not annoyed with me, sir. I have only the loftiest opinion of your work. You sincerely are the father of science."

Newton, still glaring but a shade more relaxed, replied, "I trust nobody."

"Why are you so upset? Certainly you are renowned as the master."

"They all tried to upstage me, steal my experiments, claim to have discovered things before me. Even Leibniz with calculus. I had to hide my findings for forty years so they wouldn't filch. Even my telescopes."

Isadore asked, "Why are you annoyed with me?"

"Time," Newton shot back.

"Time?"

"Time and motion. Those were my laws."

"Yes, I know that," Isadore responded.

"So why did you throw Einstein at me? You belittled me." Newton was agitated as he had been most of his life.

"Because relativity introduced changes in your laws because of the speed of light and where an observer's position would be."

"I could not measure the speed of light. I didn't have the instruments available to scientists one hundred fifty years later. I would have predicted the equivalence of energy and mass. I could have…" His voice trailed off as Isadore tried to comfort Newton by patting him on the shoulder, but Newton was gone. In his place stood Albert Einstein, his white hair in complete disarray.

"He always cried. A real crybaby, but without question the best of all of us."

"Professor, do you think he would have figured out $E=mc^2$?"

"Without question. But if *he* had conceived the energy-mass existence, our planet would probably not exist today."

"My God, professor, why?"

"Because, my friend, it would have given idiotic politicians a head start of two hundred years to activate physicists to use that equation to develop the thermonuclear power that could splinter our planet apart. Isadore, there are over forty thousand such bombs in the wrong hands today." He gave Isadore a knowing wink and was almost gone.

"Albert, wait, wait. Why, then, did you make all that known in 1905?"

Einstein winked back; his eyes, which could either sparkle or droop with fatigue, drooped. "Why," he said, "do we discover things? Because we know things and also know that others know and will soon outface us. That is competitive thinking and all humans acquired that spirit from the microbes, sea and land animals, and all creatures, including swimming and flying ones, which fairly covered the earth. As that matured, so did their brainstems, the cortex, until upright man could think. Man and his brain grew and thought, and between the instincts inherited from his forebears and his enlarged thinking apparatus, we have the mayhem and chaos that await us."

Einstein casually regarded Isadore, who slumped in his armchair, and asked, "But you already know the answer. Why did you stop me?"

"Because I have heard the other side of the answer—God's side."

"You didn't hear it from God."

"No, of course not, but from his priests and guardians and believers."

"They are but humans with the same cortex as yours. God's history was composed by man. God is the beginning, the first step, the unexplained commencement of the universe, and that will never be known."

"So there is a God, professor?"

"So there may well be, Isadore."

"Don't listen to him," Pope Innocent VIII screamed as he emerged from the sparks. "Yes, the Inquisitions were my idea, the accusations were mine."

Isadore's eyes met the red ones glaring from Innocent's ashen sockets. "And so was the torture and countless burnings of your witches and contrarians."

"The bible certifies witches. Deny witches, you deny the bible."

"I deny your ability to reason."

"Six hundred years ago that statement would have meant *your* torture and death."

Isadore asked, "Do you recant? Do you realize the turmoil, the suffering you inflicted for such a hideous course?"

"When life ends, there is no retraction, no denying. You die with your beliefs. You will find out." With this warning, Innocent turned into the flames.

The next visitor immediately entered.

"I remember you with a clean-shaven face, and here you are with a neatly trimmed white beard. Whatever you looked like, I could care less—you were my favorite," Isadore said.

"That is quite a compliment coming from someone as well read as you." Hemingway stood arms akimbo, legs apart as he stared down at Isadore.

"You said things the way they were meant to be heard. Direct—no baloney, no words bigger than yourself," said the seated host.

"True, that's the way I wrote. I had an idea and I didn't want it to get stale. No sense mollycoddling a good story. Out with it, I say. Do you have something to drink here, by the way?"

"There's an old bottle of brandy there on the shelf. Never could open it. Tried, but couldn't. Didn't want to ruin it with pieces of old cork sinking in."

Hemingway held the bottle and magically pulled the hundred-year-old cork out effortlessly, fetched two water glasses from the kitchen, and poured each glass half-full of brandy. He handed one to Isadore, clinked his glass with Izzy's, and downed the golden drink with a few swallows. "That's good stuff," he said as he refilled his glass.

Isadore merely held his drink and smiled, obviously pleased with his guest's contentment. Peering over his spectacles, Isadore broached a subject he wasn't quite sure Hemingway would appreciate.

"Why did you stop writing? You were so good."

"You had some pretty famous people in here today…who all stopped writing."

"You mean like Aristotle?"

"Don't throw him at me. He prances around like a peacock, knows everything—full of himself," complained Ernest.

"In his time, he was the best…"

"Bah! You don't have to be like those Greeks. Give me Shakespeare, Twain, Poe—there were hundreds who didn't strut."

"Ernest—I hope you don't mind me calling you that—but you were genuine. You wrote about your experiences. That is firsthand. Most of us write by researching men like you, historians of a sort. Why did you stop? I mean the way you did?"

Hemingway finished his second brandy and poured his third. "I stopped because I could no longer be personally involved in the action. I could invent, certainly, but I didn't want to be merely an inventor."

"You ran out of material?"

"Perhaps. I didn't want to struggle with the truth." Hemingway turned toward the fire, catching a glimpse of the next caller, a short dark-haired man wearing a cape, a cornered hat, a sash across his chest, and a sword protruding from his caped overcoat. Ernest bowed, put his empty glass next to the half-filled cognac bottle, and started off. As he left, he took Isadore's glass of liquor and downed it. "I forgot, you don't drink. Pity." He vanished.

Napoleon took an empty glass, filled it, and drank it down gracefully. "You know," he said, "they named this after me." He poured another glassful of the brandy, almost emptying the bottle. "Sorry to finish your bottle. I'll have Marshal Lannes send you a case."

"Don't bother, Emperor," answered Isadore. "I really don't drink; the bottles will just sit."

"As you wish," replied Napoleon.

"But you mentioned Lannes. I read he was your favorite."

"No secret at all," replied Bonaparte. "I loved him and I hated him, but to the end of his life he was a hero, the bravest of the brave. You know, I had twelve marshals, and they were all wonderful in battle."

Isadore, a true desciple of Bonaparte's history, knew he had only a short time to face him. "Emperor, you know I wrote your history. I followed your career as closely as I could over a hundred fifty years since it ended."

"It will never end," corrected Napoleon. "History itself doesn't end. It has its own life. It breathes and comes back to life every time. It is heard or read, and I *was* history for fifty years."

"What do you decry as causing the end of your career?" asked Isadore, expecting Waterloo to be mentioned.

"First and foremost, the invasion of Spain. I never saw such an enemy. They were everywhere, unprepared and untrained, but on their own land—their impossible roads, difficult terrain, their deserts, and their mountains—they were unbeatable. And intrigue, Bernadotte, Talleyrand, the Turks, the Prussians, the Russians, and the damned British navy, Trafalgar!"

"You had much in your way," agreed Isadore.

"And Moscow, leaving an undefeated Russian army in my rear. That damned country—so large and so forbidding in the winter."

Napoleon was walking quickly around the den, his hands folded behind him under the parted tails of his overcoat. "Then Wellesley—you know, Wellington—took advantage of France's condition and beat us in Spain many times and finally at Waterloo." He stopped his march around the den in front of Isadore. "But you know, he was damned lucky at Waterloo. I had him beat except for…Blücher." His voice dimmed.

Isadore wanted to resolve his feelings for the warrior and statesman slowly fading before his eyes before the great man completely disappeared. "You were a great reformer: your code, legal rights, equality across class lines, economic benefits…"

Napoleon raised his hand, quieting Isadore abruptly. "It was for the future to decide if reform was worth the millions of lives lost. I fought for reform, as you said, to end 'ancient regimes' once and for all. Now, my friend, the world has greater problems: brain-washing religions, weapons. Oh! Those weapons. And, if I'm allowed a moment of regret, I should have developed potential leaders to extend my code. I let the damned Prussians take over Europe and look what they did. Twenty times the dead. I should have…"

Isadore wiped tears from his eyes, but the blinding moisture and the bright firelight hid the Emperor as he departed. Other figures gathered behind the flames and casually seemed to wait for an opportunity to materialize, but they were suspended in their quest by a form eminent in his patience and his obvious firmness.

"Who might you be?" Isadore softly asked the faceless figure standing between him and the fireplace.

"I'll be happy to tell you, my friend, but first, let me light your pipe."

With a long wooden matchstick, its end set afire from its meeting with an ember, Isadore's tobacco-tamped meerschaum bowl was lit, and the superb odor of the glowing tobacco swirled around the duo.

"I am your spirit, the voice you listened to when you needed me, your only friend when you had no family. I am the very thoughts in your mind, the stories you wrote and told, your opinions and suggestions, yes, what you approved and disliked. I am your advisor and guide, your strength when you physically floundered, the cool breeze when heat weakened you, and the warmth when winter storms swooped. I lit your final pipe."

"My final smoke?"

"Yes, Isadore. All those guests who visited you tonight were the ones you invited back in your compositions, and there were many more wishing to come. They were a bit too late. The ones who made it were your wake visitors, your shiva callers. Isadore, you had no particular religion; all faiths came. Your stories covered a host."

"Sir," Isadore softly asked, "am I dead?"

"Oh, yes. I should say just about."

"My, this is easy."

"Approaching the end usually isn't, but the finale itself is a snap." In a more cheerful tone, the figure added, "Everybody does it, the famous and the unknown, the ugly and the beauteous. Sizes don't matter, nor do shapes. Those who languished and the accomplished one…" Their voices lowered.

As the two, each with an arm around the other's shoulder, stepped through the fire, Isadore asked a final question.

"All those I wrote about—the good and the bad—they all go to the same place from here?"

"I am only *your* soul. I cannot answer for the others."

"And I? You? Where are we going?"

They were gone.

The snow that intensely fell that night blanketed the area around Isadore's house, making it difficult to approach. The helper who came to the home each day to clean up and prepare meals for Isadore could not get to the unshoveled entry. Worriedly, she called his phone number to tell Isadore that she would come when she was able, but hearing no response to her call, she explained the situation to 911. They responded by clearing the entryway and allowing the housemaid to let the men and herself in.

The home was cold, bright light from the reflected snow shining through the windows and radiantly brightening the hallway, the dining area, and the den. The two policemen and the maid thought to inspect the upstairs bedroom first, but a glance at the den where the library and fireplace were sent the three there first.

The room smelled of yesterday's ashes, a cold and dank odor, stale, with a drifting shade of liquor blending into the mix. There in his rocker sat Isadore, snug in his blanket, still as a fencepost, silent as a snowflake, with a smile wide and assuming as a quarter moon on a wintry night spread on his face.

On an end table near his chair, an open bottle of cognac, empty except for a finger of liquid at the bottom of the bottle, sat next to its neatly removed cork and a tumbler with but a drop or two of liquor remaining in it.

A policeman examined the glass, smelled it, and remarked, "Looks like the old man drank himself a party."

The other officer added, "It's pretty obvious he drank himself to death last night."

The housemaid shook her head.

"That bottle of brandy sat on the shelf unopened for the twelve years I worked here. The cork was set in the bottle like it was cemented in there. Besides, boys, he was a teetotaler—never took a drink in his life."

"You mean until last night," an officer quipped. "Nobody came or left here in nearly twenty-four hours because of the snow, and you left just before the snow started." He winked at the maid. "Maybe it was your party."

"Well, I never," she said defensively. "Like the old man, I never took a drop. I'm a religious lady."

A sly smile was shared by the police as the maid held her breath and put a hand to her heart.

Isadore's smile never changed. It was fastened on his face like the cork wedged in the bottle for all those years.

CHAPTER ONE
The Camera Store

This story was related to me by the two main characters involved in the tale. The possessives (I, me, mine) will not be used after introducing the players and will not appear again until the last chapter. The story is theirs, though the task to recollect it is mine. One feels an emptiness when an attempt to recall the past is made, because the past seems to vanish into the blackness of night, whose winking stars are anxious to say that they hold the past and are loath to share it, but with sufficient prodding from the searcher, they will allow one more peek.

There is no question that hearing part of this life story so emotionally explained to me was memorable and important, a memory I tucked away for over fifty years. For this long period of time, I considered that knowing about the few people involved was a very personal matter not to be shared.

Vi and Leon said that they had never disclosed these incidents to anyone else. Their family consisted of just the two of them; they had no other living relatives and to my knowledge, no close friends with whom to share this information. Yet they were anxious to tell the tale as if it were a trap from which they wished to escape, or an animal growling at them and daring them to silence its roar. Strangely, it became so for me also. This unraveling story, a ball of yarn untangling, became a dream, and one I did not wish to revisit. That was a long time ago, but I remember it as it appeared in those dreams as if it were a stage play. I was given one more peek.

The years, which have long passed, leave different sentiments for folks. The happy days are cheerfully recollected, while sad times are usually erased from memory, and history, depending on its elapsed number of years, leaves a filmy curtain veiling its memory. Its flickering candle, rekindled with repetition, crashes into the calmer waters of our lives and casts us to a modern storm at sea.

To begin a twentieth-century love story by recalling a Junker born in 1815 seems illogical, but Otto von Bismarck, the great unifier, diplomat, and chancellor of Germany, set the stage for this tale. His great accomplishments of the mid-nineteenth century were the unification of the German states and the creation of the Reichstag, the congress and its rules of law. He warred against Austria, Denmark, and France, the conclusions of which resulted in increased territory for Germany. Bismarck's version of reason certainly bent the truth to suit his interpretation, and he argued that the new German areas were German-speaking ones in the first place, and that his adversaries were to blame for the conflicts at any rate.

Bismarck served as chancellor under three emperors: Frederick III, William I (whom he adored), and William II (whom he abhorred).

The chancellor was a diplomat of the highest order and an intriguer, employing his personality to conquer his political foes. He steadfastly believed in the rule of law and moderation, adhering to Goethe's statement that "Genius is knowing when to stop."

He somehow convinced his people that he was antiwar. He backed the general public in policy decisions, and after unification, justified maintaining a huge army while remaining within Germany's borders. As the calendar inched toward the twentieth century, Bismarck, an antisocialist who feared rising socialism would lead to revolution in Germany, was removed as his nation's chancellor by William II in 1895, three years before his death. Otto von Bismarck, a desperately disappointed and vitriolic man whose dreams of regaining power were shattered, prophesized the date that World War I would begin. He was off by less than two months, and his reasoning proved prophetic for the postwar period also. He never imagined that his dream for the German nation would be torn apart by a maniac who was a child in 1895.

In the years to come, Hitler would dissolve the rules of law into the fanatic soup that was Nazism. The Reichstag was abolished, cleansing by extermination followed, and world slaughter in the form of World War II was close behind. German nationalism, a condition of which Bismarck approved, would become an instrument wicked and deadly, of which he certainly would not have approved.

The players in this story were born around the turn of the century while the cauldron that was Europe was not yet boiling but merely heating up.

CHAPTER TWO
The Players and the Dream

The year was 1959; I was twenty-nine years old and a partner in an expanding super discount store business. My firm was opening one leased department store every ten days in unlikely venues such as trolley barns, abandoned factory buildings, and failed department and drug stores where space was abundant and rents were cheap.

The concept of the true discount store began to flourish after World War II with stores like E. J. Korvette and an original one, Ann and Hope, in Rhode Island, an abandoned warehouse with a huge surrounding parking lot predicting a tremendous increase in auto use, which had its start around 1948. Fixtures in the stores were crude. There were racks and tables of no apparent corresponding style. Walls were bare, and signage within the store indicated price only, but the discounted price was key, and customers flocked into these stores for the savings. Wal-Mart, Kmart, Price Club, and Costco followed many years later, giving us a competitive edge and an enormous head start.

We employed hundreds of people, but additional store openings kept us busy hiring new store and office personnel where there was a need for better financial and merchandising controls.

An ad placed in the *Wall Street Journal* produced an immediate response with resumes appearing, which I read, made inked comments, and then filed, having not yet decided on a hiree for a particularly important position.

On an early spring morning, an applicant presented herself to our receptionist, who called and advised me that a lady with resume in hand would like to be interviewed. I stepped out of my office into the receptionist's area and ushered the applicant into my office. After interviewing many potential employees, I was getting good at it, but call it luck or intuition, I was impressed with Vi at the outset. She was dressed in a dark navy suit and a white blouse that had a loosely tied bow, and though she was about five feet two, she wore black shoes with low heels. She was thin but strong and erect as she sat in the chair in front of my desk. In the first moments of an interview, appearance is very important, and I guessed her age to be about sixty. She had white hair, which hinted at past blond days, neatly coiffed with a small black hat resting on top of her head.

Her light blue eyes, which sparkled, gave her a young look even though there were thin creases in the corners of her eyes and mouth. She wore no lipstick and had a light pink complexion and a straight nose whose nostrils widened when she smiled. I thought she must have been a beautiful young lady not too long ago.

To my delight, our conversation began brightly. Vi had a German accent, but her command of English was of the highest level, and her thoughts, descriptions, explanations, and general knowledge were astounding. She had studied accounting and finance in Europe and had worked with her husband, who had a camera and optics store in Vienna near the Ringstrasse. In 1937, Vi and her husband, Leon, settled near London, where Leon worked for the British government in a scientific weapons program until the end of the war. Vi worked there also in a actuarial capacity. They moved to the United States in 1946 and opened a camera store in Newark, New Jersey.

Leon had recently retired, but Vi wished to continue working, hence our meeting.

Hiring Vi was easy. Her name was Yvonne Wiser Schoenweis, but Vi is the name she wished to be called. She lived in New Jersey, took the tubes in and out of Manhattan, and each morning, walked to our office on Thirty-Fourth and Ninth Avenue.

I spent a few days working with her for hours at a time, spending our time on the systems we used, especially actuarial ones, within that area where bookkeeping and accounting personnel were busily employed. Vi was to reorganize that area and also set up a department that would capture sales information using the new computers recently introduced to the business community.

She seized the opportunity, grasped the needs we desired, and continued working with me an hour or so each day, when we would analyze the figures she regularly presented. Her manner was intriguing because she was serious and industrious, and though it is not a good idea to personalize someone in a workplace, I felt, many times, that there was another human being inside her body, perhaps hiding another life, because at times she would hesitate, stare ahead for a few seconds, and with a delicate move, dab at her moist eyes with a handkerchief.

Her work was so good that I wanted her to be at ease on the job, but her stressed intervals bothered and interested me. Rather than approach this problem at the office, I invited her to lunch at a quiet restaurant in the New Yorker Hotel a block away from the office. That lunch was the first of many we had together, and while the conversations were mostly about business matters, I noticed that she was at ease more than usual one day. I looked at her directly on that occasion and said, "Vi, excuse me for asking, but I see at times that you stare straight ahead, wipe your eyes, and hold your forehead. You do that a lot; is there something I can help you with?"

She looked at me, said nothing for a few seconds, and then blinked. I saw her eyes were moist and faraway, but she managed a whisper. "There are a few things I'd like to tell you that neither Leon nor I have spoken of. You know we have no family and few friends, which is why we seem so quiet. You don't know my husband—I'd like to you meet him—but you'll find our personalities very much alike. I love Leon very much and you and my job mean a lot to me, so I think I would like to tell you about the part of our lives that you must be guessing about.

"You understand there were some very difficult times for us before the war began and both of us find it hard to talk abut them. They were frightening years…" Vi broke off her thought, hesitated, and then said, "…but telling you about them would actually help me."

I nodded my assent and remained silent, looking at her without changing my expression, and said, "I would like very much to hear your story."

So the show began, and my recurring dreams and my imagination were affected often. On a brightly lit stage whose dark blond boards were gleaming with reflected lighting, I dreamed of black folds of softly pleated curtains that were quivering mysteriously, straining to part at center stage, but they remained in place. There was no audience, just an empty theatre with neither actors nor sound. The pit was empty.

As Vi's story unfolded, the dream recurred often: actors took the stage, the pit became occupied with musicians, and their lovely music wafted throughout the theatre. The sound of drums softly gave rhythm to the music and ever so slightly increased their volume, introducing a sense of mystery in the offing. The curtains continued to shiver as I watched them, but with a strange, almost human desire, they stayed in place for a while, then opened slowly but not fully. A spotlight placed a circular glare on the first character, standing alone between the curtains at stage front, but it was not Vi.

Vi began describing her husband to me as she smiled at the mention of him with obvious warmth. "Leon is sixty years old, which as you know is my age also. In his youth he was extremely handsome, and to me, he still is."

I was interested more in Vi's background, so I wondered why her decision was to introduce Leon at that point. Vi guessed my feeling and with sensitivity suggested, "Leon is the most important part of my life story." She continued, "He was born in Vienna in the old Jewish neighborhood of Leopoldstadt." She digressed and added quickly, "Both of our fathers were physicians, and oddly enough, the same age. I think they were born in 1880 or 1881, and they probably knew each other later on, but that is not important."

Vi continued with no struggle to recall facts. "Leon's mother died in childbirth, leaving his father, Dr. Schoenweis, heartbroken and totally unable to care for his new son. As I understand it, a governess was hired, and as Leon remembers, she must have been kind and loving. She remained at her job for over fifteen years, never comprehending Leon's intellectual level and hardly able to assist him with his studies. So Leon was left to master his school subjects alone. He had no trouble doing that."

Vi did not have to search her memory to relate Leon's childhood because it was obvious that he often spoke of his early years, leaving her with the knowledge that a truly resolved spirit raises itself in distressed times. Vi was hardly tasting her lunch as she eagerly continued. "Leon was thirteen when his father went off to war to serve as a field surgeon in the Kaiser's army. You see, many Austrians were asked to serve, and Vienna, a city of nearly two million people, naturally had a large contingent of volunteers, even though it was not part of Germany. It was a republic then, but a German-speaking country loyal to Germany and decidedly nationalistic." Vi's voice grew emotional. "Gas was used extensively in the First World War, and Leon's father suffered for the rest of his life from the effects of it."

My interest was building. I offered no questions as Vi continued. "He survived the war, living until he was about forty-four, long enough to see his son become a high honors student mastering in physics, mathematics, and especially competent in optics, lenses, and photography."

Vi smiled knowingly. "Now you know how we got into the camera business, but his other specialties, like physics and lenses, enhanced his reputation and made him valuable to governments who were busily building their nations' war machines."

Vi relaxed a bit, had some of her lunch, and asked if I was tired of listening to her.

"Absolutely not," I said. "In fact, I'd like to know more about you and your family."

Vi smiled and raised her eyebrows. "I'm going to tell you my story, but you will be amazed by the similarity that Leon's and my family shared—except, of course, our religion."

She leaned forward, her hands folded together on the table. "My family lived far from the Jewish section in Vienna where Leon lived. It was called the Ottakring section, only one or two miles from the Schönbrunn Palace north of there, and the narrow cobblestoned streets had lovely one- and two-family homes built side by side. My father was also a surgeon like Dr. Schoenweis. His wife, my mother, also died when I was born."

The mention of her mother brought a handkerchief to her eyes, and after a moment's hesitation, she said, "We were Catholic. My father hardly observed his religion, but it was obvious that my mother had." As she said that, her hand rose to her neck, where from under her blouse she gently lifted a gold chain with a small crucifix on it.

"This was my mother's. I've worn it since I was six, when my father gave it to me." Vi took a breath. "It was then my father explained to me that my given name was Yvonne, but my mother's favorite flower was das Veilchen, the violet, so my father's nickname for me became Vi."

"It has endured," I said softly.

"Yes," she said, and added, "the strange similarities of our families continued. My father, Dr. Wiser, also served the Kaiser. His field hospital was shelled and he was badly wounded at Malmedy. He did recover, and though he was crippled by his wounds, he resumed his practice but died too early in his life."

"How old were you?"

"Oh, I was twenty-three; my life was shaped by that age." Smiling again, she recalled her childhood days. "I had a lovely nanny when my father went off to war. I was a studious little girl, reading at an early age and probably studying harder and longer than the other kids in my class."

With a show of embarrassment, she said, "I felt sorry for myself. My father's wounds kept him in the hospital for long periods, and much of my time was spent visiting him and studying. I'm afraid I had little time for friends and play. The kids thought I was a snob and some of them hated me for that reason."

It was later than the time we usually returned to the office. Both of us looked at our watches as Vi said, "I'll tell you the rest of the story, but we must go back now; a few people are waiting for me."

As I paid the bill at the table, Vi added, "I want you to meet Leon. You will like him and he can fill in the story better than me."

As we left, I told Vi that I would enjoy meeting her husband, and we arranged for the three of us to meet for a drink at the bar in the New Yorker the next evening after work.

The next evening, the three of us were sitting in comfortable lounge chairs arranged closely around a small circular cocktail table in the dimly lit bar. Leon was soft-spoken but animated after our introduction.

"Vi told me what she has covered with you so far." He leaned back, smiled, and thoughtfully added, "But you know only of the first leg of the journey. First I would like to tell you things about Vi's early years." Leon obviously enjoyed the prospect of recalling that time. Husband and wife happily interrupted each other as they recounted their youthful years, but Leon had the floor first.

"Vi went to the Laurentia Christian School, where she was always first in her class. She was absolutely beautiful when I met her, and pictures I saw of her at Laurentia showed her to be quite lovely at that early age. She had long blond hair, the bluest eyes, and you could sense the alert, intelligent child she was." Leon gladly filled in small gaps in Vi's early history, though he reluctantly discussed his childhood.

Vi explained the relationship she'd had with her father, to whom she often referred as Papa. "When Papa went off to war, I was thirteen, so you can imagine up to that time our talks were not too serious. He would talk to me about my mother in a very loving way, which also brought much love in my life for her. When I asked Papa why he had to go to war and leave me with only Nanny, he said, 'Perhaps you already understand that when people are at war, they get hurt and doctors on both sides must help. That is what we were trained to do: to attend to the sick and wounded.'"

Vi said, "I was crying when he explained his duty because I was thinking only of myself. I asked him if I would ever see him again, and he answered that the front was only hours away and that he would come home quite often. Nanny would take care of me in the meantime.

"Papa did come home a few times, but the gas damaged his throat, making his voice husky and difficult for me to understand. He coughed quite a bit and I understood how difficult it was for him to speak."

Vi continued, "Once when he returned home for a week, I asked Papa why we were fighting. I told him the kids at school were told that most of the world hated Germans and that it was time to protect ourselves, and even though Austria was not a part of Germany, we all had to fight to help our people."

Vi remembered that her father answered in a way she did not fully understand. "Papa offered a different opinion to my question. He said that world powers were in a contest to see which areas they could colonize. Papa saw my consternation, which grew worse as he further explained, saying, 'Imperial powers all act alike, wanting more land so that they will become wealthier and more powerful.'"

Vi leaned back in her chair and put a finger to her forehead as if to say she was beginning to understand. She said, "Papa finished his thought, stopping to cough. 'All countries are alike that way, but the big difference is who leads those countries and what the laws are guiding the leaders and how far they will go with their aggressiveness and their willingness to break their laws.' Papa went back to the front and I to school, where the kids all talked about bombs, gas, battles, tanks, killing, and relatives who had died or returned home badly wounded, and how Germany would win because God was on our side. I kept studying, wishing Papa would come back, and praying for the war to end. I didn't really care what side God was on. It seemed to me that He would make his own decision and I hoped He would make it quickly."

After an hour in the lounge listening to stories told by both Vi and Leon, more of the characters came to light, and after that evening, those players melded into the tale, slowly at first, but with clarity.

Felix Gruber

As a teenager in Vi's class at Laurentia, Felix Gruber was given to indiscriminate flirting simply because it was easy for him to do so. His blond crew-cut hair neatly topped his ruddy complexion, and his deep blue eyes, a broad, smiling mouth, and a narrow nose made his somewhat square face a Nordic model. He was tall for his age, his stature presaging more handsome growth in his future. His best feature was an attitude of ease, a justified hint of character and strength and an ability to enter conversations and keep them going. The girls loved him and tried to attract his attention, while his male classmates were friendly and would often try but fail to emulate him.

Felix's father was a salesman for a wine and beer distributor. His sales area and truck route stretched from the western edge of the Carpathian Mountains all the way to Innsbruck and the north of Switzerland—some four hundred miles in all, which kept him on the road constantly. During summer vacation, Felix was happily invited to join his father on these sales and delivery trips. He loved the countryside, the Alpine scenery off to the south and the hills to the north, where many small towns dotted the farmlands. The villages all had cafés and beer halls and restaurants, which were Mr. Gruber's customers. For Felix, the thrill of traveling, besides the scenery, was the freedom he felt on the road, and the banter with his father's clientele, and the friendships that were developing.

Felix worked hard unloading cases and didn't mind the work, but his real joy was when his father allowed him to share the driving, which turned his adventurous and exuberant nature into pride and true happiness. In late spring and into early autumn he had the road, while the rest of the year he had the girls and, incidentally, his studies.

There were two girls in the class who did not seem to be interested in Felix: one whose name was Ursula, by far the tallest girl, and the other was Vi, the best-looking and most intelligent one. Felix decided to exert a supreme effort to include Vi in his coterie, beginning with their final year at Laurentia. The year was 1917 and the students were fifteen or sixteen.

On a cool spring day, Felix made his move. The pines and fir trees, always green, had a particularly sweet, pungent smell, and they crowded both sides of the road to school. The maples, birches, and oaks began to exhibit new yellow-green foliage, and wildflowers on grassy fields emerged everywhere. Vi was walking alone toward her home. Felix ran up behind her, calling her name as he caught up. She turned and smiled when Felix asked if he could walk her home.

"Of course you can walk me, but where are all the other girls who are always around you?"

Felix, accepting the humor in Vi's question, smiled. "I'm giving them the afternoon off." They both laughed and Felix added, "I think they are getting tired of me. I meant to talk to you before, but you are always busy. You are very different from the others, but I think you would like to be friendly."

"You know," Vi said, "I'm sorry that I seem like that, but honestly I must act the way I feel. I really like studying. New things, especially math, interest me; it's like finding a treasure box. I don't know what's in it and I'm happy when I open it and find things inside that I could spend hours with until I find out everything about them. Does that seem crazy to you? Anyway, I'd rather discover things than do and say what the other kids do. They probably think I'm a showoff."

Felix answered without hesitation, "No, they don't have any bad feelings; they think you are different." He paused as if he did not want to say what was on his mind. "Except for Ursula, maybe; she doesn't approve of people with different ideas. She's very political, like her father, and thinks that everybody should agree with her."

"I've only spoken to her a few times."

"I'm sure, but that could be enough for her to make a decision. What's more, I think she's jealous of you—I mean your looks—and you always beat her out on grades."

Vi only said, "Oh."

"Somehow I'd be careful of her if I were you. Don't trust her."

Vi nodded and changed the topic. "What makes you happy?"

Felix told her about his love of the countryside, of the work and the people and of course sharing the long drives with his father. He added, "My mother says, 'Do what you must do and make sure what you do makes you happy.'"

"I think your mother is very smart. She must be wonderful. I wish my mother never died. I miss her."

This introductory talk was followed by many more. The two chatted about school and the mundane subjects of adolescent interest, but drifted into politics and where Germany stood in the chaos raging in Europe. On their strolls and chats, they found their ideas coinciding, their relationship blossoming, but their personal feelings, their emotional attitudes, quite different. Felix still had the girls and Vi had her studies, but they both had a friendship that each knew would last a long time.

The year 1918 was on hand, and in Vienna, the turmoil and ultimate horror of the European battlefields was well known, though the city was not physically harmed.

Vi and Felix sat and talked in their favorite coffee houses, walked the Prater Gardens, the Innerstadt, and the Ringstrasse and strolled to the Rathaus, and marveled at Votivkirche and the Gothic architecture at St. Stephan. They walked through the residential neighborhoods of Vienna and visited the Am Hof, and to passersby not suspecting the friendliness of their relationship, they appeared to be young lovers.

The slaughter went on only hundred of miles away, but the killing ended in 1918.

Vi and Felix discussed the music of Haydn, Mozart, Beethoven, and the Strausses and visited their homes in Vienna.

They held hands in the coffee houses and tried to analyze the war and the future but were unable to imagine the confusion, the disorder, and the terror to come.

Romance did enter Felix's mind and he wanted to get right to the point with Vi. He had his opportunity one day when their walk slowed in front of the Conservatory of Music.

It was 1921 during their first semester at the university, and conditions in Germany and Austria were worsening by the day. Still, the times Vi and Felix spent together walking, having coffee, or at times, at a museum or a concert, were filled with good conversation and a genuine air of friendship. Felix had many girls fond of him to whom his friends referred as his geliebte, his unending string of lovers; however, stirring at his brain and heart was Vi. Was she in love with him or he with her, and where should their closeness lead them?

In front of the Musikverein their walk slowed to a stop. They were hand in hand. The weather was perfect; a warm sun brightened the street and glistened on shop windows and the glass of slow-moving vehicles. The Gothic architecture in the area and the conservatory grounds added luster to the scene, with lively people striding in all directions. Felix led Vi to an outdoor area of a coffee house, where they sat in silence for a minute, not at a loss for words, which was never the case for them, but each seemingly knowing that the other had a serious matter to discuss and was not quite ready to begin. The white-aproned waiter took their order and appeared minutes later with their coffee.

Felix, still holding Vi's hand, said with reluctance, which was not his habit, "There is something I'd like to ask you."

Vi, guessing correctly that Felix was more serious than usual, nervously said, "Yes, I feel this is important—please go ahead."

"We see each other a lot."

"And it is always a pleasure, my good friend."

"It bothers me more than a little bit that we consider ourselves best friends only."

"And we are."

"But is that all we are ever to be…best friends?" He went on, "I mean, we kiss each other goodbye then we leave each other. I see another lady and you…I don't know what you do. You tell me often that there are no men in your life."

Vi softly broke in. "There *are* no men." Her hand was now resting on top of Felix's. Neither had bothered to sip their coffee.

Felix, hesitating again, said, "I'm not sure how to say this, but would you like me to be your man?"

Vi thoughtfully answered, "It's not as simple as that and not easy to answer. When you don't know yourself—I mean, who I really am—and the way things are around us make no sense…well, that is a terrible combination, and it confuses me."

Felix then said in an inquisitive way, "You can be strange, even eccentric. What is your future going to be? Where will you be in the next few years?"

She answered, "How can anybody know? I don't. And honestly, Felix, I can't make long-range plans now. What I am sure of right now is that I want to finish my studies at the university, and then perhaps leave the country for a while—I don't know. But Felix, I can't settle down now, I just won't…" She paused for a second and then in a lighter tone said, "Felix, you will never be without a liebhaber. The girls love you. You will never be alone." Realizing what she had just said, meant as a compliment, was actually a refusal, she immediately added, "Perhaps I am jealous of all the girlfriends you have, but please understand that I do love you. I really am confused. I need time, Felix."

The tone changed and the indirect refusal of his offer sank in to him. He felt that Vi would never seriously consider his semi-proposal, and at the same time, he felt she would forever be a loving friend.

They had their coffee, paid the bill, and in a rare silent moment, walked slowly hand in hand onto the avenue.

Felix yielded with disappointment to the lack of response to the relationship he wished existed between him and Vi. Though he deeply felt the vacancy, Felix's inner strength—perhaps it was loyalty or his ability to withstand a blighted hope that would rescue him—wrestled with his next step, a choice of going on with his education or beginning his career in earnest.

He would settle for Vi's friendship and allow his future to be decided a bit later. He would attend the university and let the girls chase him. He was still young.

Mindfully, Felix realized that his future could not be fully predicted at that point. There were complications. Many of his friends had left Austria to live in Germany when they were his own age, but that was not his wish. Vi had much to do with his decision to stay in Vienna, but deep in his soul was a resolve to steer a peaceful course and pursue a career at the same time.

Ursula Streicher and the Captain

Behind her back the students at Laurentia called her "Der Storch," but never so that she could hear them. Storks were very large birds; indeed, so was Ursula, who at fifteen years of age was about five feet ten inches tall and broad-shouldered. She had heavy legs always covered by long skirts, the fabric and the style of which were uniformly the same for all the girls. Her white blouse, which was also part of the uniform, showed no rise where her breast was concerned. Her broad shoulders supported arms that were thick and muscular. Her fingers were long and often clenched into a fist.

Ursula had short brown hair, a round face, brown eyes with lashes wide apart, a pointed noise, and brownish lips that covered large teeth. She was a good student and was opinionated and verbal in a harsh and direct approach to conversation.

Ursula's only friend at school was a chubby pink-faced lad named Eric Mann, who followed her and appeared to be her servant, obsequious and omnipresent, and hung on her words like an apple on a tree. Eric had floppy brown hair, eyes more yellow than brown, and a wide mouth under an upturned nose. He seemed to be the only person to whom she spoke in hushed tones, and they were together for almost all of their free time. He would listen and Ursula would talk.

Ursula's father was a police captain, tall and broad all over, and a known bully to his subordinates and to the district he served. He was shrewd, not brilliant by any means, but clever enough to become politically connected with a tiny Nazi contingent in Munich, where he visited often. There was a fledging Nazi underground slithering in the shadows of Vienna's evenings. Streicher accepted as God's truth where the blame for Germany's woes lay and eagerly spread this poison wherever the fangs of this venomous snake would strike. Communism and Judaism were his targets, and though it was early in the game, he hit the bullseye of the future fears and hatred that would one day cast Nazism into the gruesome monster it became.

Captain Streicher expressed his fears and prejudices to all who listened, especially in the beer halls, where he was popularly accepted as an exponent of the new faith, a man who could also prove and gladly show his strength and quench his thirst with lager for which he never paid. At home, his wife and Ursula repeatedly heard and thoroughly agreed with his creed and did not dare to question his point of view but furthered it in their own discourse. Strong men with muscle made official have the apparent attribute of a sharp mind and the actual disposition of complete loyalty to a cause, which in a dictatorial atmosphere would propel such men to prominence. Streicher was so marked.

Ursula's mother taught at the gymnasium. She was browbeaten and by no means sensitive to opposing views. She was tall and flat-chested, and her broad face was undistinguished by any handsome features, her graying black hair in a bun. She wore gray or black dresses and suits that gave her a militaristic appearance. Her shoes were black and had low heels.

Ursula was a good student and studied hard at home, her mother helping her even when she did not request it. Her friend Eric often worked with Ursula at her house, being tutored rather than sharing studies with her. He was a welcomed and familiar figure there. His father was a policeman in the same barracks as the captain's, and Streicher showed uncharacteristic restraint with his daughter and her friend.

Captain Streicher's hateful opinions were magnified by the severe problems of postwar Germany. The worse things became, the better accepted was his rhetoric; the more complex Germany's economic condition became, the less Streicher and his followers had to explain to an obviously unhappy population. The beer halls in Germany were like the ones in Austria, and the rhetoric was exactly alike, as were the attendees who came to drink and to be made constantly aware of the Nazi political agenda. The customers were young, poor, out-of-work people, jealous of the haves and eager to place blame for their lowly position and their nation's failure on Jews and Bolshevism.

The steamy halls smelling of beer and smoke were scenes of haranguing speeches, screaming preachers with armbands, and drinkers shouting their approval as they drank and spilled their lager on the long wooden tables. The scene was a filmy circus with a mob hungering for a fight, and even more so for a kill.

CHAPTER THREE
Germany 1918–1938

For twenty years following World War I (a time that Bismarck predicted), the world scene was chaotic while the spectacle in Europe was bedlam.

The Versailles Treaty of 1919 imposed terms on Germany, a defeated and desolate nation, that were harsh and degrading to a shameful degree. Alsace-Lorraine was awarded to France, the Allies occupied the Rhineland, a Polish corridor was established with West Prussia, and Posen was given to Poland. Danzig, with four million German people, was made an international city, while all German foreign colonies were awarded to Allied nations. German warships and aircraft were scrapped and the army dissolved; Germany was allowed to maintain an army of one hundred thousand men, which was plausible, but reparations of six million pounds sterling (thirty million dollars), which in 1918 was an enormous sum, was impossible for Germany, a bankrupt nation, to repay.

The printing presses created wild inflation by stamping out worthless bills, which could not buy anything because shelves were empty and food items were scarce to begin with.

Whether Germany deserved the treatment meted out by the treaty is a matter of conjecture, but the resulting unrest it caused led to a dire response. Germany had no choice in accepting the terms because if they refused, the country would remain occupied by the Allies for an indefinite period and the war would continue. In spite of the threat of occupation, the population blamed the signers of the treaty for the immediate problems the country had.

The people quickly turned those they held responsible out of office, destroyed the Reich, exiled the Kaiser, and replaced the imperial government with the Weimar Republic, which soon showed a toothless, totally weak inability to govern and to turn around the conditions existing in Germany.

Another calamity occurred in Russia in 1917. The Bolshevik revolution set its sights on Germany, wishing to cause an upheaval in Berlin as it had produced in Moscow. German nationalism disavowed communism as their past history had socialism. Retired German soldiers by the thousands organized the Freikorps, a force that roughly handled the left and actually stopped the Russian-style revolution from succeeding. The Freikorps attempted a Putsch in Berlin, which failed to derail the government, but in failing, a tiny Nazi party evolved, its swastika emblem soon to represent the terror thrust upon many millions for the next twenty-five years.

In the plot and plan of the Nazis, communism and Judaism were intermingled, and that idea was hammered into the heads of a desperate people. The Nazis screamed for the union of all greater Germany, the denial of the Versailles Treaty, and more land for the German people with food production increased to feed them all. The question of citizenship in greater Germany was answered in an ugly, heinous manner by demanding a proven line of ancestry and blood ties, which excluded Jews and Slavs.

The future leader of the small Nazi party, Adolf Hitler, was born around 1890 in Austria. He was a soldier in the Germany Army in 1914 and after the war settled in Vienna, where he failed at numerous attempts to earn a living. Well known was his attempt to become an accepted artist, but he was rejected at the art institute in Vienna and so moved to Munich, where he found a job with the city government investigating the fledgling Nazi party. He found the party to represent exactly what he believed in and joined it. His aggressive style of speaking was perfectly fitted to his anxious listeners as he spewed his hatred of all his perceived enemies and cried for the elimination of them.

In 1921, the SA Storm Troopers were organized to protect the Nazi Party and to menace those who would challenge it. The National Socialist German Workers' Party was on the way but stumbled in 1923 when Hitler and Ludendorff peremptorily tried to wrest control of the government in Munich and Berlin for their own political purposes. The police in Munich fired on the Nazis, killing sixteen of them and capturing and jailing Hitler, but the Putsch, as it was called, became a Nazi martyr's field day. In jail, Hitler wrote *Mein Kampf*, an illogical and rambling treatise on his disgust for Jews and communists. His writing displayed a warped subject matter characterized by his lunatic style, but a large and growing following nodded assent and shared Hitler's wordage and his militarism. They would soon fill the streets, cheering and adoring him, obviously willing to accept his opinions and to follow him.

Hitler realized that he needed the law to accomplish his aims and for the next few years, he would obey them while plotting to destroy and mold them to his liking.

From 1924 to 1932, the German parliament, the Reichstag, was unimpressed with the Nazis, who had about 3 percent of the seats as late as 1928, but the cold wind of depression originating in the United States blew frigidly over Europe. The Nazis benefited from the disaster as the poor, the unemployed, and the hungry yearned for immediate relief.

Unemployment in Germany stood at 15 percent with six million out of work, production cut, and shops and banks failing. The Weimar government's weakness and its inability to reduce Germany's problems found the Nazis capturing over 37 percent of the Reichstag's vote in 1932 as the population turned to the Nazis for help.

In 1933, Hindenburg, the Weimar president, who for years had held off Hitler's desire to be chancellor, capitulated and named him to the post. In the next few months, the Enabling Act, which Hitler introduced, was enacted, the Weimar constitution was suspended, and Hitler became supreme commander with the complete right to govern.

In 1933, in the Night of the Long Knives, Hitler moved to purge Ernst Röhm and two hundred of his officers, all of whom were put to death. The SA now became a part of the Reichswehr as Hitler declared himself "supreme judge of the German people."

Ernest Röhm was the leader of the SA Storm Troopers and though he and Hitler were comrades, Hitler suspected him of trying to merge the SA with the German Army (the Reichswehr) and then take overall command away from him. Rohm was shot to death on Hitler's order.

When the Reichstag building burned in 1933, Hitler blamed communists and Jews and vowed to "crush them with an iron fist." The Nazis now had 44 percent of the seats and resistance to the party was crumbling when in early 1934, Hitler turned his attention to the unemployment problem. He approached the great German production companies to finance his Nazi coffers, which would be able to build a huge army and mobilize it with production from the financing moguls. The mills would then employ those seeking jobs and the party would have served and covered two major objectives at the same time. In 1935, Germany rearmed and added 400,000 more men to its military force while England and France reduced their forces, showing no desire to enter yet another war. The Great War had ended only seventeen years before, and the Allies naively thought Germany, too, had had enough.

In 1936, with no Allied resistance, Hitler reentered the Rhineland and remilitarized that area directly on the eastern border of France. In the same year, the Axis was formally announced as a pact between Germany, Italy, and Japan. The Spanish Civil War, which was Franco's response to the Spanish Republican government (which included communists and separatists), gave Hitler and Mussolini a practice session to test their air force's ability to bomb civilians, a preliminary event to the next war.

Franco accepted the help but remained neutral during the war; however, a Nazi presence was evident in Spain during the war years.

When Hindenburg died in 1934, Hitler appointed himself the Führer.

Italy joined Germany (the Axis) and the Italian Army invaded Abyssinia in 1934.

In 1936, Hitler withdrew Germany from the League of Nations and the disarmament talks in Geneva.

In 1938, Hitler claimed that the inclusion of Austria, his birthplace, into the Third Reich was the "divine will of God," and an enormous majority of Austrians agreed when the Führer moved into that country after having infiltrated it for years. The Austrian chancellor, Schuschnigg, was warned by Hitler that if he rejected the Anschluss, there would be a civil war. Troopers were placed on the border and Schuschnigg resigned in favor of Dr. Seyss-Inquart, a stalwart Nazi who welcomed Hitler into Austria.

Austria

The Bronze Age rattled throughout the land, as did the Celts, the Germanic tribes, the Romans, Charlemagne, the Swedes, and the Turks. Maximilian, Napoleon, Maria Theresa, and the Habsburgs then added their personalities and their politics to the changing nation. The Habsburgs would include the conquest of Spain and two thirds of Europe in their record of accomplishments, while eras such as the Gothic, Baroque, Renaissance, and Neoclassical would follow. Introduced was astounding architecture of state structures, castles, and palaces while lovely residential quarters, churches, parks, and museums slowly took form.

The pastries, chocolates, and meats joined the goulashes, wiener schnitzel, and fabulous wines to make the Austrian cuisine sumptuous.

Lakes, river valleys, and the great Danube River flowing in the northern borders of Austria and through Vienna, a city of one and a half million people, added to the beauty of the country. The Tyrol, the East Tyrol, and the Vorarlberg areas of western Austria, where the magnificence of the Alps cannot be debated, joined the grand music of Mozart and Strauss, which is the chorus that permeates the loveliness of the country.

With the heavy-handed politics steamrolling into Austria in the 1930s, the personality, the character, and the temperament changed the identity, symbolically, of their beautiful land.

The Austrian Alps became an anthill, the rivers and lakes turned fetid, the food and wines spoiled, the architecture became a pile of stone, and the music became cacophonous. Past history was buried, forgotten, and rewritten as it was shattered under Nazism, buried under the corpses and smoldering landscape of a new empire called the Third Reich.

History of Austria
1918–1938

Greater Vienna, a city teeming with refugees from Northern Europe and elsewhere, held about two million people in 1910. The problems of large cities are common to all of them: overcrowding, slums, food supply problems, and racial questions spawning jealousy, bigotry, and often lawlessness and mayhem. Only five other cities in Austria held over fifty thousand inhabitants, Graz and Linz being the largest of the five, the other three being Salzburg, Innsbruck, and Klagenfurt. Small villages were scattered in the valleys and along rivers. They were known as Haufender, while thousands of scattered small farms dotted lower Austria and Alpine areas. The Alps to the south, the waterways, and the lush greenery that covered rolling hills and mountains all combined to make Austria a lovely and serene nation.

In 1918, after World War II, the Reichstag, the Imperial Parliament, called themselves German Austria and proclaimed an independent state with their own council (Staatsrat). Vienna erupted in revolutionary disturbances; at the same time, the German revolution was in effect. The National Assembly resolved that German Austria would be a democratic republic and Austria would be a component of the German Republic.

Karl Renner, a socialist, became head of a coalition government, but Otto Bauer, a virulent left-winger, became foreign minister.

In 1919, Bolshevism in Hungary led to a soviet republic there and Austrian social democrats resisted with their own troops, not wanting to ally themselves with the old order. The People's Guard was established and was successful against communist attempts at putsch. Bauer and Friedrich Adler were regarded as saviors, defeating the communist attempt (agitation) to take over workers' and soldiers' councils.

Other Austrian provinces wished to break away from Vienna, refusing to send supplies or food to the big city; they wanted provincial rights to make their own decisions. There were attempts at provincial secession. Vorarlberg voted for union with the Swiss. Tyrol wanted to secede. To save the situation, the constituent assembly elevated Vienna to statehood; the mayor was now governor. Red Vienna pursued an autonomous policy: the government was not socialist, but the reds were strict Marxists and had large representation. A national assembly and federal council (Bruderrat) were introduced in 1919.

In 1920, Otto Bauer, a firm believer in unifying with Germany, immediately inherited the rancor of the League of Nations, which firmly opposed any German unification policy. Bauer resigned and Karl Renner, who backed an independent Austria, became the foreign policy chief.

Decisions by the Allies and the League caused Bohemia and Moravia to be ceded to Czechoslovakia while German-speaking Hungary in turn was ceded to Austria. The stewpot that was that area caused a war between Czechoslovakia and Hungary, with the Bolsheviks naturally agitating for additional communist gains.

In 1921, German nationalists and social democrats became the majority voters, causing Renner to resign. The feelings of the Volk, the preponderance of German-speaking people who were workers and peasants, strongly sided with nationalism in Austria, while Vienna, with two million people, remained socialist. The Viennese benefited from aid and relief from Great Britain and the United States, creating more friction with the rest of Austria.

In 1922, inflation became rampant in Austria; however, the League of Nations and the Allies again propped up the economy, stabilizing it for the rest of the year. Up to 1926, this stabilization had the effect of keeping the radical Nazi elements at bay so that relative calm existed in Austria.

The fanatics were hard at work like wood-boring worms slowly destroying the wholesome society, which was struggling to emerge, waiting for hard times to return to their advantage.

In 1926, the new chancellor, Ignaz Seipel, played into the hands of the growing number of Nazi thugs by demanding greater authority to control the socialists, who, to their credit, had abolished the slums in Vienna. This was accomplished by taxing property, which alienated those who existed on private income.

The socialists organized an armed guard called the Schutzbund while opposing elements had the Heimwehr as a defense force. Those fighters naturally clashed often, leading to a mass demonstration by Viennese workers, who burned down the Ministry of Justice. Police fired on the crowd, killing eighty-nine workers and setting off additional fighting, which strengthened the Heimwehr cause and greatly enlarged their force, while at the same time the fascists were winning more seats in the Parliament. All the while, Seipel enjoyed more authority, which he used wantonly. The world economy was crumbling, having the effect of lessening the aid to Vienna, which in turn saw the return of inflation and a real economic crisis. The Nazis had their chance once again.

In 1930, the Austrian government, now led by Otto Ender and Johann Schober, established a customs union with Germany, which France totally respected, bringing the matter to the Hague Court, which condemned the union. Germany once again was humiliated, and the old saw of the disallowance of self-determination angered the people to the point where national socialism spread and voters increasingly flocked to their standard, making normal government untenable.

In 1933, the Austrian Parliament disbanded, leaving Engelbert Dollfuss, a follower of Seipel, in control of a chaotic situation. He was an authoritarian who called for that type of constitution. Dollfuss did not back an Anschluss (the unification of Austria and Germany), which Hitler, now Chancellor of Germany, had as his fondest wish—Grossdeutsch: a united

Germany. Dollfuss tried uniting with Italy with the verbal backing of France and Britain, who had no bite to the bark and so backed off.

In February 1934, civil war broke out in Vienna with the Schutzbund facing the Heimwehr. The rest of Austria by this time was solidly in cadence with Anschluss and the authority and strength that Hitler showed. The war lasted four days.

The country had no constitution, no rights of man; the social democrats being driven underground saw Austria become the Federal State of Austria.

By July, the Nazis seized the chancellery and proclaimed a Nazi government, murdering Dollfuss. Again, the Nazis were ahead of schedule. Those who were responsible for the destruction and murder were caught and executed while Hitler denied complicity, again understanding this as a premature action and seeing once again that obedience of the law was a needed perception.

In 1935, Germany, needing an ambassador in Austria, sent von Papen there while Kurt Schuschnigg became chancellor.

At this time, Great Britain, France, and Italy created the Stresa Front, but with typical complexities, Italy invaded Abyssinia, collapsing the union.

In 1936, Hitler marched into the Rhineland with no opposition, while in Austria, Schuschnigg, negotiating with Germany, compromised with them, which created a German State of Austria, but with Germany recognizing Austrian sovereignty. The effect of this deal set the Nazis more or less free to act, as Austrians by that time were solidly behind the German chancellor and his fanatical vision.

From 1936 to 1939—the Spanish Civil War—pro-Nazi Franco welcomed Hitler's invasion, and the Luftwaffe got practice bombing civilians.

In 1938, the Austrian police discovered a new Nazi putsch plot—this in what was supposed to be a sovereign state. Chancellor Schuschnigg then called for a meeting with Hitler, who again denied complicity with the plot but also showed sympathy for the Nazis' cause.

On February 12, Hitler dictated the terms known as the Berchtesgaden Surrender to Schuschnigg, which instructed him to hype the plot and give a general amnesty to all Nazis involved. Hitler also demanded that Schuschnigg include Nazis in his cabinet. To Schuschnigg's credit, he challenged the Führer about these terms, only to be told that there would be a plebiscite, which was put off until April 10 to allow for Nazi propaganda to air. Schuschnigg was told to resign, which he did, and Hitler accompanied his troops into Austria and announced the completion of Anschluss. The plebiscite's results surprised no one: 99 percent of the voters in greater Austria supported Hitler, whose triumphant march into Austria was greeted hysterically by the entire population. The miniscule resistance was immediately driven underground while Hitler basked in the multitudinous outpouring of support, which gave him impetus to extend his plan to enlarge his Grossdeutsch agenda.

Britain and France, though steadfastly confronting German movements, were totally unable to resist with a military presence. Britain had less than 100,000 soldiers in the twenties, and France had fewer. Also, production of guns, planes, and munitions was minimal and could not possibly be compared to Hitler's buildup of 500,000 troops by 1934. The size of his armed forces in 1939 was enormous; indeed, his losses in the Second World War were approximately five million, while his service personnel totaled nine million (more than 16 percent of the German population).

CHAPTER FOUR
The Camera Store

Vi was twenty-one years old when she met Leon at a college party. The attraction was mutual and the initial conversation naturally drifted into family history. They found out quickly enough that each had few friends and both were studious, though in different fields of study, and had strikingly similar familial backgrounds. They spoke of religion, Leon noticing a delicate gold cross that Vi wore as a necklace.

"My mother's," she whispered. "My father gave it to me when I was little. I'm not a religious person, but I will always wear it and cherish it. I know you are not Christian, so I hope you don't mind."

Leon, a foot taller than Vi, smiled down at her and said, "I don't think I'll ever mind anything about you."

"You know," she answered, "that's rather strange to hear after knowing you for less than an hour, but somehow I believe you, and I have never said this before, but I feel the same way."

Vi was much shorter than Leon; her blond hair was knotted in a bow in back of her head, which was the fashion of the time. Her eyes were bright blue and twinkled as she directed them steadily to whomever she spoke to. Her features were firmly settled on a pink complexion and her figure was well proportioned, giving a glimpse of strength to the observer. Leon liked what he saw.

He was six feet tall and had black hair, dark brown eyes set on a ruddy face, good features, and a smile that Vi interpreted as one not given easily and certainly not too often. He was thin and exuded intelligence. His well-mannered ability to handle conversation easily and with a strong thought process impressed Vi.

Both of them knew each other to be serious human beings not given to wasting time and liking the things that Vienna offered: the music, the parks, the architecture, the attitude of learning, the grace, and the appearance of a seemingly happy population.

Vi explained to Leon her relationship with Felix. "He was a school chum. We met formally on a walk home one day. We were sixteen."

Leon noticed an unease in Vi's explanation and tried to soothe her. "We all have our childhood affairs…"

Vi broke in. "No, no, it was not that at all. Leon, I want you to know that I love Felix. Don't be alarmed. I love him as a dear friend, never a lover. There never has been romance, though Felix wanted there to be."

Leon's face had a knowing expression, his eyes directly on Vi's. His shoulders drooped a bit, and he clasped his hands together as he nodded and listened.

"Leon, I think I will always love him and he me, but there now is no question that we will go separate ways." There were tears now, gently wiped away. "You are my love. I knew that the minute we first met." Vi admitted this without taking her moist eyes off Leon's.

He softly spoke. "I would like to meet him someday."

"He travels a lot and is rarely in Vienna lately," Vi continued. "There is more I want to tell you about him. We will always be able to depend on him." With hesitation, she said, "There is something else about him. He often seemed to be poetic. I mean the way he described things—perhaps a poet without a pen or paper. He said he would write a poem for me, but he never did. I think he regarded poetry as being out of character—ashamed perhaps to express himself in a feminine manner to me when he knew what my feelings toward him were.

"He thought he would be wasting his energy. Not exactly—he wasn't afraid of that. Maybe he was thinking of me, you know, not caring to push me, sort of urging me to change my mind."

"You wouldn't have." This was not a question Leon asked but a statement.

"No, I wouldn't have, but Felix was right if that was his thought. I would have felt protective of him and at the same time embarrassed."

Leon knew what Vi meant. He understood the relationship between Vi and Felix and did not intend to subject Vi to more pressure. There might have been some doubt about Vi's relationship with her good friend; there would have been a natural tendency to wonder, but Leon totally relied on Vi's fidelity and would continue to do so for their lifetime together.

Leon met Felix soon thereafter, but they were not to be great friends. Rarely was Felix to be a topic of conversation.

After three months of courting, Leon and Vi were married in Vienna. Their fathers and some older family friends came to the ceremony, as did a few of Leon's acquaintances but only one of Vi's, the outwardly joyous but inwardly saddened suitor Felix.

The early part of their life together had romantic moments, but there were never to be firefly evenings, candied apple street fairs, or canoes on moonlit lakes. The atmosphere in German-speaking lands steered Vi and Leon along the windy currents of the unfolding political scene. There was a chilling breeze always surrounding people who had a different road, a path that was not the one that the multitudes trod. Intellectuals, who were the backbone of the culture for many years, still existed, but they now had to fit into the jigsaw puzzle of emerging fascism.

In a few years, non-Aryan scientists would be banned from attending German universities, and most certainly from teaching at them. Leon, whose science background included physics, was especially proficient in optics. He would have preferred a professorship to the life of a merchant, but he heeded the warning signs. After university and marriage, the couple decided to attack a two-headed monster. They would become merchants by opening a camera shop on a side street a few yards from a corner of the Ringstrasse where a large space was available that had show windows on either side of two huge doors. Passersby could see merchandise in the windows and see past them into a well-lit and fully merchandised store. With family money at hand, financing the business was no problem. Before they signed a lease, Vi, with some nervousness, said to her husband, "Are you sure this is what you want?"

"No," Leon answered seriously, "but with you managing it, we'll do well here."

"I can manage it," Vi said. She was holding Leon's hand. "You will be busy with pre-doctorate work, however…"

Leon interrupted Vi's thought. "Yes, but there will be time enough for me to help you, but not in-store. With purchasing and planning, yes."

Leon on occasion would take trips alone, and Vi, without questioning him, realized that there would be times she needed him but she could do her job alone. There would be store help. She knew that Leon, besides studying, worked in a small laboratory a few blocks from their house. He worked there during the day to fit with school hours and his merchandising duties at the store. Most nights he was at home with Vi, often studying while she, at her desk, would be calculating and keeping the books. They were a very busy couple.

Leon's monthly trips took him to France and at times across the channel to England; occasionally a short journey to Switzerland would only take a day or two out of his schedule, while the longer ones would last a week. Leon explained to Vi that he was being paid by various government agencies.

"I deposit those payments in a British bank," he admitted.

"Why there?" Vi asked.

"Call it a premonition" was the answer. "Someday we might want to live there."

"But England." Vi's eyebrows raised a bit, but her voice was always soft. "There's the store…" she said as her voice trailed off questioningly.

"Yes, I know. I've thought of all that and I may be wrong. Perhaps one day my training— my knowledge—" he corrected himself as if he did not want to elaborate, "could make us an even better living, a better life. We could open another store if you would like, or have two and keep this one."

Vi's eyes now looked up at the ceiling. "Two stores—a chain." She softly laughed, but her even and understanding temperament produced a soft response. "We will figure all this out later on, dear. For now, I want you to be happy. Do what you feel you must do and like what you are doing." She had heard that said before.

After their wedding and the four-day honeymoon in the Tyrol, Vi and Leon found themselves attracted to each other in exactly the same way as in their courting days. When they were together, they kissed and held each other closely. Wherever they strolled together or sat at a café, they were hand in hand; at times, Leon would bring Vi's hand to his lips and softly kiss it.

Their many conversations were quietly delivered, and there were no arguments except on facts or when one wished to correct the other, always suggesting something mutually beneficial.

Vi knew that she would never be able to bear children, and Leon had been aware of this since early in their relationship. He accepted it without question and probably with some relief, for deep in his mind, he wanted nothing to disturb or distract his selfish wish to live his entire life with his wife alone. The two were sitting at the outdoor part of a coffee house one early spring day. It was cool yet sunny and Vi had a plain wool muffler on and a fisherman-style sweater over a bright red skirt. Leon, also in a heavy sweater, with no hat, gloves, or muffler, thought Vi looked especially lovely. The two holding hands and smiling at one another were a Viennese snapshot of fresh and vibrant youth in love.

Vi questioned, "We've spoken about this before, but why are we so close together yet so far apart from others?" She looked directly at Leon, who did not answer.

She answered her own question. "I really know why, dear: our childhoods—no mother and perhaps not wanting to rely on friends."

Leon now responded. "That's a big part of the reason. But to be honest, when you came along, I wanted nothing else. You know, we are very much alike in a way. We want and need each other desperately and both of us have a longing for intellectual matters so that when we are apart, we concentrate on different scholarly things: you on finance and history, and I love my sciences."

Vi was enjoying the conversation the way people who want to please each other discuss matters for which they already know the answers and warmly delight in that knowledge.

"I'm bothered by something that is related to our feelings but could interfere: the condition of the German government and ours. I know we are being propped up by the Allies and things are pretty good here right now, especially good for us and the way we live. I wish it could go on forever."

Leon broke in. "Our business can only get better, and we will always have each other. The crazies in Munich will never get anywhere. Of course, I wish they would disappear, Vi, but you know these fascist ideas have never taken hold for long in world history but have always been there."

Vi softly argued, "Now, that's my specialty. You are right; there have been many dictators, but the people never let a fascist party take over an entire country's governing system, but now there is a party and a leader somehow screaming out their hatred with so many Germans agreeing with him."

Leon picked up the thought. "If people go back to work, and they are slowly doing that, and they can feed themselves and their families, and the money they earn is not valueless, we have nothing to worry about."

"Leon," Vi said. They were sipping coffee and enjoying pastries. "We might have nothing to worry about now, but the hatred in Hitler's voice and the way he rants and shouts…"

Leon interrupted. "Try not to predict our future. Give Weimar a chance in Berlin; this is still Austria."

"Yes, but can you explain something I cannot understand?"
"I'll try."
"How can you hate someone you have never known? There are millions of Jews, your father was at the front, there are so many good German Jewish people…how can he hate them all? He says he does!"

"Vi, that makes him psychotic. I don't know how anyone can hate an entire body of people. He is afraid of liberalism, of communism, of anything approaching democracy, and he blames the entire Jewish population of the world. That makes him crazy. No decent person will ever follow him."

Vi said, "He fears those forms of government because he believes they are weak, and that doesn't fit his nationalistic approach as a strongman who has no constitution to follow and no laws to obey outside of the ones he creates."

They were earnestly pursuing the subject now. Vi continued, "I agree with you that as long as the German economy is progressing he will not grab any more influence than what he has around him, but I think he is waiting for German economic disaster to come to his rescue. And remember, Leon, he is an Austrian."

"Yes, he is Austrian by birth, and we are a German-speaking nation, so I agree that there would be a terrible correction if the Brits and the States will not support us." He went on, "You know I am as far from being a Red as you can get, but those Socialists in Vienna are making strides here cleaning up Vienna's slums and employing lots of people in public works. Our problems would be food and other supplies coming here. The countryside is very unhappy with the overpopulation in our city; we have more than one third of the entire population of Austria here, and they keep pouring into the city from Northern Europe and even from Germany."

Vi was listening and totally agreeing with his assessment. She was holding Leon's hand more tightly with both of hers. She said, "All those new people should really help our economy." This was more of a question that a statement.

"Yes," agreed Leon, "but the problems they create overturn the potential good. We can't feed them, and when one slum is destroyed, a new one springs up. The whole country has to get behind the effort. If they don't, then you are right: the economy will suffer and the government would not be able to survive."

In a lighter manner, Leon said, "You know, Vi, we might be too harsh on this subject. Like we agreed, we are doing well, and there are a lot of people here who are not bigots and toughs—for example, your old friend Felix."

Vi drew her hand back slightly but still clasped Leon's. She leaned back on her sidewalk chair and said to her husband, "Leon, dear, I don't think you ever brought Felix's name up before, but I think you probably would like to know more about us." She winked and smiled at Leon, who showed a deepening interest in the conversation. Vi's personality included an ability to be honest without creating doubt. "You surely know that Felix and I were never lovers." Leon tried hard not to blush, but he did not blink. Vi continued, "Leon, dear Leon—but we loved each other. Is that hard to understand? I'm sure you know that we were entirely different personalities. I was a loner, had no friends. He had a harem to choose from, a lovely family, brothers and sisters…how different we were. As high-schoolers, we became close friends; from the beginning we understood each other and enjoyed every minute together.

"He told me that he would like more of me; I refused, knowing full well he would never be without company. He is still exactly that way, I'm sure.

"I think I knew from the start that a deep love for him would never be my choice, but I also know for sure that if I or we ever need him, he'll be there in a flash, the same as if he needed me. Leon, he was my only friend."

Leon only nodded. He had heard much of this before, but Vi knew that he understood fully and had no doubts or hidden feelings. Their hands remained clasped. Vi said, "Let's walk home; I'm getting chilly."

Traditional intellectuals such as Vi and Leon, though not part of nineteenth-century history, started their lives steeped in Victorian backgrounds. Europe, for most of the 1800s after the Napoleonic Wars, rebuilt itself, concentrating on democratic principle and emphasizing the role the people were to play. Germany under Bismarck grew to be a militaristic nation with the union of Prussia and other Germanic people as the target.

Even though the vein of fascism threaded itself into European history, liberalism and, a bit later, Marxism became the main arteries. The ever-present mobilization of the masses, combined with nationalism and strong leadership, melted like the snows of spring into a social concept. This created large-scale confusion amongst thinking people. By far the largest segments of the masses were attracted to quick solutions of the weighty problems that naturally followed conflict.

Darwin did not help clarify the tricky conflict of liberalism vs. fascism. Survival of the fittest fit neatly into fascist thinking, such as the strong becoming the flag carriers in the all-important and necessary war that was needed to attain the perfect man theory. Anti-Semitism became a direct descendent of Darwinism, though its concepts were created long before.

Confusing historical facts were much on the minds of Vi and Leon, and generally, on the minds of builders of society, which included the rich, the artistic, entrepreneurial types, and a particular group of intellectuals. Many hours of conversation and a groping for answers entered their lives. Always the venomous serpent coiled and waited in the grass, and the builders knew it lurked but prayed that it would slither away.

Propaganda was the beating heart of Nazism. Before Goebbels took complete charge of publicizing the precepts of the Nazi party, the party itself was an unpopular vote-getter (from 2 percent of the population in Germany in the early 1920s, it rose to over 40 percent in July 1932). Propaganda and the horrible economic condition starting in the United States and quickly spreading to European countries uncoiled the snake and readied it to strike.

CHAPTER FIVE
Leon's Secret

Leon was an avid student much impressed by the new physics called "quantum" supported by the mechanics, which seemed to make a philosophical study work very well with the nuts and bolts of science fathered by Isaac Newton. The subatomic quanta world especially interested Leon, while Albert Einstein, only twenty years before, had introduced a new word, "relativity," into the scientific community. The speed of light and the significance of the interexchange of energy and mass prompted Leon to apply these innovations into his special interest of lenses and optics in general.

Many physicists are naturalists, writers, and even businessmen besides teachers of their science. Leon's ability to split his time between his studies and his lab work and helping Vi with merchandising the store would seem a backbreaking task, but he did just that, in addition to his frequent trips. The trips were often secretive.

Leon met with some well-known physicists on his journeys, including a one-hour meeting with Niels Bohr, the great Danish scientist who incidentally was responsible in 1943 for saving over 7,000 Danish Jews by appealing to the Swedish King Gustav to offer them asylum, which was immediately accepted. The 7,000 crossed the Oresund and were welcomed near Malmo only days before Hitler ordered their execution.

Leon also had short meetings with Eugene Wigner, Leo Szilard, and Edward Teller; they quickly exchanged information, and then he would conduct his buying duties for the camera store. The trail he left would substantiate the merchandising trips, but some of his meetings with the physicists were noted by Nazi authorities.

A laboratory was built by the United States Army Corps of Engineers early in 1943 (some ten or twelve years after Leon's buying trips) on a little-heard of mesa near Santa Fe, New Mexico, whose forested surroundings hid the identity of Los Alamos. At that astounding technical area, hundreds of scientists were at work under the management of Robert Oppenheimer and Leslie Groves, developing nuclear weaponry and untying the knot that was thermonuclear energy.

Almost all of the German, Hungarian, and Danish scientists who left those nations found themselves at work in Great Britain and the United States. All of them were expelled from their teaching jobs, prohibited from working in Germany, chased out, threatened, and forced to flee, which was Hitler's only good deed, as it turned out, though unintentional.

Leon was stopped and questioned one day in 1936 in a Copenhagen hotel lounge by two men in leather coats. The men did not touch Leon, but their presence was intimidating and threatening.

"Would you mind telling us what you are doing in Denmark?"

"I'm on a short buying trip."

"What did you buy from Professor Bohr, let me ask?"

"I was buying nothing from him."

"Then why did you meet him?" The more muscular of the two men moved his face closer to Leon's so that his breath could be felt.

"I was told he could help me locate lenses I wanted to sell in my store. Why are you interested in Bohr? He's a Dane…" Leon edged back away from the face close to his own.

"I am asking the questions. We can easily take you with us if you give us a problem. Let me tell you, no Jew can be trusted these days. Bohr's wife is a Jew…"

"Bohr is a Dane and I am an Austrian businessman. I told you I am on a buying trip, a business trip." Leon opened his attaché case on the bar and showed the men orders he had written for camera equipment. The bartender and a few patrons now gathered near the three men, whose conversation grew animated.

"We will watch you." The two slipped away out of the lounge after hissing their parting warning.

The bartender helped Leon put his papers back in the case. "Those bastards are everywhere," he said in English. Others agreed with his statement in Danish.

There was no question in Leon's mind that he was an object of interest to the Germans, but he had no idea of the depth of their concern. He had left no sign of his scientific experiments; all of his written work, his formulas, and his calculations were never kept at home or in the lab. His memory was a profound repository and his papers were in trusted hands. There were signs that his small laboratory had been searched but never sacked. Things were put back in place neatly, but the signs were there, and that alarmed him, though he did not want the anxiety of such knowledge to upset Vi.

As was the situation with many vulnerable people in Austria and even in Germany, financial and other personal reasons made them hesitant to leave. Their hopes and prayers were for Nazism to abate and for the thugs to realize that their habits might change with better times to come. Of course, it turned out to be naiveté proven by the death camps, Kristallnacht, the invasions, and the slaughter to follow. Their faith was broken and their conviction shattered, but Hitler was not in Austria yet, and their leader, Schuschnigg, seemed to be a decent fellow whose cause was not Nazism.

Indication of danger is often obscured by optimism, as was evident by the many families trapped by Nazism in the 1930s. For many there was no money for travel or escape to safety and there was nobody in foreign countries who even knew them, much less who could house and feed them. In many cases, folks would not leave parents or loved ones behind to the loneliness and danger to come.

For Vi and Leon, the store and Leon's mysterious income deposited in London made them financially secure and ensured that if they wished to leave Austria, there would be no problem doing so, but danger moves quickly and silently. It moves at night or in early morn and it strikes quickly like a snake whose venomous bite on its victim is felt when the poison acts, or like the rapids in a fast-moving river carrying everything downstream, a human being carried with it helplessly grasping for a branch or some object to halt or just to slow down the unmistakable disaster ahead, because the current itself cannot be diminished.

What was most obvious to many threatened people—the hatred, the restrictive laws, and the openness of the threats—particularly were noticed by Leon and others who for years had secretly guessed the fatal end of the scenario. Though Leon's conversations with his wife were masked in favor of calming her and allaying her anxiety, he planned and sided with the Allied cause and directed his knowledge and exploratory talents away from the new Germany.

He and other physicists, many of whom had already left Germany, would abandon their homeland's new policies and somehow try to aid Germany's enemies with a solemn desire to someday witness a saner Germany by defeating the present one.

CHAPTER SIX
The Plan

Ursula Streicher called her father "Captain" like everybody else who knew him, from the people on the street who greeted him to relatives and close friends. His wife called him Hans. Their house was near the Donaukanal on Backerstrasse, a middle-class neighborhood where most of the small homes looked alike and huddled together, separated by small gardens, really only patches of grass and flowers.

The family of three were home together, a rarity as the captain attended meetings almost every night, as did his daughter; though the meetings were at different places, the substance was similar. Each of them wore armbands at those meetings but removed them before the return trip home. Vienna was soon to be a part of Nazi Germany, but in 1937, it was still an independent city in a republic.

"Captain," Ursula said as she put her hand on her father's shoulder. He was smoking a pipe while sitting in an armchair. "I want to discuss—rather, ask you something." This was uttered in an uncharacteristically solemn tone. "You know Vi, the girl I went to Laurentia with?"

The captain put his pipe in a large ashtray, looked up at his daughter, and also with a hushed voice, answered, "The good-looking one who married a Jew. Yes, I remember her, and I know of her."

"Well, she has a business, a camera store."

"I know," the captain said.

"Her husband helps her run it, but he is rarely there," Ursula continued. "They do well there…"

"I know," the captain answered. "Let me tell you, Ursula, we know a lot about the Jewish businesses—more than I want to tell you about right now."

"I think I know what you mean, and that is what I want to ask you about."

"Soon, those businesses will disappear—you can count on that—and so will the Jews who own them."

"Captain, that is a very good business. To make it disappear might not be the answer."

"What do you mean by that?" Streicher scowled at Ursula. "We will confiscate all the merchandise—"

Before he finished his thought, Ursula, in a moderate yet slightly accented rise in her voice, interrupted her father's sentence. "No, don't confiscate…"

Now Streicher was perturbed. "What do you care if we take the goods?" His voice was now angry. "We will take it all!"

"Captain, I want the store and all the merchandise in it. I want to own that store and run it."

"What do you know about running a store?" the captain said directly to Ursula's face, but his voice dropped and his eyes lowered as he considered her thought. He picked up his pipe, studied it, and said while looking at the grayish smoke rising from the bowl, "You have given this a lot of thought, I see."

"Yes, Captain," Ursula said. She was hovering over her seated father, not looking at him. "I have given it a lot of thought."

"Tell me what is on your mind."

"I need to know more about the store. I must know where he gets the merchandise to sell there. It is nothing to run a store—I can do that—but I need the two of them to show me things I don't know…to teach me, Captain."

"How are you going to do that, young lady, when they will soon know that we will take what they have and throw them into jail or worse?"

"I've worked that out, Captain."

Streicher, pipe in hand, said with new interest, "Tell me."

"Jews are vanishing every day in Germany and here," she said with hesitation.

"Yes, yes, go on."

"When the time is right, Captain, and I think you know when that will be, we arrest Vi's husband." Ursula turned to face her father and found concern in Streicher's face as smoke curled around him. She continued, "Vi would do anything to get him safely back. Believe me, I know this. We keep him long enough for Vi to teach me what I need to know; we can get all the records, all the books…"

Streicher, now deeply interested, asked, "Where do we keep him? Who watches him so the others don't get involved?"

"The others?" Ursula questioned.

"There is competition among us," the captain looked embarrassed, "for the Jewish wealth…"

Ursula now had the answers to her plan obviously well conceived. "Once I get the store, no one will take it away from me." She excitedly went on, "I don't care what happens to the two of them after I find out and get what I want. My little friend Eric will guard him. You must find a place to keep our prisoner, and ours alone, away from the jails: our own cell. If the colonels get him, they'll kill him, and I'll get nothing out of Vi."

The captain, with restraint, said, "There are things you don't know about. I will tell you later, but your idea will work if we are extremely careful."

"Tell me now," Ursula insisted. "I must know details if things are to work out well. We can make a lot of money for a long time; I don't want to lose this. Please, Papa."

This was the first time Ursula had called Streicher "Papa." He caught the word, enjoyed it, and was affected by Ursula's pleading voice.

"I'll tell you something. Never, ever say a word," he warned. "Berlin knows about Leon Schoenweis and wants him, but they will wait. You see, his trips were not only buying trips; they were also selling trips, and Berlin wants to know what he is selling. So far we haven't found out, but they will wait, in Berlin, until…well, I don't know until when."

Ursula was listening carefully, selfishly. "Then we will have to act even faster than I thought." She hesitated and added, "I will get my store. Count on it."

Streicher made telephone calls to Berlin the day after his talk with Ursula, a talk that filled him with pride but one that caused deep concern. He was privy to information regarding Leon that came from Berlin, which meant that Ursula's scheme was in conflict with the government's. After considering his alternatives and giving deep thought to this puzzle, Streicher arrived at a solution. He would be honest with his superiors; after all, word from Berlin indicated that the captain would soon be a colonel and Vienna would be his area to control, a far cry from a district captain. He would not jeopardize this opportunity. Kurt Waldheim himself was involved.

Streicher and two Berliners were to meet at a location outside the Schönbrunn Castle in the gardens. A misty drizzle accompanied Streicher as he waited at the spot ten minutes before the appointment time. He wore his police captain's uniform under a government-issued raincoat, his official cap atop his head as he waited. The rain was not hard enough to soak him, but the dampness added to his anxiety.

Two men approached exactly on time. Both wore raincoats and large-brimmed fedoras. Their unbuttoned coats showed black suits, white shirts, and narrow black ties. One man was heavyset; he had a thick neck and a clean-shaven, round, ruddy face. His tall stature exactly matched Streicher's height. He did not offer a salute as he greeted the captain with a "Heil Hitler," which Streicher repeated softly, also not saluting.

The other man was thin, much shorter than the other two. He was sallow, had a limp and thin, unsmiling features, and offered a crisp "Heil Hitler," no salute, which was also returned by Streicher.

Streicher wondered why neither man was introduced by name; after all, they knew him.

The conversation started abruptly.

The thin man spoke. "We only have a half hour, so let me ask you what you know about Schoenweis, and I will fill you in on what we know."

Streicher, immediately realizing that the thin man was the more important of the two, had his answers ready. "Sir," he correctly addressed the thin man, "my daughter, who is active with us—"

"Yes, yes, we know of her. She will do well."

"Thank you, sir. She went to school with Violet Wiser, knows her well; she married Schoenweis. They opened a store in Vienna, which seems to be the best of its kind here. I don't know much about the husband—I have not been instructed by Berlin at all regarding him—but I know his habits. He travels quite a bit, buying trips I heard, but also has often been seen in England, France, and Switzerland, supposedly not really buying things."

"So we know," the thin man agreed as the bigger man nodded with no change of expression. "Go on," ordered the man.

"Sir, my daughter wants the Jew's store and has a plan to get it." Streicher then explained Ursula's entire plan, leaving out no details, but he expected no compliance. In fact, he thought there would be a rebuke. In his mind, his honesty would point to his loyalty to the party and his devotion to his job as district captain.

The two men stepped away from Streicher without excusing themselves and conferred together about ten feet away from him. The thin man did most of the talking, while the big man would nod agreement and offer a few words. After about five minutes, they once again approached Streicher.

"You have handled this correctly; I commend you," said the unsmiling thin man. "And your daughter has an excellent plan of which we approve."

Streicher did not change his expression. He clicked his heels and bowed in appreciation of the compliment and, in no small way, of the relief he felt.

"What we know of Schoenweis is this: He is a physicist and an expert in optics. He has been friendly with Jews who have left Germany, thank God, but who are quite knowledgeable in the sciences, which we, too, are interested in. We have excellent, loyal scientists here, you know, like Heisenberg and Von Braun, but we must stop these Austrian Jews from taking information out of here. We cannot do everything we would like to do here yet, but our day will soon come.

"In the meantime, we will make an effort to learn more about Schoenweis and others he is working with. Your daughter's plan fits perfectly. When you have him captured, we will concentrate on his work on hand and what you have learned. Make him believe he will be returned to his wife; then we will get all the information we require."

Streicher straightened up, bowed slightly, and said, "I will do exactly what you wish."

The big man bowed. "We must be off now."

The thin man said, "Your daughter will have her store. Say nothing about this meeting to anyone. Please do not come with us to our waiting car in front of Schönbrunn, Captain, and in the future when you hear from us we will just refer to this meeting. Heil Hitler."

"Heil Hitler, sir. But one more thing: When do you want us to take him?"

"You will hear from us. Tell your daughter only that she will have the store. You know how to do these things. We are leaving it to you to take the man, secure him. Do not allow any civilians, only our people, except his wife, to see him. Keep him until we take over, and until that time, keep his hope alive that he will be set free. We want all the information he gives you."

"Yes, sir," said the captain.

The two men quickly strode away from Streicher down a garden path to the south end of the castle to the street, where a large black limousine sped away with them. Streicher kept standing where the three had met as he was instructed to do. As he stood alone, the mist lightened and the drizzle stopped.

He knew these men were important, that they were now more familiar with him and would remember and reward him in the future. He would tell Ursula what he was allowed to say and see her contentment as she realized that her future was secure and that Leon and Vi would be out of the picture very soon.

CHAPTER SEVEN

The Arrest

A call very soon after his meeting with the SS came for Captain Streicher at his office. An officer announced it to the captain as he was busily attending to a matter that had him actively involved. Annoyed by this intrusion, he growled at the officer, "Take a message, dammit; you see I'm busy."

"Sir, it's Berlin."

"Get out. I'll take it in here." He started sweating. "This is Captain Streicher."

"About our meeting at Schönbrunn."

"Oh, yes, sir."

"Are you quite ready?"

"Absolutely, sir."

"Do you need any help?"

"Not at all, sir."

"Then do it within the next day or two."

"It will be done. He is in town."

"Do it." The phone went silent.

For weeks, Vi and Leon had talked about selling the store. The rumors in Vienna actively centered about the increase in the presence of Nazis in the city. Brown shirts were more visible, and people in the streets were talking excitedly about the attributes of Hitler's actions and the benefits that would come to Austria.

Leon made up his mind. He convinced Vi that leaving Austria would not only be sensible, but he focused on his feeling of danger closing in on the Jewish population to Vi. He told her about an offer he had in England "to continue my work there."

"You never mentioned that before," Vi said.

"Please, Vi, you must understand that I can't tell you everything I would like."

"Of course I'll go."

"There is also a position for you in London."

Vi answered, "I'm not concerned about a job, but if we leave, what will we do about the store?"

"For a few days, and I should have told you, I've been working on that. There are some people I know at university who would be interested." Apologetically, he continued, "I'm sorry I didn't ask your advice or your feelings about this, but again, I just cannot discuss everything."

"No, Leon, you don't have to apologize; I understand. For a while now I've been worried about you. Do what you can about the store; I hope there is enough time."

"Yes," Leon agreed, "time might be more important than we know."

Vi, obviously made nervous by this talk, said, "I would be ready to leave any time. Please dear, be careful."

Leon nodded.

Vi added another thought, trying not to appear anxious. "If we can't sell the store and you think we must leave quickly, we could just close it or leave it to some of our workers to run until we return."

"We will see."

"What about your lab?"

"I've spoken to some acquaintances at university about that. There's no problem with the lab."

Some of Leon's conversation about the store and the laboratory had reached unfriendly ears, which had directly caused the telephone call from Berlin to Streicher.

The summer heat simmered on the sidewalks and on the roadways that late July in Vienna, distorting the street scene with heat vapors and smoke from cars and trucks as they drove slowly by.

Inside the camera store, the usual crowd of customers did not show because of the oppressive weather. There were fans distributing air inside, but they hardly accomplished their tasks. Vi came out of the back office with a pitcher of water and some glasses for the few patrons, some of whom gladly accepted the courtesy.

Leon, who stood behind one of the counters, found himself unoccupied, hot, and bored. Vi came over to the counter and asked him why he didn't take some time off while he had the opportunity.

"I think I will. I can do some research at the university library. This order from Rome can wait till tomorrow."

"Be back around four o'clock," Vi suggested, "while it's still light outside."

Leon walked out of the store on Wipplingerstrasse on his way to Tiefer Graben. He planned to walk from there to Freyung, which ran into Schottengasse, then across to the university. If there were Brown Shirts on the street, he would be careful to avoid them. People disappeared daily, a thought that never left his mind recently. Vi and he planned to leave Vienna for the north of Italy as soon as disposing of the store could be arranged, which they were eagerly ready to do. Some of Leon's university acquaintances were interested. But what he really wanted to accomplish that day was another meeting with the interested people to alter the deal, making it a simple transfer so that it would be an easy and smooth transition—a no-cash transaction. He needed the three-quarter–mile walk to fully conceive this new plan. His friends at the university, unbeknownst to Leon, had been warned secretly not to deal with him. In fact, the heavily Nazi-infiltrated police forbade potential business-minded individuals from speaking to Leon or Vi at all. *No* dealing with Jews would be tolerated.

The spires of Saint Stephan could clearly be seen seven blocks east of Tiefer Graben, its wonderful Gothic architecture fashioned in past centuries. The Roman ruins were to the left, as was the arm of Kirche Am Hof while the Austria Fountain sprayed the street to his right. Five blocks south was the magnificent Hofburg, stretching in all directions, delighting visitors with its gardens, galleries, museums, and the Schatzkammer (the treasure house).

His thoughts of business were broken as the familiar sights of old Vienna once more appeared. Even though Leon walked these streets often, he dreamily remembered the early years strolling with Vi, the two of them deeply in love, passing often to admire the city while kissing or softly whispering their feelings. There were many strolls together, he recalled, to the Prater gardens, along the Donaukanal, and to many of the famous homes scattered about the city. They would walk from the Strauss residence, where they would hum waltzes and laugh at their inability to keep the tune, to Beethoven Plaza on Papageno Street and Mozart's area, to the museum quarter and the Rathaus, so close to the university; they attended the opera house and the Theater an der Wien and…and…Leon remembered all of the happy times, like the restaurants and wonderful hours idling at coffee houses professing their ever-growing love and dependence on each other—how sad life had been for him before they met, he recalled.

As Leon passed the Schottenkirche on the wide Freyung Street, all his memories crashed with startling and instant fear. With a mixture of summer heat and the horror of being grasped by both arms, his strength vaporized. In a flash, the sunlight disappeared; he felt a thud and then nothing after being shoved into a black limousine, which sped away. That is how simply and swiftly it happened—unnoticed, an indifferent act.

It was five o'clock in the evening, the heat slowly abating, yet still sweltering. The camera store was empty now of customers, the help were leaving one by one, and finally Vi was alone, the lights still on. She had told Leon to be back by four; it was an hour later, and he was usually punctual. Could he be on the way back from the library, which closed at five? The walk back would take twenty minutes. She would wait. She could not control her anxiety, but she had to wait, for there was nothing else to do.

At five fifteen, Vi's phone rang; she picked up at the first ring. There was a familiar voice on the line that she recognized at once.

"I know you are alone."

Vi haltingly responded, "Ursula…is that you?"

"Yes. Don't say another word and listen carefully."

Vi, now trembling, did not answer.

"Your husband will not be coming home tonight. Here is what you will do. Go home now. We know where you live. I will be there at ten o'clock tonight."

Ursula hung up abruptly while Vi's eyes filled with tears. Abject fear closed around her like a suffocating fog. She could not stop trembling as she turned off the lights, locked the doors, and cried softly while walking half-consciously part of the way home. Then she hailed a taxi to take her the rest of the way.

Southwest of central Vienna, about eight miles from where Leon was kidnapped, there was an area called Hetzendorf. A large *friedhof* or cemetery spread out on both sides of a road named Wundtgasse. On both sides of the road past the cemetery, narrow streets of short length angled in all directions, some of them like spokes coming together on Rosenhügel Square, and some of them just running into one another with no obvious design or reason.

That section in the 1930s was rundown. Buildings were abandoned; disrepair was everywhere. People avoided that neighborhood. One of the smaller buildings in terrible shape was an old bakery, its former purpose unrecognizable except for an old painted sign on the windowless side that advertised the old owner's name and DIE BÄCKEREI following it. There was a bricked-in opening next to a heavy wooden door, which was the only visible entry to the structure. There were a few windows on the face side, but no sign of life came from them.

As darkness fell, a few of the working streetlamps, obviously of low voltage, cast a shadowy yellow glare on the dilapidated quarter. The dim light hardly lit the streets, while half of the lamps did not work at all.

The men who held Leon, who was semiconscious, had him handcuffed and hooded on the floor of the limousine, his knees scrunched up, folded under his stomach. Nobody outside of the auto could hear his groans and weak cries; a kick would quiet him when his moans grew loud.

As darkness set in and the streetlamps struggled with the dusk, the limo stopped in front of the old wooden door. One of the men quickly stepped out of the car and knocked on the door three times, a signal to the only man inside to open up, which he did at once. The driver and both guards hauled a trussed Leon into the old building to a small, enclosed room fixed up as a cell next to what had been the bakery's ovens.

The inside of the bakery was musty, smelled of old clammy stone, and had a certain coolness about it that came from an open rooftop vent. The light during the day would come from rooftop openings that were covered by old filthy glass. At night, a few oil lamps glowed but certainly were not bright enough to read by unless they were placed near the prisoner or the guard.

The cell was fitted with a cot and mattress, an ancient table where an oil lamp rested, and in the corner, two buckets filled with water. One was for drinking.

The men untied Leon, un-hooded him, and placed him on the cot.

"You will remain here until you give us what is required."

Leon could only groan.

"Your guard has been instructed to never leave his station outside your cell until he is relieved."

Leon managed to utter one word. He was choking from thirst. "When…"

"You will ask no questions. Food will be provided and you will have visitation in a day or two and only at night."

The men left. Leon, in his locked cell, crawled to where the water bucket stood. He drank and splashed his face, stood up, walked to the cot, sat on it, and found himself looking at the table, on which a loaf of black bread and a jar of jam sat. He turned up the lamp and noticed the guard's face grinning at him from a barred opening in the door.

"Hey, Schoenweis, you know me?" the brown-shirted guard questioned.

"I can hardly see you," Leon managed to say hoarsely.

The guard lifted the lamp up to his face. "Can you see me now?"

"Yes, but I don't know you."

"I'll tell you then." He was short and fleshy. "You know Ursula?"

"I know of her, but I never met her."

"My name is Eric Mann. I am her best friend and comrade."

"Yes, now I know who you are."

Eric was pleased now that Leon knew him. "I was told not to speak to you, but I don't see the harm."

"Of course not," Leon agreed.

"Well, I'm a brown shirt now."

"I see that. Congratulations."

"I will be an officer one day, and then all you Jews will have to worry about *me*." Leon's silence irked Eric. He added, "Wait and see." More silence. "We'll get your store and everything else you have."

Leon ate a piece of bread dipped in the jam.

"You'll see," Eric sneered.

Leon snuffed out the oil lamp.

Vi answered the knock at the door a few minutes after ten and allowed a suited Ursula in, who quickly glanced around the room. The two women remained standing. Ursula did all the talking.

"Tomorrow night at the same time, we will take you to see him. I will be with one other man. If you try to have us followed, we will know, and you will never see him again. We will move him to an official prison."

Vi stuttered, "I have no intention of doing anything but what you want. All I want is Leon, and we'll leave Austria."

"Good," Ursula grunted. "What I want from you immediately are store records, buying records, sales—everything."

Vi softly answered, "A lot of what you want is not in the store. Some is at the lawyer's and the accountant's offices. Some will take a few days to accumulate from boxes in the basement."

"I'll wait a few days only. Start bringing the records tomorrow. Then there are things we want from your husband." Ursula was methodical now. "I'm warning you: don't hold back. I will not wait long."

"You will have to ask my husband about what you want from him; all I know is about the store and—"

Ursula cut Vi short and grabbed her arm above the elbow. "Don't lie to me, you…" She didn't elaborate but continued,

"Don't lie to me," louder now. "A few days and that's all. Understand?"

"Yes," Vi said as she rubbed the pain from her arm.

"We will pick you up at ten." Ursula turned and left.

CHAPTER EIGHT
After the Arrest

Vi and Leon lived less than two miles north of the Schönbrunn Palace in a section called Ottakring. On each side of cobblestoned streets lovely rows of three-story brick homes stood, each with garden areas and small lawns surrounding them. The streets, once lit by gas lamps, now were electrified, casting a yellow glow on the quiet neighborhood, which housed wealthy folks. An occasional barking dog broke the silence of the night.

Vi sat in the front room, lit by a single lamp perched on a mahogany end table. She had eaten nothing and waited for Ursula. She wore the same clothes she'd had on at the shop. She had not stopped trembling, and now that night had fallen, her fear increased and anxiety blocked any possibility for her to think clearly. It had been only four hours since Leon had disappeared, but thoughts of torture and even his murder filled her mind. To add to this horror, she had no one in whom she could confide.

In her terror-filled mind, Vi was anxiously reaching for help. She seemed to be space-bound, arms outstretched, praying feverously to cling for support to anyone or anything. Only Felix came to mind, and a momentary release of tension soothed her as she felt Felix's presence. His honesty, loyalty, and affection flooded her memory. Her terror eased; her breathing, which came in short gasps, relaxed. Somehow she would draw Felix into the predicament that she knew enveloped her and certainly would expand.

Vi's racing mind concluded that Felix would be traveling; he was on the road quite a lot during the summer. How could she contact him? The Nazis surely watched her house and her movements; to use her phone would be dangerous, and to implicate her old friend would be unfair and terribly dangerous. She cried and held her head in her hands as she moved from chair to sofa in the darkened parlor, expecting Ursula's knock at her front door at any minute.

At precisely ten o'clock, a soft rapping at the door made Vi jump. The terror in her breast returned, and with difficulty, Vi approached the door and opened it as Ursula's large body pushed passed her. The door was silently shut. Ursula looked to either side of the parlor.

"Is anyone else here?"

"No one." Vi could only whisper.

"Anyone in the house, upstairs?" Ursula gestured with an upraised arm.

"No, nobody." Vi, followed by Ursula, walked to the sofa next to the end table and sat on it. She looked up at the towering figure standing over her.

"Is Leon all right? What has happened to him?"

Ursula wore a dark raincoat and a floppy black hat that folded down, concealing a part of her face. She stepped now into a more shadowy spot, still hovering over Vi, whose trembling hands once again covered her face. Ursula's height emphasized her unspoken dominance as she stared down at Vi.

"I will be here only for a few minutes, so listen carefully to what I say and do not interrupt. Leon is all right for now and will stay that way if you do exactly what you are told."

Without wavering, Ursula continued her admonition, quietly but with a menacing warning in her tone. "Leon will be guarded day and night under lock and key in a cell. He will be fed and otherwise taken care of by the guards. Nobody except me and a few others know his whereabouts, and he will not be harmed as long as you obey."

Vi did not say a word but regarded this huge figure of authority with a growing hatred cloaked with terror. She nodded assent.

"You people must understand that all Germany will soon be united—that, of course, includes Austria. I tell you this so that you understand our authority will be universally obeyed in all German-speaking areas. Jews will have no right to exist anywhere in Germany. Your biggest mistake was to marry one; to us, you are a Jew." She glared at Vi for a moment and continued. "But I will make a deal with you and I think you will accept it."

Vi now listened more intently.

"Berlin wants your husband's written plans and all his models, blueprints, etc., already constructed or plotted in writing. If we had them in hand, this meeting and arrangement would not be necessary. We want all the research he has been working on for the last twelve years. We do not know where that work is, but we think you can produce it, and of course, you must. Most probably, you are beginning to get the point, but you haven't heard the whole deal yet.

"You must give us what I ask quickly," she went on. "The second part of the deal is this."

Vi didn't move a muscle.

"You must give me all the following information about the camera store." Ursula handed Vi a list of items that included volume of sales broken down by category, all figures, including markups, inventory, and all purchase figures, and a complete list of the merchants the company dealt with. "I want the store and I will own it and run it. You will meet me when I tell you at the lockup where Leon is so you can see for yourself that he is well as long as you cooperate. When we are certain that you have given us everything, we will give you two days of freedom to leave. You can take some clothing and money with you. One more thing," Ursula demanded. "You are not to touch the bank accounts of the shop or your personal accounts. When you leave here, you will leave everything the way it is now."

Vi mumbled, "Everything?"

"That is the deal. I will get in touch when you must accompany me to Leon's cell," Ursula added with a sweeping motion of her arm. "You will be watched every second. If you do not comply…I don't have to tell you, but we will get all you have anyway. Go to the store every day, make an excuse for Leon's absence, and wait for my message. Remember: freedom for what I ask." Ursula walked to the door, opened it, and left without another word.

The panic Vi had felt before left her now. She could think again knowing that Leon was alive. She believed what Ursula said was true. The Nazis wanted Leon's work—his inventions, his plans, whatever those were—and they would keep him alive until they got all they wanted out of him…and then what? She doubted they would ever free him. She did not consider her own welfare. In fact, at that moment, her welfare, indeed her own life, did not come to mind.

Ursula craved her wealth. Her jealousy and hatefulness and her vicious Nazi disposition left no doubt of the brutality of which she was capable, and the police force, Streicher's club and shield, was her armed force.

Vi would have to obey the order she had been given; they would watch her, perhaps follow her, but she would be a target if she did nothing, and that was not Vi's nature or her intention. Ursula had told her to remain at work in the store and gather information for her until she was satisfied. Vi thought that was a loophole; there was room for a plan. The store would provide a little free movement in the tiny area she was given, and she would wiggle through that narrow space and come up with a plan, something, anything…she must.

Saturday
Even though there were eight people employed at the camera store, Vi only trusted one woman, who had been with her since the store opened. Her name was Fanny Mayes. She was an older lady, perhaps seventy, and Vi had met her when she was a patient of Dr. Wiser years ago and engaged her to keep the store tidy. She was Vi's first employee when work was difficult to find, and Fanny's need for some income was obvious. Her loyalty to Vi was never in question, but with the situation at hand, where Vi

felt she was constantly observed, great care was essential in carrying out a plan, yet a gamble must be taken.

Vi wrote a note on an invitation card, enclosed it in a small unaddressed envelope, and slipped it to Fanny with a separate tiny piece of paper with Felix's address on it. The note without disguise read, "They have Leon. I am being watched and need help at once. Need to buy lenses." Felix would understand.

Vi instructed Fanny to deny knowing the note's contents or to whom it was addressed if she was approached. She was just to say, "I was told to leave it on a certain park bench." Vi would be the only suspect. Fanny was to destroy the addressed slip of paper before anyone could see it. Vi knew the risk for Fanny, and of course for herself, but this was the only opportunity she had, and she seized it. Fanny, though not a knowledgeable person, sensed the danger but took the note and the slip and quietly said, "I will do it."

Vi answered, "Do it tomorrow morning as soon as you can. Please, Fanny, do not contact me." It was Saturday afternoon and Felix never traveled on Sunday. His clients generally did not open for business on Sunday mornings.

On Monday morning, the store opened at nine thirty to let the salespeople enter. Fanny was not in when Vi opened the store, but she never arrived before eleven A.M. Vi then locked the door and went to her back room office, which she always did each morning. This particular day she was unsteady, nervously imagining the worst. Had Fanny been picked up? Had she destroyed the address slip if she was? What could she now do since her only plan began with Felix and ended with him? She knew the next few hours would be exasperating, a torture. She was so upset she forgot to put the coffee on. The girls could have a cup if they wished…

A few minutes after ten, the first visitor entered the store and waited patiently at a front counter after placing a briefcase on the glass top. A salesgirl approached him, cordially greeted him, and asked if she could help him. The man handed a business card to the girl and with a smile said, "I would like to speak with the buyer or the owner. I understand the store needs replacement lenses. I can assist you for that."

The salesgirl agreed. "We do need a reorder for lenses. The buyer will not be in this week, but I'll tell Madame Schoenweis that you are here." She hurried off to the back office with the business card in hand.

The professional gentleman wore a dark business suit, vest, white shirt, and blue tie. A felt Hamburg fit neatly over gray hair finely barbered on his head. He wore round steel-rimmed glasses that slightly magnified his blue eyes, while a neatly trimmed moustache above his upper lip was joined by a small goatee under his chin. Though appearing older, he stood straight, tall, and quite motionless as Vi emerged from the back office and approached him. The salesperson accompanied Vi to the front counter and motioned to the gentleman as if she wanted to introduce them. The three now stood together. Vi thanked the girl for bringing her to the salesman, whom she did not recognize. The salesgirl remained standing at the counter as Vi extended her hand to the visitor while he looked at her directly.

Without changing her expression, she was overwhelmed as she marveled to herself, "Those blue eyes. Those are Felix's blue eyes." She wanted to scream out loud. Felix kept an unsmiling countenance.

"I am here from Düsseldorf; your supplier agent there told me to see you a few weeks ago. I tried getting in touch with your husband but was not successful reaching him."

"Oh, it's quite all right to deal with me. I would offer you coffee but it wasn't put on this morning."

"I would love a cup, but I came right over this morning first thing, no breakfast, and at noon I must be on my way back to Düsseldorf. Could we go to a coffeehouse? I see there is one around the corner on the Ringstrasse."

Vi looked at her salesperson, who had not moved away since the introduction. "Martha, we'll be back soon. If you need me, we will be around the corner at Karl and Freddie's—and if you would, Martha, put the coffee on for the girls." Martha said nothing and moved away as Felix retrieved his briefcase from the counter and escorted Vi out of the store.

Once outside, Felix, without looking at Vi, said, "Don't say anything until we get to the shop. We will know then if we've been followed. I don't think so." They looked like client and salesman.

Inside the coffee shop, Karl, one of the owners, greeted V_1, who often had a snack there with Leon.

"I have not seen Leon in a while."

Vi answered calmly, "He has been away on one of his longer trips. You will see him soon."

"I hope so. Two coffees?"

"Yes, please."

The coffee shop was empty. It was late for breakfast. Felix and Vi chose a small table near the front window. Felix opened his briefcase and placed some literature in front of Vi, as well as an order form and two pens. Vi immediately perused the slick pages illustrated with lenses while she turned to see if anyone was near enough to hear them. Satisfied that she was as safe at that moment as she could be, she whispered to Felix while still gazing at the booklet in front of her.

"Dear, dear Felix, how can I thank you?"

"Don't try."

"They have him. Ursula came to our house."

"Ursula. I should have known."

"They will take me to see him. She wants the store."

"A trade for Leon."

"Yes, but they want more from Leon."

"I knew that months ago. I was sure the both of you would have left."

"We talked about it."

"It's too late for that. Here's what I want you to do. Keep looking at the book and start writing an order. When you know where Leon is, a delivery man will make a partial delivery of the lenses you are now ordering. When you pay him, give him the address or location of Leon's prison. Vi, if it's possible to get him out, we, my friends and I, will do it."

Vi, with great caution, explained that he would not be in a formal prison until they got what they wanted and Ursula was assured of getting the store.

With trepidation, Vi added, "Felix, if we don't get him soon, I think they will kill the both of us. I'm sure of it. I feel it."

Felix put his hand on Vi's writing hand. "You must stay calm; we will get him out."

Vi's eyes were on the order pad. "Felix, I want to hug you. I know I shouldn't ask how you will do that."

Felix said, "No, you shouldn't. If this works, someday you will know."

"Felix, even if we fail, I owe you my life and my love." She kept writing orders.

Felix let his cover dim for a moment. "You owe me nothing. Our friendship was my profit. In fact, I still owe you something."

"What in the world do you owe me?"

"A poem, remember?"

"Oh, my God…"

Felix admonished Vi. "Keep writing," he said.

With an unsteady hand, Vi finished the order. Felix paid for the coffees.

Vi's orders were in Felix's case and she had copies of them in her hand. They bid farewell to Karl as they walked out of the restaurant. At the corner, they parted, but not until Vi stared directly into Felix's blue eyes, magnified by his little round glasses, and said, "I love you. I've always loved you."

Felix said nothing, but the smile on his face was genuine. He walked straight ahead, knowing Vi would turn left and return to the store.

A few moments after Vi arrived at the store, a steely-faced Fanny Mayes came in to work. She stopped to greet Vi, who still had the orders in her hand, and with little change in her demeanor, said, "I hope you had a nice Sunday."

"I did," answered Vi. "How was yours?"

"Perfect," said Fanny.

Vi smiled and thought to herself, A great secret agent. Vi felt better than she had for days. She handed the order copies to a suspicious Martha.

"Martha," Vi said in a plain and steady voice, "do me a favor and file these orders. The merchandise has been promised to me very soon."

CHAPTER NINE

The Imprisonment

Ursula was accompanied by a tall, broad-shouldered companion. The knock on Vi's door was answered quickly. She let the two into the hall of her house. Ursula did the talking. The man was intent, a sullen look on his face, a face ominously projecting a strong authoritarian image. He stared straight at Vi as Ursula proclaimed her thoughts with haste.

"This will probably be the only chance you will have to see your husband here. We will keep him here only a few days. If you and he produce what we are after, he will be free to go. If you do not, this whole situation will be out of my hands. Now, what do you have for me tonight?"

Vi had a small attaché case ready. It was in the hallway, ready for Ursula to take. Vi had anticipated this proclamation. "There is quite a bit of the information you want in here." She pointed at the attaché case. "But I could hardly get everything together in such a short time. I will have much more for you soon."

Ursula demanded action. "Soon must be only a day or two—no more. Do you understand me?"

"I naturally will do my best. Yes, I understand."

Ursula explained, "We will drive to the holding place, where you will see your husband for a few minutes only." Her voice commanded, "Do not attempt to be sly. Do not try to trick us. Give us what we want; do as we say."

Ursula felt she had Vi in her grip. The feeling of power, of brawn versus weakness, became more obvious with every demand. There was no conversation, no question and answer, no give and take—just muscle and sinew applied to the powerless. Ursula knew Vi was defenseless and sublimely vulnerable, and she enjoyed her potency.

With every passing minute, Vi grasped the lurking terror and awfulness of the situation. She knew there would be no freedom or deal to be made. Vi would rely on the thread of hope on which her plan hung. She needed a sturdy rope, or better still, a chain, but she held only a thin string.

The hallway's light turned off as Ursula stepped out and looked about in the darkness. The man took Vi's arm and hustled her to a car parked in front of the house. Ursula, who carried the case Vi had given her, sat in the back seat with Vi. The man drove.

The route he followed headed west past streets Vi knew well. He drove out of the busy Ringstrasse area past the Neubau District toward the Schönbrunn Castle, then south across Altmannsdorf Street, then west again to Hetzendorf.

Vi trembled and sighed, which Ursula judged to be rising fright. It was not. Near this area and close to the castle was her childhood neighborhood, the house where she was born, where her mother had died in childbirth in a hospital not ten blocks away. The *friedhof*, the cemetery where her parents were laid to rest, was only blocks away. In fact, the road they were on cut straight across the middle of the cemetery.

Vi could not catch her breath. An omen, she thought. Mother and Papa watching, guiding me. She shivered and wept openly. Her fingers reached for the tiny crucifix attached to the thin gold chain around her neck.

Then the car drove into the area Vi had been told not to go near as a child. It was a factory area and had been beginning to decay thirty years before. Now, in the dim glow of the streetlights, it appeared decrepit. My God, she thought as she trembled. This is where they are keeping Leon.

The car stopped in front of the bakery. The driver got out of the car at the same time as Ursula, and Vi clumsily emerged from the rear door. Ursula, towering over Vi, stood about ten feet back from the old wooden door as the man rapped three times with the butt of a pistol. As the door opened, the man stepped aside to let the women in. They were facing a grinning fat man in a brown Nazi uniform. The swastika on his armband and the luger in a leather holster suspended on a shoulder strap were proudly evident.

"Eric Mann," Vi gasped, "this is what you are doing?"

Eric, still grinning, answered gleefully, "And we will do a lot more; you will find out."

Ursula, easily a foot taller than the guard, said to him, "Keep quiet. Do your job and open the cell."

Without a word, Eric, key in hand, opened the door to the room with the light from the oil lamp casting hideous, shimmering shadows on the dark walls. Leon stood by the wooden table, tears streaming down his grimy face, his clothes filthy and disheveled, as Vi rushed past Ursula, the man with his gun drawn, and a grinning Eric, to embrace Leon. They kissed repeatedly and hugged while both cried shamelessly.

Sobbing, Vi cried to the three, "Leave us alone for a few minutes."

Ursula gave the order, "Shut the door, Eric," and then to the prisoner and Vi, "Two minutes." She shouted, "Tell him what we want. Tell him he will be free to go after that." The cell door was slammed shut and locked by a delighted guard. The stench inside the cell was strong.

Ursula instructed Eric that he was relieved for the night. "Otto here will stay until you return tomorrow night at nine." She quickly added, "This arrangement will only last two or three more days." Eric's smile indicated awareness.

Inside the cell, Vi wiped Leon's face with her handkerchief, then embraced him again and whispered, "Darling, only listen. Act as if you believe what they say. Tell them you will cooperate. Help will be coming very soon, but I can't tell you more about that now—only that there is an underground, and they will help. Stay hopeful."

Leon could say very little, but through his tearful sobs, he said, "Whatever happens, know that I will love you till my last breath. That is something these devils can never take away from me."

With those last words, the door swung open; Eric swiftly moved in and roughly pushed Vi out to a waiting Ursula. The strong man stayed while Ursula drove away with Vi and Eric in the back seat.

"I'll come by the store tomorrow," Ursula announced. "Have the records ready."

Vi said nothing.

Eric hissed, "You'll see." A crooked smile appeared again on his face.

The next morning as the store opened for business, a deliveryman was waiting. Vi saw him waiting outside, walked to her office, and brought a checkbook out with her. "Tell me what I owe you for this delivery. I'll write the check out right now," she said, which she did. With a swift movement, she turned the check over as if to dry the ink. There was a complete description of Leon's location on the back of the check, including advice to knock three times on the wooden door. "You must hurry to cash it," Vi said with a smile.

The man quickly glanced at the reverse side of the check, folded it, and put it in a wallet inside his coat pocket. He thanked Vi, and seeing nobody close by, whispered while he wore a false smile, "Somebody will pick you up at ten thirty tonight. His name is Heinrich. Everything is set. Smile."

She did.

Around noon, Ursula walked into the store. Before talking to Vi, who was in the rear office, she spied Martha, the salesperson, who approached Ursula.

"How can I help you?"

Ursula answered, "Is everything all right?"

"Yes," answered Martha.

"Has anybody contacted her?"

"No, she doesn't even talk to customers."

"We have the phones tapped," Ursula confided.

Martha asked, "Anything there?"

"No," said Ursula, "except she speaks to the accountant, but it's business talk. What has she been doing in the store, and does she leave it?"

Martha paused while she collected her thoughts. "She spends a lot of time in the basement and in the office gathering papers, and she never leaves the store. She sends me out to bring in lunch or whatever, and her husband usually writes the orders, even though she does occasionally."

"Anything coming in the store?"

"You mean merchandise?" asked Martha.

"Yes."

"This is the slow time of year; summer always is. We needed lenses. They came in. A box came in this morning."

"Let me see the box," said Ursula.

"It is already opened. The girls are putting out the lenses now. I'll show you."

Martha pointed out the lenses as if she were selling them to Ursula, who just said, "No, thank you. I want to speak to Mrs. Shoenweis for a moment."

Martha knocked on the office door, which Vi opened to let Ursula in and closed it again. They were alone.

"What have you ready for me?" Ursula demanded.

"Quite a bit. You will find many of our vendors' orders, and if you look at the dates on the orders, you will know when to place them."

"What else?"

"I would like to ask a favor," Vi pleaded. "Leon looks terrible. I don't know how long he can stay healthy in that terrible place."

Ursula was turning some of the pages that Vi had collected for her. "I don't care what he looks like," she said with indifference, and then casually looked at Vi and added, "Where are the daily figures and the comparatives, the year-to-year ones?"

Vi sensed the futility of her plea, but she was playing a game to fashion herself as an exhausted pawn surrounded by superior chess pieces that could surely conquer her and win the game. Ursula played with a heavy hand. All the jealousy of her school days, all the hatred that envy begets, coupled with the strength an upper hand brings, made her callous, ruthless, and cruel.

There was no forthcoming reply to Vi's seemingly pitiful request. "Give me all the records, all the numbers. Ask for nothing. Where are the bank records?"

Vi gave her another batch of receipts and papers, which added up to a considerable pile. She arranged them, banded some together, and put what she collected in the large suitcase.

"I'll have more for you tomorrow; come later in the day. It will be ready." Vi then offered, "If you want me to help you go over some of this—"

Vi was crudely stopped in mid-sentence.

"I don't need your help. I can read as well as you. Be ready for me tomorrow."

Ursula picked up the heavy suitcase with little effort, opened the door, and with long steps marched down the length of the store and out of the front door.

At five o'clock on that sultry day, Vi locked up the store for the last time in her life. The camera store was in no way a prime thought as she began her journey home. Ten thirty that evening was now her next concern.

CHAPTER TEN
The Escape

The underground unit of which Felix was an active member was immediately receptive to the rescue plan for significant reasons. Felix's relationship with Vi was of minor importance compared to Leon's activities in scientific circles and his connections and links to his fellow physicists. Though a few of the group were German, all were virulent anti-Nazis, and all were intent on freeing those held by Nazis, risking their lives in that effort.

Most of the young elements of those secret groups were ordinary men and women who objected to various Nazi beliefs, but many were nationalists who would show allegiance to their country by actually fighting for it—a strange situation, but one that can be understood when a number of segments are analyzed while the puzzle cannot wholly be solved one way or the other. Of course, some underground participants stayed the course, died, escaped, or were fortunate enough to live through the war and resume their pursuits.

The sultry summer night was cloudless; an oval moon cast its white shine on Vienna. The city was alive at the Prater, whose glowing lights would compete with the moonlit sky. But on the far western side of town, an eerie silence pervaded the quiet neighborhood where Vi nervously awaited the two-man team of rescuers.

She had been told to be ready at precisely the time the grandfather clock now showed. She would carry only some money in a small purse, no clothing except what she wore, and no other personal effects. Two brown shirts would pick her up in a black limousine. Vi waited by a curtained window next to the front door. Directly across the street, Vi could see her spying neighbor obscured by filmy curtains, which partly separated as she watched.

The limo arrived less than a minute late and stopped quietly in front of Vi's house. One brown-shirted person knocked at the door, which opened immediately. The brown shirt took Vi's arm, opened the rear door of the car, and ushered her in while he climbed in next to the driver. They were off in seconds.

"My name is Heinrich and that is Artur driving. We will get Leon out of his prison, deliver both of you to Felix, and be off." Heinrich was well built, a sturdy man with handsome features. A crew cut was hidden by his cap. In the darkness of the auto, Vi could only partially see him. "We will not be going with you."

Though Vi had many questions, she asked none.

Heinrich said, "You will stay in the car while we get Leon out." He guessed at Vi's question. She only nodded.

The limo came to a silent stop twenty feet from the bakery's entrance. Both men exited at the same moment, slipped revolvers out of their holsters, and proceeded directly to the large wooden door, where Artur knocked three times with his gun.

A voice from within growled, "Is that you, Dieter? You are early. You were to come tomorrow night."

Artur said only, "Ja, ja."

The door opened instantly, revealing a burly brown shirt and a grinning Eric Mann standing three feet to the right of him. The large guard did not recognize his replacement in the few seconds left in his life, for as he reached for his luger, Heinrich shot him in the eye. Artur had already slammed the door shut as a fumbling Eric, his weapon only halfway out of his holster, was hit by two bullets to the head, one from each of the rescuers.

Both guards were killed where they stood. Heinrich and Artur turned the bodies face up as they searched for the cell keys, which Eric had on a chain tied to his belt. Artur pulled the key ring from

Eric. There were only four keys on the ring, and one of them unlocked the cell door. The dim lantern glow barely exposed a ragged and frightened Leon in a corner behind the cot. He could not speak but allowed himself to be led out of the cell, where he stepped over Eric's body and nearly tripped over the other dead guard. Artur and Heinrich each helped Leon to the car, where a wide-eyed and open-mouthed Vi could only gasp Leon's name as she hugged him and brought his head to hers.

When Leon was ushered into the waiting car, wet towels cleaned and refreshed him. A clean pair of pants and a shirt was provided, and he struggled into those clothes as the auto sped away. He was allowed to relieve himself when the car stopped for that purpose on a lonely, untraveled part of the twenty-minute ride to Felix's truck at the tavern.

"You will have a twenty-three–hour trip to Bregenz and another two hours to the Zurich outskirts. If the Nazis are unaware of what happened at the bakery for a day or two, you should have no trouble."

Leon advised the men, "Nobody came there in the mornings. At about one o'clock, one of the guards would relieve the other and bring food."

Heinrich quickly answered, "We should be in luck, with the guards out of the picture. We may have no problem with the timing."

Leon asked, "Are there any of you coming along?"

"No, only Felix. Vi will be up front with him. The problem is Felix makes this trip a few times a month, and he always gives rides to soldiers or SA. They know him and wait for him."

Artur added, "But they shouldn't be able to see you. Stay absolutely quiet; don't even sneeze," he smiled.

When the car stopped, Artur and Heinrich, both in their brown uniforms, stayed in the car. Felix was standing with Vi at the front end of the truck. The tavern lights barely lit the scene. Leon did notice that Vi had on a black wig with bangs and wore dark glasses.

Heinrich said, "Don't greet her. Go right to the back of the truck where Felix will be waiting. Good luck."

As Leon left the car, he said, "May God bless you both." He closed the car door and glanced at Vi, who was on the step of the truck lifting herself into the front seat. Leon quickly walked to the rear of the truck where Felix was waiting. There was a short ladder with only two rungs on it, which Felix helped Leon to climb and then hoisted him into the back end.

About five feet of empty space in the rear was preceded by a full load of cartons, barrels, and boxes of wine bottles. There were ten cans of petrol there also. Between this tightly filled collection of wares, there was a narrow aisle provided through which both men slid. At the end of the aisle was Leon's living space. On the floor, a few rugs of heavy material would be Leon's mattress. Tucked in the corner against the wall that was the back of the driver's cab, a jug of water and a little food was stored.

"Lie down," whispered Felix. "I'm going to fill the aisles with cartons." He did so as he worked his way rearward. Leon was now invisible in his wooden cave.

There were some opened cartons of wine in the empty space in the rear. Felix stepped over them, jumped to the ground, and closed the truck's rear gate by lifting the hatch and slamming it shut and securing it. He stepped on a fender ledge and jumped neatly into the driver's seat.

A black-haired and dark-bespectacled Vi sat next to Felix and said, "Is he all right?"

"Just fine. We'll be picking up some men, perhaps soldiers, soon. Play along."

"Where will they sit?"

"In the back of the truck, and one perhaps up front with us."

"But Leon?"

"They won't see him. Relax. We have a long trip in front of us. There is plenty of petrol in the truck in case you're wondering." As he put the truck engine in gear he said, "There's a bag of fruit under your feet if you get hungry."

"I won't be!"

They were off.

They headed east out of the Vienna suburbs on good roads and flat farmlands for about three miles. Towns like Mödling and Baden were off to the south, where Felix took a detour and picked up two men. He warned Vi that they were SA in street clothes whom he would let off at Salzburg and then pick others up there.

One of the men sat next to Vi, while the other climbed into the rear. They were off again.

The route would take them first to Linz, about 140 kilometers west, where Felix always picked up some German soldiers from the border and dropped them off at Salzburg, about 100 kilometers south of Linz. From Salzburg, it was only a 50-kilometer ride to Bischofshofen, 60 kilometers to Kitzbühel, another 150 kilometers west to Innsbruck, and then München was less than 150 kilometers north.

The plan was to meet another one of Felix's trucks in Bregenz, which he would drive to Zurich in Switzerland. The other driver would take the first truck, deliver the wares, and head east back to Vienna. That driver was part of the underground, but he was a Swiss national.

The British who were waiting in Zurich for Vi and Leon would fly them to England, but that was twelve hours away over 700 kilometers of driving, which would see the truck on level roads for a while. It would then head southwest through the Tyrol, where mountains as high as 8,500 feet would rise on both sides of the valley highways. There would be no snow in August except on mountaintops over 7,500 feet high, where snow would embrace those heights all year long.

In Linz, one man got off the truck, but three were waiting for Felix at the place he usually picked the men up.

The man sitting in front next to Vi saw the three new potential riders and groaned.

"That's the captain. He's a sonofabitch. He'll want the front seat; I'll get in the back."

All the new riders were in civilian clothes and all carried small bundles. The captain had a suitcase. He waited while the fellow now in the front seat got down off the truck. The captain handed him his suitcase as the two bowed to each other, and he climbed into the now vacant front seat. He immediately eyed Vi.

Now three men climbed into the back. One man left, thanking Felix, who said, "Have some wine. There is plenty there for you."

The men laughed and immediately opened some bottles. Felix said to the captain, "I have your favorite. I'll give you some when we get to Kitzbühel."

"I'll take her, too," the captain said, pointing at Vi, "when we get there."

"Sorry, Captain, she's mine."

"You have plenty more where she came from."

"She'll explain to you, Captain."

They drove off.

"Fraulein, you would come with me when we get to Kitzbühel?"

"I cannot."

"He wouldn't mind," he said, gesturing at Felix.

"He better mind."

"Why is that? You're not married to him?" A question.

"No, but I am pregnant. I am going to Klagenfurt for an abortion."

"Herr Hitler frowns on abortion," said the captain.

"Herr Hitler isn't pregnant," answered Vi, and the two men laughed.

After about half an hour, Felix asked the captain if he would mind driving to Kitzbühel.

"I'm tired and still have a long way to go before I deliver this load. You would do me a big favor."

"No, I don't mind."

Felix joked, "You can drive faster than me; nobody would dare give you a summons."

The captain enjoyed Felix's little joke. The truck stopped and Felix and the captain exchanged seats. They were off again. Felix immediately began to fall asleep in the passenger seat.

"Where are you from? What's your name?"

"My name is Hannah. I live near Vienna."

"What do you do?"

"I work in a tavern. Felix sells beer and wine to them. That's how I met him."

"Why are you so interested in him? He has many girls."

"I don't want to talk about that."

"There are other fish to fry."

"If I can't get an abortion, he'd better marry me."
"You love him."
"Yes. Very much."

Felix was not quite asleep, and what he heard made him a very happy man.

The captain, not put off by the conversation, put his right hand on Vi's thigh, moving her dress up a bit. She stopped his hand by putting hers on top of his. He forced his hand upward now under her dress.

"Captain," she shouted. "Stop that. I'm very nervous and not in the mood for this."

Felix, now awake, addressed Vi.

"Hannah, stop shouting. I know how anxious you are. Calm down. For Christ's sake, I'll marry you."

Vi threw her arms around Felix and kissed him full on the lips. The captain's hand flew off Vi's thigh, his intent destroyed and his chance of conquest totally shattered.

After emptying twenty gallons of petrol into the tank, Felix again took over the driving. When they reached Kitzbühel, the captain got out, thanked Felix for the ride, accepted two bottles of his special wine, and disinterestedly bowed slightly to Vi.

"I hope you two will be happy," he said.

Vi was beaming, but Felix smiled at the Captain and gave him a knowing wink. The captain said, "You devil," and left.

A mile down the road at a closed petrol station, Felix stopped the truck, knowing that the unattached rest rooms would be open. He let the men out of the back of the truck and found them to be drunk or approaching that state.

"I think you are all going as far as Innsbruck, where I usually pick up German soldiers and let them off at Bregenz. You men had better be sober there in case an officer sees you."

They nodded and thanked Felix, used the facilities after Vi emerged, and climbed back in the truck to sleep it off. It was only eighty kilometers to Innsbruck in the province of Vorarlberg, probably the loveliest section of Austria, but there would be little to see in the dark.

When they arrived at Innsbruck, they had driven over 450 kilometers—close to 300 miles. It was after four o'clock in the very dark and silent early morning. The beautiful area could not be seen at all. There was an oval moon that clear and cloudless night, but all the riders in the truck had seen the city and its surroundings many times before. With that familiarity came complacency, which made all the occupants interested only in finishing the trip and routinely undertaking what the new day would offer.

Felix was anxiously hoping that the next hour would bring this plan to a successful conclusion. He fervently prayed that his other truck would be at the right spot, that there would be no problem at the border, and that the identity of Vi and the hidden Leon would not be discovered. If by long-shot chance the Nazis would be at the border and question them, all three could be detained, arrested, and probably murdered soon after.

Vi had similar thoughts and feelings of apprehension, but her tension was not visible. Her restraint and her ability to clearly think and act made her a candidate for the stage. The way she had managed the captain an hour before was pure Hollywood.

Through all his courage, Felix marveled at Vi's calmness and actions in such a tight spot. His newest perception of his old friend magnified the feeling of warmth he had for her, and though he faced potential difficulties, his ardor for Vi remained foremost in his thoughts. He must save this precious person.

At Innsbruck, all the previous riders got off, and two German soldiers, both of whom had been thankful passengers of Felix in the past, had been advised of his route and had called his office in suburban Vienna only a day before to request the ride they were about to get. The expert planner that Felix was suggested that they were to be at a certain place on the road a few hours before Felix planned to be there. If he had to wait for them, he might miss the other truck or upset the scheduled flight from Zurich. He would not refuse these soldiers a ride in any case for "political purposes," he amusedly thought. Riders were always waiting for one of Felix's trucks in appointed places on Tuesday or Wednesday nights, which routinely were his travel days all year long.

Everybody knew this carefree and helpful spirit along the route. He was famous for his untroubled and charitable manner, for the free transportation, and for the always available open bottles of wine. His business prospered, aided by his amiable reputation, yet in truth, Felix would have it no other way.

The soldiers were tired and worried that Felix had forgotten them, but when his headlights shone on them and the truck stopped to pick them up, they cheerfully thanked him for remembering. They were usually on guard duty at various entry spots to Germany, and for the next weeks, they would be in Bregenz guarding one of the border areas just north of the city.

"I'll be transferring with another of my trucks to Zurich," Felix told them as he helped them to a bottle of wine. They had not yet boarded the truck.

"We will leave you in Bregenz," one soldier said.

"You won't be at the Swiss border, then?" questioned Felix.

"No," the guard answered. "There won't be any of us there until Austria is an official part of Germany."

"It won't be long now," the other soldier offered.

"I hope not," Felix lied.

"No, it won't be long," the soldier said, taking a long drink from the wine bottle. "We were told that within a year, our entire unit would be moved to the Austrian border. You know what that means."

Felix agreed. He was happy to stretch his legs, even though it was four thirty in the morning on the side of a lonely country road a mile from Innsbruck. The three men were relaxing, standing as they conversed while Vi was fast asleep in the cab.

"We will have to invade Austria," the soldier said. "They have panzer units, which were transferred to the SS—tough group—which are supposed to assist us."

"You won't need them," Felix said. "Austria is completely ready to be annexed."

"We hear Schuschnigg is opposed."

"He is, but he's got real trouble with Seyss-Inquart, who is with us," answered Felix.

"We will find out soon," the other soldier said.

"We'd better be going."

"We will sit in the back," one soldier offered. "I see you have Der Liebhaber in front. We won't bother you; also, we can stretch out and rest that way."

"Fine," Felix agreed. He poured more petrol into the tank. Bregenz was about 130 kilometers away. They would arrive there in less than two hours, perhaps six thirty in the morning. There would be the first light of sunrise, and God willing, the other truck would be there. The soldiers had said no German guards were stationed on the Swiss border. All these thoughts rushed through Felix's mind. He would seat Leon in the cab; he would look disheveled, unshaven in over a week, and he would pass as a worker, a loader of crates they were picking up in Zurich. There were good Swiss vintage wines in that town, but Felix thought, I'll take a few bottles, maybe an open crate with me. You never can tell.

The truck arrived in Bregenz, a city of only 20,000 German-speaking people. Bregenz was a lovely town on the Bodensee, a large lake with water so pure it was drinkable. Mountains surrounded the lake, their reflection mirrored on the calm surface of the water.

The soldiers left the truck in the center of town and thanked their benefactor, who gave them each a bottle of wine. Vi was pretending to sleep in the driver's area. She never greeted the soldiers, and they never got to see her. Leon, lying on his canvas mattress piled high enough to provide a soft bed, was advised by Felix through a slit in the wooden wall separating them to stand and stretch. "Move your legs and arms."

"I will." Leon accepted the advice. "Is Vi all right? When can I see her?" he hoarsely asked.

"In a few minutes. You will sit in front with the two of us. You will be a helper."

"Leon," Vi whispered through the narrow slit. "Poor Leon. Are you feeling okay? We must act the part, dear Leon. We will cross the border to Switzerland and drive to Zurich."

"I know. The men in the car at the bakery told me. I will be okay if I can get my arms and legs to work. They are still quite stiff."

"Exercise them," Felix said to the wall. "You must be able to walk."

"I will."

The truck was moving again. The streets were empty. There was no traffic the short distance to the crossing area, the border of Austria and Switzerland.

At the crossing, Felix looked anxiously for the other truck, which was not in the designated spot but stood in front of the pole stretched across the border; the driver was talking to two Swiss guards who had rifles slung over their shoulders. There wasn't another person or vehicle in sight as Felix pulled up next to the guardhouse, where one guard recognized him and waved.

"How long will you be in Switzerland?" a guard queried Felix.

"We'll be back in a few hours. I have to pick up some cases at the winery; they're for some German customers."

"I see you have a new girlfriend."

"Oh, yes," Felix said with a bored expression. "She is going to visit her sister here for a few days."

"And him?" the guard said, pointing to an unshaven Leon.

"He's going to help me load. They might keep him at the winery for a few days."

Felix opened the rear of his truck and left a half case of good wine at the shack. Pointing to the driver of the other truck, he said, "He will take this truck and deliver the goods in it."

One guard stood at the back of the open-ended vehicle, peered in at the load inside, and helped the new driver slam the gate shut.

"Good trip," he said.

Vi and Leon waited at the second truck while Felix finished his talk with the guards.

"You have a good-looking friend there," one guard said.

"Thanks."

"I hope the tall guy can do the job."

"He's strong as an ox. Had too much wine last night."

"See you later," a guard said as he lifted the striped pole. The three Austrians got into the truck's cab. Leon was a bit unsteady but managed to get in with a little help from Vi, who got in last and sat at the window. Felix drove through the open gate, starting the last leg of his journey: another 120 kilometers or 75 miles to Zurich and a small airport with a 2,500-foot runway two miles northeast of town.

Vi cried as she hugged Leon, who also wept. They said nothing; just held each other and cried for a few minutes. Felix drove intently and fervently prayed that the plane would be waiting for them on the strip.

At eight thirty, they arrived at the airstrip. There was no building and no tower. Worst of all, there was no airplane.

"There is nothing we can do but wait," Felix said. Vi thought he had never looked as worried as he did at that moment.

"Of course we'll wait."

Leon turned to Felix and put his hand on the shoulder of a man he admired and envied secretly. "Felix," he said, "whatever happens, I want you to know that you and your friends are the bravest men I can imagine." There was no answer. Leon went on, "Leave the truck here. Come with us to England."

"No, I could never do that."

"Why not? What could stop you? If those bastards ever find out your part…"

"I'm not worried about them finding out."

Vi broke her silence, tears streaming down her face. "Why not, Felix?"

"There are too many reasons."

"What could they be?"

"Vi…" He looked at Vi and with a steady voice explained, "A few of the reasons are these: I am Austrian. I consider myself a German and probably always will. True, I hate what these Nazis stand for, what they represent, and what they are turning my country into. I would love to fight and destroy them, but I would be destroying myself at the same time. I would be destroying my country, my life, my business, my future. I'm terribly confused with this problem; many of my friends are in the army now, and some have the same feeling as I have. How can I destroy them? How can I walk away from all the things I know and do?

"Maybe someday this whole mess will straighten itself out, but right now, it gets worse every day. Every German seems to love that crazy lunatic; they'll do whatever he asks of them. They are not thinking of the millions of people he would murder; they are thinking of their stomachs and they are thinking of a great big important nation that slob has promised them. A nation of assassins is what they will be. Perhaps I can help build something better here one day."

"Why can't you build all that in the future?" Leon asked.

"I'm not smart enough to predict the future. I am here, Leon, and I must stay here. In the meantime, I and thousands like me must do our best to help people who can't help themselves, but we must remain Germans."

"Will we ever see you?" Vi pleaded.

"You must not try to contact me," Felix honestly answered. "If you do, it would be very bad for me—maybe fatal."

"We would do nothing to harm you."

"That I know well," Felix said, gazing straight into Vi's moist blue eyes.

"Are you in trouble now?" Leon asked.

"No, they know nothing about me, and as far as the bakery is concerned, it is my bet they haven't discovered what happened there yet. I'll be back in Vienna when they do." He looked up at the sky, shielding his eyes from the early morning sun rising in the east, where he suspected the plane would come from.

"Nothing yet," he said. "Not a sound."

As he said that, a twin-engine early Douglas fixed-gear plane soundlessly made a crosswind approach very low in the sky with its two cut engines, glided into a short approach to the short runway, and noiselessly landed. The pilot taxied to the end of the runway and swung the plane around in the opposite direction. There was no wind on this clear, calm day. The propellers were spinning; the engine was not turned off. A hatch door swung open with a few stairs on it. A man emerged, quickly stepped down, and ran to the waiting trio.

"You must come quickly. Are the three of you coming? We were told only two."

"Only two are going. I am staying."

"Hurry," the copilot insisted.

Vi grasped Felix, hugged him, and said, "I'll always love you; you know that."

"I know, and you are my love," he whispered in her ear.

Leon grabbed Felix's hand, drew him close, and hugged him. "Felix," he said, "I love you, too. You are the finest man I've ever known. You are our family."

"Hurry, please," the copilot repeated.

The three ran to the plane, Leon struggling to keep up. He was helped up the few stairs, then the hatch was pulled closed. By this time, Felix was in his truck and back on the roadway heading to the winery. Tears in his eyes did not help his visibility, but he managed. He would always manage.

The plane carefully skirted German territory, flying only a short distance over Switzerland, then northwest to France, where it refueled twenty kilometers south of Paris, took off once again, and in less than an hour, landed in Dover. The ordeal was over for Vi and Leon, both of whom had nothing to do from that day with the planning of their lives until October of 1946. The years before their flight from Austria were nerve wracking but productive years for the both of them. Vi, in business, would build and lose a successful store, and Leon would become a sought-after though surreptitious physicist believing that the Germans knew little about that part of his life. Of course, he was mistaken, but as happenstance would have it, he found himself as happy and safe as possible in England with the woman he loved. He wanted nothing else.

Vi was relieved, to say the least, but her thoughts were heavily concentrated on those whose valor had saved her and Leon. She especially thought of Felix and wondered, for the rest of her days, if she had merely cared for him or if she had truly loved him. An answer came much later in her life, but she was never to see her childhood sweetheart again.

After Felix completed the trip, he returned to suburban Vienna. The scene at the bakery violently greeted Ursula, who ran back to her car, stopped at the nearest telephone booth, and called her father. She was out of breath, horrified, and crying openly.

CHAPTER ELEVEN
Streicher's Office

"Get over here as fast as you can," he roared. She did. "He's what?" he screamed at his daughter as loudly as he was able.

"Gone," she cried, terror-struck to be in front of her father explaining the state of affairs.

"Jesus Christ, he can't be gone!" This he screamed even more loudly than before. Ursula was in tears, her large frame quaking, her shoulders quivering. "And those two idiot guards are dead."

"Yes," she gasped, "and one was Eric."

"How long have they been dead?"

"The doctor said two days."

"And nobody checked the goddamned cell for two days."

"I went there when I was supposed to. The guards relieved each other, I thought. And I was busy the day before."

"Doing what?" the captain yelled at the ceiling. "What was more important?"

"I was going over the store records."

"Vi was the only one who knew the location."

"Yes, Captain."

"Why the hell did you take her there?"

"That was the plan—to frighten both of them."

"You see how goddamned frightened they were."

"We watched every move she made. I even had an agent in the store."

"An agent." Streicher grinned.

"A spy, Papa."

"Don't 'Papa' me, you idiot."

Ursula was crying openly now, slouched in an armchair in the captain's office at the police station. "I'm sorry, Captain; I didn't think she could go in there, shoot two men, and free him."

"She didn't, you goddamn fool. She had help. I'll find them."

"She spoke to no one." Ursula was sniffing.

"Bring that stupid neighbor in here."

Ursula went out and brought back the parting-curtain spy from across the street from Vi's house. The captain questioned her rudely.

"You only reported people we know as visiting the Schoenweis home."

"I did not know you knew them."

"Jesus Christ, one of the people you reported was my daughter here."

"I couldn't see clearly."

"And her bodyguard, who, by the way, was killed."

"I didn't know."

"Nobody else?"

"Only the brown shirt SA man. I didn't think I should report him."

"What brown shirt?" he screamed.

She began to cry. "The one who picked Schoenweis up that night."

"What goddamn night?"

"Three nights ago, and don't scream at me. I have relatives who are SA."

"I don't care if your relatives are Churchill and Roosevelt. The man you saw was the killer. What was he driving?"

"A black car."

"License or what he looked like?"

"I could not see."

"Oh, my God." He picked up his phone. An adjutant answered. "Get my intelligence officer in here. Get all my officers in here."

Five men stood in front of Streicher, whose face now was a reddish purple as he screamed at them, "I want the killers. I want Schoenweis the Jew; I want his wife. I want anybody who had anything to do with this!"

One brave lad had the temerity to say, "Sir, we don't even know where the jail was or who the guards killed were."

Streicher did not answer. Instead, he shouted directly at Ursula. "Tell them what you know. I want a full report tomorrow, lieutenant, do you understand me?" There was more purple than red now.

"Yes, Captain, I understand."

Streicher screamed after the men leaving his office. "You'd better come up with answers, you hear me?" Then, with his hands in the air, he yelled, "This is the worst thing that could happen to me. Nothing could be worse. Nothing."

A secretary hurriedly ran into Streicher's office.

"What the hell do you want?"

"Sir," she said, "Berlin is on the phone."

Streicher was slumped in his chair at his desk. The purple face slowly faded to red and then to the whitish pallor that generally accompanies abject fear. The voice was clear and the words were uttered slowly and deliberately.

"Is what I heard about the Jew scientist and his wife true?"

"Yes, sir. I'm working on it right—"

"You are working on it," he repeated in a deriding, sneering tone.

"Yes, sir."

The voice grew quite loud. "If we traveled to Vienna to discus this matter, don't you think it was quite important?"

"Yes, sir."

"Don't yessir me," he said, now screeching. "You called yourself a district captain; you should be a district street cleaner."

"But sir—"

"Shut up and listen to me, you idiot. I want those two back, you hear me? I want them back, and if there were others, I want them. I want all of them. You are making a playground—no, a zoo—out of our intelligence department. If you don't get results, you won't even be a district street cleaner."

"Yes, sir." Streicher's uniform was dark with perspiration, his hands shaking so hard he had difficulty holding the phone and pen.

"Now, Captain Yessir, I'll send a man down to oversee this mess. Heil Hitler."

"Heil—" Before Streicher could get to "Hitler," there was a loud click at the other end. Berlin had slammed the phone down so hard, it probably splintered.

That same evening, a rather short man wearing a black suit, white shirt, and black tie stood before Streicher, who sat behind his desk but immediately stood when the man marched into the office ahead of the secretary, who supposedly was to introduce him to Streicher. The man's round face was pale, but his cheeks were reddish. His lips were dark brown, his hair black; his nose, which supported the round frames of his glasses, was a smallish stub of a specimen. His black eyes seemed to protrude, perhaps due to the tightness of the buttoned white collar of his shirt.

"Heil Hitler." A short click of his heels and no salute followed as he sat on the only vacant chair in the office. He leaned forward in his chair after Streicher repeated, "Heil Hitler." The office door was closed.

"Captain, Berlin is angry."

"I know. I spoke to them, sir."

"Address me as Colonel."

"Yes, Colonel. Can I get you something to drink, Colonel?"

"This is not going to be a cocktail party."

"Yes, Colonel."

"Within the next fifteen minutes, I want all your officers above the rank of patrol here, and I want your daughter here also. Give the order now."

Streicher went out the door and told his second-in-command whom to assemble. He then told the secretary to call Ursula and tell her to come at once. Then he nervously reentered his office, where the colonel sat smoking a cigarette attached to a long black holder.

"Streicher," he hissed, "has anything been touched at your jailhouse?"

"No, Colonel, the bodies are where they fell. We covered them with sheets."

"That is the first smart thing you have said."

"Thank you, Colonel."

"We will go there after this meeting."

"Yes, sir, I'll have a car ready for all of us."

"I want to be called Colonel."

"Yes, Colonel."

"Have you found anything since Berlin called?"

"I have been to the cell, collected fingerprints, and questioned people working near the cell."

"What have you found?"

"Very little, Colonel. Whoever worked that operation knew what he was doing. I know only that he wore a brown shirt and drove a black car."

"And the neighborhood?"

"Nobody saw anything, Colonel. There really is nobody working there, and at night it is dangerous to walk there, so the streets are empty."

During the investigation, which turned up nothing, the question of friends of the disappeared couple came up. That also brought no answers, as Leon's schoolmates knew only of his studious habits, his small lab that now was a ransacked clutter, and his devotion to his wife.

"What about old friends?"

Ursula said she had not known Leon until recently, but she had known Vi for many years. "We went to Laurentia together. We were in the same class. She was friendly with a boy named Felix, and they stayed friendly for a few years, I heard."

"Who is this Felix?"

"His last name is Gruber. I haven't seen him for over fifteen years."

One of the officers at the inquest offered, "I know him. He has a wine and beer distribution business. He does quite well…has five or six trucks and a warehouse in—"

"Bring him here. We will speak to him."

Calls were made; Felix was on the road and would be back in a day. A person in his warehouse was told to make sure he would be at the police station as soon as he returned.

"Of course" was the answer.

The next day the investigating Berliner was advised that Gruber was back and would be at the police station that afternoon. The colonel had already done his work regarding Felix, whose background had been checked—his habits, family, religion, and general whereabouts scrutinized by Nazi intelligence personnel.

"Mr. Gruber, I understand you know Vi Schoenweis."

"Oh, my God, I knew her years ago. She married a college friend about fifteen years ago."

"A Jew?"

"I think so. She was Catholic."

"Have you seen her?"

"Years ago she opened a camera store. I dropped in to wish her well."

"You haven't seen her since?"

"No. I am a busy man. I travel four or five days a week. I have little time."

"You have time for women?"

"If I didn't I wouldn't want to be alive."

There was laughter in the office.

"We understand you often pick up soldiers when you travel."

"Yes, but they are never women."

More laughter.

"You are very popular on the highways. We have checked you out."

"It seems you have."

"And we have been told that many times you have a girl with you."

"Those trips can be lonely, sir."

"Has your old friend Vi Weiser ever been in a truck with you?" This surprise question sprung on Felix was asked to see if there was a twinge or any slight charge in his movement or facial expression.

Felix feigned a look of incredulity. He answered, "I don't remember ever seeing her since the store opened. No, I doubt if she ever saw one of my trucks."

"She has disappeared with her husband."

Felix shook his head in disbelief but said nothing.

"If you happen to spot her or hear anything about the two of them, call in immediately."

"Certainly."

There was an air of disappointment in the room. No clues turned up, a dead end, a blunted investigation, a dismal meeting. With disheartenment, the colonel dismissed the meeting and turned to Streicher.

"Come to your office with me."

Streicher anxiously followed the colonel. Only the two men were in the office. The door was shut; the colonel spoke to Streicher.

"We will keep investigating, but in the meantime, Herr Streicher, I want you, *alone*," the colonel said, emphasizing "alone" and pointing at Streicher, "to go back to the cell *now* and paint a Jewish star, a communist emblem, and a hammer and sickle on a wall in there. Nothing else. Use lime and a little water for paint. I want it to dry fast. Do not touch the bodies. Be back here in an hour."

Streicher left the office, drove to the hiding place with a jar of calcimine quickly concocted, did as he was told, and came back. He found the colonel now addressing his men and an aide of the colonel whom he had not seen before.

The colonel turned to Streicher and said with a vacant stare, "Tell us what you found in the building, Captain."

"On a wall in the room where the men were murdered there was a Jewish star and a communist slogan painted, Colonel," he obligingly answered.

The colonel, now standing in front of the gathering, quietly snorted. "This was the work of the Jews; I knew it all along. Communist Jews." He turned to his aide. "I want pictures," he ordered. "Go to the building with the captain; see what he describes. I will have reporters here soon. The country must know what is going on here."

The propaganda line used a hundred times before would soon poison, to a greater extent, the atmosphere in Austria. Much was made in the Nazi-controlled press of the two men brutally murdered and dumped in an old abandoned bakery, a building obviously known and used by Jews and leftists. Pictures of the wall highlighted the story. There was no mention of Vi or Leon, or that the building was a prison.

Before the colonel left for Berlin, he spoke to the captain alone on the street in front of the police station. It was two days later.

"Well, we have made the most of a bungled operation, haven't we, Captain?"

"Yes, Colonel—there will be no more mistakes."

"Good, I believe that. So no more about this case to the press or to anyone. I will handle this important news event myself."

"I understand, Colonel."

"Heil Hitler."

"Heil Hitler, Colonel. I would like to ask a favor before you leave."

"What is it?"

"My daughter wants that store I spoke to you about, the one that Schoenweis owned. They are no longer here, Colonel."

The colonel, without hesitation and eager to move on, said, "Tell her to take it right away, change the name, and advertise a new ownership. I will clear this."

"Thank you, Colonel; she will be pleased. Heil Hitler," Streicher announced to the colonel's back as he slid into his waiting limousine.

Back at the police station, the meeting had been dismissed. Two officers who had been at the cell were talking alone.

"When we were there, I didn't see any paint on the walls."

His friend and colleague answered quietly, "I wouldn't bring that up if I were you."

CHAPTER TWELVE
England and the United States

The English people with whom Vi and Leon became friendly were reserved yet amiable, not given to idle chatter. Most of their acquaintances were informed, bright, and interested in folks up to a certain point, but they would not venture too deeply into the personal backgrounds of others. Vi and Leon were like that also; they considered that many men and women in their milieu came from circumstances similar to their own or even more tragic ones. Some had lost close relatives and were reluctant to talk or even think about the horror that was the Third Reich after 1938.

The Schoenweises were lucky not to have lost friends or relatives to the Nazis, lucky not to have an extended family like most of the émigrés in their community, lucky to have had Felix and his brave companions whom they respected and would defend forever if need be, and they considered themselves fortunate—not particularly lucky, but blessed—to have been saved. This awareness made them contrite and eager to stay their course quietly and industriously, and even though they enjoyed intelligent conversation and joined it, they were not inclined to elaborate on what they thought were personal matters. They would never speak about their loss, their store, their home and the possessions inside it, and what money they had. Those were insignificant items compared to what others had lost.

Once in the suburbs of London, where a group of scientists and their wives gathered one evening, relaxing after a not-very-fancy dinner, the talk drifted to the German personality.

"They are a sticky bunch, those Germans."

"How do you mean?"

"They flow together, all of them, like a brook heading downstream."

"All of them?"

"Doesn't it seem that way? I mean, they flocked to Herr Hitler. I know there were reasons early in the game, but like sheep to the shepherd, no matter what his idiotic policies, they flocked after him."

"And you think *all* of them flocked to him."

"Yes, all of them. Did you see the pictures of him in the open limousine riding along Unter den Linden? There were millions of them there."

"All of them were not there," Vi broke in.

"It looked like that."

"Leon and I met some who weren't there."

"They probably weren't Germans."

"They were Austrians, but they were Germans nevertheless."

"Impossible. They are all intent on murder, killing civilians, mayhem…"

Leon replied with a quiet resolve, "I'm sorry, but you are wrong. There are many good human beings there helping very unfortunate people to survive. I don't want to go too deeply into that."

"Why?"

"Because those few deserve our secrecy. They are Germans, but you must agree that amongst any collection of people, there is a difference in genealogy, family values, education, just their basic intelligence, and the building blocks that allow them to use their mentality humanely—in our eyes, correctly."

"You make it sound hopeful, Leon, but the throng following the Nazis are many…"

"We will beat them because we must."

"Very dramatic."

"Maybe, but work we are doing here and in the States, where they have ten times the amount of scientists that we have, will one day guarantee success."

When tea was served along with cakes, the conversation broke off into sections, the women discussing mundane things that concerned their daily lives, their children, schools, food shortages, and the progress of the war, while the men gathered in another room, had their whiskies, smoked, and quietly discussed the business of their lives.

There were many more evenings of dinners and conversation. The topics would vary, but personal experiences were never a subject willingly brought to the table. They talked about the air battle of Britain, the night air raids that Goering thought would bring England to its knees, the buzz bomb designed by a colleague, Werner von Braun, who would stay in his homeland and develop the hideous bomb-laden drones that would burn out of fuel and sail and explode without aim on random civilian neighborhoods of London. (Von Braun, the ardent Nazi, was saved from Russian capture by the U.S. military in 1945, which secreted him to the States, where he worked for the Allies in his special field of rocketry, later to be treated as a hero.) His buzz bombs killed many men and women and children on London's streets.

As the end of the war in Europe happily neared its end, the future of the scientists and their families became an important and oft-repeated conversational theme. The Americans still had Japan on their hands, which turned out to be concluded in a year, notably due to much of the work of these British scientists who contributed to the development being completed at Los Alamos and Alamogordo on the fission bomb, and the future fusion of hydrogen, which would lead to the test at Eniwetok—a test that would manufacture a weapon one thousand times as powerful as the atom bomb.

While Leon worked on his special project and Vi was busily at work in the same London suburb, they joined each other almost every evening after their workday was finished. Five times in the forties, the British War Office was requested by its American counterpart to send a number of scientists working in Great Britain to Los Alamos for weeks at a time. The Manhattan

Project, a name plucked out of the air to disguise the top-secret task of developing the atom bomb, was well under way. Work on the same type of project was nearing its conclusion in Germany, although they were approximately a year behind the Americans. The Germans, in a highly secretive scientific alliance with Japan, started that country's endeavor to manufacture the bomb; however, Japan's attempt was immature and hardly under way when Hiroshima and Nagasaki were destroyed in 1945.

While in New Mexico on his trips there in 1943 and 1944, Leon renewed his acquaintance with Edward Teller, the father of the hydrogen bomb, and Leo Szilard, and was introduced to Robert Oppenheimer. It was during those few short hours of meetings that the subject of Einstein's non-participation in the Manhattan Project was brought up. Leon was carefully advised not to participate in a movement well-known to the physicists, which started with Einstein and Bertrand Russell, to never use the weapon dependent on the chain reaction of uranium 235 and plutonium on human beings.

"None of us want to witness the destruction we know will occur, but the Germans will have that ability. So there is no argument" was the gist of the anti-movement.

The truth is that Einstein did change his stance and urged Roosevelt to use whatever was necessary to destroy Nazi Germany, but after seeing his groundwork used, he once again became a pacifist and lectured for the rest of his life on the global devastation inevitable with the competitive use of fission and fusion weapons. Einstein claimed, at one point, that if FDR had lived, he would not have used the bomb. Truman was a realist.

Leon's taste for the United States was sharpened in the years he traveled there, and although Vi never visited the States then, she was influenced by her husband's desire to live there.

Their last name was changed by British intelligence in 1937 for reasons never explained to the couple, and though there was no objection, their wish to one day reassume the name "Schoenweis" reached the appropriate ears. When an arrangement was made in November of 1946 to immigrate to the United States, they immediately applied for U.S. citizenship under the Schoenweis name.

Five years later, as new Americans, they settled in a Newark suburb and once again started a business they were qualified to operate: a camera store and an optical supply business in downtown Newark. The business was only moderately successful, keeping the two comfortable financially and happily occupied working together once again. Leon's scientific background was now a hobby, and though he was not yet sixty years old, the stress he had endured made him look and feel older then his years. Vi, on the other hand, who was the same age as her husband, was far more spirited. She had a disposition that prompted resolve and motivation.

CHAPTER THIRTEEN
The Return to Vienna

Early in 1956, Leon became ill. His dizziness, his uncertainty as he walked, and his halting speech indicated a light stroke, which was diagnosed at St. Barnabas Hospital. The doctors were only half as worried as Vi and Leon, suggesting the mildness of his condition would only require some medication, some bed rest, and a more relaxed working schedule in the future.

"Vi, I decided there would be *no* working schedule. I'm going to leave the business; sell it to my employees."

"That's a good idea."

"I think so. There is a critical time in everybody's life when we should know to slow down without a doctor to tell you."

"Will you be bored? You could go in one or two days a week."

"No, I'll find things to do," he seriously insisted.

Vi would find things to keep Leon occupied, things that would not tire him. Soon she would consider a position for herself—everything in the proper time—but she began nurturing the thought, one that would mature in the future. She was only fifty-six years old, the same as her husband. "But I want to say involved. I'm healthy and feel great," she would remind herself.

In 1957, a now retired Leon, fully recovered except for some fatigue, listened carefully to his doctor's advice regarding a more relaxed lifestyle. With the store closed and the medical suggestions in mind, he and Vi traveled by car to nearby vacation spots, museums, and upstate festival occasions. They drove into New York to see shows and operas and hear symphonic music, which they loved, especially the lilting works of Strauss, Schubert, and Beethoven. Music transported them back to the wonderful, embracing ambience of Vienna in the twenties, when the delicious interval of their student days had separated them from others so that their jealous decision to enjoy the city and their love for one another would be theirs alone.

The year after Leon's illness and the store closing presented all the joys of freedom to the couple, but Vi harbored a desire she thought she had kept hidden from her husband, and as the year happily moved on, the merriment subsided. She would talk to Leon about her wish: The voices of Vienna were whispering to her, urging her on one hand to revisit the good days and on the other hand in a more adventurous, daring manner, to test her spirit, her courage to summon the horror of the past. The ugliness of 1938 secretly pursued Vi and challenged her recollection.

Leon sensed Vi's inner notion to solve and resolve, but there was a difference in their personalities. He was content with the present and upset with the portion of his past that certainly gnawed at him but was best forgotten. He would never forgive the dread and fright visited on him and Vi, but to face the scene again would unnerve him. Yet the hints Vi left with Leon were unmistakably evident of her wishes.

"We could see the new Vienna."

"Vi, I know what you're getting at."

"We would see the new people, the new mood. Leon, it was twenty years ago."

"How could we be there and not feel the way it was?"

Vi considered her husband's uneasiness and his condition, and though she always bent to his satisfaction, there was something essential in her plea.

"You are right about that; there is no forgetting, no real forgiving."

"I've thought about that. Forgiving, I mean. The way I see it, things turned out well for us even though it was never meant to be like that. They would never have let us leave or live."

"I know that, dear, but—"

Her thought was discontinued by Leon as he finished his reasoning. "But we did leave. And Vi, you know that providence—call it that—appeared in our lives then, or maybe providence stepped in between Ursula, the Nazis, and us. Whatever, but the result was we did get out, so…" Leon collected the meaning of his reasoning. He hesitated. "So, maybe there is no reason to forgive, no reason to go back. It would break our hearts."

"It might," Vi agreed.

"That bunch might all be dead. Who knows?"

"Leon, dear Leon. I don't want to upset you, and I see that you are."

"Not really. I've got to tell you the truth. I know you want to go there. I've known it for a long time, and I think you know that I would probably be afraid to stand in front of our old store or the bakery cell. But I'm thankful for what we were given. That's it, Vi. I would rather be thankful than hateful."

Vi accepted her husband's thoughts and respected the reality of his argument, but there was an abject wish for closure buried deep in her chest. She said, "Leon, I think we must go. I won't let you get sick over this, but I believe that when we see the new city, the new people, you will feel better—probably even good—about this trip."

Leon's negative sense was wearing away, eroding because he would not battle Vi's feelings together with a question that truly bothered him like a sore that does not heal. He often wondered about the righteous heroes who had stepped between the Nazis and him and Vi—good people who never knew him. Were they alive? He reasoned not. Perhaps he could find out.

Leon changed his course like a stream whose flow diverges after running into a boulder blocking its way. He was hardly transformed; merely modifying his stance so that Vi would be satisfied. He bent.

Some days later, after Vi had not broached the subject, he said, "Vi, I've been considering this trip to Austria. Do you think we could avoid the trouble, if it appears, of seeing the old Nazis?"

"Vienna is a city of almost two million people, new people who have found a lovely home for themselves. I really doubt if we would come across anyone we knew."

Leon thought of something else. "Do you think anyone at the university would know me if I dropped in there?"

"That's a wonderful idea. See the old place. You had good years there."

"But if…"

"I know what you're thinking, dear, but the old fellows have probably retired or died. That was almost twenty-five years ago, and the young professors and students would certainly not know you."

"And the store," he said as he studied Vi's reaction. "The store you were so close to. It was like a child of yours."

"Yes. The store." Something stirred in Vi's memory. "I wonder if it's still there, and if it is, who owns it. If Ursula is involved, I don't know how I would react. I have thought about those things often." Vi hesitated. She knew what Leon meant. "If anyone from the old days is there, I promise you I won't cause trouble. Leon, I promise. No, I swear it."

"I know you won't," he conceded softly.

"I feel something like you do," she admitted. "We made it—no thanks to the Nazis, but we made it—and for that alone, like you, I am thankful. I will not make trouble." Again, Vi paused, and to a silent Leon she brightened, smiled, and said, "But I want to see our old house, the neighborhood, your lab, and even that rotten building they kept you in. Leon, it will be like a victory celebration. We will laugh about it."

Laughter would not visit Leon.

From Kennedy Airport in New York, the plane crossed the Atlantic after flying over Newfoundland. It skirted over southern Ireland and western England and landed at Heathrow, where the plane refueled. Passengers were allowed to debark and stretch in a special area where refreshments were available.

"Vi, if it weren't for you, I would go back to the States right now."

Vi laughed. "You know you wouldn't. You are probably as anxious as I am to see the change in Austria—the cities, the people, the places we remember." Leon offered no response. "You would never forgive yourself for not going on" Vi was still smiling.

Leon finally confessed, "You are right. I wouldn't. I'd be ashamed of myself not to have the courage you have, but I'll be on edge until we are back in New Jersey, so don't let me shake myself to pieces."

"I'll watch you every inch of the way."

The plane left Heathrow, had a short stop in Frankfurt, and then made a nonstop flight to Vienna's city air terminal. After a passport and baggage check, a porter trailing behind them delivered their baggage to the taxi area. The terminal was crowded, with heavy traffic everywhere, people rushing about in many directions, and nobody paying attention to other scurrying travelers. Well-lit, busy shops lined the corridors with an active combination of serious shoppers, just-looking pedestrians, happy travelers, and souvenir hunters.

The first surprise to Vi and Leon was the bustling mob that cared not, in their merry haste, about race, color, ethnicity, or nationality. In the late summer afternoon, they emerged from the air-conditioned terminal and tipped the porter, who helped load the taxi with baggage and its human cargo.

"Grand Hotel Wein." Leon's German and his accent were perfect. The cab traveled on Park Ring, Schubert Ring, and made a right on Kartner Ring, and after a trip of less than a mile and a half, let its fares out at the Grand. The check-in was fast, their room lovely, and the excited but voiceless couple were fascinated. Finally, Leon announced, "What a change."

"No Nazis, no war," said Vi.

"No brown shirts, black shirts, armbands."

"No fear."

"Vi, I'm glad we are here. Let's spend the next four or five days sightseeing. No turmoil for a few days." An impassioned plea spoken jokingly.

"Absolutely." A firm agreement endorsed with a kiss given softly.

After breakfast, a short walk found the couple in front of the huge and ornate Vienna State Opera house; a block further was the Zweig Institute, a section of the university where Leon had studied for a short time. They would stand and remember. It was too early that Saturday morning to enter those places, but a few blocks west, they were surprised to see many early morning pedestrians gathered in front of one of the truly magnificent sections of the city. To the right and for blocks around spread the old palace, the Hofburg, a seat of government, along with the Rathaus, less than a mile away. Across the Burgring, the museum quarter spread for five blocks along the Messe Platz on Museum Street.

Vi and Leon would spend the next two days exploring the museums and enjoying the attractions at the Museum Quarters. When they last visited those wondrous places they were a young married couple whose eyes fell mostly on one another, missing the art and history on which they now would concentrate. Perhaps their concentration might be distracted by a memory, by feeling, so many years later—the softness of each other's clasped hands, the romantic arm about the waist, the whisperings, and the tender stolen kisses.

The memories were gentle, perhaps stirring, but they were travelers now, adventurers making this sunny, lazy morning a time to explore. They knew that soon enough there would be ugly reminders stridently hurled at them, but they delayed those moments by prolonging the superb current charm of attractions.

They would see the Spanish Riding School, hear the Boys' Choir, and visit the Albertina Collection, the library, the treasury, and the Imperial Apartments. The next day would be spent at the Museum Quarter again, strolling the halls and exclaiming over the paintings and sculptures.

During the lunch and dinner hours, they tried to find the old coffee houses they had known in their youthful days, but they could not. A few old famous ones were still there, as were the older hotels, but those places had not been their haunts in the old days. Instead, they had their coffee and strudels at new sidewalk cafés, admiring the ambience and unbridled peace that pervaded the fast-moving crowds. Theirs was an admiring silence.

The third day they taxied to the Rathaus, walked across the park to the National Theater (Burg Theater), and strolled the

Volksgarten bordering the Parliament and Palace of Justice. Leon examined the old university where, in 1937, Jewish professors were advised to leave and were summarily expelled, jailed, and probably exterminated after the Anschluss one year later. His stomach weakened and his desire to see more of his old school faded, so he located Vi in front of the Burg Theater. The two taxied to Saint Stephan's, walked around and in the old church, gasping at its Gothic beauty, lunched at a café, and again taxied, this time across the Donau Kanal (the Danube Canal) to the reconstructed Jewish Temple Israel and then to the Prater, where in the early evening, the active amusement part was alive, its lights sparkling like the red-hot soaring embers of a log fire.

On Sunday they walked the streets of Leopoldstadt, the section in which Leon's boyhood and early manhood was spent. The long taxi ride to Vi's old neighborhood ended in sadness, for Dr. Wiser's house still stood, though its age saddened Vi the way seeing old folks, relatives, or friends after many years is a reminder of the joys of youth and the beauty of what once was. The Great War back in 1914 was recalled distinctly, as was the presence of her father, his war years, his suffering, and his advice to his tender teenaged daughter.

The ghosts of the late summer swirled and howled around their old home, screaming at Vi as she remembered a scowling, menacing Ursula demanding all their family's possessions, pressing Nazi bite and sting into Vi's terror-filled heart. Leon was imprisoned and Vi had been mentally tortured by threats of her husband's fate. She wondered who lived there now.

"I don't care who lives here; I'm leaving."

"It's not Ursula?"

"It can't be. There are children playing outside." Vi was weeping.

"You've had enough?"

"Yes."

"No more, then." They got back into the taxi, but Vi gave directions to the driver.

"Why?" Leon argued.

"I want to drive by the old bakery—just drive by it. It's on the far side of my parents' cemetery. We have to drive through it." Leon's arm was around Vi.

The cab stopped in the cemetery at the spot where Vi knew she could walk to the graves of her parents. She asked Leon to stay in the car. He watched Vi as she obviously found the burial site, stood by it with her hands clasped in prayer, and seemed to speak to the stones.

"How long ago did they die?" the young cab driver asked Leon.

"More than thirty years ago."

Vi stepped back into the cab. She was no longer crying as she said to Leon, "I spoke to Papa and to my mother. I said, 'See, Mama? I wear your cross.'" Then she cried again but brightened as the cab approached the street where the bakery stood.

A surprised Leon said, "There are only row houses here."

"They're new," the cab driver announced. "They're still building more. This whole neighborhood's been torn down and new places built. You want me to stop?"

"No, never mind. Take us to the Grand."

"I'm glad not to see it again." Leon was looking at Vi, waiting for her reaction. "They destroyed it for us."

"I am glad."

"Are you disappointed?"

"You know, Leon, I think we have been told something today. We've been told there really is a new world out there. I don't know how long we will live, but I hope it is long enough to see more of the misery of the past disappear just like that filthy building did."

The momentarily uplifted couple sat in silence until they reached the hotel.

Leon asked, "Is there anything else you want to see today, dear?"

"No, let's just relax. Tomorrow we'll see the store."

Before Leon and Vi turned the corner of the Ringstrasse, she said to Leon, "I want to stop here for a moment."

"Why here?"

"Because that old coffee shop was where Felix and I had a coffee and discussed the escape."

"My God."

"Yes, he was disguised. You were being held."

"I remember the coffee shop. I had breakfast there a few times," Leon recalled.

"I was in there often. It was owned by two nice gentlemen. Let's see who runs the place now. It was Karl's."

They went in about ten thirty in the morning, after breakfast and before lunch, the time of day when few people frequent eating places or spend working hours in there. Vi led Leon to the same table at which she had sat with Felix twenty years before. A white-haired, aproned man, holding menus, edged near and looked quizzically at Vi, demurred for a second, and picked up the courage to address her.

"Excuse me for asking, madam, but you look familiar to me. I am Karl. I own this shop."

"My God." She trembled as she spoke. "Karl, I am Vi Schoenweis. I owned the camera store around the corner."

Before she introduced Leon, Vi stood up in front of Karl, extended her arms, and put them around the old proprietor.

"It's nice to see you again." She hugged Karl and said, "This is my husband, Leon. He came in here a few times many years ago."

Karl stammered, "I'm sorry, but I don't recognize you. But I saw you both looking in, and Madam Schoenweis I knew right away."

"Please sit with us," Leon offered.

"I will, but let me bring you coffee first."

He returned with the coffees, removed his apron, and immediately sat between these two old customers. They exchanged life stories.

"The war." Karl was idly fingering silverware, his voice low and sad. "My two sons never came back from it."

Vi touched his hand. "I'm sorry. What a terrible loss."

"Yes, it is terrible. My wife and I can never get over that. They were our only two children. I want to tell you about our feelings." Karl was still looking at the fork and spoon, seemingly addressing those objects and hesitant to speak directly to his guests. An embarrassed uncertainty held him back, but he did find words.

"A lot of us in the neighborhood knew you were Jewish or married to a Jewish man. We all knew what was coming."

He looked up at Leon, then shifted his eyes to Vi. "Nobody did anything about it. Everyone knew of the edicts, the Nuremberg laws, but what nobody knew was how serious this would get to be, and…the truth is, nobody cared; things in Austria were bad, and we believed the reports that Jews and communists were the trouble."

Leon placed his hand on Karl's arm as if to steady it. The gesture spoke for itself. It said, "If this is too difficult for you to recall, don't upset yourself." Out loud, Leon said, "We, all of us, have discussed this very often. We can imagine your feelings at that time—"

Karl interrupted. "We felt a need for Hitler. He was our knight, our protector. We felt he was exactly what Germany and der Grossdeutsch would need. We joined the cause. If I wasn't too old, then I would have enlisted like my two sons did."

As Karl related these events, it became obvious that he was crying out to be heard and understood.

Vi said, "Have you had a chance to tell people all this?"

"Never to Jewish people," he admitted. "I'm sure many Jewish visitors to Vienna have been in here, but I would hardly just start a conversation with people I don't know."

"We understand."

"You I knew then, and so you are giving me the opportunity to excuse myself, to tell you how sorry I am for you, to apologize to all of you who suffered." Karl's moist eyes suggested the truth. "You came into my shop almost every day, so when you stopped coming in, I asked about you at your store. They told me you sold the place to another woman."

Vi listened intently. Karl continued, "But I know you can't sell a business so fast, so I figured it was taken away from you somehow. And then you disappeared."

Vi would not disclose the circumstances of that summer. She would always protect her and Leon's rescuers.

"Yes, they did force me out. We left Austria soon after."

"You were very lucky," Karl said. "But again, I must admit, nobody around here, including me, paid attention."

The mood of Austria in the thirties was evidently a selfish, self-serving one, as admitted by Karl. Leon was silently enthralled by Karl's confession, yet he always knew the background and the design of the Germans. Accepting Karl's apology, Leon at the same time could not forgive a time of racial hatred. This ex-Viennese couple saw firsthand the new, young Austrian citizens who were babies at the time of Anschluss and who were quick to tell outsiders of their guiltless situation and of their repugnance for Third Reich policies. The American couple would accept the denials and rejection of this new generation; their apologies for parents and other older family members was a salve for wounds of the afflicted and a release for German youth.

Karl continued to recant in a humble and contrite manner. He spoke about knowing the plight of the Jews, Slavs, communists, crippled, and mentally ill, but Vi was after a different piece of information.

"Who does own the camera store now? We are going to visit it next, and we might introduce ourselves."

"She never comes in here. I just know her name: Hannah Kranisch. She's a middle-aged woman, maybe sixty, but she had heart problems, I heard. But she's back to work."

"We'll drop in, Karl. We are very sorry about your sons."

Karl shook his head. "The hardest part," he said, "came later, when my wife and I realized that they, with millions of others, died for a terrible cause. But we didn't know that then. We were all patriots."

His voice trailed off. Leon shook his hand and Vi hugged Karl again. More people came into the shop.

"Let's hope for better times. God bless."

"God be with you," replied Karl.

Vi took Leon's arm as they nervously but resolutely walked to the corner, turned left, and approached the camera shop.

As Vi and Leon neared the camera store, Leon, whose arm was locked with Vi's, stopped, causing his wife to stop also.

"You're not afraid?"

"No, not afraid. Yesterday was very difficult for you. Is this going to be too much?"

Vi sighed. "No," she smiled. "I can handle this. First, let's look over the outside, the windows."

The name, in neon red block letters, read, "Der Kamera Austausch" (The Camera Exchange).

Leon started walking again and stopped in front of their old business. They were on the edge of the sidewalk, backing up almost to the busy street, looking up.

"Two floors now." Leon marveled at the doubled size. "We were amateurs." The well-lit windows promoted a full assortment of cameras, lenses, and all kinds of equipment to service those items. New computer items designed recently, born to the world perhaps six years before, were exhibited in abundance, as were services for those things. TVs and accompanying supporting items, as well as some office supplies, were for sale on the second floor.

"They covered all the bases."

"I wonder who's managing all this."

"It couldn't be Ursula."

"Well, there's no time like now to find out."

Leon pulled open one side of the double door and held it open for Vi, who entered first. Showcases lined the walls of the wide carpeted floor, and behind those counters, salesgirls waited on customers, some of whom were examining the merchandise. The store help were young and energetic. None of them looked familiar. The interior was cool and had an odor peculiar to retail stores reflecting the type of goods sold in them; this one had a musty air-cooled breath, cigarette smoke, a trace of oil, the warm smell of fluorescent lights, people, and carpeting all mingled together and unnoticeably circulated.

There was no sign of a floor manager, and sales people were all busy with customers. Vi and Leon studied the cases.

"Stock looks good," Vi admitted.

A young saleslady leaned over her counter area and offered her help.

"Can I show you anything?"

"We would like to see the owner."

"I can help you with anything on this floor," she condescendingly implied.

"I'm sorry," Vi apologized. "I'm sure you could. But we just came in to see the owner." Vi summoned a great deal of courage to say that and not tremble.

The saleslady answered, "Madam Kranisch is not well. She is here but asked not to be disturbed. The buyers are not in today."

"We just want to see her for a moment. We are old acquaintances, not here on business."

The saleslady said, "Come with me. I'll ask her if she can see you." She led them to the rear of the store, where she had them wait at a large mahogany table while she softly knocked on the office door. The sign on the door read, "Hannah Kranisch, Proprietor." Vi, standing closer to the door than Leon, could hear the short conversation.

"What is it?" The unmistakable voice and tone of Ursula Streicher, no matter what name she called herself, was obvious.

"There are two people here who said they are old acquaintances of yours and would like to say hello."

"I'm not seeing anyone today. Ask their names," she said in a hoarse but strident voice.

The girl came out and asked their names.

"Tell her it's a surprise."

The girl timidly reentered the office and delivered the answer.

"Tell them to come back tomorrow; I'm busy." A rasping quality but a definite inquisitive accent colored her sentence, while to the girl she insisted, "I'm in no mood for surprises. I'm feeling weak."

As Ursula hesitated, a gnawing, curious appetite began to move her. She was struggling to rise from her chair as Vi and Leon slowly walked toward the front of the store. Their intent was to return the next day. Ursula, now standing outside her office by the mahogany table, stared at the backs of the departing couple.

The salesgirl caught up to them. "Madam is outside the office now."

As slowly as they could, Vi and Leon turned around; they were ten feet from Madam, now facing this immense gray-haired figure, whose large features were surrounded by creases lining her pallid face. Her long arms covered by the sleeves of her dress hung down at her sides but slowly rose to her face in an attempt to cover her eyes. In abject terror, she whispered a name—"Vi, Vi, Vi,"—repeating it as she sank to the carpeting, her lips still moving. The aging Nazi, the bun in her gray hair unraveling, lay in a large dark pile on the floor.

Sales help and customers gathered around the unmoving mound. Some tried to help.

"Water. Get water."

"It's no use."

Vi and Leon were already on the busy sidewalk, hurrying off. They hailed a taxi and headed back to their hotel. Once there, the concierge was instructed to exchange their flight reservation for one that would leave as soon as possible.

"Is everything all right? Was your stay a good one?"

"It couldn't have been better." Leon nodded in agreement to his wife's answer, yet neither was smiling.

CHAPTER FOURTEEN
The Ending

In 1967, life became hectic. Our business grew big and tall like a sprout watered regularly. Time was spent on Wall Street and uptown at the office, but hardly ever on the road. We had supervisors and supervisors for the supervisors doing the traveling then. Our company was "going public," issuing shares to be sold to public investors, raising cash to finance our operation and perhaps some with which to buy other companies. That was what Wall Street was created to do: be a major financier to the business community. Wall Street would go astray many times, and it became obvious that it needed supervision and regulation—whatever any business or government needs to guarantee success and its honesty. Our executives put those requirements in place. For much of that work, Vi would get the credit. She was a worker whose spirit and intelligence motivated many of our achievements, and though she approached seventy years of age, her energy and reliability were as solid as a brick wall. But the wall cracked and fairly collapsed that year when she discovered that colon cancer attacked her. She began to receive treatment at Sloane-Kettering Memorial Hospital. She was in and out of the hospital, spending about a week in, and then out for a week. She could not come to work during that time, and while she was an in-patient, many visitors from the office would keep her company, including myself, whenever I was able. What Vi had put in motion at work was smoothly running.

On an Indian summer day in late September, while New York trees had not yet shed a leaf, I was at my desk looking at the warm street scene below, an iced drink in front of me, when my phone rang. It was Vi, speaking from her hospital bed, which, unfortunately, she had occupied for longer stretches of late. I knew she might be leaving the hospital soon, so it surprised me to hear her say, "I'd like you to come down to Sloane." She was weeping and spoke with pauses.

"There is a man here you must meet. He will only be in town a few more hours. You don't know him, but you must hear his story. Leon is here also."

Nothing I could think of would keep me away. "I'll take a cab; be right there."

I was in her room in less than twenty minutes.

The back of her chair faced the East River, a busy waterway of fast-moving, choppy wavelets and faster-moving barges and tugs. The Triborough Bridge spanned Randall's Island and Ward's Island, supporting high rise residential buildings. The busy scene sparkling in the sunlight outside behind Vi was in deep contrast to the hospital room, whose yellow light and egg-white walls filled and surrounded a tense and emotional group of three individuals crowded around an unoccupied hospital bed, which took up most of the space.

On one side of Vi's chair, an overspread array of colorful flowers filled a tabletop, while to her right, Leon stood, his suit wrinkled, adding more depression to his dejected appearance. He was holding Vi's hand, bending slightly to do so. Vi's eyes were a moist blue as they sparkled through the creases on the corners of her eyes and on her cheeks. She happily received me.

Springing up from the hospital bed on which he was sitting, a man I did not recognize now extended his hand to greet me. Leon also smiled; his handshake was a gentle one, and I patted his shoulder with my left hand.

The fellow whom I did not know was a husky, white-haired gentleman, bespectacled and ruddy, taller by a few inches than me. He looked to be seventy-two years old and in good physical condition. He continued to hold onto my hand as he introduced himself as Orlando Gomez—this said with perfect English with a decided German accent exiting from a man with a Spanish name.

With some confusion, I introduced myself, obviously spoken with a perplexed expression brought about by Orlando's mixture of nationalities. Vi smiled.

"Let him explain what is obviously puzzling you." In a more serious tone, she said, "I'm emotional right now. It's hard for me to talk after speaking to Orlando and hearing his story." She sat back and repeated, "I'm not up to it now."

I told her to relax as I turned to Orlando to relate or rather repeat what had been said to Vi and Leon before I arrived. Orlando's lips spread slightly as he managed a smile and began his explanation.

"I was born in Austria, went to war as a German army soldier, and was lucky enough to return in 1945. I stayed only a few months to visit a couple of relatives and a friend or two near Vienna." He took a breath and clarified what I already imagined. Regarding Vi, knowingly, he said, "I told Vi and Leon all this two hours ago, but they insisted I repeat it for you.

"I left Austria, not wanting to remain there another day. I'll explain. I went to Rome and booked passage on a ship to Brazil, not pretending to know what I would do there. There were many Germans there, and I joined a group who were importing items and selling them in the larger South American cities. As time went by, I made numerous trips to the States, which explains my fluent English."

I interrupted Orlando, excusing my rudeness. "In all those years, you never contacted Vi and Leon?"

"I had no idea where they were or if they were even alive, and if they were, in what country they lived." He again looked at Vi, shifting his eyes between her and me. "I tracked Vi and Leon down less than two weeks ago. I changed my name in Brazil as soon as I could. Now you know about my name, my accent, and my English." He smiled at the three of us and continued.

"I knew Vi and Leon for less than one hour of my life before today."

That incredible statement shocked me. My mouth must have been wide open; no words followed my consternation as I awaited Orlando's accounting. Still sitting on the edge of the bed, his arms behind him supporting his sitting position, he carefully chose his words and said, "There were three of us in Vienna who were close friends in the thirties. We were drawn together for a very specific reason, but for a reason and a motive that made it impossible for us to allow anyone to know that we knew each other, let alone that we were friendly. The Nazis were everywhere in Austria and especially in Vienna, which became more evident each day. Everybody knew the Nazis would be marching into the country at any moment. If anyone opposed the movement openly, it would be dangerous and even fatal."

Vi's complexion, which was once lovely and vibrant, had turned to an ashen pallor. Her eyes were moist and more deep-set than just days before, but she shifted them from Orlando to me. She knew the story and it affected her deeply once again.

"One of the three of us was Felix Gruber."

At the mention of his name, Vi gasped.

"He always kept Vi from knowing of our friendship. I know that he didn't even see Vi for years."

"That is so." Vi could only whisper.

"We hated the Nazis with all our hearts and with all the bones in our bodies, but almost everyone around us loved Hitler. It was savior worship. The beatings, the kidnapping, the murder; how could anyone approve? But they did—all of them did.

"The three of us kept silent. We were with the underground. We kept our business strictly to ourselves. We were German, we felt German, but not the way others felt. We were not going to run away."

Vi and Leon had heard the same pleas, the same reason for some to stay in a nation whose politics were hated. Vi remembered hearing it on the airstrip in Zurich. Felix could easily have stepped into that plane with them, but he refused to cut and run. He would stay to see a better Germany, perhaps to make it better. He would lay his life down to make it better, thirty years before.

"Instead, we decided to help as many people as we could, people who were in trouble and wanted to get away. They were mostly Jews. Among the three of us, we had transportation, printing equipment, arms, money, and clothing—things we needed to help those in trouble—and we used those items a lot of times.

"One day, Felix reached me and said that some very special friends were in desperate trouble. One was locked up, he said, and the word was he was soon to be killed, along with Vi here, his wife." Orlando looked at Vi as he spoke. Leon sat on one of the arms of the chair and held Vi's hand. Orlando continued.

"I remembered that Felix often mentioned Vi. I hope I'm not offending you, Leon, but Felix probably loved Vi."

Leon said, "I know," and momentarily closed his eyes as Vi, as she had said many times before, murmured, "We loved him, too," including Leon in her admission.

"The four of us agreed that we must act immediately to save both of them. Felix, in his disguise, met with Vi in her store and pinpointed the exact time for action. The delivery man, you recall, Vi, got some very important information for us, and we made our plans to move that very next night."

Orlando clarified, especially for me, the events of the critical night.

"That next night, as I said before, was the one hour in my life that our paths crossed."

He again looked at Vi and Leon. Vi buried her face in both her hands and cried as Orlando described the rest of the tale, which he recalled vividly. He, for the first time since we met, was overtaken with emotion. He paused, took a breath, and now tears appeared running down his cheeks.

"Give me a minute," he said as he wiped dry his tears. It became obvious that he had told this story for the first time in Vi's hospital room and repeated it for me, his emotional response reappearing for the second time.

"Felix drove the loaded-down lorry and waited for the rescue to be completed by me and Artur." He hesitated, again breathed deeply, and said, "You all know most of the night's events, I mean before Leon was delivered to Felix, but since that evening and for the rest of my life, I never shot men again like that. What is worse, I remember having no remorse. The job had to be done. It happened so fast—you see, they were enemies."

Orlando was apologizing for acting as he had. He was contrite, almost regretting it.

"A thousand times, I dreamed of killing those two. They might have been Nazi thugs, but we killed them." His conscience was bared like a skinned animal. He repeated once more, "There was no feeling; it was painless."

My interest, my concern was deep, as I felt remorse for this tortured soul.

"My God," I said. "You were Heinrich, the man in the brown shirt."

"Yes," Orlando said. "I was Heinrich."

We all remained silent and looked at one another vacantly, relaxed, sorrow mixed with victory. I left the room to buy and bring back a tray of coffee for all from the dispensing machine down the hall. We sipped our coffees, holding very hot Styrofoam cups gingerly. Nobody said a word.

I picked up the cudgel, breaking the silence. "Of course, Vi and Leon know the story. Vi had a good listener in me for quite a while, but…" I queried, seeking Orlando's attention, "Could you tell us more about you and your friends after the rescue?"

Orlando was staring at the ceiling as if to ask it where to begin.

"I told Vi and Leon only a little of it, but I will go into detail." His thoughts collected, he began. "When Hitler triumphantly marched into Austria, the mood of the people was of hysterical pride and happiness. Their outright joy created in the monster the strength of knowledge that anything he wished, after the Anschluss, would automatically be accepted by the population of my nation. The Nuremberg laws immediately went into effect, and mayhem soon followed in the countryside and especially in Vienna. Jews were rounded up immediately and disappeared from the streets while looting of their homes and their businesses took place wantonly."

He said thoughtfully, after a sip of coffee, "There would be no more work for the three of us. Truthfully, there were no more people to save, and our fate was similar to all young men in

Austria. We were drafted right away, conscripted into the German army. I was sent to a communication detachment, Felix went to the transport section, and our other friend went into an infantry unit.

"Felix and I knew of each other's units and we were both in the force invading Russia; the last I saw of him was in May of 1941. Barbarossa, Hitler's invasion of Russia, was about to begin with, believe it or not, three million troops."

Orlando gave us a quick history lesson. "We had three million, but what Hitler didn't realize was that Russia had five million troops, four times as many trucks, and twice as many airplanes." He continued, "In 1942, at Stalingrad, German losses were almost three hundred thousand men. We surrendered in January of 1943. The saddest part for me was hearing that our handsome, brave, and poetic truck driver friend was killed in action there. He was with the Sixth Army, driving a supply lorry."

I expected to hear this news from Orlando, but the sadness of that moment was overwhelming. Orlando said, "This is a poem he gave me in 1941. I've kept it and made numerous copies. Whenever I read it, I see him happy as a lamb driving his truck on the road to Innsbruck."

We didn't read it just then but heard Orlando mumble, "He was my best friend; he died thirty-four years ago and he is still my best friend. Our other friend also didn't make it through the war. I'm not sure where he was killed, but family members told me about him."

"And you," I said, "I'm glad to see you made it." Tears were flowing.

"Just barely," he admitted.

Orlando had told Vi about Felix before I came, which accounted for her pallor and emotional state. When she could speak, she admitted their love for each other; however, she wanted Orlando to know a bit more about his best friend. She was crying as she spoke.

"We were in love, you know, but how do you love somebody without the desire, perhaps the lust, that usually follows?" She wiped away tears, which were freely flowing down her cheeks. "The best way to describe my deepest feeling then is to say for me it was like the profound love parents have for their special children. For a true artist, perhaps it is the joy and emotional fulfillment of seeing a perfect sunset or Tyrol Valley at dawn with its cover of shadows on the snow."

She broke off for a short time. Orlando was totally silent.

"Felix, beautiful Felix, brave and good, loyal to the fullest extent—oh, how I loved him. It's impossible to picture him dead in the snow at Stalingrad, and for what cause? A cause he hated, but for the country he loved."

Orlando's head sank beneath his shoulders. "I survived but just barely," he admitted. "I was at Kursk in July of 1943; we had seven hundred thousand troops there and the generals thought we had a topical advantage. The Russians had one million three hundred thousand men there and more tanks than you can imagine, which immediately went into action against the German armor. This was the largest tank battle of the war," he mused.

"We now know that Hitler didn't believe the losses we had at Stalingrad, but we pulled out of the battle when we learned it would be won by Russia. The Americans and Brits had launched the invasion of Sicily after Africa was finished, so we were on our way to Italy." He gave a short chuckle and said, "They were on their way, but I wasn't."

Orlando maintained his train of thought. "My unit was one of the last to withdraw; the communications truck I was on was hit by a tank shell and sent reeling off the road. My arm and shoulder were badly mauled. I passed out and later found that the ambulance that had picked me up made it to Czechoslovakia and into Germany. Another ambulance picked me up and we wound up in Bavaria in a little town called Eichstadt, where the nuns of Abbey St. Walburg not only saved my life but also my arm. I finally went back to Austria in 1945, stayed only a month, and somehow got transportation to South America, where I settled down with lots of other Germans and went into business."

"What a story," I said with a whistle. "Did you go back to Vienna?"

"No," he answered. "What was left of my family lived in a small town near Baden; I see them only seldom. The Viennese acceptance of Anschluss sickens me to this day. It's a beautiful city, but I can't get 1938 out of my mind."

He got up to leave, saying, "I want to say goodbye to Leon and Vi, and then I'll be driving to Newark Airport and on to Chicago, then back to Rio. I have a rented car."

He and Vi were crying when he hugged her goodbye and gently kissed the top of her head. He shook my hand and Leon's with a firm grip. I said the last words before he left the room. "I want you to know that you are a true hero. I am only sorry that everybody in our country doesn't know your story."

"Thank you," he said, and left Felix's poem, which Vi held.

Tears were rolling down Vi's face and mine, but I was able to say to her, "Let's read the poem together. It is almost thirty years old. It's about time." The poem, as we found out, was written in German. The copy we had was the translation Orlando had made of it.

Blest are those who have seen the world
Silent streams and waves that curl
Mountains high and sheathed in snow
Sweating deserts with breathless sands
All these I have come to know.

Magical cities with mystical streets
Quiet towns with sounds discrete
Foreign tongues and foreign ways
Not meant to startle or impress
But natural as the sun's caress
As the winter's bite or summer's haze.

Friends had I to a large degree
All sizes, shapes and pedigrees
Goodness I sought in every soul
And found it easily or deeply mined
For it was always there to find
And always a pleasure 'twas to unfold.

My journey left me memories
Of smooth and fine and boiling seas
And on my sails and pennants too
In letters bold when flappings cease
Read and know that I'm at peace
And have but love for you.

    There was a note on the bottom of the page. It read, "Heinrich, if ever you should run into Vi, give her this poem. I'm off to Russia."

    Orlando had been Heinrich back then, as we all now knew. Felix kept his promise and Vi had his poem.

    The recurring dream I had so many times finally ceased. It is unbelievable, but the shivering black curtains finally met at center stage, and as music no longer came from the orchestra pit, the theatre darkened.

EPILOGUE

Vi passed away in the fall of 1965; Leon died ten months later. Following his wife in death as in life was a natural occurrence. She was a leader, willful, strong, and intelligent. He followed of necessity, benefiting from her virtues while being brilliant and important in his own right. Both lived to be about sixty-five years of age.

Merely to stay alive in Nazi Germany under their circumstances was a success, but their now forgotten existence is a triumph. Trumpets should have sounded.

Dr. Wiser and Dr. Shoenweis lived until the mid-1920s.

Ursula died in the middle of her ill-gotten store in August of 1957. She was a Nazi to the end. Her father, who became a colonel in 1938, disappeared at war's end, as did many officers of the Third Reich, probably to Brazil or Argentina, never to be heard from again.

Eric Mann, Ursula's friend, was shot dead in the baker's cell in August of 1937.

Felix Gruber, Vi's dear friend and consummate hero, died in the winter campaign in Russia called Barbarossa along with close to three hundred thousand German troops near Stalingrad. He loved Vi with his last breath, a love that was not unrequited.

The other pre-Anschluss hero was killed in the war, leaving only Heinrich, who, except for the hospital visit, was never heard from again.

There remains no question that the new Vienna in no way resembles Hitler's Germany. Austria now tries to exist and prosper in a democratic channel; the hatred once dominant in the country might still be cellular, but it is not prominent. Mankind on our planet, which began its pulsating and boisterous life four and a half billion years ago, evolved from minute organisms, which in turn grew to water specimens, which became land animals. Two hundred million years ago, humankind, from these origins, began its march. It is obvious that the mind of man had its roots (like DNA and RNA) in the early stages of earth's development.

This is not an excuse for the depravity or lunacy of Hitler or that ilk, but an indication that buried deep in our brains and bodies remains the possibility of antisocial and cannibalistic symptoms borrowed from our ancient forebears.